SECOND WIND

SECOND WIND

*Sometimes, the end is
actually the beginning.*

Buck Dopp

ISBN: 9780578994925

Library of Congress Control Number: 20210927223407

Published by Buck Dopp
Lake Havasu City, Arizona

This book is dedicated to all veterans. Many of my friends who served their country in the military have contributed to this book in one way or another. I give them my heartfelt thanks.

Second wind: The renewed energy, strength, or endurance to continue in an undertaking.

This is the most profound spiritual truth I know: that even when we're most sure that love can't conquer all, it seems to anyway. It goes down into the rat hole with us, in the guise of our friends, and there it swells and comforts. It gives us second winds, third winds, hundredth winds.

—Anne Lamott,
Traveling Mercies: Some Thoughts on Faith

1

When Caleb Sinclair started his shift at the Ax Handle, the bouncer had no way of knowing this day would trigger a series of events that would change the course of his life. Sinclair checked IDs from the front door of the comedy club and sports bar, dodging the advances of flirtatious women who found him handsome and mysterious. He focused on preventing minors from entering the club, breaking up fights, and removing unruly customers.

The twenty-six-year-old stood six feet tall, with bright blue eyes and short black hair. He weighed 190 pounds and was more lethal than his thin frame suggested. Anyone picking a fight would soon regret the folly of tangling with the fierce fury unleashed by this quiet man. His situational awareness, honed by three combat tours in Afghanistan, enabled him to respond to threats with lightning-strike quickness that rendered opponents defenseless in seconds. The army had taught him to fight, and he'd learned his lessons well.

The sports fans gathered at the Ax Handle for ladies' night on a pleasant December evening two days before Christmas to watch games with cronies and hopefully hook up with members of the opposite sex. Some customers came to get high while enjoying the big screens; others came to watch the games going on at the alehouse.

Colored lights sparkled from several Fraser firs; the Christmas conifers filled the bar with pine scent and joined the aroma of cinnamon and vanilla from the table candles. Bartenders and scantily dressed servers—all women—wore Santa hats as they scurried to take and deliver drink orders and food. Mistletoe hung from the ceiling in a corner, attracting couples intent on engaging in public displays of affection. The Ax Handle, located in the historic district of Briggs Lake, a western Arizona desert town, served the best chicken wings in Mohave County and offered sauces that met every taste. Buckaroo, the house craft beer, light and tangy and always a customer favorite, augmented a wide assortment of foreign and domestic brews.

A skinny seventy-four-year-old man, perched alone at a corner table, sipped spring water from a straw. His thin, unkempt white hair barely covered his large ears and glowed every few seconds from the multilayered ceiling lights when they changed colors over his head.

Folding his long, bony fingers on the table in front of him, he scanned the busy bar scene. His drooping shoulders, long nose, and gray eyes, which darted from person to person, resembled a bald eagle searching for a slow-swimming salmon.

Suddenly an explosion of glass captured everyone's attention. Customers and servers turned toward the sound in time to see shards of glass skimming across the bar and raining onto the floor below. A drunken man clutched the neck of the broken beer bottle he had just used to shatter a pitcher full of beer.

Caleb leaped to the rescue of the bartender, who had ignited the man's ire by cutting him off from alcohol. The drunk pointed the broken bottle at the bouncer as if it were a pistol. "Mind your own business, pretty boy, or I'll shove this bottle right up your sorry ass."

The man, in his early forties, with a receding hairline and a soul patch on his chin, had a long brown ponytail that extended to the middle of his back. His tank top drooped over narrow shoulders to the waist of his cargo shorts.

"Hey, man. Be cool," the bouncer said as he held up both hands. "We don't want any trouble here. You've had enough for one night. Why don't you go home and get some sleep?"

"Why don't you kiss my ass?" The drunk cocked his arm and squinted.

Relieved to see the drunk's anger redirected at Caleb, the bartender retreated to the other side of the bar under a light that illuminated her reddish-brown hair. She turned and smiled at her knight in shining armor.

Caleb glanced in her direction.

Without warning, the bouncer felt numbness creeping down his forehead, followed by a hot liquid gushing from the gash on the crown of his head. Rivulets of blood poured down his face, blurring his vision and stinging his eyes. Tasting his blood, he pivoted away from an oncoming punch, grabbed the arm and shoved his hip into the man's midsection, then pulled him to the floor. When the man got up, the bouncer held the attacker in a bear hug.

Caleb yelled to the bartender, "Ashley, call the cops!"

2

A shley pulled a phone from her hip pocket and dialed 911. Its glittering pink case reflected the colors of the ceiling lights as she held it to her ear. The operator asked her to stay on the phone until the police arrived. Turning to the other bartender, she said, "Rosie, please call Joyce."

"Sure."

Rosie punched in the boss's number. "Joyce, sorry to bother you at home. A drunk guy smashed a pitcher of beer and hit Caleb over the head with a beer bottle. Caleb's bleeding bad. Ashley called 911, and we're waiting for the cops."

"I'll be right down."

Caleb pushed and carried the patron backward out the front door and onto the sidewalk. A stream of onlookers poured out of the bar behind them—drinks in hand—as if they were watching a sporting event. Young women drawn to the bar that night by the ladies-only drink specials and the handsome bouncer eagerly anticipated the ensuing spectacle.

Still holding the broken bottle, the man elbowed Caleb, then jerked to the left and right, attempting to free his arms. The bouncer won the tug-of-war and smashed the beer bottle against the wall. The inebriated customer headbutted Caleb, who responded with a throat punch that rocked the man backward against the wall. He followed up with a series of left-right combinations that started blood flowing from the man's nose and mouth. He slid down the wall to the ground, unconscious, in a bloody heap.

His right fist held high and still clenched, Caleb stood over the man he had just knocked out. "Stay put, you piece of shit."

Sirens announced the arrival of two police cruisers. The officers kept their blue lights flashing and ran through the mob.

"Break it up," one cop shouted. "Go back inside. We'll handle this."

Joyce Benson arrived and approached the officers with a calm and confident demeanor. The attractive middle-aged woman had long legs and short red hair. Her commanding presence projected strength and wisdom.

"Officers, I'm Joyce Benson, the owner of the Ax Handle. This man is my bouncer, Caleb Sinclair. The customer had too much to drink and became violent when the bartender cut him off. He had to be removed for his safety and the safety of others."

They ran toward the bouncer. She followed.

"What happened?" one of the officers asked.

"This guy got bombed and demanded more booze. When the bartender cut him off, he swung an empty bottle at a full pitcher of beer, sending glass and beer everywhere. I asked him to leave. Then he hit me over the head with the bottle. I moved him outside so he wouldn't hurt anybody."

"Was anyone else injured?" the senior officer asked.

"Not that I know of. Just me."

"What about him?"

Caleb shrugged.

The man regained consciousness. "I'm going to sue you, skin-head, and this bar for everything you're worth."

The bouncer glared at the man—his fists clenched at his sides. "Good luck with that, you asswipe."

The other cop handcuffed the groggy troublemaker and gave him the Miranda warning. "I'm taking you in for assault, battery, and making a terroristic threat. We're going to the ER first to get you patched up, then we're going to the police station."

After hearing him speak and getting a better look at him, Benson recognized the drunk as longtime customer Derek Snerd. She'd bought the Ax with many years of sweat equity as head bartender and had several run-ins with him.

Snerd and his friends frequented the watering hole and were big tippers. Joyce Benson appreciated his business, although he could be a problem when intoxicated. He hadn't been at the bar recently, so the new bouncer had never seen him before. She thought Snerd spent more at the tavern than he could afford on his income as a realtor, but somehow, he always had money to spend, even when house sales were slow.

Before leaving, the officer who had taken Caleb's statement said, "We may need you to come to the police department tomorrow for questioning. For now, you better get to the hospital. We'll call an ambulance."

"I'll take him." Benson put her hand on her young employee's bloody shoulder. "Come on, Caleb. Let's get you to the emergency room. You're going to need some stitches."

"I'll be fine, Joyce."

"We're going to the ER."

As Benson escorted him to her car, the skinny old man stepped out of a shadow. His smile grew wider with each passing second. His eagle eyes caught everything, and he liked what he saw.

3

Caleb pressed a towel against the top of his head and limped into the examination room behind PA Kerry Donnelly. With the cheerfulness of a waitress doling out the day's first cup of coffee, the medical professional asked about the accident as she cleaned the wound.

"I've been doing this for about nine years, and you're not the first busted-up bouncer I've patched up, and you probably won't be the last," she said with a smile. "You were lucky. The X-rays showed no skull fracture or brain bleed."

"It was a good thing he hit my head, ma'am. There's not much he could hurt. You should have seen the other guy, but they must have taken him to another hospital."

After sticking a needle in his head, she slowly moved it around. "I'm going to numb the area around the cut. This will sting, but it won't last long. I want you nice and numb."

"I've been a numbskull all my life, so it will feel natural."

"There are worse things to be called."

"I've been called those too."

She laughed. "There's nothing wrong with your sense of humor."

"Am I going to need stitches?"

"Staples."

"Staples?"

"For this injury, staples will work much better."

"I've never heard of using staples before."

"They won't hurt. You'll feel pressure but no pain."

"You'll make sure I won't have a scar, right? I wouldn't want it to hurt my acting career."

"No pressure, huh? I'll see what I can do." She set up the stapler and began the process of closing the cut. For the next few minutes, the only sound in the room was the heavy click of the staple gun.

"It may bleed some tonight, so I'm going to give you a box of gauze pads. Just press them lightly on the wound, and the bleeding should stop. How are you feeling?"

"Fine. Remember, I'm a numbskull."

"I remember."

"Thanks, Kerry. You'll be glad you did such a good job when you see me on *The Bachelor*."

"Looking forward to it, Mr. Sinclair. You should have your doctor remove the staples seven to fourteen days after the cut is healed."

"I don't have a doctor."

"Then you can come to the ER. One of us will take them out for you."

"Thanks. In the future I'll try to avoid swinging bottles."

"You do that." She looked into his blue eyes and smiled.

4

Later that night, Sinclair sat on the couch in his apartment, cradling a bottle of Bud Light in one hand and a TV remote in the other. The doorbell rang. Caleb set his beer on the crate he used as an end table. On the way to answering the doorbell, he tripped over his shoes and stumbled to the door. When he looked through the peephole, he saw only darkness.

"What do you want?"

No answer.

The doorbell rang again.

"Get out of here."

The doorbell rang a third time.

He released the deadbolt and cracked open the door, leaving the chain in place.

"Surprise!"

The bartender Caleb saved earlier stood outside his door holding a pizza box in one hand and a bottle of wine in the other. She wore a faded pair of cutoffs and a tight-fitting orange crop top that blended with the red streaks in her brownish hair that she had pulled back in a ponytail behind a Boston Red Sox cap.

"Ashley Bivens! What are you doing here? It's a little late for angels to be traipsing about."

"On a mission from God—making a house call to check on the patient. I thought you could use some nourishment. You can't live on just Slim Jims and pork rinds, you know."

"I know."

"Aren't you going to invite me in? Some host you are."

"Oh yeah." Unlatching the chain and opening the door, he smiled. "You're a fine one to talk about eating habits. Look how skinny you are."

She raised her arms until they were parallel to the floor. "You got a problem with this?"

"No. You look great."

Glancing at the TV as she dropped the wine and pizza on the kitchen counter, she placed her hands on her hips and shook her head. "Are you betting on games?"

"Channel surfing. Trying to find something good to watch while I drink myself to sleep. I've had kind of a rough day at the office—you know, saving damsels in distress."

Her smile disappeared when she got a closer look at his head. His swollen face had the beginnings of two black eyes. "Look at all those scratches on your arms. I'm so sorry this happened to you, Caleb. Thank you so much for helping me. I don't know what I would have done."

"Just doing my job, ma'am."

"Did you get stitches?"

"Nope. Staples—twelve of them." He leaned over so she could see the crown of his head.

"You're still bleeding, Caleb. There are tiny drops of blood oozing out of the staples."

He straightened up and pressed a gauze pad over the wound. "The bleeding has almost stopped."

"You took one for the team—and for me. Thank you, sir."

"That's why I get the big bucks, you know."

Ashley's green eyes lit up, and her smooth, pearly white skin glowed. "You did more than your job." She stretched out her arms and wrapped them around his neck, pulling him to her. She placed her lips on his and kissed him several times. When she opened her eyes, she locked them on his. "You were amazing."

"Thank you."

She took his hand and led him to the couch. The wine never did get opened, and the pizza wasn't eaten until the following day. Cold pizza never tasted so good.

18

5

The next evening the mysterious old man returned to the Ax Handle, requested the same table as the previous night, and again ordered water.

Caleb entered through the front door and headed straight for the bar. When Ashley saw him, she beamed.

"I hope you made it to work on time, Ashley."

"Of course. How are you, Caleb?"

"Good. Thanks for last night."

She smiled. "I thought you were off today."

"I am. Joyce wants to discuss what happened last night."

"She's probably going to give you a bonus or a raise."

"I could use it. You have gorgeous blue eyes."

"Um…I thought they were green."

"Green or blue, whatever color they are, they're beautiful. Did I tell you I'm color-blind?" He smelled the fragrance of her lavender perfume, and it reminded him of their night together.

She stared at him with a big grin.

Caleb looked around at the tables. Seeing the old man, he turned back to her. "Wasn't that dude here last night?"

"Yep."

"He's Albert Einstein with a drinking problem."

"Water is all he drinks."

"Why come here just to drink water? He can do that from home."

"He's lonely. That's why a lot of people come here—just to be around people."

"I think he comes here just to look at you. I know I would."

"He tipped me a hundred bucks last night. That man can come here every night of the week as far as I'm concerned, and he can stare at me all he wants."

"Copy that."

"Where did you get the 'copy that' business?"

"The service. 'Copy' or 'roger that' means 'message received and understood.' 'Affirmative' means 'yes.' 'Negative' means 'no.'"

"Oh, I see. Copy that," she deadpanned.

"You got it."

"I'm a quick learner." She winked.

"I noticed. Any plans after work? If Joyce gives me a bonus, I might need help celebrating."

"I can move a few things around."

"I'll stop by at closing and pick you up. Sound good?"

"Affirmative."

6

Joyce Benson promenaded through the bar in a colorful cactus-print pantsuit. Upon seeing her bouncer, she motioned for him to join her in the office. After she closed the door, she pointed at a chair. "Sit down, Caleb. Thanks for coming in. You know, I really appreciate what you did last night."

He sat down, put his elbows on the armrests, and looked around. "No problem."

"How's your head doing?"

"It's doing. Good thing the drunk hit me there. Being hard-headed finally paid off."

"Glad to hear it. I've been worried about you. Take the rest of the week off and give yourself some time to heal."

"Yes, ma'am."

"We do have one little problem. The guy you punched last night is an old regular who hasn't been here in a while. His name is Derek Snerd. He plans to sue you and the bar. I've been on the phone with my lawyer most of the day trying to resolve this."

"That's bogus. We should be suing him. He threatened Ashley and hit me over the head with a beer bottle. When we got outside, he headbutted me. See this?" He pointed to a lump on his head the size of a golf ball. "If that isn't assault and battery, I don't know what is. And look, I have two black eyes."

Benson frowned. "I know what you're saying. You did punch him, though. In fact, you beat him up and knocked him out. He went to the ER for treatment and wants his medical expenses paid as well as money for pain and suffering—and he wants you fired."

"He started it, and he hit me first—twice, in fact."

"Don't say anything about this to anyone. I'll try to make it go away."

"Whatever you say, Joyce."

He left her office and took a seat at the bar.

Ashley finished taking a drink order, then hurried over to him. "What happened? Did you get a bonus?"

"Nope."

"Did you get a raise?"

"Nope."

"What then?"

"She wants me to take the week off—to heal."

"You could use some healing time. You look bummed. What's going on?"

"I guess I'm a little tired."

"Do you still want to do something when I get off?"

"Of course. You're part of my rehab plan."

"Good."

He turned his head toward the white-haired old guy and his glass of water. "Take good care of the old dude."

"For sure."

7

Later that night, Caleb returned to the Ax and checked the messages on his phone while he waited for Ashley's shift to end.

When she got off, Ashley grabbed her purse from under the bar and pulled up a stool next to his. He put his hand on her thigh. "Want a beer before we go?"

She patted his hand. "Sure."

He motioned to the other bartender to get her attention. "Rosie, a Bud Light here and a PBR for the lady, please."

"Sure, Caleb." Rosie went into action, pulling the bottles from the fridge.

After examining the crown of his head to evaluate the wound, Ashley looked him in the eye. "How are you feeling?"

"I'm good. Couldn't get you off my mind for some reason. Don't know why."

"I have that effect on men."

"I'm not surprised."

"You've crossed my mind a couple of times today too, mister."

"Glad to hear that." He raised his bottle. "Here's a toast to my favorite bartender."

She raised hers. "And to my favorite bouncer." She took a pull from the longneck bottle. "That hits the spot."

"Busy night?"

"Too slow, Caleb. Without you, no crowd. No drunks. No fights."

"It was the discounted drinks for ladies' night, not me."

"Yes, and you too. You're a babe magnet."

"I wish."

"Those chicks last night kept asking if you were in a relationship."

"What did you tell them?"

"I said you were happily married."

He gave her a gentle shove. "You're pure evil. How were the tips tonight?"

"Not bad. The old guy gave me a hundred bucks again. He kept asking all about you—

your name, where you're from, stuff like that."

"What did you tell him?"

"That your name is Caleb Sinclair and you just got out of the army because that's all I know about you, dude."

"That's all you know about me?"

"You're a pretty good kisser, but I thought I'd keep that to myself."

"I should get to know the old guy. I could use a big tipper like that in my life. The only tips I get are girls' phone numbers. You can't get money for those."

Jealousy shot through Ashley like a lightning bolt. She didn't think that was funny and wondered why he felt he needed to bring up other girls' phone numbers. "Are you bragging or complaining, dude?"

"Just stating a fact. After last night, there's only one chick on my mind, and that's you."

"Yeah, right. You're so full of it."

"The heart wants what it wants."

Her face turned as red as a stoplight, but her heart signaled green. "You and I have only been together one night, mister. How can you say that?"

"I just know. My head was split open, and it still hurts, but I've felt good all day long because I'm thinking about you and not my head."

"Don't give me that crap." She gently slapped him with a careless wave of her hand, yet her heart raced faster.

Ashley studied Caleb as he opened his billfold and put cash on the bar. She didn't know much about this ruggedly gorgeous man, but she knew he'd rescued her, and she felt safe with him.

She had come to expect the attention she received from men who found her attractive and lavished compliments on her. Caleb had always been friendly, yet she'd never felt she was on his radar screen. It pleased her to realize she had finally attracted him.

"I'll be right back." He slipped off the stool and headed for the restroom.

She put both hands around the bottle, now nearly empty, and studied the label. *I think I'm falling in love with this man. He's such a good guy. I don't want to jump into this too fast, but I don't want to lose him either.*

She'd witnessed his gentle side last night, and it was something to behold. Externally the bouncer projected toughness, yet on the inside, he was as tender as a puppy's eyelashes. She remembered his velvet touch and delicate embrace last night. Yet, only hours earlier, he had knocked out an aggressive drunk. She was falling hard and couldn't help herself.

Returning to his stool, Caleb finished his beer and slapped the bottle down on the bar. "We sure had fun last night, didn't we, Ashley?"

"Sure did."

"While I was gone, were you thinking about me?"

"Maybe."

"Thinking what a cool dude I am?"

"No. Asking myself what was I thinking to spend the night with someone like you." She cracked a slow smile.

"You were tired and fell asleep."

"You could have woken me up and sent me home, you know."

"I was sleeping too."

She patted him on the back. "Problem solved. We spent the night together because we were too tired to do anything else. Nothing more."

"That's our story, and we're sticking to it."

They touched knuckles in a slow-motion fist bump, each feeling a tingle.

8

Caleb slid off the barstool. "How about going for a ride on Riverside Drive? It's a beautiful evening. We could get to know each other better. Maybe you'll even learn to like me."

"Don't get your hopes up, dude. Why don't you follow me home so I can change?"

After dropping her car off, she emerged from her apartment in cutoffs, a tank top, and flip-flops. As Caleb steered his weatherworn Frontier pickup truck to scenic Riverside Drive, her lavender perfume filled the car and transported him back to last night. The full moon lit the landscape and sent a beam of light across the river. There was a cool breeze that calmed the desert landscape.

"I just thought of something, Ashley. It's Christmas Eve. It doesn't seem like it when you live in the desert, does it?"

"No, it doesn't. Merry Christmas, Caleb."

"Merry Christmas, Ashley. Just think, this is our first Christmas together."

"You're optimistic. How do you know it's not our only Christmas together?"

"I just know."

"What did you think of me before last night, Caleb?"

"I thought you were cute and sweet and a good bartender. You're confident and calm during bar rushes."

"Thanks. I try to have my crap together most of the time."

"Your turn, Ashley. What did you think of me?"

"I thought you were a nice guy, good-looking and strong. You were always friendly in a coworker sort of way."

He laughed. "What's a 'coworker sort of way?'"

"You were cordial in your interactions but businesslike, as opposed to sharing personal things. Don't get me wrong. That's not a bad thing. I'd rather have a colleague act professionally than hit on me. I get hit on a lot."

"I don't doubt that."

"If you thought I was cute and sweet, why didn't *you* ever hit on me—or ask me out or try to get to know me better?"

"I thought about it. Not sure if I'm ready for a relationship with anyone right now. This is my first position after getting out of the army, and I want to concentrate on doing it well. This job is all I've got right now, and I can't afford to blow it."

"Work comes first for me too." She pressed out a wrinkle in her cutoffs with her hand. "Mama told me, 'When you're at work, work. Don't talk religion, politics, or sex.'"

"What else is there?"

She laughed. "Tell me about you. I want to get to know you."

"There isn't much to tell. Mostly boring stuff."

"Where were you raised? What are your parents like?"

He scratched his head. "Ever heard of Des Moines, Iowa?"

"Where the tall corn grows, right?"

"Right. I spent my childhood there. Never knew my real parents. I was raised by foster parents. They were older but cool."

"What happened to your parents?"

"They were drug dealers, so Child Protective Services took me away from them after they nearly overdosed. They could be dead by now for all I know—or care. I tried looking up my dad by taking a DNA test, but nothing came up showing any close relatives."

"That sucks."

"My foster parents loved me, and I have no complaints about how they raised me. They taught me right from wrong, and they taught me how to work."

"Those are good things to learn. My parents did that for me too."

"When they retired, we moved to Briggs Lake because they loved the warm weather in Arizona. I graduated from Briggs Lake High. After a while, they got bored, and so my foster dad worked for the Parks Department part-time and my foster mom cleaned houses for extra money to make sure they had enough to give me the things I needed."

"They sound like hardworking people."

"Yeah, they were…are. They're in a nursing home now in Fort Dodge, Iowa. When I left home, they went back to Iowa to be closer to their extended family."

"That must be a shock to their system every time winter rolls around. Any other family?"

"That's it. They're the only family I have—that I know of. What about yours?"

9

"My family is Welsh-Irish. We ended up in Marin County, California, because of my dad's job. He works for Wells Fargo in San Francisco."

"Your family must be rich. Why are you working as a bartender?"

"They're not rich, just comfortable. Banking salaries are generally on the low side. My parents raised us to be self-sufficient. We've all had to work our way through school. They say it will mean more to us if we have to work for it."

"They didn't want to raise spoiled brats."

"No danger of that. I'm studying to become a registered nurse and paying all my school expenses with the tips I make bartending. I take classes three days a week. When I'm not working or in class, I'm studying."

"I've had to work for everything too. My foster parents had modest incomes—Dad worked for the city water treatment plant, and Mom was a secretary. They did what they could to help me, but they couldn't do a whole lot."

"Have you ever been to Marin County, Caleb?"

"Never have."

"It's like a garden, constantly blooming and covered with vegetation, a far cry from the desert. Every morning the fog rolls in from San Francisco Bay through Mill Valley. It's glorious. I was so blessed to be raised there."

"You should have stayed. What brought you to the Arizona desert?"

"A guy I was dating got a job as a test engineer at Fiat Chrysler Automobiles at the Arizona Proving Ground. He was ingenious and ambitious. I'm sure he'll be the plant manager someday."

"Why did you break up?"

"It's complicated."

"It always is."

"He cared more about his job than me. I'm the jealous type and didn't want to share him with anyone, not even a car company like Chrysler."

"Was he seeing someone else?"

"No, he wasn't. Though I accused him of it all the time. It was my own fears and head trips. He couldn't take all the drama. My jealousy drove him away. Pun intended."

"He didn't have a girlfriend after all?"

"No. He had a mistress. Her name was Fiat Chrysler Automobiles, and I just couldn't compete with that. He was more interested in building cars than building a life with me. Here's something you need to know about me from the start. I want to be the most important thing in my man's life."

"I get that. Do you believe that someone can have only one true love and if they don't find that person, they'll be single all their life?"

Ashley brushed her hair back with her left hand. "I never thought about it that way. I've either been interested in guys who weren't interested in me, or I've had guys who were interested in me, but I had no interest in them. I guess I'm looking for a man who loves me as much as I love him."

"That's what we all want."

"I can't spend the rest of my life wondering if I should have hooked up with Mr. Fiat Chrysler. He had his chance, and he made his choice. I'm not wasting my time with a man who's more in love with cars than with me."

Caleb pulled into a scenic overlook so they could enjoy a bend in the river that offered a spectacular view of the moon and the spotlight it beamed across the majestic Colorado River. They opened the car windows to feel the wind on their faces and smell the fresh desert air.

They talked late into the night. When they ran out of things to discuss, Ashley felt his gentle embrace and velvet touch when he pulled her close to him and kissed her. He kissed her for a long time, and she kissed him back. Time stood still.

"I wish I could do this with you all night, Caleb, but I can't stay up any longer. Some of us have jobs and have to go to work tomorrow."

"Copy that."

He drove her home, walked her to the door, and kissed her good night. They hugged each other for a few minutes without saying a word.

"Thank you, sir, for the beautiful evening. Merry Christmas."

"You're welcome. Merry Christmas. You're my Christmas present this year. Santa was very good to me. Can I see you tomorrow after work?"

"I'd like that."

After closing the door to her apartment, she leaned back against it. *I love this man.*

10

Caleb picked Ashley up after work for the next few nights. The new couple usually went out for a bite to eat, then returned to her apartment to watch TV. It got harder each night for Caleb to leave. They lingered at her door, saying good night over and over and kissing each other repeatedly, not wanting their time together to end.

The old man with the white hair came to the bar every day, always drinking water, tipping a hundred dollars, and asking about Caleb.

On Friday morning Caleb got a call from Joyce Benson to meet in her office at five o'clock p.m. When he arrived, he saw Ashley talking to the old man. He waved as he passed them. She looked up and smiled.

Once inside Joyce's office, Caleb felt tense. A sensation came over him that something was wrong.

"How's your head, Caleb?"

"It's good, Joyce. I'm ready to go back to work anytime."

"Here's the thing. That guy was so wrong to hit you over the head like that. It was uncalled for. He was drunk and didn't realize what he was doing, and just so you know, he did apologize to me."

"He should have apologized to Ashley and me. What an ass."

"No doubt about it, he was wrong, and he felt bad about it afterward, but you shouldn't have punched him out either."

"Joyce, the imbecile opened a six-inch gash in my head and would have done more if he had the chance. He could've hurt Ashley or a customer. What was I supposed to do? I had to stop him. I was doing my job—protecting an employee and customers from an out-of-control guy trashed out of his mind."

"Removing him from the bar was fine. Holding him for the police was fine. Hitting him was against company policy." She shook her head. "You didn't just hit him once. You punched him several times and knocked him out and sent him to the emergency room. His lawyer is saying he may have received permanent damage to his eyesight. You knew the policy from the day I hired you. Under no circumstances can you hit customers."

"It won't happen again."

She tapped her forefinger on her desk. "Mr. Snerd and I have come to an agreement. He won't sue us."

"I'm glad it worked out."

"Yes." She took a deep breath and looked around the office. "There is just one other thing. Unfortunately I'm going to have to let you go."

"Let me go? Get real, Joyce. I was protecting the people in your bar. You hired me to do that. I'm a bouncer. That's what bouncers do. What don't you get about that?"

"You exposed my bar to potentially expensive litigation that could have bankrupted me and closed the Ax. I've spent years building this business and worked too hard to let something like this ruin it. The bottom line is that you violated company policy, and that's grounds for dismissal."

"But—"

"You signed the policy. It's in your personnel file." Benson opened her top desk drawer and handed Sinclair a check. "Here's your final check. I'm sorry."

"No sorrier than I am." Caleb rose to his feet, folded the envelope, and stuffed it in his front jeans pocket.

Benson stood and moved close to him, appearing ready to shake hands. He was not so inclined. He straightened up, threw his shoulders back, and walked out of the office.

Although she was in the middle of taking a drink order, a glance in his direction told Ashley something was wrong.

Once outside the bar, Caleb paused and exhaled. *Wow. I can't believe this. I just got the axe for doing my job. Now what?*

The front door opened behind him, and the old white-haired man caned his way out. He extended his hand. "Hello. Let me introduce myself. I'm Richard Stockbridge."

"Hi. Caleb Sinclair."

They exchanged handshakes.

"I watched you deal with that thug the other night. I'm impressed with the way you handled yourself."

"Glad someone was. I just got canned."

"Why? After the way you took care of that drunk guy, I would have given you a raise."

"Apparently, coldcocking a customer who threatened to kill a bartender is against company policy. Who knew?"

"I'm so sorry to hear that, Caleb. However, this could turn out to be a good thing for you. I have a proposition for you."

"What?" Sinclair asked as he stepped back.

"I'd like to offer you a job working for me."

"Doing what?"

"Is there someplace nearby where we can talk?"

"There's the Blue Onion, a restaurant not too far from here." Caleb pointed up the street. "We can walk there."

"That's fine, but don't walk too fast. As you can see, I use a cane."

As the six-footer with the short black hair and the much shorter old man with the long white hair trudged up the street, they drew stares from other pedestrians who wondered what enterprise had brought this odd couple together.

11

Once seated inside at a table in the back, the old man leaned his cane against the chair next to him. Servers hurried into the kitchen with dirty dishes and jingling silverware while others bounced out the other door with trays of steaming hot food and soups. Mouthwatering aromas from clam chowder to fried onions hovered over the dining room like a cloud.

A waitress bounded to their table and took their drink orders. When she was out of earshot, Stockbridge folded his hands in front of him and began his pitch. "I need someone to do errands—to visit people from my past and give them the things they need most."

Caleb adjusted his chair closer to the table. "You want me to pass out money to your old friends?"

"Something like that. In some cases, they may not need money. Your job is to find out what they need most, and I'll see they get it."

"Everybody needs money."

"Not really." Stockbridge lowered his voice. "I don't need money. I need health. I'd give away all my money to have my health back."

"What's wrong with your health?"

"I'm dying."

The waitress brought iced tea for Stockbridge and black coffee for Caleb. They both ordered the salmon sandwich special. After writing on her pad, she fixed her eyes on Caleb. "Is there anything else I can do for you?"

He caught the flirty expression in her eyes and shook his head.

She maintained eye contact with him a few seconds longer before looking in Stockbridge's direction. The old man waved her off.

"That's terrible about you dying, Mr. Stockbridge. I'm so sorry to hear that."

Stockbridge took a sip of his iced tea. "I'm not too happy about it myself. I have a rare disease. My doctor told me to get my affairs in order."

"Cancer?"

"No, I beat the big C a couple of times. This is different. It's a long story for another day. I've accepted the diagnosis and am making the most of the time I have left."

"That sucks."

"Tell me about it." Stockbridge leaned forward. "I want to do something for a few folks I've known in the past. That's where you come in."

Caleb sipped his coffee. "I'm listening."

"I own several businesses, and they have been profitable beyond my wildest dreams. I started with nothing, and now I'm wealthy and have more money than I know what to do with. Of course, with my diagnosis, money isn't going to do me much good."

"You could invest your money in research for a cure."

"Caleb, I don't have that kind of time. I'm at peace. I've lived a long and fruitful life. I'll be seventy-five soon. With the time I have left, I want to distribute my wealth."

"I get that. But why can't you do that yourself—what do you need me for?"

"I don't want the people to know where the money is coming from."

"Why not?"

"It's complicated. I have my reasons. I understand you were in the army, right?"

"Affirmative. Army Ranger School and Special Operations Command."

"Good. There's some risk. I have to tell you that up front. I have no way of knowing what kind of reaction you're going to get from them or the situations they find themselves in. I don't expect them to be criminals or anything like that, but I don't know for sure what you're going to run into."

"Whatever you got, it couldn't be harder than three Afghanistan deployments fighting the Taliban. I can handle myself."

Stockbridge's eyebrows rose. "I saw that the other night. How's your adjustment to civilian life going?"

"When I got out, I partied every day for a couple of months straight, using alcohol to dim the images of war I couldn't get out of my brain. I was self-medicating to numb the pain. And I have a lot of bad dreams—one in particular keeps coming back. Before I knew it, I ran out of money and had to start looking for a job."

"I imagine it was hard to transfer some of your military skills to civilian jobs."

"Affirmative. I can think quickly on my feet and make good decisions under pressure in life-or-death situations. I'm having trouble convincing companies that those leadership skills can apply to civilian jobs."

Stockbridge imitated a company recruiter. "Your skills are impressive, young man, but we don't really have an opening for someone good at killing another person with his bare hands."

Sinclair laughed. "Not exactly, but something like that. All I've been looking for is a chance to show a company what I can do. The army tried to get me to stay in and go to Officer Candidate School."

"Why didn't you?"

"The last time I was wounded, I felt my luck was running out." He pulled back his shirtsleeve to expose a scar that ran from his shoulder to his elbow. "When I got this, I tasted my own mortality for the first time. Up until this, I thought I was invincible. And I guess I was. You know, when you're eighteen, you know it all. The sniper bullet almost killed me, and I realized it was time to quit."

"I don't blame you. The work I have in mind is more like a messenger, a go-between. You won't have to shoot anyone, and nobody will shoot you. At least I hope not."

"Good to know."

12

The waitress returned with their dinners. Sinclair and Stockbridge scarfed down their sandwiches in silence. At the same time, instrumental versions of '60s rock hits played softly from the speaker system, interrupted periodically by the sounds of the swinging kitchen doors.

When finished, Stockbridge took a sip of iced tea and wiped his mouth with a napkin. "I'll pay you a hundred grand a year and cover all your expenses. I'm not sure how long it will take you. Probably a year. Could be more. Could be less. It all depends."

"Holy shit. That's a lot of money. Nothing illegal, right?"

"Oh no. Nothing like that, Caleb. You'll need to do some traveling, though. I'll reimburse you for your expenses, of course."

"How do I find these people?"

"I've researched them and will give you their contact information. You may have to do some digging into their lives a bit to see what they need the most."

"And that means what?"

"That means you'll have to spend some time talking with them. Get to know them. If they need money, how much and why. If they don't need money, find out what they do need. Let me know, and I'll make it happen if I can."

Caleb looked away and gazed at a middle-aged couple at a nearby table while trying to process this new information from Stockbridge. He noticed that the couple wasn't speaking to each other, and he wondered why. They didn't seem happy.

Looking back at his dinner companion, Caleb took a breath. "I can't just walk up to strangers and ask them personal questions.

They'll think I'm crazy or that I'm stalking them or something. They'll call the cops."

"You'll have to invent a reason."

"I can't lie to them."

"You don't have to lie, but be creative. Explain your interest in the people in a logical and believable way."

"What do you mean?"

"Caleb, have you ever thought of writing a book about your war experiences?"

"Sure."

"Then you can tell them you're thinking of writing a book. That's not a lie if you've thought about it before."

"I see what you mean."

"Strike up a conversation the way you would with any new acquaintance. Sincerely compliment what they're wearing or what they're doing—be authentic and honest. It doesn't matter how you start the conversation, then ask questions and listen. When they trust you, they will share their hopes and dreams."

Caleb looked away in thought. "With all due respect, that's easier said than done."

"Yes. But I believe you can do it." Stockbridge put both palms on the table. "That's the job. What do you say?"

"I'll give it a try."

Stockbridge reached across the table, and they shook hands. "Good. Welcome aboard."

"How will we communicate?"

"Using secure cell phones." He reached into his pocket and pulled out a phone. "This is yours. Nobody can eavesdrop on our conversations as long as you're using this. We can meet in person sometimes and use snail mail too."

"Do you live in Briggs Lake, sir?"

"Yes. I bought a place along the Colorado River. It's secluded and private. I also have a home in Fort Myers, Florida."

Stockbridge folded the napkin on the table in front of him. "Your first assignment is local and should be easy. Her name is Danielle

Stevens. She works at the Starbucks in the Briggs Lake Bookstore." He slid a card across the table containing her name and the address of the Starbucks.

"Got it."

"Any more questions?"

"No. I'm good."

Stockbridge stacked a pile of cash on the check, got to his feet, and extended his hand.

Caleb shook it. "Thank you, sir. I appreciate the opportunity. I won't let you down."

"I know you won't."

13

Ashley Bivens ducked into the passenger's side of Caleb's pickup and fastened her seat belt with a click. He closed the door and came around to the driver's side. After he began backing up, she turned to him. "What's wrong, Caleb?"

"What do you mean?"

"You don't look good. I can tell something's wrong."

"I'm sure you heard."

"Heard what?"

"Joyce fired me." He exhaled, relieved to say it out loud.

She put her hand on his thigh. "That's why Joyce called an all-staff meeting tomorrow. Oh, Caleb, I'm so sorry."

"Thanks."

"She's a bitch."

"She may be a bitch, but the Ax Handle is her bar. She can do whatever she wants."

"I don't understand. The drunk threatened me and could have hurt me badly if it wasn't for you. You were hired to prevent things like that."

"Except I wasn't supposed to hit the guy. I signed paperwork agreeing to all company policies, and that was one of them. She had me dead in the water."

"What are you going to do for work?"

"I already got a job."

"Really? Doing what?"

"Visiting people. Finding out what they need. Then communicating the need to my boss, who will get it for them."

"Excuse me, but what the hell kind of job is that? Does your boss think he's Mother Teresa?"

He looked at her, and they cracked up.

"Good one. You're a funny lady."

"It's one of my gifts."

Still smiling, he continued. "Look, I know it sounds weird, but I think he's legit."

"Let me get this straight. You're working for a guy who has his own version of Make-a-Wish, only it's for grown-ups?"

"You got it."

"Who in heaven's name is this?"

"You know him. He's the old dude with the shoulder-length white hair who looks like Moses who's been tipping you a hundred dollars a day for serving him spring water."

"Stockbridge. That old geezer is your new boss?" She laughed out loud. "You've got to be kidding. That's not a job. That's a fairy tale."

"No. He's for real. He's rich, and he's dying, and he wants to give away his money before he passes."

"Caleb, he's probably a horse's ass and wants to make amends with people he's screwed over but doesn't have the spine to do it himself."

"He didn't say that was his motivation, but it could be in some cases."

"He's a good tipper. I'll say that for him."

"He's promised me a six-figure salary plus expenses—says I won't have to do anything illegal. I don't have anything else going for me. I might as well give it a shot."

"Remember how I told you he had been asking me all sorts of questions about you? Turns out he's been coming to the bar to do research on you. But why you?"

"He said it was because of the way I handled myself that night with the drunk." Caleb turned the radio on and changed the subject of their conversation. "I like all music, but my favorite is the blues. What do you want to do tonight?"

She took her hand off his thigh and pulled her hair behind her ear. "I'm kinda hungry. I know a good all-night coffee shop we haven't been to yet. Let's get something to eat, then go to my place."

"Sounds good."

They rode in silence for a few minutes, listening to signature riffs by blues legend **B.B. King**.

"Can you do me a favor, Ashley? Don't share anything about Stockbridge or my new job, please."

"Sure. It's in the lockbox." She twisted her thumb and forefinger in front of her mouth.

They parked the truck in a neighborhood even Mr. Rogers wouldn't have visited, in a rundown section of town. Caleb's danger instinct on full alert, he got out of the Frontier and eyed the surroundings with caution.

Once inside, they ordered a couple of burgers.

"Caleb, what do you really think of me?"

"What do you mean?"

She raised her voice. "What do you think of me?"

"You're smart, cute, and sweet."

"In that order? Keep going."

"I was done."

She kicked him under the table.

"Ouch! Some date you are. Kicking me in the shins."

"Watch yourself, young man. Don't let these good looks fool you. I can be fierce when I want to be."

"I don't doubt that for one minute, lady."

"You have beautiful eyelashes, Caleb. Has anyone ever told you that?"

"Nope. You're the first."

"They're even longer than mine."

"Come to think of it, I guess my eyelashes are awesome. Thank you for noticing."

She threw a wadded-up napkin at his face. "Telling you that was a big mistake. It's obviously gone to your head."

"What's gone to my head is you. I've got a bad case of Ashley Bivens, and there's no cure."

"I'm like a disease. Is that what you're saying, dude?"

"If what I feel for you is a disease, I hope it's chronic and lasts for the rest of my life."

"What a charmer you are. You better stop that talk right now, or I might fall in love with you."

As they ate their burgers, the couple shared funny stories. Each tried to outdo the other until the tales became so far-fetched, it became harder and harder to believe they could be true. At a certain point, it didn't even matter if they were true because they were hilarious. Ashley loved seeing his face light up when he laughed. He had a good laugh, and she added that to the growing list of things about him she liked.

14

After finishing their meal, Ashley and Caleb headed to the parking lot holding hands. Out of the darkness, they saw Geno Schlubb, a tall man with a high-pitched voice, and his partner, Lenny Colleti. The strange duo appeared to be in their thirties, and they blocked the path to Caleb's pickup.

Colleti, a short, chunky bald man, folded his arms. "What's up?"

"Your time talking to us. Get out of our way," Caleb said through gritted teeth.

Lenny answered, "Aren't you the funny one? We lost our wallets and need you to borrow us some cash for the drive home."

"Sorry. I guess you'll have to walk."

"You got money. You just came from a diner."

"Get your fat ass out of our way—now!"

Lenny grabbed Ashley's arm. "Not so fast. Hey, hottie. Let's get acquainted."

"Get your hands off her, scumbag," Caleb growled.

Geno launched a roundhouse right. Caleb ducked and rammed a knee into his groin, causing the tall guy to squeal like a wounded female cougar. Caleb followed up with a left hook that sent the goon sprawling on the ground, moaning in agony. In the next instant, Lenny felt a numbing kick to his elbow and heard his bone shatter. He involuntarily let go of Ashley's wrist and cradled the limp arm, screaming profanities at the young veteran.

Caleb grabbed Ashley's hand. "Let's get out of here."

They ran for the truck as fast as they could and drove away. As Caleb merged with the traffic, he looked over at his girlfriend. She quivered from head to toe. "You all right?"

"I'm fine. I can't stop shaking, though. Sorry. I was scared to death. That was horrible. I'll never go to that place again."

"Me neither. The food's not bad—the neighborhood's another story."

"Where did you learn to fight like that? You hit them like lightning strikes."

"The army…Ranger School…we're good at that stuff. Fighting is what we do."

"I'll say. You really know how to kick butt, literally. Forget bouncing; you could make a living as an MMA fighter. On second thought, I don't want to see your pretty face messed up. I'd rather you became my personal bodyguard."

"I hope the pay is good. I don't work cheap."

"The pay isn't much, but the fringe benefits are amazing." She put her head on his shoulder. "You *are* my knight in shining armor."

When they got to Ashley's apartment, they polished off a bottle of Zinfandel and chatted all night. As the sun peeked over the horizon, they were talked out and tired.

"Another all-nighter," she said. "Being with you has been hazardous to my sleep schedule."

"You can kick me out anytime you want."

"I know. C'mon, Caleb. Let's go to bed."

He followed her into the bedroom and detected the scent of lavender. Ashley pushed down her daisy dukes and stepped out of them. She yanked her blouse over her head and tossed it toward a chair. It missed and fell to the floor. Unsnapping her bra and letting it drop at her feet, she slid under the covers while Caleb, mesmerized, stood staring at her.

"C'mon, let's get some rest," she said while holding up the blanket for him.

Seeing this gorgeous girl beckoning to him to climb into bed filled him with desire. He wasn't tired anymore. Leaving his clothes in a twisted heap, he slipped under the blanket next to her. He felt her soft skin against his chest and heard her heart beating. At that moment nothing else mattered but to be with this woman. He wanted to touch her, kiss her, and hold her forever. He wanted her in every way. He pulled her close and gave her a long kiss.

15

The next day, Caleb called Stockbridge. "I took my girl to a restaurant last night, and two guys approached us in the parking lot. They picked a fight with me so that they could rob us. I beat the crap out of them, and we took off. I'm telling you this just to keep you in the loop."

Stockbridge replied, "Thanks for the information. Glad you're okay."

"I enjoyed our dinner the other night. The more I think about working with you and helping people get what they want, the more I like the idea."

"It should be fun helping people's dreams come true. Especially since we want nothing in return from them, not even a thank-you, an acknowledgment, or public recognition. That's the best way to give, don't you think?"

"Sure is. I'll let you know what happens with Danielle Stevens."

"Looking forward to hearing about her. Thanks for calling, Caleb. Be careful out there."

The next evening a couple of visitors stopped by Derek Snerd's house. He was sitting in his bathrobe having a drink and watching TV. "How did it go last night, boys?"

"It didn't go so good, Mr. Snerd," Geno said, looking at the floor. "We had some complications."

"You're not going to give me excuses, are you, Geno?"

"We followed them to a restaurant. When they came out, we got in their faces to rough them up, like you said."

"What happened?"

"He was fast and trained good in fighting. He whacked us before we knew what hit us."

"I warned you he was a bouncer and an army veteran. That should have told you something, Geno."

"We didn't have enough preparations for fighting him. He kicked me in the family jewels. I'm not going to be able to walk without a limp for a week or so. As you can see, he broke Lenny's arm, and he'll be in a cast for the next six weeks."

"Look at you, Lenny, you fat fart. You're as worthless as tits on a bull."

Geno leaned into his boss. "Give us another chance. We'll take care of business next time."

"Before you try to get him again, there's another job I need you guys to handle, but don't screw this one up. One of our distributors is holding out on us. He's got a cash flow problem, but that's not my problem. He's got a balance due, and I want you to collect."

"You can count on us, boss," Geno said. "For all intensive purposes, it's a done deal."

Snerd wrote down a name and address, a number, and an amount, then handed it to Geno.

"We got this, Mr. Snerd."

"Another thing, Geno: you guys keep a low profile and stay away from the Ax Handle for a while."

"Low profile. Got it."

Snerd closed the front door after his gangsters left. He walked into the kitchen, poured himself a shot of Jack Daniels, and tossed it back. *I'll get you, bouncer boy. You're going to wish you'd never messed with Derek Snerd.*

16

Caleb entered Starbucks looking for Danielle Stevens, his first assignment from Stockbridge. He loved the smell of coffee in the morning even more than its taste. His mouth watered, ready for that first cup. Danielle worked alone, so he waited until she'd served the other customers before stepping up to the counter. The thirtysomething had black hair styled to midlength and wore a black blouse and shorts. Her fingernails were painted black, and she had a semicircle of small diamonds pierced into both ears and silver rings on her fingers. Her pale complexion, accentuated with powder, was in stark contrast to her heavy black eye shadow and liner. He noted that she didn't wear a wedding ring.

Stockbridge should have told me she was a witch.

She filled an empty urn bag with coffee, started the water, and looked up at him.

"May I help you?" Her voice, soft and tender, didn't seem to match her dark and jolting appearance. He got a whiff of patchouli oil when she moved toward him.

"I'd like your regular blend, the largest size you've got."

The Goth girl snatched a cup from the tall stack that was set upside down. "Should I leave enough room for cream or sugar?"

"No thanks. Just black." *Like your hair, your nails, and your blouse, sweetie.*

She smiled as she filled up his cup. "Here you go."

"Thanks." *What a smile. This girl must love her job. Either that, or she's flirting with me.*

"Working all by yourself must keep you busy."

"I won't fly solo for long. I'm the manager, and one of my employees called out sick. Someone's on the way to help."

"That's good. You're the manager, huh? Doing this long?"

"About seven years, the last two as manager. I like coffee, and I like the business. I'm going to school part-time, taking business management courses—saving up to buy my own coffee business."

"Good for you. Just curious, what does a coffee franchise cost?"

"Depends on the company. I'm figuring a half million. There's the licensing, the capital needed for the building, and enough fluid cash to keep it going until the customer base gets built up."

"That's a lot of money. How long is that going to take you?"

"At least a couple of years. I'm saving all I can with every paycheck. At some point, I'll get a business loan. On the side, I write children's books. If one of them takes off, I'll be able to get the cash sooner."

"Sounds like you've really thought it through. I admire your commitment to your goal."

A customer drove up to the window for a latte, which sent Danielle back to her coffee makers. Caleb watched her quick movements and saw flickers of light reflecting off her jewelry.

Shapely body underneath all that black. There's a tattoo on her neck. I can't quite make it out. A cross?

When she finished, she looked around to see if any other customers were waiting, then bounced over to his table again.

"Go ahead and sit down. If you've got time. I'm enjoying our conversation. I recently got out of the military, and I don't have a lot of friends to talk to."

Danielle looked around and sat down. "Don't mind if I do. I've always got time for my customers. Thanks for your service. My name's Danielle Stevens. What's yours?" She stuck out her hand.

"I'm Caleb Sinclair. Pleased to meet you." They shook hands.

"So, were you in a war?"

"Yes, I was."

"I'm so sorry. I don't believe in war. I don't blame our soldiers, though. Killing isn't the answer to anything."

"I know what you mean. I've seen a lot of bad stuff I'm trying to forget."

"Then let's change the subject. Are you working?"

"I have a temporary job, but I'm not as focused as you are with what I want to do long-term. I feel like I'm floundering a bit trying to plan my future."

"I sometimes flounder too, Caleb. You just have to listen to your heart and trust."

"Trust what?"

"Your gut instincts. That's what I do. I have confidence in myself that I can do anything I set my mind to."

He took a long sip from his coffee cup. "Your vision for your life is so clear. I wish I had that. I'm not sure what I want to do yet. I just know I don't want to kill anyone—or be killed, for that matter."

"That's a good plan!" She laughed, and her face lit up with a toothy grin.

He noticed her light blue eyes, bright and piercing at the same time. "Say, if I wanted to buy one of your books, how would I do it?"

"They're available on Amazon—wait." She got up and went behind the counter, pulling a business card from her purse before coming back to join him at the table.

"This card has my number and PO box. If you send me your address, I'll sign one for you and send you a free copy."

"Excellent."

She noticed a group of three retired guys who were coming for their weekly bull session over coffee. "I have to go. I've got customers. Good meeting you, Caleb."

He watched Danielle wait on the three regulars like they were old friends. They loved the attention she showered on them, along with the coffee she poured into their cups. At one point she looked over at Caleb and smiled. He smiled back and lifted his cup to toast her.

At a table in the back sat a man in a business suit with a white shirt and no tie. Caleb had not noticed the man when he came in. His ponytail faced the wall behind him, and his dark eyes, both swollen and bruised, were hidden behind a pair of sunglasses.

This is my lucky day. There he is: the bouncer boy. I could strangle that piece of shit right now with my bare hands. I might have to take care of him myself if my boys can't get their act together.

17

A week later, at the end of Danielle's shift, the owner of the Starbucks stopped in.

"Danielle, we need to talk," he said in a severe tone of voice.

"Yes, sir," she said, her heart thumping. "We can meet in the reading section of the lounge. Follow me." She led him to the back of the store. "No one is usually here."

"You're right. No one is in here reading—or buying books, for that matter. That's the problem. The Briggs Lake Bookstore is closing. They're going bankrupt. We're on a month-to-month lease to operate our coffee business. When they close, the space will no longer be available to lease."

"How soon?"

"Three weeks. I'd like to be able to sell the business to someone willing to relocate it. If not, I'll just close it and retire."

"Seven years—"

"I'm sorry. You'll get unemployment, and I'll give you a good recommendation."

"Mr. Harvey, I can't live on unemployment. My daughter and I are on our own."

"I'm sure you'll catch on somewhere. You're a talented girl."

Danielle's mind was spinning. *Now what am I going to do? I've got a four-year-old daughter with no daddy and no family who cares about us.*

When Danielle arrived at the day care center, her daughter was waiting in the lobby, her yellow and orange backpack strapped to her back.

"What took so long, Mommy?"

"Mommy had a meeting, Lacy. I'm sorry. Do you have all your things?"

"Yes. In my backpack."

"Good. Let's go."

Danielle and Lacy stopped at the post office on the way home so she could get her mail. She brought it back to the car and looked through it before leaving. Among the bills, there was an envelope with no return address. She opened it and read the note inside: "To purchase your coffee business. Good luck." Then she saw the cashier's check for $500,000.

"Mommy, why are you crying?"

18

Caleb and Ashley had been apart for a few days. She worked a couple of double shifts while he ran errands. Although they texted and spoke on the phone before going to bed, those things never quite satisfied their craving for each other's touch.

Deciding to do something different on her day off, they rented Jet Skis to picnic at one of the lake's secluded coves.

"It feels like we have the lake to ourselves, Caleb," she said as she throttled up, taking the lead. Caleb struggled to keep up on his Jet Ski. He didn't have much experience with personal watercrafts of any kind. However, he felt no need to disclose that fact to Ashley. "Fake it till you make it" was his motto, and it usually worked for him.

A competitive swimmer and surfer from her youth, Ashley could outmaneuver any man in a boat or on a Jet Ski. Growing up near the ocean, she'd spent summers at Marin County's beaches—Stinson, Muir, and Bolinas were her favorites. After moving to Briggs Lake, she spent every spare moment on the lake on her Jet Ski or cruising the Colorado River in a rented pontoon boat.

Caleb followed her zigzags and managed to keep from falling off as he bounced through the rough water caused by the collision of her wake with the whitecaps. The gusting wind added to the challenge. He hung in there and followed her, dazzled to see his girlfriend in a new light—in her element on the water. Watching the synchronization of her back, arms, and legs as she balanced and steered her way through the water captivated him. Seeing her bikini-clad body in the bright sunlight and her brown, orange-tinted hair flowing behind her like a celestial fire gave him an even greater appreciation for her fitness and physical beauty.

Upon reaching a secluded cove, they pulled their Jet Skis halfway out of the water, laid a blanket in an area shaded from the wind and sun by a large boulder, and gobbled up their lunch.

"I'll make you a river rat yet, Caleb. I came to this spot when I first moved here. It's a place I can get away by myself and think. I've made my important decisions here. See that rock?" She pointed to the gigantic boulder overhead.

Caleb followed her finger. "Very cool."

"I call it Decision Rock."

"Very peaceful. I like the privacy too."

"Caleb, would you rub some sunscreen on me? Mine washed off on the way over here. With my fair skin, I have to keep it protected all the time."

"Affirmative." He grabbed a tube from the tote bag, sat down behind her, and with a circular motion of both hands, smoothed the white cream into her neck and back.

"That feels soooo good," she purred.

He removed her top and continued massaging the sunscreen, telling himself that if he was to do a proper job, all her fair skin should be protected from the sun's rays. She made no effort to resist. When he finished, she leaned back against his chest and moaned. "Thank you, sir."

Caleb responded by wrapping his arms around her and gently squeezing. She melted in his embrace. She turned around and kissed him as she pushed him down on his back. They kissed passionately, filled themselves with each other's love, then drifted off to sleep.

Caleb's buddy Nick is shot and crumples to the ground a few feet away. Ducking under a blizzard of steel projectiles, Caleb presses a bandage against Nick's stomach to staunch the blood. When the UH-60 Black Hawk finally lands, the helicopter is greeted by a hail of bullets. Caleb cradles Nick like a baby in his arms and charges through the gunfire toward the chopper. Crew Chief Big Jim Robinson hoists Nick inside at the door, and Caleb jumps in behind, nearly falling out as the chopper lifts upward with a roar. Rocket-propelled grenades detonate around the rising copter, engulfing it with smoke and the smell of sulfur and ammonia. The explosions launch shrapnel into Caleb's right leg. He's so focused on encouraging Nick that he doesn't feel the steel shards lodged in his calf. When they land at the field hospital, Nick is dead.

Caleb sat straight up. "No!"

Ashley woke with a start. "What's going on, Caleb?"

He waited until he could catch his breath before answering. "I'm sorry, honey. I had a nightmare."

"In the daytime?"

"I get them night and day."

"What's it about?"

"It's a flashback of the time my buddy Nick took a bullet in the stomach and bled to death before we could get him to the field hospital. I feel guilty that I failed him. I should have done a better job stopping the blood."

"Those things happen in wars. People get killed. It's not your fault."

"I tell myself that sometimes, but that doesn't help Nick. He's dead."

"All I know is that you're a brave man and I admire you. Don't be so hard on yourself."

"Thanks, honey." He laid back down and drifted off to sleep.

19

She'd been with many men but never one like him. He was strong and brave and so handsome. She felt safe with him. Yet he was gentle. His touch was soft, and his voice, though deep, always held a kind tone. She studied the large scar on his arm that slanted from his shoulder to his elbow. Not able to resist the temptation, she ran her forefinger along it to see how it felt.

He woke up again. "What?"

"I just wanted to feel your scar."

He ran his hand backward over the top of his head and blinked his eyes.

"How did it happen, if you don't mind telling me?"

"A firefight. It was over, actually. Out of the blue, a sniper got me. A bullet took a chunk out of my arm. A few more inches, and I would have been dead."

"It must have hurt."

"Knocked me down, and I bled all over the place, but it could have been worse. Thankfully, a medic attended to it before I bled out."

"You were lucky."

"I'll say. Someone was looking out for me."

"Why'd you get out of the army?"

"Felt my luck was running out after getting shot, and it was time to bail. Courage gets built up through training, education, and experience, sort of like deposits in a bank account. Then every close call or near-death experience you have chips away at your confidence and makes withdrawals from your courage account. I just couldn't build the courage account back up anymore. I no longer felt invincible and knew if I didn't get out, I would get killed."

"I've never heard it stated like that. I don't blame you."

"Another thing that went down—ROEs changed," Sinclair added. "I thought those changes would get me killed."

"What's an ROE?"

"Rules of engagement. Politicians in Washington restricted our ability to shoot at enemy targets. You can't engage the enemy unless you follow the rules they lay out. While you're deciding if the conditions allow you to use your weapon, the bad guys can get a free shot at you. It got so bad that they had to be shooting at us almost before we could fire our weapons." He took a sip of his water. "When they changed those rules, we started losing a lot of guys. What do you expect when you can't shoot until they're shooting at you? If the enemy always gets the first shot, you're not going to survive many gun battles."

"That's just common sense. Why would the politicians do that to our troops?"

"They were worried about civilian casualties. That happens in war and can't be avoided. It's called collateral damage."

She patted his arm. "I see."

"Afghanistan's government went bonkers every time there were civilian deaths and put the pressure on our guys. Of course, a lot of those so-called civilians were Taliban in disguise."

"That's terrible."

"The trouble is, the enemy doesn't wear uniforms or signs. They dress pretty much like the civilians. They blend in with them, and innocent people get caught in the crossfire. Sometimes they use civilians and children as human shields and even set up headquarters in hospitals so we can't bomb them."

She gently touched the scar on his leg. "What's this from?"

"A piece of steel got lodged in there and had to be surgically removed. It's called shrapnel, and they are put in bombs and explosives to inflict maximum damage to humans when they go off. I got that the day Nick died."

She bent down and softly kissed the scar. "Do you regret it?"

"Getting out?"

"No. Going in. Are you sorry you joined the army?"

"No. I'd do it all over again. It's weird, but I felt like it was a calling to enlist in the army and fight for my country. Like I was supposed to go. I worked a couple of summers in construction. I saw guys have serious accidents, and one guy got killed on the job. I felt that it would be safer to go in the army if that's what my gut was telling me than to continue in construction. I believed that I was supposed to go in the army next. I never thought I'd get killed."

"And you weren't."

"Right. But after that sniper wounded me, it changed everything. I felt my number was up, and if I stayed, I'd end up dead. I know it all sounds crazy, but that's the way I looked at it."

He bounded up to a half-eaten bag of chips and started munching on them. "You want some?"

"No thanks."

"Can we change the subject? I'd rather not talk about the military anymore. Tell me about you."

"What do you want to know? I already told you about my dad working for Wells Fargo and Mom teaching. They could probably retire, but they love what they do. I have four sisters."

"Are they all as beautiful as you?"

"Of course not."

"I'm glad your old boyfriend was into Chrysler instead of you. His loss is my gain. It opened the door for me. I wouldn't be able to spend this beautiful day with you learning how to be a river rat."

"And I wouldn't be able to kiss the boo-boo on your arm and make it better." She bent over and kissed the scar, starting from his elbow and moving up his arm to his shoulder, and then she kissed his lips. "Feel better?"

"I feel much better. Thank you, Dr. Bivens."

"Enough serious talk. Let's go for a swim." They had contests to see who could hold their breath longer underwater and swimming races—all won by Caleb. When they got back to the campsite, their discussions turned serious again.

20

"You told me your first assignment was here in the city. How'd that go?"

"It went fine."

"Did you give someone money?"

"I can't get into the details."

"How can we have a relationship if such a big part of your life is kept from me? I need someone to talk to about my work. You need someone to confide in too. How can we do that if you keep secrets?"

"I hear you. I'll ask Mr. Stockbridge if I can share stuff with you. How's everything at the Ax?"

"Joyce reinstated Derek Snerd, the guy you threw out that night. He's a low-life scum. I can't stand that little turd. He taunts me with things like 'Miss your boyfriend, sweetheart?' or 'Nice ass.'"

"Nice ass? What kind of a sick bastard is he? I'll go down there and have a talk with him."

"Don't do that. I can handle him. You don't need any more trouble from that guy. He's bad news."

"How's school?"

"Good. I'll get my nursing degree in about a year if I can keep taking classes."

"That's great."

"What about us, Caleb?"

"Good question. I'm not exactly sure, honey."

"I love you, Caleb Sinclair. I've fallen head over heels."

"I have feelings for you too, Ashley."

"Where do we go from here?"

"I'm not sure. I know I need to work and make enough money to get myself set up. I'm broke. I've got bills to pay. As for the future, I have more questions than answers."

"I said I love you. I need to know you feel the same way about me. I want to be with someone only if they want to be with me as badly as I want to be with them. Do you know what I mean?"

"You told me that before."

"You said you have feelings for me. What does that mean?"

"I want to be with you. You're the best thing that's happened to me since—I can't remember when. I think about you when I go to bed at night and when I wake up in the morning. You're on my mind all day long too."

"That's good to hear, mister. Then let's take our relationship to the next level—make it exclusive and consider moving in together. What do you think?"

"I hear what you're saying, honey. We definitely have chemistry and so much fun when we're together, but—"

"But what? You don't want to move forward?"

"I wasn't going to say that; you interrupted me. We've only been seeing each other for a few weeks. Don't you think you're rushing things?"

"Rushing things? If something's right, it's right, dude."

"We've just started to get to know each other."

"You don't want us to be in a committed and exclusive relationship? You want to keep dating other girls and see if something better comes along. Is that what you're saying?"

He looked down at the ground. "Oh, Ashley, I don't know what I'm saying. With the new job, there's a lot on my mind. It will involve some travel, and I'm not sure what I've gotten myself into or where this is going to lead."

"Let me go on the journey with you, Caleb. We'll figure it out together."

"I know I love hanging out with you. I can't remember when I've had so much fun, but can't we just take it one day at a time and see where it leads?"

"Sure." She looked down and started playing with a small rock. "How come I have the feeling you just blew me off?"

"All I'm saying is that with my new job and uncertain future, my life is up in the air, and I need some time to figure things out."

"And I said we can unpack things together. That's what couples do."

He found a big rock, heaved it into the lake, and watched the rings spread out.

"If that's all you can give me for now, fine. I'll wait until you decide on your course in life, but I'm not going to wait forever. We have something special. We should build it and protect it. If you're not using something, you're losing it. That's all I'm saying."

"I get that. Like I said, let's have fun and take it one day at a time and see where things go."

She tipped her half-full water bottle and downed it in one gulp. "If that's how you feel."

He looked out at the lake. "I do have feelings for you, Ashley. It's not that."

"Of course you do."

"What does that mean?"

"You tell me."

"It's been a perfect day. Let's not ruin it by getting into a fight."

"Caleb, how is talking about our relationship getting into a fight?"

"I know. That's not what I meant. We disagree on a couple of points, so let's not beat a dead horse."

"So discussing moving in together is beating a dead horse?"

"I have to get up early tomorrow and finish the work on the Frontier before my next assignment."

"Then let's go home."

When he drove to her apartment, she kissed him and gave him a hug. "I can get out here. Thanks for a lovely day, sir."

Once inside her apartment, she poured herself a glass of wine. *Caleb and I are not on the same page. I have a decision to make, and I think it's going to break my heart.*

21

The next day, after returning from a jog, Caleb grabbed his phone to check his messages.

It's me. Why didn't you pick up when I called this morning? Are you blowing me off? I didn't sleep last night. I've been doing a lot of thinking about us. I've told you I loved you and wanted to take things to the next level. You're not ready to do that, and I don't want to pressure you into something you're not ready for. So let's take a break. I'll give you some space to figure things out. Goodbye. I love you.

After hearing Ashley's message, he went to the refrigerator and got himself a glass of orange juice. Sitting on his couch, he punched number one. No answer. When her voice mail greeting started, he hung up.

That night Caleb called the Ax and asked to speak with Ashley.

"This is Ashley."

"Ash, I've been trying to reach you all day. I want to talk about the message you left me. I think you got the wrong idea from our conversation yesterday. We need to talk."

"We've talked enough. It's obvious you're not ready for a relationship. I heard what you said. You want to have fun together and take it one day at a time, but Caleb, I have to be honest with you. I want more than that."

"All I've said, honey, is that we need to go slower. I don't want to disappoint you or waste your time by making commitments I'm not sure I can keep."

"Like I said, Caleb, I'm ready for a relationship and you aren't. That's the bottom line. I'm not interested in rehashing the same issues over and over."

"Neither am I, but we aren't seeing eye to eye. I think we should talk things out."

"Now suddenly you want to talk? Yesterday you didn't want to beat a dead horse. Which is it? You and I look at our relationship differently, and we each have different needs. I need an exclusive relationship, and you need time to make decisions. I get that. We're done. There's nothing more to talk about. I have to get back to work. Goodbye."

The next day, Caleb got a call from Stockbridge directing him to a local gun club adjacent to a state park and within about seven miles of the Colorado River. Alvin Larsen, the subject of this assignment, had a relationship with a war correspondent of particular interest to Stockbridge. Caleb brought his Glock 19 to practice on the firing range, which was open to nonmembers. After target practice, he asked the range officer about Larsen.

"Comes here every month when we have the trap and skeet tournaments. The old guy's a pretty good shot—a bit nutty—but a good man," he said. "He'll probably be here Saturday for a competition, but other than that, I don't know how to contact him. He keeps a low profile."

"Thanks. I'll stop by Saturday."

When Saturday arrived, shooters within a hundred miles showed up to test their mettle against local sharpshooters. The men and women of diverse ages and backgrounds shared a love of firing their shotguns, rifles, and pistols. The Arizona desert sun blazed as hot as their gun barrels, so everyone wore hats, and the smart ones added a generous coating of sunscreen.

With his ear protectors on, Caleb sat in a lawn chair close to the competitors, smoking a cigar. It was easy to pick out Alvin Larsen. Not only was he the oldest guy at the range, but also he was the most colorful. Larsen kept his gray hair in a buzz cut, but he sported a handlebar mustache that balanced his protruding nose and prominent chin. His rail-thin, mid-seventies body, barely more than about 145 pounds, moved with agility and the fitness of a much younger man. For shooting, he wore a camouflage baseball cap, rattlesnake-skin boots, and a plaid Western shirt.

The finals came down to Larsen and Dewy Beech, a man from Brainerd, Minnesota, who had hunted deer since he could hold a Remington .30-06. Now his firearm of choice was a Remington 870 12 gauge. In the final round, each shot at twenty-five clay pigeons; Larsen shattered twenty-four clays to Dewey's twenty-one. The $200 prize money went to the old guy. When the group congratulating him thinned out, Caleb approached to offer his compliments.

"Good shooting, Mr. Larsen."

"Thanks, kid. Call me Alvin." Larsen removed his cap, wiped his forehead with a red handkerchief, and replaced his cap with a black Stetson he had parked at the registration table during the competition, a favor always granted by the scorekeeper. The Stetson had a personality all its own, from its pheasant feather sticking out on one side to the rattlesnake band, and appeared to be as old as Larsen and just as weather-beaten.

"My name's Caleb Sinclair. I was wondering if I might talk with you about your experiences in Vietnam. I heard from a guy working at the gun club that you're a veteran."

"Don't usually talk about that. It was a long time ago."

"I'm a combat veteran too. I'm having kind of a tough time adjusting to civilian life. I have a lot of bad dreams and thought it might help to talk to guys who've been through it. Maybe I can learn something. I'm also thinking of writing a book about war."

"I guess we could talk awhile, but I left my dog at home, and I need to let him out. You're welcome to follow me. It's not that far. We can talk there."

"Sure."

22

Caleb steered his Frontier behind Larsen's beat-up Dodge pickup truck to his trailer in an RV park near the Colorado River. Once inside, he met a huge black Lab who licked his hand with large strokes while drumming a nearby chair with his tail.

"Friendly, ain't he? Name's Budweiser. Speaking of Bud, you want a beer?"

"Sure. I'm guessing that's the house brew?"

"Ya got that right. I stock PBR if ya'd prefer. We got none of that low-cal, light stuff around here."

"Gotcha. Bud's fine. You and my girlfriend are the only people I know who drink PBR."

"I like her already." Larsen popped open a couple of beers. After setting them on a small kitchen table, he turned to Budweiser. "C'mon, Bud, let's go. We'll be right back."

Caleb seized the opportunity to look around the trailer—dirty dishes in the sink, a saggy couch with rips in the upholstery next to a green leather recliner placed in front of a wide-screen TV that dominated the tiny living room. Next to the recliner sat an end table with a large ashtray full of cigarette butts propped up vertically like tombstones in a crowded cemetery. On the main wall hung a large velvet portrait of Elvis as a young man, handsome and thin. The brass nameplate under the portrait contained only two words: "The King."

The aluminum door, missing a spring, slammed open, hitting the wall. Bud leaped inside and jumped on the couch. Larsen sat at the table across from Caleb. "That was quite the shoot-out, wasn't it? Dewy and I have gone at it more than once; I usually win, though.

He can't take the pressure." Larsen took a big gulp and did his best to stifle the belch that would not be controlled. "Excuse me."

"I'll bet you learned to shoot straight under pressure in Nam."

"It sure motivates ya to shoot straight when someone's shooting back at you. Nothing makes a man concentrate more than saving his own ass."

Larsen got up from the kitchen table and pulled out a pack of Marlboro Reds and a Zippo lighter from a jacket pocket. In the next instant, he flipped the lighter open with a finger snap that sparked the flame to life. After lighting his cig, he took in a deep breath, exhaling in a long cloud of smoke toward the carpet.

"Smoke?" Larsen held out the pack.

"No thanks. I just quit a few months ago. I only smoke cigars now."

"Did you know Marlboros have been the most popular cigarette in the world since 1972?"

"No."

"What do ya want to know?"

"What unit did you serve in?"

"The First Battalion, Ninth Marines. We saw some tough action at Con Thien, a battle that lasted from May to September 1967, one of the longest battles of the war. We walked into a buzz saw on July 2. North Vietnamese ambushed us, and eighty-four marines died. They called us the Walking Dead after that. I could be wrong, but I think that's the most marines killed in one battle in the whole Vietnam War. I thought I was going to die too. It was a shit show from beginning to end."

"How did you survive?"

"I've asked myself that question a thousand times. Lucky, I guess."

"Do you feel guilty about being one of the survivors?"

Larsen took another long drag and looked at Budweiser on the couch. "What do you think?"

"Did you ever have war correspondents in your outfit?"

"Yeah, two. Don't remember much about the first one. Good guy, I guess." Larsen scratched the side of his neck. "I got some kind of bug bite. It's driving me batshit crazy."

"What about the other writer?"

"The other one was an ignoramus—couldn't find his butt with both hands and a magnifying glass. The clown followed us around for six months, getting in the way. One time I almost got dusted for his stupidity."

"What happened?"

"We got ambushed. It got hairy, bullets flying everywhere. Definitely FUBAR. Then this pansy gets scared and wanders away from our squad. Sarge told me to go out in the jungle and get him. Dodged my way back and forth through several jungle trails. When I found him, three Vietcong were closing in. I shot them all, bang, bang, bang. One shot, one kill. Oorah!"

"That must have been something."

"It surprised the hell out of them; I can tell you that. They didn't know what hit them. I've always been a good shot—hunted since I was a kid and all that. That reporter was one lucky dude. A couple of seconds later, he would have been sliced and diced. We radioed for air support, and a Phantom roared in and rained death on the rest of the VC in the area. Lit 'em up like a Christmas tree."

"That writer must be your best friend for life."

"Not exactly. We got ahold of some of his articles, and he made us look like a bunch of soulless killers. Whiskey, tango, foxtrot?"

23

Caleb took a swig from his can. "Was he lying about you in those stories?"

"His facts were true, but they didn't reflect the context of our actions and what they were doing to us. His writing was slanted in favor of the Vietcong. I tried to look at things from his perspective, but I couldn't get my head that far up my ass."

"What do you mean?"

"He emphasized the atrocities we committed but didn't say anything about what they were doing. The Vietcong were trying to kill us any way they could. They dressed like civilians, and we couldn't tell them from the citizens. We were fighting for our lives. It was either kill or be killed."

"And you guys were just doing your jobs."

"Exactly. I never believed in the devil until I went to war. Now I do."

Alvin got up, grabbed a flyswatter, and paused for the triangular horsefly to land on his coffee table. His catlike reflexes turned the fly into black bits in an instant. He used the swatter to scrape the remnants of the fly off the table to the floor, leaving a liquid spot.

"When the commander in chief orders ya to go somewhere and fight, you go. We were a bunch of jarheads humping through the jungle, killing the bad guys before they could kill us. We were in the jungle so deep, we shoulda brought our own oxygen tanks to breathe."

"I hear you, man."

"Guys like that writer turned the American people against the war, all right, but they also turned them against us. Hell, we didn't start the war. When we returned home, we were treated like shit. Some called us baby killers and all that. It really sucked."

"If I ever write that book about war, I won't misquote you or put a bad perspective on what you say. I promise."

"That don't matter no more to me. People who know me know what I'm about. No book is going to change their minds about me one way or the other. As far as I'm concerned, anyone who doesn't like me can go to hell and kiss my ass on the way."

Caleb laughed.

"You write whatever you want, kid. At my age, I don't give a rat's ass."

"Got it."

"Here's the deal. If America sends us to war, they better be prepared for deaths—accidental deaths of civilians, deaths by friendly fire, atrocities, and fragging. Ya know what fragging is, right, kid?"

"Yes. Shooting your own men, usually NCOs and officers."

"Damn straight. Some were fine, but you had ninety-day wonders and some shake-and-bake NCOs fresh from the NCO Academy that got guys killed because they didn't know shit."

"Did you see that happen?"

"What?"

"Fragging?"

"One night, this new sergeant blew himself up in his tent with a hand grenade."

"How did he do that?"

"He had help, my friend. He had help. Somebody decided it was better to take him out than risk losing a bunch of guys due to his stupid decisions." Larsen took a long drag on his cigarette. "Yep. War is a nasty business, son."

"For sure."

"I have a couple of good memories from Nam. I met this young Vietnamese woman from a village called Phuoc Lam Long An, only twenty-two miles from Saigon. Her name was Beti Huynh, and she was a cutie. Got grazed by a bullet on her way to school during the war. Didn't even know it till a teacher asked why her leg was bleeding."

"That's a shame."

"One time while she was babysitting her nephew, an American helicopter peppered the rice fields around them with machine gun bullets. Beti saved his life by dragging him to a nearby tunnel and shielding him with her body.

"I snuck out to meet her a few times until our outfit was pulled out of the area. Our last night together, we spent most of the time crying. When I left, she gave me a Vietnamese Hai Nghin Dong worth about one thousand dong."

"How much is that in American money?"

"About four cents, but that's not the point. When she handed it to me, she said, 'Now, Alvin, no matter what happens, you'll always have money. Remember that.' I kept it all these years. One of my prized possessions."

"That's awesome."

"I told her I'd be back for her after the war and we'd get married. That never happened. Afterward I was too screwed up to do anything for a while. Where in Afghanistan were ya stationed, son?"

24

"Spent most of my time in the Hindu Kush. Ever heard of that, Alvin?"

"No. Not really. I'm not that up on geography."

"It's a lot of mountains near the border with Pakistan and China. Did three tours there. Just got out over a year ago, felt my luck running out."

The old leatherneck lit up another cigarette from the one he had been smoking. "Good thing you got out when you did. When you start to feel the fear, it's time to get out if you can."

Larsen got up and tossed his empty can into a garbage bucket dangerously close to overflowing and swung open the refrigerator door. "Want another beer?"

"Sure." Caleb tilted his can to finish the last of it before handing the empty to his host.

Holding the refrigerator door open, Larsen stood looking at his young visitor. "We were damn good fighters too. In a firefight, there was no difference between regular army, draftees, or marines. We fought as one—Blacks, Hispanics, and whites. Our skin may have had different shades, but our blood was the same color—red."

"Same with us. We fought for each other."

After sitting down, Larsen continued his thought. "People shouldn't blame the military for the wars; it's the politicians who send us to war in the first place. In my day we had the draft. I had a low draft number, so I knew I was going no matter what. I thought, if I was going to go anyway, I wanted to go as a marine. They have a good reputation for fighting hard, and I liked the look of the dress blues. Still have mine, and I can still fit into 'em too."

"We all volunteered too, Alvin. Some guys enlisted after we were attacked on 9/11."

"At least you had a choice. A lot of the guys I served with didn't want to be there. They were drafted, and it was either go to war, go to Canada, or go to prison."

"Hey, Alvin, you got PTSD?"

"I don't think so." Larsen belched so loud, Budweiser lifted his head off the couch and stared at his master. "But I probably got a slight drinking problem."

Caleb laughed until beer came out of his nose. "I've had some problems with bad dreams and memories. Do you have them?"

"I just learned to live with them. What are you going to do? You can't go back and change anything."

"That's right. We've been treated better than you guys were, Alvin. I get thanked all the time for serving. Some guys resent it when people do that. I don't. I appreciate it."

"Nowadays, I get thanked a lot too, kid. It sure beats being called a baby killer. Listen, you'll get over those dreams and memories. It takes time. You may have 'em, but they won't hurt as much. Leave the past behind, onward and upward. You gotta turn the page, or you'll go crazy."

"Thanks, man. And someday I hope to write this book for those who were there and for those who weren't there."

Alvin took a drag off his cigarette.

"Are you still working, Alvin?"

"I'm on social security and a disability pension because I got some crotch rot and headaches from Agent Orange. I do odd jobs around the trailer park for extra money, and I enter every shooting contest that comes around. I'm usually in the money."

"Sounds like you're doing fine."

"Yeah. I started out with nothing, and I still have most of it."

"Is there anything you wish you had?"

"A house. I had a streak of bad luck, and my home was foreclosed on. Since then, I've had to live in this trailer. It's not too bad, but it's small and leaks when it rains. I'm praying for a new house from the big man upstairs."

Alvin stood, kneeled at the couch, and petted Budweiser. Then he got up for another beer. "Ya ready for another?"

"I'm good." Caleb looked around the trailer. "I appreciate the hospitality and the beers. You were deadly with those clays. Cool under pressure."

"It's much easier to shoot when the target isn't shooting back at you."

"Stay off the skyline. Is there a way I can stay in touch?"

"I don't use the computer. Too much trouble. You can call or write anytime." He reached into his jeans pocket for his wallet and pulled out a wrinkled business card. "This has my address and number on it."

Alvin walked Caleb to his truck. Budweiser ran ahead of them until he saw a rabbit and disappeared. "If you ever publish that book, could I buy a copy? I'd love for my grandkids to read it. I have trouble explaining war to them."

"Affirmative."

Alvin handed Caleb his prized 1,000-dong note. "Here, son. Take this. Now, no matter whatever happens, you'll always have money. Remember that."

"Thanks. Oorah!"

Taking a last look at the old marine in his rearview mirror as he drove away, Caleb saw Alvin standing tall and straight, saluting him.

Semper Fi, Lance Corporal Larsen. Semper Fi.

Two weeks later, a local bank officer contacted Alvin and informed him that an anonymous donor had gifted him a house and an annuity to cover maintenance costs. Alvin looked at the ceiling and then at the bank officer. In a throaty voice produced by a few too many Marlboro Reds, he uttered, "Whiskey, tango, foxtrot…that's an answer to a prayer. Oorah."

25

It was a big night at the Ax Handle. Nancie Echeverria was booked for Saturday night as part of her From Your Mouth to God's Ears Tour. Although the show started at nine, patrons began taking their seats at seven thirty and ordering drinks.

Promptly at nine, Nancie took to the stage amid thunderous applause. She paced the stage like a lioness wearing a colorful dress. "How's everybody doing tonight in Briggs Lake, Arizona?"

The crowd yelled different unrecognizable things.

"I'll take that as a 'good.' I like to tell dad jokes. Sometimes he laughs."

The crowd loved it.

"The past, present, and future walk into a bar. It was tense."

The audience applauded.

"A cliché walks into a bar, fresh as a daisy, cute as a button, and sharp as a tack."

The crowd laughed.

"What do you call a joke that isn't funny? A sentence."

At first silence, then laughter.

"You finally got that one, huh? How about this one? What do you call a robot that drinks water? Rusty."

Some laughter and then applause.

"How do you know if you're meeting someone who ran a marathon? They'll tell you."

Laughter throughout the audience.

In the next room at the bar, Derek Snerd, drunker than a sailor on shore leave, insisted on talking loudly and sharing his opinions with those seated around him. The more he drank, the louder he got.

Ashley, working the bar that night, politely asked him to tone it down so others could hear Nancie's stand-up in the adjoining room.

Snerd glared at Ashley. "Don't you be telling me what to do, Red. We've been down that road before."

"First of all, my name isn't Red, and second, stop threatening me. If you're in our bar, we expect you to treat the staff and customers with courtesy, or you can leave."

"Calm down. Just trying to have some fun. Speaking of, I saw your boyfriend the other day at the coffee shop. He's a real player, isn't he? You should have seen him hitting on that cute little number who runs the Starbucks. Her name is Danielle, and she always wears black. She's as cute as a kitten. I'm sure Caleb thinks so too."

"What's that supposed to mean to me? I couldn't care less."

"Maybe you should care. It looks like he's cheating on you."

"I haven't got time for your nonsense. I have other customers to wait on. Please keep it down. Before I leave, can I get you anything to drink?"

"I don't want you serving me anymore. Where's Crystal? I want her to serve me, not you."

"I'll get her." Ashley found Crystal Glade in the kitchen smoking a cigarette. "Snerd wants you to serve him. He's all yours."

"I'll be right out." She went into the bathroom and freshened her lipstick and makeup. She popped a mint into her mouth and turned in the mirror to see how her bottom looked. She thought it looked pretty good.

She went out to the bar. "Hi, Derek. Can I help you?"

"Let's talk for a minute. How you doing?"

"Fine."

"You know, I like women with big butts."

"Yes. You told me, Derek."

"And you have a nice big butt."

"Thank you, Derek."

"Would you get me a couple of shots of tequila?"

"Sure."

"Good girl. Before you get them, come here. I want to smack that booty."

"Not now, Derek. Not in front of all these people. Stop by later after work, and you can smack it all you want."

"That's my girl. See you later."

Crystal left to retrieve his drink order.

26

Returning home to his apartment after a long run, Caleb sat down with some Chinese takeout until he heard a knock on his door.

"Shoot. Now what?" He groaned and got up to look out the peephole. It was Ashley.

"Come in, honey. You're just in time for dinner. Have a seat."

Tossing her purse on the couch beside her, she pranced in and looked around with her hands on her hips. Her pink crop top glistened and made her breasts look like ripe peaches. With no hat, her long hair cascaded down her shoulders like a crimson waterfall.

"It doesn't look like you've done much cleaning since the last time I was here, mister."

"I've been kinda busy. Want a beer or a glass of wine?"

"You got a PBR?"

"Of course. I stock it just for my favorite bartender. Give me a minute." He went into the kitchen, opened a bottle, and handed it to her. "Want a plate of General Tso's chicken?"

"No thanks. I ate earlier."

"I thought you were working tonight."

"I took the night off. I'm not feeling good."

"What's the matter?"

"Snerd was in again last night and said something that ticked me off."

"What did he say, honey?"

"He said you have a girlfriend, some Goth girl who runs the Starbucks named Danielle. He said he saw you two canoodling one morning."

"Wait. What? Canoodling? What does that mean?"

"Flirting and cuddling."

"That wasn't what was happening. I was doing my job. Danielle Stevens is one of the people Stockbridge wanted me to contact to see what he can do for her. She's one of my projects, that's all."

She tilted back her PBR for a long sip and then slammed the bottle down. "Must be a fun project. Snerd said the two of you looked like you were really enjoying yourselves. I guess now I know why you aren't ready to take our relationship to the next level."

He darted to her side and put his arm around her. She shoved it away. "Stay away from me. I told you already: we're through."

"Ashley. That's crazy. You've got nothing to worry about. You can trust me. Why do you believe Derek Snerd over me? He hates my guts. He's just trying to hurt you and ruin our relationship. Can't you see that?"

She blew her nose into a tissue. "I don't know what to believe anymore."

"It was strictly business. Honestly. I'm with you. Not seeing anyone else."

"You're not seeing me either. I broke up with you. Did you forget that already?"

"You just said you were giving me time to figure things out. Let me explain about Danielle."

"That black-cloaked barista must really make you happy—even Snerd noticed."

"I was asking her questions to understand what she needed."

"Oh, I see. Then I suppose you were going to meet her needs... all of them."

"No. So Stockbridge could help her with what she needed."

"And what did you find out?"

"I can't talk about it. Stockbridge doesn't want people to know what he and I are doing."

"If you're doing nothing wrong, Caleb, there shouldn't be any need for secrecy, right?"

"I gave my word to him to keep his business private."

"And I told you that I'm the jealous type and won't tolerate any fooling around. All I know is that I wanted to take our relationship to the next level, and you kept stalling. Now I know why."

"What do you mean?"

She gathered up her purse to leave and noticed a book on the counter. "So now you're reading children's books? I see you've finally found something on your reading level."

"It was a gift."

"From who?" Ashley opened it and read the message on the front page out loud. "Hi, Caleb, here is my first children's book. Enjoy. Love, Danielle."

"She writes children's books besides working at Starbucks. She sent it to me as a friend. That's all it is."

"I see. That's why she wrote 'Love, Danielle.' I better get out of here so you have time to read her book."

"Ashley, please don't do this. You still love me, don't you?"

"We're through. It's over." She slammed the door on her way out. Caleb sat stunned and speechless.

27

A few days later, Stockbridge and Sinclair met for lunch at the Onion.

"Now that you have two assignments under your belt, are you getting more comfortable with what we're doing?"

"Yes. I think I'm getting the hang of it. It helps to know we're changing their lives in good ways."

Stockbridge laughed and struck the table lightly with his hand. "It's fun to help people, isn't it?"

"The assignment with Danielle did create a problem with my girlfriend, though. She dumped me. The drunk I kicked out that night saw me with Danielle and told her we were getting it on."

"What did you tell your girlfriend?"

"That I was just doing my job and that Danielle was one of my assignments. When she asked about it, I told her I couldn't give her any details."

"Good. I asked you to keep this confidential, and I wish to remain anonymous."

"I told her that, but she thinks I'm hiding something from her. When my girlfriend got up to leave, she saw a children's book Danielle sent me that she signed, 'Love, Danielle.'"

"Oops. I'll bet that went over like a match in a dynamite plant."

"Something like that."

"Caleb, I'm so sorry. Is there anything I can do?"

"Not now. She doesn't even want to speak to me. She's been hurt in the past by unfaithful boyfriends and is very jealous and insecure. I wasn't ready to take our relationship to the next level, and she thinks the reason is that I still want to play the field."

"That guy you threw out is a grade A jackass."

"He should be in the turd hall of fame. But to Joyce, he's a good customer for the business and threatened to sue the bar, so I get fired and he's back there."

Stockbridge's smile faded. He took a bite of salmon and began chewing slowly. Caleb sipped his water, and both were silent.

Stockbridge looked back at Caleb. "If you're serious about this girl, I don't want your work for me to in any way hurt your relationship. What's her name?"

"Her name is Ashley Bivens. She's really a sweetheart, and I don't want to hurt her. She may be the one—who knows? You know who she is. She's the red-haired bartender with the killer body."

"Ah yes, Ashley. I do know her. I always ask for her when I go in there. Except her hair is actually auburn, Caleb."

"Whatever. I'm kinda color-blind."

"Why don't you arrange a meeting with me and Ashley, and we'll set some ground rules for sharing information with her? If you think she might be the one, you don't want to let her get away."

"It's kind of too late for that, sir."

"All right. If things change and she gives you another chance, let me know. We'll arrange a meeting. Ready for your next assignment?"

"Affirmative."

"There's a guy living in the Las Vegas area named Clinton Devers who's in a wheelchair. I know a lot about him. He's paralyzed from the waist down from a war wound. See if Clint needs anything. Make sure his home is wheelchair accessible; if not, we'll get the remodeling done for him. If his house doesn't require renovations, see what else he needs."

He handed Caleb a large envelope with pictures of Clint and some biographical material.

28

A week later, Caleb sat in the bleachers of a YMCA gymnasium in Las Vegas watching a wheelchair basketball game. As the young men and women rolled up and down the court, the crashing sounds of the colliding chairs reverberated throughout the gym.

With only a helper to retrieve errant basketballs, the lone referee followed the action, doing her best to keep up and not get run over. Except that they were pushing their chairs forward with gloved hands while in a sitting position, the wheelchair athletes dressed like any other group of twentysomethings playing a pickup game of hoops— sweatbands, shorts, and tees.

When the game ended, Caleb walked down to the court and caught the eye of the nearest wheelchair athlete. "Is there is a Clinton Devers playing in this game? If so, can you point him out?"

"Sure. Clint's over there." He indicated a young man with a full beard and a shaved head crowned with a camouflage sweatband and a matching tank top emblazoned with the words "Rangers Lead the Way."

"Hey, Clint. This guy needs to speak with you," the man yelled, pointing at Sinclair.

The young man looked up from a conversation with two other athletes, then rolled his chair toward Caleb.

"Nice meeting you. I'm Caleb Sinclair."

The man in the chair extended his fist, and they touched knuckles. "Clint Devers."

"I like your shirt, man. I'm a Ranger too."

"Scrolled? Seventy-Fifth Ranger Regiment?"

"Affirmative."

"Cool, brother. In Afghanistan?"

"All over, places like the Hindu Kush, near the border of Pakistan, wherever."

Clint locked the wheels on his chair. "That's awesome. My last action was in Syria as part of Operation Inherent Resolve."

"Clint, the reason I want to talk to you is that I'm doing some research for a book I'm writing on war. I'd like to interview you about some of your war experiences."

"Sorry, bro. I did stuff I can't talk about, ever. I'd have to kill you." Clint's ambiguous tone and grim expression left some doubt as to whether he was kidding or serious.

"I know. Same here. I won't ask for specifics on where you served or what you did. I understand there are things you can never reveal. I'm only interested in your personal story."

Clint glanced around the room, tapping his right hand on the wheel for a few seconds. "I guess so. But why me? You don't know anything about me."

"I have a friend who has heard of you, and he thought you would be a good guy to talk to."

"Who's that?"

"I'd rather not say, if you don't mind. He's a private person. I just want to talk to people who served, and he's given me a few names of those who might be good to interview. You were one of them. It's nothing weird."

"I guess so. I got nothing to hide. But I got nothing to brag about either. I did my job and was blessed to be able to come home alive. Not much else to tell."

"I get that, but I think people should hear what our soldiers have to say about war instead of hearing only from politicians and those who never served."

"Only thing is, that stuff's in my rearview mirror. I'll talk with you for a few minutes. There's a place across the street that makes sandwiches that are out of this world. It has a drive-through, which is easier for me."

"Perfect. My car's in the lot. I'll follow you."

"Another thing. I'm meeting a guy for a game of eight ball at a local pool joint. Do you mind if we eat our sandwiches there?"

"Negative."

He pointed at his tank top. "Follow me. Remember? Rangers lead the way."

"Lead, follow, or get out of the way, brother. I'm right behind you."

After getting their lunches, they drove to Mr. Lucky's Bar and Billiards. Clint unlocked the wheels on his chair and spun it around, facing the rear of his van. He opened the back door with a remote control and wheeled his way to the lift that lowered him.

Caleb watched in amazement. "That's a pretty fancy rig you've got there, Clint."

"High tech, baby. Nothing but the best for the man."

As Sinclair held the front door for Clint, he noticed a sign that read "No Gang Colors Allowed. Leave Your Colors and Attitude at the Door."

"What's that all about?"

"Nothing. Kevin, the owner, runs a clean place and doesn't tolerate biker gangs or anyone else who is looking for somewhere to fight and cause trouble."

Everyone at the bar turned toward them when they entered. A large man with a bald head approached them. Several shouted greetings to the young man in the chair. "I thought you weren't going to show."

"Kiss my ass," Clint snapped. "Caleb, this jackass is Wally Butts. He's a fellow veteran."

"Army?" Wally asked.

"Hooah!"

"Clint and I are known as the bald brothers." He turned around to patrons at the bar and yelled, "Clint found us some fresh meat, everybody." There was a smattering of claps and cheers—a few raised mugs in the air.

"I haven't played in at least a year. Besides, I'm only here to have lunch with Clint."

Wally bobbed his head. "Hear that one before, Clint? 'Haven't played for at least a year.' Yeah, right. He's a ringer."

"He's not here to play pool, knucklehead. Besides, I don't need any help beating the likes of you," Clint said with a smile. "I've got your number, bro."

"You think you have my number."

The two army Rangers and Wally Butts scooted to a table for four in the corner with three chairs, always reserved for Clint and his buds—and he had many. A grinning petite blonde hustled to the table to take their drink orders.

"Hey, Diana, please get my friends and me some Coors Lights, a cup, and my cue."

"Sure thing, Clint." She nodded at Caleb, and he smiled back.

He turned to Sinclair. "Don't let her petite figure fool you, bro. I've seen her put gang members in their place for getting out of line. You don't want to mess with that little lady if you know what's good for you. She'll kick your ass."

"Copy that, bro."

"As the saying goes, 'Don't give her any attitude and keep your hands off.'"

Wally laughed. "Wasn't there a song like that?"

"From the Georgia Satellites, bonehead."

Diana returned with a pool stick and handed it to Clint.

"Thanks, Diana." He set the base on the floor and then held the stick in a vertical position like a golden scepter. "It's a regulation stick and all, bro, but it's longer, which helps me on the long shots. That way I don't need to use the granny stick."

"Awesome, dude. It's tremendous you can still play pool."

"I lost the use of my legs, not my arms and brain, bro."

"Yeah," Wally added. "He likes to remind the ladies about all the body parts he can still use."

Caleb and Clint laughed while Diana stifled a grin as she shook her head and left to get their beers.

"Wally's right. I can do everything I used to do except use my legs. I focus on what I can do, not on what I can't. If a man adapts and adjusts, he can do almost anything he makes up his mind to do."

Caleb gave him a thumbs-up.

"Hey, Wally, we're going to eat our lunches and chat for a few minutes about the war before you and I play pool. You're welcome to stay here with us and drink your beer."

"Naw. I wanna practice before we play."

"Suit yourself. You probably need the practice before playing me."

"Shut your face."

Diana handed Wally his beer and brought the other two beers to the table with a cup.

"You having coffee too, Clint?"

"Naw, that's my spit cup."

29

After gobbling down their sandwiches while discussing the similarities and differences of the Middle East climate to the Southwest, Caleb started the interview.

"I'm writing a book about war, and as I said before, a guy told me you were a veteran and had a story to tell. I want the perspectives of the men who were actually there in combat."

Clint opened a can of Copenhagen and offered it to Caleb. "Want some?"

"No thanks, bro. I'm off the chew and cigs. I'll smoke a cigar if you have one."

"Sorry. Don't have stogies, and you can't smoke in here anyway. You were saying you're writing a book?"

"I'd like to hear your story and maybe put it in my book."

"My story's pretty simple. Not much to tell. While on patrol, my squad's armed personnel carrier rolled over an IED, killing our sergeant and all but four of us. After the blast I couldn't move my legs. I thought it was all over for me."

"Was that before they put the heavy armor underneath APCs and Humvees?"

He shook his head. "It was after they put on the heavy armor, not before. This IED must have been the mother of all IEDs."

"What happened next?"

"Before I go on, promise you won't mention my name in your book."

"Promise."

"Good. But I want you to put the names of the three guys in the story because they saved my life. And make sure you spell their names right. They maintained suppressing fire to keep the bad guys away until we got rescued."

Caleb pulled out a notebook and carefully transcribed as Clint spelled each man's name and dictated the actions each Ranger took to save them from being overrun.

"After I got to the field hospital, I asked the doctor, 'Will I still be able to play the piano?' He said, 'Sure.' I said, 'Good. I always wanted to play the piano.'"

Caleb laughed suddenly, spilling beer on his shirt. "I'm sure he'd never heard that one before."

"Probably did, but my setup, delivery, and timing were excellent, bro. The sawbones laughed out loud just like you did, even though he may have heard it a hundred times."

"Have to admit it. You did make me laugh. How's the adjustment to civilian life going?"

"The worst part was leaving my guys. I wanted to get back to the action as soon as I could, but unfortunately it didn't happen. My rehab took longer than expected, and I got washed out instead of a return to duty. Forced to take a medical discharge and retirement."

"The comradery of the guys is the only thing I miss."

"That's right, Caleb. We're brothers in arms. Earning the Ranger tab was one of my proudest accomplishments. Not many people can say they did that."

"I think the failure rate at Ranger School is about sixty percent. If you can get through the training, it gives you confidence that you can go through anything."

"That's for sure. What got me through combat situations and rehab was a phrase I learned in Ranger training: 'This too shall pass.' I kept repeating it to myself over and over."

Caleb wrote down everything word for word. "With all the training they gave us, they embedded into us some pretty choice curse words along the way, didn't they?"

"When it comes to profanity, I have an extensive body of work in this field."

"Me too. The other tough part of adjusting to civilian life is this dream I keep having. It comes at random times, usually when I'm stressed. It's about the day my best friend, Nick, was killed in action. He died before we could get him to the field hospital. I think I could have saved him if I'd reacted quicker before he lost so much blood."

"I've had some of those bad dreams too." He reached into his pocket and grabbed a piece of shrapnel. "The docs cut this bad boy out of my back and gave it to me. I keep it nearby, and when I start getting flashbacks, I hold this piece of metal in my hand and remind myself that war couldn't kill me and it's not going to stop me from living the life I want to live."

"That's awesome."

"You need to remind yourself of that too."

"Thanks. I'll keep that in mind, Clint."

"Remember to put in your book that we fought for each other. We'd give our lives for the guy next to us, and he would do the same for us. People need to know that. Despite our differences, we always fought as one and had each other's six."

"Got it. I'll make sure to make that point when I talk about how your buddies helped protect you."

"And one more thing. We all had limitations going into the military, and we all had limitations coming out. In my case, I can't use my legs. Yet life goes on. You can't quit and wallow in self-pity. Focus on what you can do and not on what you can't do. Here's my motto: 'start where you are, use what you have, and do what you can.' That's how to approach life. Put that in your book."

Caleb spent a few minutes writing down these last statements. "I've got enough for my book, Clint. Thanks so much. Anything you need? I mean, did the government make your home wheelchair accessible?"

"It's all good. My experience with the VA couldn't have been better. I've heard horror stories about bad VA hospitals, but to be honest, the people I work with here are the best. Our local here in Nevada takes good care of everyone. Got no complaints." He took a big gulp of his Coors to polish it off.

Caleb took a sip and exhaled. "Your positive approach to your injury is inspiring to me. What do you do for work?"

"I'm a computer forensic specialist. I go online and impersonate children and catch those piss tubes who prey on innocent boys and girls. I work closely with the federal government to root out child pornographers. They even trained me in Virginia."

"That's cool."

"I started a foundation to honor my grandfather. He was an investigative reporter who busted a ring of child sex traffickers and pornographers in the San Francisco Bay area. In those days, everyone hid those child molesting predators under the rug. He exposed those perverts and helped bring them to justice. He was up for a Pulitzer but never received it. The mob gunned him down in broad daylight, and they never found out who did it."

"Sorry to hear that, Clint."

"It sucked, what happened to my grandfather, but he inspired me to continue his work."

Wally waddled to their table. "Hey, bro. Getting bored. Are we going to play pool today or not?"

"Cool your jets, baby. I gotta go to the shitter. We're done, right, Caleb?"

"Yeah. Thanks a lot, Clint."

"I'll be right back." He rolled to the restroom.

Wally sat at the table with Caleb. "Did he tell you what happened?"

"He told me about the blast under the APC and how he couldn't move his legs, so these three guys who survived the blast held off the bad guys for hours until he could be airlifted to the field hospital."

"What? That's not what happened."

"What do you mean?"

"He's feeding you a BS sandwich."

"Why do you say that?"

"What really happened was that everyone was killed except Clint, who lost the use of his legs, and three guys, all who were seriously wounded."

"He said that."

"They were trapped in the vehicle, and it was on fire. Clint managed to free himself using only his arms. He dragged himself out and extinguished the fire, or they would have all burned to death. Then he propped himself up—"

"Wait a minute." Caleb pulled out his notebook and took this new information down. "Go ahead."

"He propped himself up against the vehicle, and when about a dozen Taliban moved in on them, Clint engaged them in a firefight, killing five of them, even though he was wounded a second time in the shoulder. When he ran out of ammunition, he threw grenades with his good arm. When he ran out of grenades, he fired a flare gun at them. He held them off until help arrived, saving his life and everyone else's."

"Judas Priest!"

"If I'm lying, I'm dying. One of those guys he saved came here one time and told me all about it. Clint got the Silver Star for courage under fire. Those three guys worship him. They get together every year. He's badass, man."

The door to the restroom opened, and Clint wheeled his way to the table where Wally and Caleb sat.

"Caleb, I have a gift for you." He pulled the piece of shrapnel out of his pocket. "Take this. I don't need it anymore, but you do. When you think of that bad dream, pull this out as a reminder that the war didn't kill you and that it's not going to keep you from living a good life. Keep the faith, my brother in arms."

Clint and Caleb said in unison, "Hooah!"

Caleb quickly left so that Clint wouldn't see the tears streaming down his face.

One week later, Clint received a cashier's check from an anonymous donor for two million dollars for his foundation.

30

Ashley arrived fifteen minutes early for her night shift at the Ax to replace her friend Rosie.

"How'd it go today?" Ashley asked as she set her purse under the bar.

"Really busy, but tips were good. I've got everything stocked up for you." Rosie washed her hands and dried them with a fresh towel. "Joyce hired a new bouncer. Name's Chad. He's a stud muffin. Joyce brought him around and introduced him to the day staff."

Ashley smiled at Rosie. "Thanks for the heads-up. Can't wait to meet him. When does he start?"

"He'll start tonight on your shift. You can't miss him. He's the tall blond eye candy who'll be standing by the door with the bulging biceps. Wait till you see him."

"You sound infatuated with him. Doesn't matter to me what he looks like. All I care about is that he does his job and isn't a jerk."

"Yeah, right, Ashley. Whatever you say. Trust me, you'll feel the same way I do when you lay your eyes on him." She smiled. "I'm outta here. Have a good night."

"You too, girlfriend."

A few minutes later, Joyce came into the bar to introduce the new employee. The blond-haired, blue-eyed bouncer carried himself with confidence, and his eyes sparkled.

"Ashley, I'd like you to meet Chad Blake, our new bouncer."

"Pleased to meet you," she said and extended her hand. She looked Chad in the eye, and he returned her gaze. They both felt an instant connection.

When Joyce took Chad into the kitchen, Beth Ann, one of the servers, approached Ashley. "Did you notice the way he looked at you? He likes you."

"You sure read a lot into a handshake, Beth Ann. He was being polite, and so was I. That's all it was."

"I think it was more than that. Just sayin'."

"Do you think you might be projecting?"

Beth Ann shrugged and returned to lighting candles on the tables.

At closing time, Caleb showed up. The new bouncer stopped him at the door.

"Sorry, man. We're closing in a few minutes."

"I'm coming to see Ashley."

"What's your name?"

"Tell her Caleb's here to see her."

Chad went into the kitchen and came out followed by Ashley, who marched up to Caleb with a grim expression.

"What can I do for you?"

"Can we go somewhere and talk?"

She hesitated. Feeling the eyes of her coworkers and the last couple of patrons staring at them, she spoke softly. "Give me a few minutes. Wait here by the front door."

Sinclair eased into a seat nearby while Chad eyed him suspiciously, wondering if he was Ashley's boyfriend.

Caleb squinted at the new bouncer from his chair near the door. *It didn't take Joyce long to replace me. I'm not impressed with that dude. Is that the best she could do?*

Time dragged on for both men, each feeling the need to not let the other out of his sight. Ashley breezed out of the kitchen. "Let's go."

Caleb followed her to the parking lot until she turned and said, "Let's go to the lake and talk. Follow me."

When they arrived at a scenic parking area, he pulled up next to her and parked. She motioned for him to get in her car. After he settled into the passenger seat, she asked him, "So, what do you want to talk to me about?"

"Us."

"There is no us. You don't feel the same way about me that I felt about you. I think I've wasted my time, believing that we had something special. Maybe it was just wishful thinking on my part. So there's nothing to talk about."

"We do have something special, Ashley. We both feel it. Let's not throw it away."

"You're the one who threw it away, mister. I gave myself to you and told you I was willing to go on your journey with you. I bared my soul. I was vulnerable—totally honest. And you responded by blowing me off. If you think we can be friends with benefits, you're wrong; I'm not that kind of woman."

"You said you love me."

"Loved," she corrected.

"But you said you loved me."

"Yes. And what did you say? Nothing. You didn't say you loved me back, did you?"

"I said I had feelings for you. I just didn't want to rush things. Why can't we just have fun and enjoy our friendship before getting serious?"

"It doesn't work that way, at least not with me. Find some babe who just wants friends with benefits, if that's your game. I don't play that way."

"It's not that I don't care about you. I'm just confused with everything up in the air in my life right now. It's not about you. It's about me and my search for direction and meaning."

"Fine. Take your time. But I'm moving on with my life. I'm not waiting for you."

"Just like that?"

"Just like that."

"What if I told you that Mr. Stockbridge agreed to meet with us to talk about what things I could share with you? Would that make a difference?"

She sat in silence and rubbed her fingers on the steering wheel. After about thirty seconds, she turned to Caleb. "I'm sorry. It's too late for that now. I've made up my mind."

"I only asked for more time, Ash."

"And I'm giving it to you—the whole rest of your life."

"Ashley, come on now. This is ridiculous."

"We're done here."

"Ash—"

"I said we're done here. Get out."

"Fine." He snapped open the lock, stepped out of her car, and slammed the door.

She sped off, her tires squealing.

He sat in his truck and stared into the river for an hour before heading home.

31

Caleb's next assignment took him to Salt Lake City, Utah. His message from Stockbridge was to get a hotel room in the city and wait for a couple of days for further instructions. *I'll bet it has something to do with Mormons. They have plenty of money and think God is on their side. I can't imagine what they would need from Stockbridge.*

On the first day in Salt Lake, he woke up early, before the hotel served breakfast, so he decided to take a walk. The sun was rising over the horizon, and the streets were barren, although car traffic increased with each passing minute.

The two-lane streets and sidewalks were wider than in any city Caleb had seen. At crosswalks, orange flags were available in buckets for pedestrians to make themselves more visible to drivers by carrying them across the street.

A man approached, pulling a rolling suitcase, the kind of carry-on executives use when zipping through airport terminals, except this man wasn't going on a business trip. He was homeless. The suitcase contained his worldly possessions.

When they met on the sidewalk, Caleb greeted him with a warm, "Good morning."

The man replied with an expressionless nod.

At Central Park, where the city government offices were located, he counted eighteen homeless men, either sitting on park benches or stretched out on sleeping bags on the grass.

Welcome to Salt Lake City! Where are the women?

Two men sat on a park bench carrying on a conversation. From a distance, they looked like they could be discussing the sudden drop in crude oil and how it might affect the market. As he got closer, their dirty, ragged clothing gave them away. Their shabby attire stood in sharp contrast to the manicured flower beds surrounding them. Except for a cursory glance or two, the homeless men who weren't sleeping paid no attention to the stranger walking near them.

Nobody's asked for money so far. I wonder why?

Caleb hiked up the street to Temple Square. He checked his watch. It was eight o'clock a.m., and the traffic was steady and beginning to fill the streets with cars. Pedestrians paraded up and down the sidewalks. Inside the entrance to Temple Square, two lovely young ladies who appeared to be in their early twenties approached.

"Ever been to Temple Square?" the taller girl asked.

"No, I can't say that I have. I'm just visiting. Arrived yesterday."

The tall girl had bright eyes and a name tag indicating she was from Nairobi. "I'm Anne, and this is Sharon," she said, pointing to her partner, who smiled.

"We're here to answer any questions you have about the buildings, and if you'd like a tour, we can help get you scheduled."

"I'm Caleb, and I'm just taking a walk. I really don't have time for a tour."

Anne smiled. "Isn't this a beautiful place?"

"Sure is. They've done quite a good job planting the flowers. It's really more awe-inspiring than I expected." He pointed at a large building behind a wall. "Is that the temple over there?"

"Yes, that's it."

"Do you ladies work here?"

"We're on a mission. We're volunteering to serve for eighteen months."

"So, you guys are Mormons?"

"Yes. We're Latter-Day Saints, or LDS for short," Anne replied.

"How do you like it?"

"We love it and have been so blessed to volunteer here," Anne said. "We meet so many wonderful people—like you."

"How do you support yourselves if you're volunteering your time?"

"Our families help, and we saved up before we got here."

"If you could sum up the Mormon—excuse me—the LDS beliefs in a word or two, what would you say?"

"Jesus Christ!" Sharon said.

"Cool," he said as his heart began to race. He tried to slow it down by breathing deeply.

"Do you have any more questions about the Latter-Day Saints?" Anne asked.

"Not really. I guess you don't believe in polygamy anymore, right?"

"No. That was made illegal many years ago," Anne said with a smile.

Sharon nodded in agreement.

"Do you get that question a lot?"

"Sometimes."

"Have you ever seen *Big Love* on HBO? The main characters are Mormons."

"We're not familiar with American television. What's it about?" Anne asked.

"A guy with three wives. He takes turns sleeping with them. They even had kids together."

Anne and Sharon glanced at each other. Caleb looked away from them, across the lawn at a building. *Why did I say that? You dummy. You're supposed to be making conversation, not trying to embarrass them.*

"We believe that husbands should have only one wife. Why don't you go to an LDS meeting sometime and see for yourself, Caleb? I think you would really like it."

"Maybe I will, Anne."

Sharon moved closer. "Do you have any other questions about our church?"

Caleb saw from her name tag that Sharon was from the Philippines. "Nothing comes to mind, Sharon. Wait—do you think the world's coming to an end?"

"When?"

"Anytime soon."

"It will come to an end at some point," Sharon said. "But no one will know in advance."

"I guess if we knew when the end was coming, we'd all quit working and just sit around and get stoned."

Anne and Sharon looked at each other and giggled.

Oh crap. Why did I say that? They must think I'm a big ignoramus.

Anne folded her hands in front of her waist. "You're probably right about that, Caleb."

"I enjoyed talking to you, ladies. I'd better be going."

Anne looked into Sinclair's eyes, and he smiled. "Here's a brochure, and there's a number on it you can call if you have any questions or want to set up a tour or go to a meeting."

Caleb's eyes teared up as he accepted the brochure. "Thank you. You're both very nice girls. Good luck on your mission."

"Thank you," they replied in unison with matching smiles.

I'd better get outta here. I think I'm falling in love.

Sinclair walked out through the entrance of Temple Square toward the street. While still under the arch, he glanced over his shoulder for a last look at Anne and Sharon. Now they were talking to a young boy who had walked up pointing his finger at them as though he had recognized a couple of superheroes. Maybe he had.

32

When he got back to the hotel, there was a blinking message on his phone. The front desk had an overnight package for him. He picked it up, returned to his room, sat on his bed, and opened it.

> *Caleb, I want you to go to the Miss Utah Scholarship Pageant at the Capitol Theatre. The final night of competition starts at seven, so get there by six thirty so you can get a ticket. Karmen Klosser is one of the contestants. After the pageant, catch up with her and ask if her grandmother is there. The website says her grandmother is on their scholarship board, so my guess is that she'll be at the pageant. Karmen's grandmother's name is Helen Moberg. Give her grandmother this envelope. It contains a cashier's check for one hundred thousand dollars made payable to her. If Helen Moberg is not there, give it to Karmen to give to her. Thanks, Stockbridge*

As directed, Caleb got his ticket by six thirty and found an empty seat in the middle of the theater. People flowed into the auditorium until the humming sound increased to a gentle roar that bounced throughout the room. Promptly at seven, the house lights dimmed and a spotlight hit center stage. A nine-year-old girl, who was shorter than four feet tall, hopped from behind the curtain into the center of the spotlight. After a short pause, the master of ceremonies asked everyone to stand for the national anthem. The little girl with the big voice belted out "The Star-Spangled Banner" a capella. She hit the high F note toward the end that everyone anticipates and nailed it with a flourish. The audience responded with a loud, sustained applause until she finished the final note. The little girl made a deep bow and exited stage left.

When Caleb heard the national anthem, tears flowed. He couldn't help himself. Embarrassed, he wiped them away in a hurry, glad that the house lights were off.

The contestants sang and danced their way through choreography designed to give them all several opportunities to be close to the audience at center stage under the bright lights.

After the opening group number, each contestant sashayed to the mic and introduced herself to the audience. Every introduction spawned explosions of earsplitting cheers and applause booming from supporters.

Eager for his first glimpse of Karmen Klosser, Caleb gasped when she sprinted to the microphone near the end of the introductions. *There she is.* Although shorter than the rest, her boldness and confidence made her seem taller. Speaking the four syllables of her name as if each sound was a separate note of a flute solo, she paused while her supporters showed their appreciation.

Though fewer in numbers, her backers made up for their smaller size by their enthusiasm and energy, jumping up and down as they cheered on their girl. The young beauty tossed her blond mane to the side as she strutted off stage left, keeping her eyes on the crowd and holding her sassy expression until she passed out of sight.

The fast-paced music and well-rehearsed presentations allowed over fifty girls to introduce themselves in less than ten minutes. Next, the top ten finalists were announced, and Karmen made the cut. Then the emcee explained the purpose of the swimsuit competition: judges would use the event to evaluate each contestant's health, confidence, and overall fitness.

Caleb grinned. *Fit and healthy, huh? I can judge fit and healthy.* He thought he would be good at judging the swimsuit competition since he had been judging women's bodies for many years, mostly in bars, under poor lighting conditions, and with his senses impaired by alcohol.

The emcee continued, "These contestants are earning money for college while they volunteer for service in their communities. For these young women, scholarship pageants are their sport, and they work just as hard at it as any other student athlete."

When the first girl came out, Caleb couldn't imagine anyone else being able to top her. However, each succeeding contestant looked just as good in a different way. Karmen looked exceptionally fit, and he liked the firmness of her muscles. He soon gave up trying to pick a winner.

They're all fit and healthy and gorgeous, and they're all winners in my book. These ladies have a lot of guts. I'd rather take my chances facing enemy gunfire than wearing only a swimsuit and high heels in front of a bunch of strangers gawking at me.

The evening gown competition reminded Caleb of a commanding officer's formal reception he once attended in his dress blues. One by one the girls came down the stairs in their gowns, some so tight at the waist it looked like they had been sewn on. At the bottom of the stairs, they were escorted to the center of the stage by uncomfortable young men whose grim expressions ranged from confused to terrified.

When the spotlights hit the sequins at a certain angle, a kaleidoscope of diamond-shaped colors flashed into the audience, sending Caleb into a panic attack. He reached for his AR-15 but instead grabbed the knee of a woman sitting next to him.

"That's my leg!" The woman shot him a look.

"Sorry, ma'am. I thought it was my armrest." *Caleb, get ahold of yourself, man. You're not in Afghanistan, and those aren't incoming RPGs. They're only lights. Heart, stop beating so fast, will ya?*

Seeing Karmen appear at the back of the stage caught his attention enough to distract him from war memories and bring him back to the evening gown competition. Studying the lovely lady posing at the top of the stairs waiting for her turn helped him to slow his breathing and allowed the adrenaline to filter harmlessly through his body.

"Karmen Klosser!" the emcee announced.

She stepped down the stairs like an angel descending from heaven. Her long golden hair shimmered under the lights and shined as it floated on her shoulders like ocean waves cascading on a beach. She walked rhythmically to the beat of the music, displaying confidence and poise. She again showed the same smile—both sassy and mischievous—she'd displayed during her first introduction to the audience.

Karmen's royal blue dress featured a slit up the side that went all the way to the middle of her thigh, revealing a toned and tanned leg. The neckline was cut low enough to hint at her cleavage, but it was high enough to be modest and show good taste.

Caleb admired the way she turned to walk to the opposite side of the stage with a dramatic flair. Her smooth gait was a cross between the gracefulness of a ballerina and the rhythmic stepping of a drum majorette. She took her time, soaking up the limelight, making use of every minute of exposure. Her grin, which continued to burst out spontaneously as she recognized people in the audience, radiated the joy she felt at the attention she was receiving.

He noticed how she carried her arms and pointed her fingers in a controlled manner. *This girl's going to win the crown tonight for sure.*

By the talent completion, Caleb was no longer an objective observer. He was emotionally invested in Karmen and rooting for her to win the Miss Utah pageant. Her talent was classical ballet. Caleb knew nothing about dancing, let alone ballet. But he knew what he liked, and he liked what he saw.

Nevertheless, rooting for Karmen didn't diminish his enjoyment and appreciation of the other ladies' efforts. There was a tap dancer, singers, piano players—lots of piano players, this was Utah, after all—a violinist, a ventriloquist, and even a girl who did stand-up comedy. Caleb forgot his troubles and war memories and focused on the contestants who gave their all. He imagined they performed only for him and felt certain they were all trying to make eye contact.

Karmen made the top five, which qualified her to be part of the onstage question competition—the last event of the evening. When asked who inspired her most, she smiled and looked toward her family. "That's easy. My grandmother, Helen Moberg. She's here tonight. She had a baby when she was seventeen. The baby's father abandoned her, so she raised my mom as a single parent and put her through college by working three jobs. Grandma's always been there for Mom and me. She taught me the importance of working hard and putting others above yourself."

Caleb slipped his hand in his pocket to make sure the check was still there.

While the judges tallied the scores, several soloists performed. At last they were ready to crown Miss Utah. The emcee began by announcing the fifth-, fourth-, and third-place contestants. "Now for Miss Utah and the first-place runner-up who will assume the duties of Miss Utah if tonight's winner is unable to complete her year of service."

Karmen Kloss and a striking brunette named Amanda Evans were directed to the front center of the stage. They faced each other, holding hands, each hoping for her name to be announced as the winner. Karmen made it a point to place her hands on top of Amanda's, a trick she'd learned from her friend Julie, who made a study of this and determined that the odds of winning the crown were better that way. "Make sure your hands are on top," Julie had admonished.

The auditor walked the sealed envelope to the stage and handed it to the emcee, who opened it. After a short pause, which seemed like a half hour to the two young ladies, he finally said, "The new Miss Utah is…Amanda Evans!"

33

Pandemonium broke out. The outgoing Miss Utah attached the crown on Amanda's head as she held the palms of her hands to her cheeks in ecstasy. She then made a victory lap around the stage, blowing kisses and waving to cheers and applause, while the flashes of hundreds of camera phones lit her up like sparklers on the Fourth of July.

The emcee thanked everyone for coming and said good night. And just like that, it was over. Amanda, surrounded by the hugs of her fellow contestants, waved to her family, who made their way to the front of the stage as the curtain closed.

Throughout the auditorium sad-faced families consoled each other with emotions from sorrow to disappointment to relief. A few minutes later, the contestants were out in the auditorium surrounded by their families. Some contestants were immediately proposed to by their boyfriends on bended knees.

Caleb smiled. *Those girls are getting married. That must be the consolation prize.*

An attractive woman with short, spiky hair stepped up to the mic. "Miss Bonnie here. I have some words of advice for you girls who are sad right now. Remember what I told you: lipstick fixes everything. Congratulations to all the newly engaged couples. I have some advice for the future mothers of the groom: show up...shut up...and wear beige." With that, she marched off the stage as the audience erupted into laughter.

He saw Karmen's family head for a side door leading to an alley next to the theater. By the time Caleb got there, the group hug encompassed Karmen, who wept as she held a bouquet of flowers presented to her for her second-place finish. He caught the tail end of the conversation.

"I'm sorry I let you down, Grandma."

"You didn't let me down, dear. I couldn't be prouder of you."

"I know, but I wanted to win this for you."

"You competed fairly and with your whole heart. That's all I could ask of you."

"I don't understand what happened. I thought I was going to win."

"Dear, the judges were looking for a different type tonight. You were true to yourself, which is the important thing, and you did your best. Only one girl was crowned tonight, but there are no losers. You're all winners. One of these days, whether it's in a pageant or a job interview, the person deciding will be looking for your type."

Karmen's mom, Haley, put her arm around her daughter and simply said, "Grandma's right. We're so proud of you, dear. You've got nothing to feel badly about."

Caleb walked up to them. "Excuse me. Congratulations, Karmen. I'm impressed with everything I saw from you tonight, and you're beautiful. Is this the grandma you mentioned on stage?"

"Yes. This is she." Karmen gestured toward her grandmother and mother. "This is Helen, and here is my mom, Haley."

"Hi, Helen. I'm Caleb. Pleased to meet you."

"Pleasure meeting you, Caleb. Thanks for coming."

"I just want you to know that your granddaughter is so cute, talented, and smart, I would have voted for her."

"Thanks for your kind words," said Helen. "We're so proud of her."

Reaching into his pocket, he pulled out Stockbridge's envelope and handed it to Helen. "Here's something from an anonymous friend given to you with love."

"Who's it from?"

"The person wishes to remain anonymous."

"Shall I open it now?"

"No. Open it later at home."

"Wait. I have something for you too." Helen opened her big purse, and after stuffing the envelope she got from Caleb in a side compartment, she pulled out a five-by-seven-inch headshot of Karmen and a Sharpie. Handing them to Karmen, she said, "Dear, would you sign this for the young man?"

"Sure, Grandma. Caleb with a C or a K?"

"C."

She signed it with a flourish and handed it to him. "Thank you very much."

"No. Thank you, Karmen," Caleb said.

"The person who sent you, do I know them, or is it—"

Helen, interrupted in midsentence by a group of Karmen's friends from the high school dance team, turned her attention away from Caleb to the girls. As loud and boisterous as a gaggle of geese, these well-wishers surrounded Helen, Haley, and Karmen with another chaotic congratulatory group hug.

Caleb seized the moment to make his escape. He walked up the alley ramp to the street and hailed a cab. On the way back to his hotel, he stared at Karmen's headshot, then imagined Helen opening the envelope and seeing the check for a hundred grand. *I'd love to see the expression on Helen's face when she sees that check. Now that would be a picture worthy of framing. It will blow her mind.*

34

When Caleb returned to Briggs Lake, he met with Mr. Stockbridge for lunch at the Onion.

"How'd it go at the pageant, Caleb?"

"According to plan, Mr. Stockbridge. Helen Moberg was there, and I gave her the check for one hundred thousand dollars. She looks pretty good for her age. Her granddaughter came in second in the pageant. Karmen is a stunner. Frankly, I think she should have won. Must be politics."

"You think there is politics at play in beauty pageants?"

"They call them scholarship pageants, sir. Yes, I do. It's the only way I can explain why Karmen didn't win."

"Don't you think everyone blames politics when their favorite girl doesn't win?"

"Maybe. All I know is that Karmen was spectacular, and it's a shame she wasn't crowned."

"Were you pressed on who gave the check?"

"No. Helen didn't have the chance to ask for more details. A bunch of girls came to congratulate Karmen, and I slipped away before anyone noticed."

"How's everything going with you and Ashley?"

"It's not. She broke it off. She's more ready to settle down than I am, I guess. She's not interested in keeping things the way they were. She wanted us to go to the next level and stop seeing other people."

"If you love that girl and she loves you, what's wrong with that? Compromise."

"I tried that the last time I was here, and she flatly told me that we were done. She meant it."

"Don't give up so easily."

Caleb shrugged.

"Too bad for you. I like her," Stockbridge said.

"She likes you too."

"She does?"

"Yeah."

"You just made my day, Caleb."

"I'm glad, Mr. Stockbridge."

After finishing their meal, Stockbridge handed him a check for his salary and reimbursement of his expenses for his work to date. "Take a couple of weeks off and get some rest while I do some research on the next project."

"Actually, that will work out perfectly for me. I have an old army buddy in New York City who asked me to babysit his dog for the next two weeks. I've spent some time there between deployments and enjoyed the bar scene, especially on the Upper West Side."

"The change will do you good, Caleb. I'll give you a call when the next assignment is ready."

As they got up to leave, Stockbridge grabbed Caleb's arm. "Don't forget what I said about Ashley. If she's the one, fight for her. Remember, you can share the generalities of your work. I won't have a problem with that. I don't want her to think we're doing anything illegal or creepy."

"Got it."

Before Caleb reached his car, three men lunged at him from an alley. Caleb felt a blow to his head that dazed him and then radiated pain. The pummeling he received knocked the wind out of him, and he nearly blacked out. His hand-to-hand combat training took over, and he began hitting vital body parts with precision and force. As one of the guys limped off, another grabbed him from behind, so Caleb drove a heel into the man's groin area. The third man came straight at him until Caleb's kick landed on his chin, causing blood to gush from his tongue when his upper teeth sliced into it. The remaining two retreated in the same direction as the first attacker.

What was that all about?

He managed to stumble to his car, leaving a trail of blood that dripped from his nose onto his clothes and the sidewalk. By the time he arrived at his apartment, the nosebleed had stopped, but both eyes were swollen, which made seeing difficult. After struggling to get his key in the lock, he went to his bathroom to clean up and assess the damage.

A broken nose, a couple of shiners, and a bump on my head. Could be worse. He took a hot shower and dried off, which made him feel better. After the aspirins dulled the pain, he called Stockbridge.

"Mr. Stockbridge? This is Caleb."

"Hello, Caleb, what can I do for you?"

"After I left you at the restaurant, three guys jumped me and beat me up. I managed to fight them off, but I'm not feeling so hot."

"Oh no. Is there anything I can do for you?"

"No. I gave those guys some things to remember me by. But I wonder if there's a connection between them and you."

"You don't think I had anything to do with it, do you?"

"No. I just wanted to see if you had any enemies out there who might want to discourage me from helping you."

"Could be. There are things you should know. I didn't want to talk about them unless I had to."

"I want to know everything from now on. Don't hold anything back."

"Don't worry. We'll talk soon. I'll make some arrangements and get back to you."

35

A few days later, Caleb got a letter from Stockbridge.

Meet me at the Briggs Lake Public Marina on Saturday at nine in the morning at the pontoon rental. We'll go for a boat ride far away from prying eyes. Make sure no one follows you.

On Saturday Caleb loaded a small backpack with trail mix, a cell phone, sunscreen, water, and his Glock. The temperature, already in the nineties, made everything hot to the touch. He left early, allowing plenty of time for the thirty-minute trip to the marina. When he arrived, he parked in the covered garage. It was more expensive than the general parking, but it was out of sight to passing traffic.

Grabbing his backpack, he jogged to the pier, where Stockbridge waited on a rented pontoon boat. "Hi, Caleb. Hop in. Let's get out of here."

Caleb pulled the nylon loops over the poles holding the boat next to the pier and threw them in the craft. He shoved the boat and jumped on board.

Stockbridge started the motor and steered the vessel out to the lake, slowly at first until they passed twin orange buoys marking the no wake zone. After clearing the buoys, Stockbridge pushed the throttle forward, and the boat lunged with a roar, sending waves angling away from the craft on either side.

Caleb relaxed as he looked out on Briggs Lake, a man-made body of water caused by damming up the Colorado River. *I wonder what's up with Stockbridge. Keep your guard up, Caleb. You don't know anything about him.*

After cruising at full speed for about thirty minutes, they came upon an inlet surrounded by creosote bushes and rock formations encompassing a flat, sandy beach where the pontoon boat could be safely set aground and anchored.

Stockbridge revved up the motor to pick up enough speed to drive the pontoons into the sandy shoreline, then cut the engine and pulled it up so it wouldn't hit the rocks in the shallow water.

"Caleb, take the anchor and walk the bowline up the hill as far as you can," Stockbridge said and pointed in the general area to guide his first mate.

Caleb hauled the anchor up the hill as directed before returning to the boat to grab his backpack while Stockbridge locked the motor and lifted a small cooler from a storage bin.

They sat at a nearby concrete picnic table with a wooden roof, shielding them from the scorching Arizona sun.

"Remote location, Mr. Stockbridge. No eyes on us here unless you count coyotes and kestrels."

"I know," Stockbridge said as he fetched a ham sandwich and a can of iced tea from the cooler. "It's definitely off the grid. I love this spot. You want something to eat?"

Caleb shook his head. "I'm good. I brought some water and trail mix. That's all I need. Ashley has a spot like this where she goes to think and make decisions. She calls it Decision Rock."

"Any good news with you and Ashley?"

"The short answer is no. The long answer is hell no."

"So, tell me what happened after we met the last time." Stockbridge took a bite out of his ham sandwich.

"Three guys jumped me. I was stunned at first and thought they were trying to rob me."

"I see you've got a couple of black eyes," Stockbridge said between bites.

"I'm good. At first I thought my nose was broken by the way it was bleeding and swelling, but it's doing better today."

"That's good."

"They didn't ask for money. It started me thinking they may in some way be connected to my visit with you. Not that you were behind it but that you had enemies who wanted to stop what we're doing. If that's the case, why would anyone want to keep us from doing good things for people?"

Caleb waited for Stockbridge to answer, but the old man sat in silence and offered no explanation.

"What's going on? You haven't told me the whole story, have you?"

"Everything I've told you is true. I just haven't told you all of it. Mainly to protect you."

"Protect me? If getting beaten up is protecting me, I'd hate to think what not protecting me would look like."

"It's true that I'm suffering from a fatal illness and don't have much longer to live. It's also true that I've made a lot of money legally running businesses. And yes, I'm trying to help some people from my past."

"Then what did you leave out?"

"What I didn't tell you was that I worked for the government for several secret organizations, including the CIA."

"Why would they be going after you if you were legit?"

"It depends on who 'they' are."

"I don't get why folks in our own government, who you worked for, would treat you like that."

"Revenge or to scare me from talking to anyone or to silence me forever. I was a whistleblower, and my testimony not only got a few people fired but also sent some people to prison. Their coconspirators have been out to get me ever since."

"Can't you be protected by the FBI or somebody like that or go into the witness protection program? You must have contacts in the government who can help you. After all, you were working for them."

"I wish it was that simple. Yes, I still have contacts in government intelligence at the very top, people I worked with who I trust, and they have been helpful in other situations and will help me again if asked. Except that there were some projects I was involved with that were deep cover. When it came to those jobs, things were different."

"How so?"

"For heightened security, I had only one contact. He assigned projects, and I turned over the information he needed. The fewer people involved, the safer it was for all of us. One day my contact didn't show. I think someone murdered him."

"Isn't there any way you can find out who's after you?"

"I've been trying for years."

"Were you a spy?"

"I gathered intelligence."

"What's the difference?"

"I guess not much when you come to think of it," Stockbridge said with a laugh. "It depends on who you're talking to and who you're gathering the evidence from. In my past life, I was an investigative reporter and got pretty good at digging out the facts and researching my subjects. It came in handy when I started helping the government get information."

"I wish you would have told me all this at the beginning."

"Honestly, I didn't know you would be a target, Caleb. I guess they are more serious than I thought. I haven't had any strange incidents for many years, so I figured whoever was out to get me had given up. If you want out, I'll release you from working for me. No hard feelings."

Caleb inhaled, then turned his gaze to a small flock of teal, who were bobbing around the shoreline like a convoy. He thought about this frail old guy who had to enlist the help of a total stranger because no one else he knew could be trusted. Caleb's inclination to protect others always dominated his instinct for self-preservation.

"I'll stay for now. I want to help you if I can. And I do need the money."

"I'm so delighted to hear that."

"Remember, nothing illegal. And by the way, I'm not fond of getting my head bashed in. I could have stayed in the army if I wanted to get knocked around all the time."

"Absolutely. I understand. Your safety is my primary concern. Do what you have to do to protect yourself."

Stockbridge gulped the rest of his iced tea, dabbed his mouth with a napkin, and put the trash in his cooler. "I'll wire funds directly into your checking account from one of my Swiss bank accounts so it won't be traceable. You'll have what you need to carry out the assignments, you'll get your salary, and we'll primarily communicate on the secured phone I gave you."

36

A few days later, Caleb took the Briggs Lake shuttle service to McCarran International Airport in Las Vegas for his trip to New York to see his army buddy, Anthony Victorino. After boarding and stowing his carry-on, he leaned back in his seat, thinking about his fellow veterans, Alvin and Clint. *They served their country and are asking nothing in return. They're doing the best they can. I'm glad we could help them.*

Putting his phone in his pocket as the flight attendants prepared the aircraft for departure, Caleb dutifully moved his seat to the upright position as commanded by the captain. Still coping with stress while flying, he double-checked his seat belt. He shut his eyes, trying not to think about the many narrow escapes, the times his team—extracted by choppers from hot landing zones—dove into the birds seconds before takeoff.

He filled his mind with thoughts of Ashley Bivens, picturing every detail of her physical appearance, from her reddish-brown hair to her beautifully formed feet. He thought of her hair, magnificent any way she wore it—down, up, in a ponytail. It was as thick and rich as her soul. Oh, how he longed for her touch, to hear her voice. He loved the way she called him dude, with a touch of attitude, sass, and affection. Her voice had a melodious quality, sounding almost like she was singing her words. Lean and strong, there wasn't an ounce of fat on her. Her complexion was perfect. He had never seen anyone with skin so much like porcelain.

Ashley's physical attractiveness aside, it was her desire to take their relationship to the next level that he couldn't forget. He pictured the way she argued that they could go on the journey together no matter how many questions he had about his future. At the time they discussed these things, he didn't appreciate how valuable it was to have a woman like Ashley on his team with the desire to help him forge his future. *I wish I would have understood that earlier. Now it's probably too late to salvage our relationship. Hopefully I've learned something and won't take my next girlfriend for granted the way I did Ashley. The man who wins her affection will have a charmed life.*

His reverie was interrupted by an announcement from the captain that the plane had reached its cruising altitude and that beverage service would soon begin. Passengers were told they could use their electronic devices. The captain advised everyone to keep their seat belts on in case of any unexpected bumps.

"Are you visiting family in New York?" Startled, Caleb turned to the woman next to him. When he'd boarded, she was staring at her smartphone, so he hadn't paid much attention to her. She occupied the window seat, he sat on the aisle, and the seat between them was vacant.

"No. I'm visiting an army buddy. Going to babysit his dog while he's away on business. What about you?"

"I'm going to spend a month in New York to attend some auditions. I'm an actor."

"That sounds epic. On Broadway?"

"Yes. Hopefully, anyway. Three of my auditions are for Broadway shows, and one is for a smaller theater in the city."

"I guess that one's off Broadway," he said, pointing his finger at her.

She chuckled. "Off Broadway. You got it. You know the lingo."

"That's insane you get to do that. I've never met an actress before."

"Now you have." She punctuated the comment by batting her eyes in an exaggerated manner and tilting her head back in mock arrogance.

And I've never seen someone with such beautiful eyes either. They're enchanting. Boy, I lucked out. I could have been next to some bore ass or a screaming baby. Instead I'm sitting next to an actress with Bette Davis eyes and a cute nose who isn't wearing a wedding ring.

He held out his hand. "I'm Caleb Sinclair."

She took it and squeezed it warmly. "I'm Lily Lofton."

"Awesome name. Is it your real one?"

"Of course. Is Caleb your real name?"

"Yes."

"I like it. Does Caleb mean anything?"

"I don't know. Someone told me it means 'bridges.' Maybe I'm a bridge to nowhere."

She giggled. "I think it means you're a nice guy."

37

After giving their drink orders, Lily peered out the window while Caleb opened his seat tray. The flight attendant returned with a plastic cup of water for Lily and a can of Coors Light for Caleb.

When she took the cup from the flight attendant, he noticed her manicured nails and long, shapely fingers as well as the graceful way she moved them.

A few minutes later, the plane hit a wind shear and suddenly dropped one hundred feet. The static-filled voice of the pilot boomed from the speakers. "We're expecting some turbulence for the next half hour. Please fasten your seat belts. Flight attendants, take your seats."

Caleb shook his head. "Now you tell us."

A few rows behind, Caleb heard a man yelling at a flight attendant. "I want off the damn plane."

"Sir, please fasten your seat belt. We're expecting turbulence. The captain wants everyone buckled up."

"Then I need to speak to your captain." He pushed her out of the way and rushed toward the flight deck. Caleb, hearing the drama unfold, stood in the aisle, blocking the man's path.

"Out of my way, boy!" The man raised his arms to shove Caleb to the side.

Caleb slipped his arms under the passenger's armpits and locked his hands before lifting the man off his feet and walking him back to his row. Setting him down in his seat, Caleb said, "Now stay put, sir."

It happened so fast. The man sat in stunned silence, trying to figure out what had just occurred.

The flight attendant snapped the passenger's seat belt in place. "Thank you, sir. I'll take it from here."

Caleb walked back to his seat and buckled up.

Lily looked at him with astonishment. "What do you do?"

"What do you mean?"

"What do you do for a job? Are you a cop or an air marshal?"

"I used to be a bouncer, if that's what you mean." A smile slowly crept across his face. "As you can see, I've had some experience handling drunks."

"So I noticed. You must have been good at it."

"Too good, as a matter of fact. That's a story for another day. Are you from Las Vegas?"

"No. I'm from a place called Parker in Arizona."

"You're kidding?" He stared at her. "I live only about an hour away. I'm from Briggs Lake. What are the odds that we'd be sitting next to each other on this flight?"

Caleb took a good look at Lily. He noticed her blond hair for the first time, in an organized tangle, like a wheat field on a breezy day. He liked her cheerful tone of voice and the way words floated from her mouth like dancers—artful, smooth, and purposeful. He continued to study her face as she expounded on Parker and her summers skiing on the Parker Strip, competing in Jet Ski races. He kept firing off questions to keep her talking so he'd have an excuse to continue studying her face.

After a while she stopped. "It's your turn. I don't want to do all the talking. That's not polite, and I'll bore you to death."

"I'm not bored. You're interesting."

"That may be, but I'm not going to do all the talking. It's your turn. Speak." Then she frowned.

"Don't pout. I can't resist a woman who pouts. What do you want to know?"

"Tell me more about what you do for a living, Caleb."

"I'm not a bouncer anymore. In my current job, I help a guy change people's lives. I'm like his messenger, sort of, except he keeps his identity from them. He's really big on not letting them know who he is."

"Why is that?"

"He has his reasons."

"And they are?"

"I will say this: it's been interesting to meet the people he's sent me to help. In a way I sort of feel like an angel swooping in to save them."

"Save them from what?"

"Their problems."

"Do you give them money?"

"Sometimes. Not always. Depends on what they need."

"Everybody needs money."

"I used to feel the same way, but I'm learning that money isn't always the answer. For example, my boss has plenty of money, but it can't make him well, so what good is it when what he needs is to have his health back?"

"Good point."

"Did you always want to be an actress?"

"As long as I can remember. I took dance and piano and put on shows for my parents and their friends. They encouraged me to make this trip to New York and give it my best shot. If it doesn't work out, I don't know what I'll do. Acting is all I've ever wanted to do, and I don't care much about anything else."

Caleb smiled.

"What's so funny?"

"Nothing. I just think you're so good-looking, I'd hire you even if you couldn't act. You know, just to sit there in the scene to keep everyone's attention."

She laughed. "What a charmer you are, Mr. Caleb."

"I'm serious."

"Then thank you. I've won you over. That's a start."

"And I can be highly critical."

She continued to smile and glanced quickly out the window. "I'm sure you can. Thanks for your vote of confidence."

The flight attendant interrupted them and asked if either needed a refill. Caleb nodded and Lily shook her head.

"What about your parents, Caleb?"

"They're good people. Dad worked for the city of Des Moines, Mom for an insurance agent. When they retired we moved to Briggs Lake, which is where I went to high school. Now they're in a nursing home together in Fort Dodge, Iowa, so they can be near their families."

"What did you do after high school?"

"I worked highway construction in the Phoenix area for a few years, got a couple of deewees. Decided to join the army and get away from it all."

"And they sent you to war, right?"

"I volunteered to go to Afghanistan—for three deployments. Strange as it may sound, I liked it at first—to be trained in something, to have a purpose in life. I felt like I was serving something greater than myself. I believed that it was my calling and that I would be safer doing that than staying in construction. I felt invincible."

"And now?"

"A lot of doubts, I guess. I couldn't help asking myself why. Why the destruction? Why the killing? Lives are ruined by war. When I realized war could be hazardous to my health and my luck was running out, I knew it was time to get out. Now I don't know what to do next."

"You were probably right to get out when you did. I can't imagine the horrible things you must have experienced."

"I try not to think about them."

"I've enjoyed our conversation, Caleb. I'm going to try to take a nap before we land."

"Me too."

She moved her seat back, positioned her pillow, and turned toward the window.

He inserted his earbuds and listened to his favorite blues playlist, drifting off to sleep to B.B. King singing "The Thrill Is Gone."

38

Caleb's buddy Nick is shot and crumples to the ground a few feet away. Ducking under a blizzard of steel projectiles, Caleb presses a bandage against Nick's stomach to staunch the blood. When the UH-60 Black Hawk finally lands, the helicopter is greeted by a hail of bullets. Caleb cradles Nick like a baby in his arms and charges through the gunfire toward the chopper. Crew Chief Big Jim Robinson hoists Nick inside at the door, and Caleb jumps in behind, nearly falling out as the chopper lifts upward with a roar. Rocket-propelled grenades detonate around the rising copter, engulfing it with smoke and the smell of sulfur and ammonia. The explosions launch shrapnel into Caleb's right leg. He's so focused on encouraging Nick that he doesn't feel the steel shards lodged in his calf. When they land at the field hospital, Nick is dead.

"Are you okay?"

Caleb turned to look at Lily. Her mouth was wide open, and those alluring hazel eyes reflected her concern.

"You were talking to yourself and saying, 'Stay with me. Stay with me.' Your head swiveled back and forth, and you're soaked in perspiration."

"I'm fine. No worries. I must have had a bad dream. Sorry if I alarmed you."

"Look." She pointed down at his right hand. He had squeezed his empty Coors can flat in the center.

"I have flashbacks from my war experiences; that's all it is."

"I'm so sorry, Caleb."

"It's okay."

They gazed into each other's eyes for a moment without saying a word. The captain's voice blasted through the speakers, announcing that the flight was making its final approach to JFK and would be on the ground in thirty minutes. Lily moved her seat to the upright position and put the novel she had been reading in her purse.

Caleb felt something like a twinge in his stomach. This amazing woman would be out of his life forever within an hour. *What if she's the one and I'll never see her again? It's now or never. What have I got to lose?*

"Lily, I have an idea."

Her head swung toward him. "What?"

"I was just thinking. If you would like to, maybe we could get together for a drink sometime while we're in New York?"

"I'd like that, Caleb, except I have no idea about my schedule. If you give me a day or two's notice, I'll try to meet you somewhere. I'll give you my phone number, and you can text me."

She took a paper pad out of her purse, wrote the information down, made a big happy face on the bottom of the note, and handed it to him.

"Can you read my writing, Caleb?"

"Yep. No problem."

"Are you on Instagram?"

"Yeah, but I don't post many pictures."

"I do. I have some pictures I think you might like. My headshots are on there. I'm Lilyjetski. Can you remember that?"

"I'll have to check them out." *That's a good sign. She wants me to see her pictures. She must have some interest in me, at least. She's probably just promoting herself. Actresses are good at that. It comes with the territory and doesn't mean she thinks I'm unique in any way. Am I flirting with Lily, or is she flirting with me?*

She raised her armrest and scootched to the middle seat. "Here, I'll show you some of them before we land."

"These are beautiful. You're a knockout. Stunning."

"Thanks." She grinned.

Lily continued to swipe her phone to show picture after picture. Suddenly he felt her right knee pressing against his left knee. He glanced down to see if it was accidental or intentional. It felt to him like she held it there on purpose, but he wasn't sure. In any case, he decided not to move his knee.

When the aircraft stopped at the gate, Caleb took his bag out of the overhead storage bin. "Do you have anything up here?"

"Yes, a burgundy rolling suitcase."

He hoisted it out of the bin and lowered it to the seat between them.

"Thanks. Great meeting you."

"You too. Good luck with the auditions."

"Thanks. Good luck with the dog sitting. How old's the dog?"

"I think he said he was ten. You know it takes goldens and Labs about four years to slow down and some even longer. This one's apparently trained and obeys commands, so walking him should be easy. That's the only responsibility I'll have besides cleaning up after myself. Should be a restful time in New York. Not much rest for you, I imagine."

She shook her head. "No. I'll be swamped—running to auditions, memorizing scripts, and spending time with the agency that's representing me. I'm looking forward to it, though. I've been dreaming of doing this all my life."

"It must be satisfying to know what you want to do—and to know what you're good at. I still don't know what I want to do in life, but I'm searching for the answer."

"You'll find it. What is that old saying, seek and you shall find? I think that's true."

"I hope so."

They waited in silence for the passengers ahead of them to deplane. Then he slid into the aisle and took a step back to allow her to go first. He stopped and let others go ahead of him to help an elderly lady get her bag down from overhead. By the time he exited the ramp to the concourse, Lily was a hundred yards in front of him.

At the baggage claim, he caught up with Lily and saw her standing with her girlfriend at the carousel. Not wanting to interject himself, he kept his distance, yet he felt her glancing at him more than once. After collecting her bags, Lily and her friend headed toward him.

"Caleb, I'd like you to meet my friend Jenny," she chirped. "Jenny, this is Mr. Caleb Sinclair. He's an army veteran."

Jenny extended her hand. "Pleased to meet you, Caleb. Thank you for your service."

"You're welcome." He took her hand. "Are you an actress too?"

Blushing at the compliment, she smiled. "No. I'm in marketing."

"Have a grand time in the big city," Lily said and with mock seriousness added, "and be sure to behave yourself now."

"Yes, ma'am. Good luck with the auditions. Do they still say break a leg?"

"I don't know, Caleb, but I'm sure I'll find out. Bye now."

Lily and Jenny walked toward the Uber pickup area, laughing and talking. He watched until they disappeared into the crowd. Letting his suitcase make several lonely revolutions around the carousel, he wondered if he would ever see her again.

After collecting his luggage, he sat down to text Lily. *Hi Lily, so nice mtg u. U made the flight gr8. GL Caleb.*

"Caleb."

Glancing up, he saw his army buddy Anthony standing over him. Caleb jumped up and hugged him. "You look better than ever, bro. How's life treating you?"

"Can't complain. Working hard, but I love what I do. Hey, we better get going, or I'll get a ticket."

Anthony Victorino stood a lean and fit six feet, four inches tall. His curly black hair matched his perpetual five o'clock shadow. Unlike Sinclair, Victorino had made the adjustment from army life to civilian life quickly. He'd known that he wanted to work in finance and that New York was the place to do it. He was hired by a small but growing firm and advanced to the acquisitions team. He ran the numbers on companies his firm wanted to buy.

As they ran toward the car, Caleb continued talking. "I'll bet you're making money hand over fist."

"As a matter of fact, I am, but I'm not attracting women the way you do, stud."

"What are you talking about? Women go crazy over you. I don't know what they see in you, though. It must be some Italian vibe."

"Ha ha! It didn't take you long to bring the Italian thing up. Go ahead; you're dying to say it."

"If you insist. As that woman in the Georgia bar said to you, 'You're good-looking, Anthony, in an Italian sort of way.'"

"You had your fun. But remember, she was Italian, so it really was a compliment."

"If you say so. But it sounded like a qualifier to me."

"What were we thinking, hanging out with those babes?"

"We were desperate."

"That's right, and it was closing time. Their loss."

"Affirmative."

They unloaded Caleb's suitcases at the apartment and met Flash, Victorino's golden retriever.

"Flash is baring his teeth," Caleb said as the dog approached with a scrunched snout.

Victorino chuckled. "He's not going to bite you. That's Flash's way of trying to smile like a human. He wrinkles his nose trying to mimic us. He's so vicious, he might lick you to death."

Flash's tail whipped back and forth like it was attached to an engine and thumped on a nearby coffee table. He started licking Caleb's hands in an attempt to coax the visitor into petting him, and it worked.

"How old is Flash?"

"He's ten but acts like he's six."

Like many New York apartments, the one-bedroom home on West Eighty-Seventh Street was small, but it had everything a single guy and his dog could want, and it was a short walk to Central Park. After a quick tour and some lessons in operating the cable TV remote, the former comrades in arms hit the street for the walk to the Amsterdam Ale House.

Caleb was mesmerized by the activity—cars, buses, bikes, dog walkers, and children being pushed in high-tech strollers by their nannies. Besides the sights, there were the sounds of garbage trucks, honking horns, and sirens. He felt the intensity of a lot of people doing many things in a hurry. Being in New York energized him, and he liked the vibe. He could see how living there could get addictive.

"This place is like an adrenaline rush compared to Arizona."

"I love it here. There's something for everyone and all kinds of people from all kinds of places. I like the energy. You can feel it, and there's always something to do. I never get tired of it."

Once inside the restaurant, the men took seats at a small wooden table. The server waltzed over within seconds and, after giving them menus, took their drink orders. "I'll be back in a few minutes with your beers. My name's Shannon."

"You don't sound like a New Yorker, Shannon," Caleb said with a flirty look in his eye.

"What are New Yorkers supposed to sound like?"

"I don't know…I mean, you sound like you're from the South, that's all," Caleb stammered.

"Born and raised in Richmond, but I've got New York in my DNA," Shannon replied in a courteous tone with a touch of Southern sass. "You got a problem with that, son?"

"No. I like the way you talk."

She smiled, tossed her head, and strutted off to get their drinks.

After Shannon left, Victorino burst out laughing. "'No. I like the way you talk,'" he said, imitating his army buddy.

Caleb took a half-hearted swing at Anthony's head, but he leaned back out of reach. "You dimwit."

"You're still the world's biggest flirt, and yet you can't keep a girlfriend. Maybe that's why—ever think of that?"

"What are you, my shrink?"

"Shannon may have a Southern twang, but she's got a New York tongue and Big Apple attitude. Don't mess with her, jack."

"Good to know, Father Victorino. Thanks for the counseling. When are your hours? I have a lot of confessing to do."

"You're a lost cause, dude."

"I could tell she's attracted to me. She couldn't help it, poor girl."

"You wish, ladies' man. She's just doing her job; that's why she has to be polite to you."

Shannon returned with a couple of beers, and the look in her eyes made Caleb feel they could be good friends someday, maybe more. That may not have been the look she gave him, but that was his interpretation. When it came to women being attracted to him, Caleb always gave himself the benefit of the doubt.

"We've got a couple of hours, and then I have to hit the rack. The Uber is coming at five a.m. for my flight to California, so let's talk serious stuff. Tell me about your gig."

"I'm not supposed to say too much about it, Anthony, but I need to talk to someone. I know I can count on you to keep this between us. Right?"

"Who would I tell? My dog?"

39

"Remember when I told you how I lost my job for beating up an out-of-control drunk? What I didn't tell you was that there was this old guy who waited outside the bar after I was canned and made a proposition—"

"You were propositioned by an old fart?"

"This is serious; let me finish. He asked me to do errands for him, to visit people from his past and see what he could do to help them."

"Why?"

"He's rich, and he's dying. He wants to take care of some people who helped him along the way, and he wants to make amends for some that he hurt before he croaks. He hasn't said that in so many words, but that's my take on it." Caleb sighed. "It's been weird but kind of interesting. Not doing anything dishonest, strange, or creepy, just meeting people and discovering what they need the most and then telling my boss, and he gets it for them."

"I never heard of such a thing."

"Neither had I. I think it's kind of cool that he wants to use his money to help people from his past while he has a chance."

"Why doesn't he meet with the people himself instead of using you?"

"Everybody asks that. He said that it's complicated and that he has his reasons. I think some of them he doesn't even know or he isn't on speaking terms with them. I'm speculating that it's one of those two things or both."

The friends sat in silence for a few minutes, watching a rambunctious group of college-aged students blowing off steam at the other end of the dining room. Victorino thought about his friend's new job. *The old guy had no way of knowing this, but Caleb is the perfect guy for this assignment. In combat he was the first to volunteer for dangerous missions and could be trusted to carry them out despite all obstacles and bring his team back alive.*

Anthony broke the silence. "Yep. I can see you doing something like that."

"Why do you say that?"

"You like to help people and can be trusted to follow through when asked to do something. I've seen you do that many times. Does it pay well?"

"It pays enough."

"I'd love to get you working in my company. If you can handle the corporate culture nonsense and politics, it's a pretty sweet gig."

"I couldn't sit in an office all day. I'd go batshit crazy. This job keeps me moving and out with people. I'd like to be outside helping people when I grow up."

"Assuming you do grow up someday."

The friends were distracted by a patron at the bar getting boisterous with Shannon.

"Miss Richmond has her hands full with that clown," Caleb said.

"No worries, buddy. That dude is going to find out he has his hands full with Miss Richmond. She's a hundred twenty pounds of whoop ass. He'll wish he'd never been born."

They laughed.

"You seem to know a heckuva a lot about Miss Shannon. Do you come here to hit on her, hoping for a miracle? Or do all women still find you repulsive?"

"Shannon and I are just friends. I'm not her type. I work too many hours. I can't keep personal commitments, so I don't even try. What about your love life? I want to hear everything about Miss Ashley Bivens. From what you told me, you're head over heels. I can't wait to meet her."

"She broke it off."

"What? You had the girl with the perfect body and a heart to match, and you blew it?"

"Yep. I think I did. She wanted us to move in together and take our relationship to the next level. I told her I just wanted to be friends and wasn't ready to make a commitment."

"You'd rather keep on being the world's biggest flirt than be with the woman of your dreams. What a dumbass."

"It's just that I'm starting over, doing this job, uncertain about my future. Everything in my life is up in the air now, and I needed time to sort some things out."

"You're going to lose her, bro. You can't expect the woman you've described to me to wait around while you try to sort your life out." He swung his arm and pretended to give him a backhanded slap. "What a dipstick you are. She probably gets hit on constantly."

"I know. Ashley's a spitfire, but her heart is tender. She's a knockout. Beautiful long brown hair with reddish highlights that seem to glow in the sunshine. Her green eyes—which seem blue to me—go right through my soul. It's not just her looks. She makes me glad just to be in the same room with her. I've never felt that way about a woman before."

"Buddy, then get on the next plane to Arizona and marry that gal. There will be broken hearts from Hoboken to San Diego, but hey, isn't a relationship more fulfilling than flirting with women and playing superficial mind games?"

"I see what you're saying. We hadn't been dating that long, though. I think she was rushing it. I wanted us to have fun and just enjoy each other without the pressure of taking it to the next level. She didn't agree. That's why she broke it off."

"I get that. If you lose her, you know I'm going to say I told you so."

"Of course. You'll rub it in like you always do. What about your dog, Flash? Who normally takes care of him?"

"I hire dog walkers. I have two who are pretty good," he said. "But for a two-week trip like this one starting tomorrow, I need someone at home with him." Victorino was lying. When he got the call from Caleb about being fired, he thought his pal was down on his luck and wanted to give him a place to go to. Taking care of Flash was only an excuse. "You better hang out with Flash. He gets separation anxiety."

"So do I."

"Good. You'll be a great match."

The rest of their dinner was spent sharing old war stories about their time in Afghanistan. Normally Caleb made it a point to keep his war experiences to himself. Victorino was an exception. Talking about the war with his friend helped him get a lot of things off his chest, and it worked for Anthony that way too.

"I better get back. I've got the early flight, Caleb. I do want to ask you one more thing. Are you still getting the dream about Nick?"

"I had it on the flight coming here. Scared the hell out of the girl sitting next to me."

"You did all you could do to save Nick. It's not your fault. You've got to remember that."

"I know. I try to tell myself that. It was just so terrible the way it went down. It's hard to erase the images of that day."

"You may not be able to erase them, but don't allow yourself to dwell on them. Keep your thoughts on other things. Do you think you should reconsider talking to a shrink?"

"We'll see. If I can't handle it, I probably will."

"Promise me you will."

"I will. If I can't deal with it myself."

"Good. One last thing. When you take Flash to Central Park for walks, be really careful. Watch your six."

"Why do I need to watch my back?"

"The park is more dangerous than it used to be. There's been a lot of muggings—people getting beaten up and robbed. Homicides are on the rise. The police have gotten so much flak from politicians and the media that they aren't proactively policing anymore. They're standing down, protecting their careers instead of the citizens, and I don't blame them, but it's more dangerous here."

"That's crazy."

"The cops are scared of outside protestors and activists who stir up angry mobs who come out and destroy stuff whenever there's a cop-involved shooting—even if justified. When cops get shot in the line of duty—crickets. In this city the punks are given the benefit of the doubt, and there's a rush to judgment against the cops before the facts have come out."

"Not good. I don't blame the cops for avoiding the drama. Doesn't anyone care about the increased crime and murders?"

"The people who actually live in those communities do. The politicians running the city turn a blind eye. They have private security or live behind protective gates. They're even cutting police budgets. There are dirty cops, and they should be dealt with. No one hates a dirty cop more than a good cop, but you don't degrade the police department and put the citizens at risk to score political points with activist groups."

"Thanks for the heads-up. I didn't realize I was going into another war zone. That's all I need."

40

The next morning Caleb woke to the warm breath of the golden retriever on his face. The dog's hind legs were on the floor, and his front legs were on the couch. The pooch's tongue was hanging out, and drool was dripping on his new dog sitter.

"Hi, Flash. What's up?"

Flash barked twice.

"The sky? That's an old one, Flash. Get some new material. You'll have to give me a minute to wake up and find my clothes, big boy."

Fifteen minutes later Flash pulled Caleb toward Central Park until they came upon a man sitting in a chair, smoking a cigarette in front of an old apartment building across the street. His German shepherd sat at his feet.

"How old's your dog?" the man yelled as Caleb and Flash approached.

"Ten."

"Huh?" The man held his hand to his ear.

Caleb repeated, "Ten! How old is your dog?"

"He's ten."

"Handsome dog. What's his name?"

"Kaiser. What's your dog's name?"

"Flash."

The man lit another cigarette off the burning embers of the one he had just finished. "You know, they say German shepherds can be overly protective and not good with kids. Kaiser is friendly with kids. It's how you raise 'em, you know."

"I know. Later."

"Hey, what's your name?"

"Caleb."

"I'm Buzz."

"See you, Buzz."

I better get going. This guy will keep me talking all day. We still haven't gotten to the park. Keep walking, or he'll ask another question.

The entrance from Park Avenue West had a stone stairway that led to a path toward the Jacqueline Kennedy Onassis Reservoir. There was a variety of people and dogs sharing the ritual of the early morning walk in the park. Some owners, coffee mugs in hand, were catching up with their friends while their dogs sniffed the ground in search of the perfect spot to do their business. When they finished that, they started sniffing each other. Some owners entertained themselves on their smartphones while keeping a careful eye on their dogs.

Professional dog walkers holding leashes for several canines skill-fully guided their pooches through the winding paths of the park. Joggers hurrying home to avoid being late for work raced past nannies with Caribbean accents talking on phones while pushing expensive baby strollers.

I had forgotten how big this park is and how exciting it is to be with all kinds of different people traipsing around or just hanging out. In a strange way, I feel a kinship with these folks. It's like we're all in it together and we're here because we have dogs to care for or we're taking a break from the big-city lifestyle with its brick, steel, and concrete to spend time on grass and dirt, walking under trees, and watching black squirrels and birds.

After noting the landmarks around the entrance so he could remember the way back, Caleb took Flash on a long walk down a path until it forked, at which point he took the trail that went deeper into the park until he came upon tennis courts.

"Flash, let's watch some tennis," he said and guided the canine to a bench where he had a good vantage point. A man was hitting tennis balls to a young boy and instructing him on the proper swing and best way to grip the racket. As Flash plopped to the ground, Caleb's mind drifted back to Arizona and Stockbridge with his rare disease and his mission to finish his business before the disease finished him.

"Can I pet your dog?" a woman asked.

Caleb looked up to see an old lady, about eighty, with a scarf around her head and a twinkle in her eye. Age and gravity had combined to give her spine a permanent curvature. Her smile revealed teeth that appeared to be newer than the rest of her.

"Sure. He's ten. His name is Flash," Caleb said, gesturing toward the dog, who sat up expectantly when he heard his name.

The old lady extended a wrinkled arm and stroked Flash's head down to the middle of his back with slow motions. "It's funny how friendly dogs are compared to cats. Cats don't give you the time of day."

"I know what you mean."

"Another thing: how can a person feel lonely, even with all these people around?" Then she answered her own question. "Because being alone and being lonely are two different things. We aren't alone because there are all these people around today, but lonely is a feeling that has nothing to do with what's going on around us. It's from the inside."

"Interesting. I've never considered it that way."

"I've given it a lot of thought. Before my husband died, when we were apart, there were times when he left me alone, but I never felt lonely. I knew he was traveling for his job or at a company training session—things like that—and we'd be together again when he returned."

"I don't really have anyone, so I guess you could say I'm alone and lonely." He laughed.

"I guess we're both in the same boat for different reasons. What's your name?"

"Caleb."

"I'm Lucy. I better get on with my walk. Good day to you."

"You too, Lucy."

"Bye, Flash." She shuffled toward the path, steadied by a cane that appeared to be as old as she was. Caleb watched her sway along the trail until she disappeared behind a tree.

Why did I say I don't have anyone? I have Ashley. Oh wait. I don't have her.

He dialed Ashley's number and then hung up.

Caleb stared at joggers on a path several hundred yards away. When Flash lunged for a black squirrel, the leash snapped Caleb's arm and mind, jolting him awake from thoughts of Ashley and the difference between being alone and loneliness.

"It's time to head back, Flash. Let's go."

He stood up and led Flash toward an exit to Park Avenue West. When they crossed to the next block, he saw the man still sitting in his chair smoking a cigarette, the dog at his side. When Caleb and Flash got close, he smiled and waved.

"How old's your dog?"

"He's ten."

"So is mine. What's his name?"

"Flash."

"Mine's named Kaiser," the man said with a tone of pride. "Do you live here?"

"I'm visiting from Arizona, helping a friend out."

"I've been to Arizona. I love the petrichor after it rains."

"I'm not familiar with that term," Caleb said, shaking his head.

"It's that pleasant smell after a rainfall. Rain in the desert is a refreshment to dried-up senses and gives off a delicious fragrance. In Arizona, the smell is distinctive because of the sweet scent of the creosote bush."

"Another reason it's distinctive is because it hardly ever rains in Arizona."

"True," the man said and took a long drag on his Salem. "The creosote leaves smell like candy but taste like crap—keeps animals from feeding on them. Creosote bushes can also survive the droughts that kill other shrubs and bushes. In fact, some of those creosote bushes are thousands of years old. You ever hear of King Clone?"

"Can't say that I have."

"It's in the Mojave Desert, near Lucerne Valley in California. They say it's eleven thousand seven hundred years old, which makes it one of the oldest living organisms on earth."

"I didn't know that. Thanks."

"How old's your dog?"

"Ten."

"So is mine."

"Cool. See you." With a wave, Caleb led Flash back toward their apartment until he caught sight of a street vendor. *What the heck? Might as well get something to eat.*

While waiting in line, Caleb couldn't get over how much food the guy had packed in his cart: doughnuts of all kinds, bagels, rolls, and bread. The man's movements were as graceful as a swan gliding in a pond, and his voice was as rough as tree bark. He called all the men buddy and all the women sweetie. This clearly was a guy who had no time for political correctness.

"What'll you have, buddy?"

"Coffee."

"What kind?"

"Regular coffee."

"You mean cream and sugar?"

"No. Just black."

"So you want black with sugar?"

"No. I just drink it black."

"Buddy, you're in New York now. If you want black coffee you say, 'I want coffee, black, no sugar.'"

"Got it. I'll have a bagel too."

"What kind?"

"What do you have?"

"Plain, chocolate chip, hazelnut, sesame seed, onion, and pepper flavored."

"Plain with cream cheese."

"Then you say, 'A bagel with a schmear.'"

"I want a black coffee, no sugar, and a bagel with a schmear."

"There you go, pal." He handed over a box containing the coffee and bagel.

Caleb juggled the food while he walked the short distance to the apartment. After feeding Flash, he sat down to enjoy his breakfast. He noticed that the sounds of the city were muted once he got inside, except for ambulances and garbage trucks. He could always hear those. The heater had no thermostat, and the radiator ran constantly and was only regulated by the building management.

Petrichor, what a word. Funny how that old dude knew so much about the creosote bush, and yet he couldn't remember how old Flash was. Buzz, his dog, Kaiser, and an old woman named Lucy. She taught me about loneliness, and Buzz taught me about petrichor. New Yorkers are giving me an education already. But what am I going to do about Ashley?

41

Rosie wiped off the tables as if they were her own, careful to leave them spotless. She had extra time because business was slow, and only a few regulars had showed up. The Ax Handle's new bouncer arrived early for his shift.

"Can I give you a hand, Rosie?"

"Thanks, Chad. I think the rush will be coming later when the happy hour specials kick in. I'm using the time to clean up and get organized so we'll be ready. Please go into the kitchen and ask them for the carpet sweeper. It would be helpful if you could touch up the carpeting under the tables while I wipe them off."

"No problem." He bounded into the kitchen and returned with the sweeper. The sight of the muscled twentysomething pushing the carpet sweeper put a smile on Rosie's face.

"Thanks, Chad. I appreciate the help."

"You're welcome. Are you working a double?"

"No. I'm working past my shift to help Ashley with happy hour, and then I'm going home. I got the sitter to stay late with my kids."

"Is something special going on in town?"

"There's a personal watercraft race this weekend. Joyce said when that happens, we usually get slammed around dinnertime. She's the owner, so she should know."

Chad worked fast, moving chairs away from the tables, sweeping up the crumbs, then moving them back. His diligence impressed Rosie, and he was easy on the eyes. With every backward stroke of the sweeper, his triceps flexed and stretched the short sleeves of his green polo shirt.

"Say, Rosie, is Ashley with anyone? A guy came in to see her the other night. Otherwise she seems to be single."

"I don't know, Chad. I know she dated Caleb, the guy who had your job. I haven't seen him in a while. They seem to be on a time-out."

"He's the guy who got in a fight with a customer and got canned, right?"

"Yep. There was more to it than that. The guy smashed a full pitcher of beer and some glasses and threatened Ashley."

"Joyce said the previous bouncer lost his temper and let his emotions get in the way of his judgment. She wanted to make sure I wouldn't lose it like he did. She also told me he's got PTSD from the service, right?"

"I don't know anything about that. I know the guy smashed a broken beer bottle on the crown of Caleb's head, sending him to the ER. His head may have been split wide open by that drunk, but he prevented everyone else from getting hurt. That's the important point."

"Yeah."

"I always liked Caleb. He was good to me, and when I was around him, he always handled himself professionally."

"I'd like to get to know Ashley better. Do you think she'd go out with me if I asked?"

"Why don't you ask her yourself?"

"What does she like to do—movies, dinner, sporting events, rock concerts?"

"Chad, I'm sorry I can't be much help on the details of her likes and dislikes. I'm not her agent." She shook her head. "The best thing for you to do is talk to her yourself."

"I will. It's just that we're always so busy in the evenings. I hate to bother Ashley when she's serving customers, and we all want to clean up and go home when the night is over. I think she likes me. She smiles whenever I come near her."

Rosie continued wiping tables.

He cleaned the last table and said triumphantly, "Finished. Piece of cake. Need anything else?"

"Nope. We're good. Thanks a lot."

Ashley walked in the front door, and with her came a ray of sunshine. She surveyed the empty dining room, and her gaze stopped at Rosie. "Where is everybody?"

"I don't know. I guess Chad and I drove them all away."

Ashley turned her head toward Chad, who beamed back at her. "Is that right, Chad?"

"No. It was empty when I got here. We were wondering why. That personal watercraft competition is this weekend. It doesn't make sense." He looked at Rosie with a smile.

Rosie shrugged. "You'll probably get slammed as soon as I leave."

"You're right. That's the way it always goes." Ashley ducked under the bar to put her purse away.

Joyce rushed in. "Good. You're here, Chad. Could you fill out some paperwork? You'll be eligible for medical coverage since you've been here a month, and I need to go over all the forms with you."

He followed her back to her office like a puppy dog trailing after his mother to the food dish.

"She probably just wanted to get him alone in her office so she could stare at him up close," Rosie said.

"Probably why she hired him. He's a good-looking guy. I'll say that for him. I don't think he'd drive anyone away. If anything, the dude's a babe magnet. You seem to be getting close to him yourself, Rosie."

"I wish. I'm afraid it's you he likes. He was asking a bunch of questions about you—if you're seeing anyone, what you like to do, that kind of stuff. I think he's going to ask you out."

"Really?"

"He wanted to know if you're still seeing Caleb."

"What did you tell him?"

"I said I didn't know and to ask you."

"Good." Ashley didn't feel pretty today, and hearing that a handsome guy showed interest in her made her feel a whole lot better.

"Are you?"

"What?"

"Still seeing Caleb?"

"No. We're done."

Rosie's shocked expression required more of an answer.

"It's complicated, Rosie, and it's a long story."

"It's just that you haven't said anything about breaking up with him."

"I don't like to spread my personal life around to coworkers. Relationships should be private. You're different. You're my close friend, and I trust you."

"You didn't say anything to me either."

"I know. I was going to. Just haven't had the time."

"You can count on me to keep a zipped lip."

"I know, Rosie."

"Chad also said Joyce told him Caleb had PTSD and lost his cool that night with Derek Snerd."

"What? Why would she say that?"

"So the new bouncer wouldn't make the same mistake, maybe?"

"Caleb doesn't have PTSD. He gets nightmares, but I've never seen him act like he's got PTSD. Remember, Snerd threatened to kill me that night, and Caleb came between me and a broken beer bottle."

"I know what happened…um, yeah. That's Joyce for you. Caleb probably would still be working here if Snerd hadn't threatened to sue."

"I know."

Once alone behind the bar, Ashley started typing a message to Caleb. After being interrupted to prepare a Manhattan, she came back to her phone and deleted the text.

42

Happy hour turned out to be as slow as the day shift. Ashley sent Rosie home to her kids when the rush didn't materialize, explaining to her coworker that she could handle the bar by herself with help from the two servers if necessary. Ashley noticed the bouncer texting. She didn't blame him. It was an unusually slow night, and texting helped him pass the time. She came out from behind the bar to his stand at the front door.

"Say, can I get you a soda or something to drink?"

He glanced up with a big smile. "Diet Pepsi. Thanks." He watched her walk back to the bar. She was wearing a pink blouse and tight red jeans, both of which fit her like a glove, and her long crimson hair fell like a waterfall to the middle of her back. He kept his eyes on her as she filled his glass and brought it to him. She pretended not to notice, but his attention made her heart smile.

"Thanks, Ashley. Much appreciated. I hope we get busy soon."

"I heard the Jet Ski association had a meeting that went long. We'll be slammed before you know it. Enjoy the quiet while you can."

"I don't know how you feel about socializing after hours with coworkers, but we should have coffee sometime. You seem interesting, and I'd like to get to know you better."

"Not that interesting, Chad. Trust me. Maybe we could do that sometime, but I'm taking nursing classes, and that keeps me pretty busy when I'm off work."

"I believe in the importance of continuing the learning process and trying new things. I'm helping out at my gym as a part-time trainer, and I'm taking online courses to be a certified fitness instructor."

"Gym rat, huh?" She smiled.

"Sort of. I think it's important to be healthy and fit."

"Undoubtedly."

"You seem really fit. Do you work out?"

She blushed. "Not really. I should do more to stay in shape."

"If you ever want help on a physical training program, let me know. I'll get you started."

"Thanks."

"As I said, you look fit already, but I could show you a few exercises that would help you maintain."

They looked at each other.

Joyce came out of her office and saw them talking. "Good. Just the two people I was hoping to find. The Ax Handle is sponsoring a team for the upcoming cancer walk along the lake. I'd like you both to be cochairs. Get a team of volunteers signed up who can solicit donations from friends supporting their participation—design a T-shirt for them. It should be fun and build team spirit besides raising money for cancer research."

Chad extended his arms, palms facing Ashley. "I guess we've been volunteered."

"Guess so," she said with a forced smile.

Joyce clapped her hands. "Good. I appreciate your help. I'll give a hundred dollars to the person who raises the most money for the cancer walk and another hundred for the best shirt design." She waved and sauntered back to her office.

Chad and Ashley eyed each other with sheepish grins. He spoke first. "I guess we'll have to get together now for coffee to plan our strategy. How about tomorrow at ten? I'll meet you at Hoochy's Bar and Grill."

"Well…"

"C'mon. It's for a good cause."

"Let's make it nine. I have some appointments. I can only meet for an hour."

"That's fine. Tomorrow at the diner at nine."

The door pushed open, and the rush was on. The bouncer directed everyone to form a line and started checking IDs. Ashley scooted to the bar and readied herself for the flood of customers that would be coming her way.

43

Hoochy's Bar and Grill served a signature breakfast special of three eggs, one pancake, juice, and coffee. The noisy diner, noted for good food at cheap prices, seemed to Chad like the perfect place for first dates. Its family atmosphere and sunny decor never failed to put women at ease. Chad prepared himself to wow Ashley.

Arriving a half hour early, he asked for a table in a quieter area of the dining room. His rock-hard biceps ruthlessly stretched the fibers of his shirtsleeves while his shorts strained to contain his quadriceps. As soon as Ashley entered, he caught her eye and waved her to their booth. He stood up as she sat.

Ashley spoke first. "Here we are."

"Yes. Here we are. Thank you for coming."

"No problem."

He pushed a handout he had prepared across the table. It announced the walk for cancer research along the lake and invited Ax employees and patrons to volunteer to walk and to get people to sponsor the walkers. The sheet also contained tips for soliciting donations and details about the shirt design contest.

Ashley studied it for a few minutes. "You really put a lot of thought into this already, Chad. You seem to have covered all the bases."

"Just a rough draft to get us started. Feel free to change anything you don't like or to suggest anything I should add or remove."

"It's a good start indeed. Let's ask Joyce for fifteen minutes at the next staff meeting. You can share the details of the walk, and I'll talk about the shirt design contest and the prize for getting the most donations. Tonight I'll go over this again and see if I can add any improvements."

When their food arrived, the conversation switched to personal subjects, and Ashley realized she liked Chad a lot. She saw him as good guy, a straight shooter, and it impressed her to see how politely and respectfully he treated the server.

"Have you lived here all your life, Chad?"

"Yes, for the most part. I spent a spring semester studying in France near Normandy and then hitchhiked around Europe the following summer."

"What were you studying?"

"Art. That was my major. I wanted to be an artist, painting in oils and watercolors, but I got sidetracked by that cruel reality of needing money to live. Jobs don't always help you to become the best van Gogh, and besides, my interests changed. Now I spend a lot of time at Bible studies."

"Really?"

"There's an inspirational fellowship here in Briggs Lake, and we get together several times a week. We're all seekers, trying to understand why we're here and what this life is all about. We come from all denominational backgrounds."

"I was raised Catholic and went to Catholic schools growing up."

"Do you have horror stories about the nuns?"

"No. My teachers were so sweet and set good examples by the way they lived their faith. Always strict but fair, they taught me to respect my parents and others. I still practice things I learned and even quote them sometimes."

"My parents didn't believe in God or religion, but I've always been curious about the meaning of life—why we're here, how to have a fulfilling life, that kind of stuff. I thought there must be more to life than working, getting married, having kids, and then dying."

"Life sounds kind of bleak when you see it that way."

He laughed. "I guess so. I think it's bleak without God. What do you think?"

She took a bite of her pancake and chewed slowly. "I'll tell you one thing. You were right to recommend the Hoochy's breakfast special. This pancake is incredible."

"What'd I tell you?" he said in a whisper.

"As to the meaning of life, I think it's about doing your best to be a good person, not hurt anyone, and always be ready to help those in need."

"If more people tried to be a good person, this would be a better world; that's for sure," Chad said. "How do you like the bar business?"

"It pays the bills. I like people, so it's fun to meet all the interesting folks out there. How about you?"

His eyes went to the ceiling. "I can't say that when I was in sixth grade and the teacher asked us to write a story about what we wanted to do in life, my essay was titled 'Why I Want to Be a Bouncer.'"

"Good one," she said with chuckle. "I know what you mean. We set goals, and then life happens."

"My career choice then was astronaut. You know how it is, Ashley. A person has all these dreams and goals—"

She finished his sentence: "And then life happens."

"Exactly."

"At one time I thought I would be a professional tennis player. Then I discovered boys."

"I'm so glad you did," Chad said. "Let me extend a heartfelt thanks on behalf of our gender."

She wrinkled her nose. "Now I'm studying to be a nurse, which reminds me—I've got to do some reading for a test. I've enjoyed this." She reached for her purse. "Let's split the tab."

"It's already been paid. My treat."

She smiled. "Thank you, sir."

"My pleasure."

As Chad led the way out of the restaurant, all the heads turned in their direction and stared as they marched toward the front door. Ashley felt the jealous eyes of every woman as if they were judging whether she was good enough to be with a man like that.

Eat your hearts out, skanks. I'm worthy, bitches. Believe me: I'm worthy.

44

After four days on the Upper West Side, Caleb acclimated to the rhythm of the city and the noises that punctuated each day. In the morning, the clanging of metal on metal and the roar of the heavy engines of garbage trucks as they accelerated down the street no longer startled him. Still, the blast of their hydraulic brakes when they screeched to a halt usually woke the veteran up if he happened to be asleep.

He decided to call Ashley this morning to say hi. He had thought about calling her every day since arriving in New York but chickened out each time, not wanting to take the chance of being rejected. Today he felt ready to handle the rejection if it came, his desire to hear her voice more powerful than his fear of her blowing him off.

After making eggs and toast, he sat on the couch to make the call. Before he could punch the number one on his speed dial, his phone rang.

"Hi, Caleb. This is Lily from the plane. Remember me?"

"How's it going, Lily?"

"So far, so good. I've made a lot of new contacts, and people have been very helpful. I haven't landed a job yet, but I think I'm doing okay with the auditions. I've had four so far, and more are on the schedule."

"That's good to hear."

"I'm calling to see if you'd like to get together for dinner or something. My Saturday is open, and I could use a break."

"Sure. I'd like that. I'm clear Saturday night—and Sunday, Monday, Tuesday, Wednesday, Thursday, and Friday too. Just sayin'."

"Good to know. I'll make a note of that. Do you know any good dinner places?"

"My buddy Anthony suggested I check out a dive bar that serves delicious food at fair prices. On Saturday nights they have an old blues piano player named Ivory Williams who used to play with Louis Armstrong."

"Satchmo?"

"Yes."

"Wow. She must be a hundred years old. What's the name of the place?"

"Al's Place."

"Al's Place? Really?"

He cracked up. "My buddy didn't say it had the most original name, only that the food was tasty. Why don't we meet there at eight p.m.? I'll text you the address. Ivory starts playing at nine. It should be fun."

"Do you remember me?"

"Sure. I'll just look for the most glamorous woman in the place."

"Yes, now I remember: you're quite the charmer. See you then."

Caleb tossed his phone down and shook his head. *I didn't think I'd ever hear from her again. She must be lonely to want to get together with the likes of me. I guess I better get a haircut tomorrow morning. First impressions are lasting impressions. No. I already gave her the first impression on the plane, so this is the second impression. I'm good.*

Flash sensed something was going on. The big golden retriever always wanted to be in the thick of things. He tail-wagged his way to the couch, then rested his head on the edge of the cushion where Caleb was reclining.

"Flash, I've got a hot date tomorrow night. Do you think you can watch the apartment while I'm gone?"

Flash licked his arm.

"I'll take that as a yes." He put his arm around the pooch. "Flash, you get me."

45

Caleb arrived at Al's Place ten minutes early after a terrifying cab ride through Midtown. It felt like being choppered into a hot LZ. *Relax, Caleb. You survived three tours in Afghanistan; you can live through a New York cab ride, even though it seems more dangerous.*

Waiting not so patiently for Lily at Al's front door, Caleb gasped when Lily stepped out of the cab. She glowed like she had just been announced as the winner of an Academy Award. Wearing a white sweater with intricate embroidery over a pair of formfitting black slacks gave her a look of sophistication and casual elegance.

He didn't know what to say at first, so he just said, "Hi, Lily. I'm glad we could get together."

"Me too. You're much taller than I remember."

"That's because I was sitting down."

She smiled. "Good point."

"You're even more attractive than I remembered."

"Thank you. I clean up pretty well."

"How are the auditions going?"

"Exhausting and discouraging, but I'm persistent and hopeful."

"If I was a director, I'd hire you."

"Thank you again. I'm soaking up these compliments. It's been a long week."

"Are you hungry?"

"Sure am. I hope you brought plenty of money."

"I have enough, Lily, and if I don't, I know how to wash dishes if push comes to shove."

"Oh, you do, do you? That piece of information will come in handy someday."

"I'm a highly qualified individual. I'm also a good dog walker."

"Good to know that too. Wow, you're a man with many skills."

"Yes. In New York dog walking is a profession, you know. It's a thing."

"I've noticed," she said with a grin. "Shall we have dinner?"

"Oh yes, dinner. I almost forgot. Come on in."

Entering the dining room, they approached the hostess stand. The hostess picked up a couple of menus and led them to their table. After they were seated, the busboy filled the water glasses, and the server came for their drink order.

"Good evening. My name is Michael. I'll be your server. What may I get you to drink?"

"Lily, would you like to share a bottle of wine?"

"Sure. Whatever you like is fine with me."

Caleb studied the wine list. He didn't know anything about wines. The name Silver Oak cabernet sounded impressive. It wasn't expensive, but it wasn't the cheapest wine on the menu either.

"We'll have a bottle of the Silver Oak cabernet."

"Very good, sir. Anything else?"

"I'd also like a bucket of ice to keep the wine cold," he said with an air of authority.

Michael eyed him for a few seconds before deciding not to correct him in front of his date. "Of course. I'll be sure to bring an ice bucket with the wine, sir."

After Michael left, they sat in silence for a few moments, adjusting their place settings and silverware. The aroma from trays filled with hot food floated in the air like a natural perfume.

Caleb took a sip of water. "I'm glad you called. New York has so many people, interesting people, and it's fun meeting them, but it's a refreshing change to be with someone I've already met."

"I know what you mean," she said as she brushed her blond hair away from her eyes. "Has living in the city given you any inspiration on what you'd like to do next in your life?"

"Not really. I can't see myself picking up dog poop forever."

"I'm with you on that."

Michael returned with the Silver Oak cab and displayed the label to Caleb before popping the cork and giving him a taste.

"It's good," he said. "Thanks."

With no trace of judgment, Michael poured the wine, placed the bottle in the ice bucket, and left.

"Let me propose a toast. To your gigantic success as an actress in New York." They touched glasses.

"Thanks, Caleb. To be honest, I also feel some uncertainty about my future. I hope something comes of this trip. If it doesn't work out, I guess I'll go home. If I don't catch on anywhere, at least I know I tried. In the end, that's all we can do: try and do our best. Right?"

"Right. I'm trying to live in the present, not the past. Sometimes a person has to start walking to find the right path. You don't find a way forward sitting down."

"That's for sure."

They talked about the noisy garbage trucks, the good food from street vendors, and the energy of the people in the city until Michael interrupted them to take their food orders. After he left, Caleb leaned toward Lily. "Did you notice that he didn't write anything down? He must have a superior memory. I've never seen that before."

"Neither have I. We'll see if he screws up our orders."

When Michael returned with their food, they saw that he remembered everything. He placed Lily's chef's salad in front of her with a flourish and then floated Caleb's T-bone under his nose before landing it gently on the table.

"I don't go out to eat that often, so when I do, I like getting steak."

"Oh, I understand. No need to apologize to me. I have to watch my weight for auditions."

"As you can tell from this," he said as he patted his stomach, "I don't plan on going to any auditions anytime soon."

She laughed as she picked up her fork and tossed her head to the side. "It looks like you have six-pack abs under that shirt to me. Bon appétit."

When Ivory Williams started playing, conversations stopped. The diners clapped enthusiastically after each song. She acknowledged their appreciation with a nod and a smile.

Pausing in the middle of her set, she glanced around the dining room. "I used to hang out with Louis Armstrong and his band when they came to town. Sometimes even cooked for them to give them a break from road food. Louis was a sweet man with a big heart. I visited him the day before he passed. His wife and I were good friends too.

"His nickname was Satchmo, but I always called him Pops. He had charisma, and could he ever light up an audience—that man was a cool cat. He faced discrimination coming up like the rest of us, but he never played the victim, never played the race card; he only played the trumpet, and that was good enough for him. A lot of Black folks criticized Louis for not being more vocal against discrimination and segregation. But you know what? He was the first Black musician to cross over to white audiences, and that paved the way for the rest of us. In my book, he did his part for our race.

"The song I'm going to play now won Louis a Grammy for vocal performance in 1964. It's a number called 'Hello, Dolly!' This is for you, Pops."

Everyone listened until she finished, and then the room exploded with applause and cheers from every table.

"Caleb, did you notice she sang that song with Louis Armstrong's voice? She didn't just impersonate him. She channeled him."

"I did. Ivory must be in her late nineties and still can play and sing. I've always loved smooth jazz and the blues." He took a sip of wine. "How did you like growing up in Parker?"

"I had a blast boating and swimming on the Parker Strip. I love the sun and water."

"So do I."

She added, "It gets hot in the summer, of course. We got used to it. Practically lived in the river growing up and spent a lot of time in our friends' pools too."

"We like to brag that Briggs Lake has more than three hundred days of sunshine a year. Do you ever remember coming to Briggs at night?"

"Not really. We probably visited friends once or twice, but nothing sticks out."

"The reason I ask is that except for a few main streets and the highway, we don't have streetlights."

"Why not?"

"The founder wanted people to be able to see the stars at night."

"How do you find your way around the city at night? Without streetlights you can't see the street signs."

"Good question." He laughed. "It gets tricky. You have to know where you're going from driving there in the daytime, I guess, or flash your bright lights at every corner to see the street signs. But now with the GPS on our smartphones, it's a lot easier than it used to be."

"Everyone must have gotten lost in the old days."

"You'd be surprised how we adapted. We somehow found our way. Another thing kind of unique about our city is that the neighborhood is laid out in cul-de-sacs, so you can't go around the block if you get lost. You have to go all the way back to the street you turned on."

"Why would they design the city like that?"

"The founder wanted everyone to have a good view of the lake."

"I never heard of such things—no streetlights and no city blocks—but it makes sense if you want people to see the stars and the lake."

"You should come sometime at night, and you'll see what I mean."

"Maybe I will. If you give me a tour."

"I'd love to."

"Deal."

"What does your boyfriend think about you spending this time in New York?"

"What makes you think I have a boyfriend?"

46

"I can't imagine that a woman as attractive as you would be single and not in a relationship."

"Strange as it may seem to you—and thanks for the compliment—I am single. I was in a long-term relationship with a guy from Parker who has a commercial real estate business. We were together almost five years, but I broke it off. He didn't support my acting career and didn't like the idea of me going to New York."

"You felt he was holding you back?"

"If two people really love each other, they should each want to help support their partner's dreams and goals, don't you think?"

"Yeah."

"I don't need a man just to have a man. My mom taught me not to ever settle—you know, lower my standards just to be with someone. What about you, Caleb? Do you have a girlfriend?"

"I did. She dumped me recently."

"Why?"

"She was ready to take our relationship to the next level and get more serious. I just got out of the service, and I don't really have a career yet. I don't even know what I want to do in life. I didn't feel ready to settle down and make a commitment that I wasn't sure I could keep."

"If you and this girl are in love, you can go on the journey together. She can help you discover what you want in life. You can explore life's options together."

"That's almost exactly what Ashley said."

"Ashley. That's a beautiful name. What's her last name?"

"Bivens. Her name is Ashley Bivens."

"I like her name. What's she like?"

"She's beautiful on the outside as well as on the inside. She's got auburn hair and green eyes, which seem blue to me because I'm color-blind. She's a bartender where I used to be a bouncer, but she's studying to be a nurse. I didn't notice her initially, but after we spent our first evening together, I haven't been able to get her off my mind."

"I can tell by the way you talk about her that you really love her."

"I do, but I have a hard time convincing her of that."

Lily passed on dessert, again citing the need to keep her weight down for auditions. Caleb wanted to make the most of the big night, so he scarfed down a Dutch chocolate cake. Neither really wanted to end the evening, but Lily felt she needed to keep a regular bedtime schedule.

"Caleb, I better get some rest. I really enjoyed being with you tonight. Thank you very much." She reached her hand across the table and patted his.

"You're welcome. I would like to do this again sometime before I go back to Briggs."

"So would I."

"Can I call you a cab?"

"Sure."

They left the restaurant, and he walked out to the street holding up his hand. A cab stopped five minutes later, and he opened the back door. She paused before getting in and hugged him. It was an embrace that lingered, and it was better than a kiss. They both felt something special, and he smelled her strawberry perfume for the first time.

"Thank you, Caleb." She gave him another quick hug.

"No. Thank you, Lily." He held the door until she got in and then closed it. The cab sped off.

47

The huge crowd on Saturday night filled the bar to capacity with people primed to party. The multitude swamped Ashley, keeping her too busy chasing lucrative tips to think about Caleb. During the cleanup, her thoughts turned again to her ex-boyfriend. She wondered where he was tonight—what he was doing and who he might be with. She missed him and felt a pang of jealousy.

Chad helped clear glasses and bottles from tables and noticed her sad expression. "Is everything okay, Ashley?"

"I'm fine. I guess I'm just tired. We were nonstop hustling most of the night, and now it's hitting me."

"You worked your tail off. I don't know how you keep all those drink orders straight. I couldn't do that."

His sincere compliment went down like candy. "Thank you for your kind comments. I really appreciate you saying that, Chad. With practice you could do the same thing. It's not rocket science."

"When someone's good at something, they make it look easy."

"That's an intriguing observation."

"Say, my friends are playing in a club nearby, and I promised to stop by for a while after work. Would you like to join me?"

"Sure. I can't stay too long, though. I'm beat."

"Me too. We'll just make an appearance and leave."

"Let's do it. Sounds fun."

Chad and Ashley arrived at the Upper Room in time for the band's last song before the final break. The club, filled with positive vibes, felt cozy and comfortable, a stark contrast to the chaotic atmosphere at the Ax. The audience showed their respect and appreciation for the band, who called themselves Armor of God.

During the break, the band members pulled up chairs to Chad and Ashley's table. "Hey, guys. This is my favorite coworker, Ashley Bivens. Not only is she a fantastic bartender, but also, as you can see for yourselves, she's beautiful."

Blushing, Ashley held her hand up. "Stop. You're giving me a big head." She noticed the deep respect these guys had for Chad, and she felt privileged to be the woman he brought to meet them.

Chad made individual introductions all around, starting with his roommate. "Artie and I have known each other forever, and now we're living together. He's one of my best friends."

"Chad and I used to go to school together," Artie said. "We were both in eighth-grade English."

"Was he a good student?" Ashley asked.

"Chad didn't know the meaning of fear," Artie said. "In fact, there were a lot of words he didn't know the meaning of."

Everyone laughed, especially Chad.

Artie was on a roll. "Chad could have been a Rhodes scholar except for his grades."

"Artie's taught me a lot," Chad said. "Like never again to room with a struggling musician if you want help with the rent."

Chad proceeded to introduce the rest of the band members, sharing a compliment or quick story about each.

"Are you all Christians?" Ashley didn't have to ask, but she wanted to hear how they would answer.

Chad spoke up. "We're all Christians. How could you tell?"

"You're so nice to each other, and I know it's not fake nice. It's genuine."

"It is," Chad said. "Thanks for the compliment."

She turned to Artie. "I love your band. You're all really good musicians."

"I hope you'll stick around for our last set," he replied.

"Chad and I are tired from work, but I think we can stay for your last set. Right, Chad?"

"Right."

After the show, Chad held her car door and waited until she was settled in and belted before closing it. She leaned back in her seat and took a deep breath. "This was fun. Thanks so much, Chad. I needed to get out and do something."

"It was fun for me too. Thanks for coming."

When they got to her car, which was parked at the Ax, she turned to him and patted him on the shoulder. "Thanks again. You're a good man. See you tomorrow."

He gave her a thumbs-up. "And you're a good woman, Ashley Bivens."

"Bye now." She jumped out, turned back, and waved before walking to her car.

48

A few days later, Chad and Ashley were contacted to attend a meeting of the coordinators for the walk for cancer research to plan the schedule and go over the rules. Joyce arranged their schedules so they could both have the night off, and Ashley drove them to the training.

Louis Strollo, chairman of the walk, who also happened to be the chief of police, conducted the training. His first wife lost her brave battle against cancer, and he had volunteered every year since to honor her. Wearing a crumpled gray suit and sporting a mustache that twitched every time he spoke, he went over all the rules and procedures, urging chairpersons to immediately begin recruiting walkers and then have the walkers get sponsors as soon as possible.

As the meeting broke up, Isabella Rodriguez, an old friend of Ashley's, approached and gave her a hug. "Hi, sweetie. Long time no see. What's new?"

"Good to see you, Isabella. I didn't know you were a part of this. Glad you're doing the walk too. Not much new with me. Still taking classes for my nursing degree and working. My life's pretty dull."

"How can it be dull with a hot boyfriend like him?" She snapped her head sideways toward Chad, who stood with a group of guys, laughing at a jokester they all knew.

"He's not my boyfriend. He's the bouncer at the Ax and my team cochair."

"Oh. Too bad. He appears to be the cure for all things boring."

"I will say this. He's a real gentleman."

"Then introduce me to him now. What are you waiting for?" She tossed her head in his direction, grinning from ear to ear. "Let's get this party started."

Ashley sidled over to the gaggle of guys and grabbed Chad's arm. "Chad, there's someone I want you to meet."

She took his hand and led him to Isabella. "This is my longtime friend, Isabella Rodriguez."

"Hello. I'm Chad Blake." He gave her the elevator eyes. He couldn't help it. Standing about five feet, five inches, she was a stunner. Her long black hair and dark eyes, bubbling with mischief, beckoned him. He made a conscious effort to slow his breathing, but he couldn't stop his heart from thumping against his chest.

"Aren't you a tall glass of water?"

"If I'm a tall glass of water, you're peach sherbet with whipped cream and a cherry on top. You look too sweet not to be anything else but a dessert."

Her face turned red. "What a gentleman. Ashley was right."

"You've been talking about me, huh?"

"I told her you're a gentleman. Women appreciate that."

When she observed the way Chad and Isabella were staring at each other, Ashley felt a tingle in her stomach. She regretted introducing them. *Isabella's a big flirt, and he's falling for it. She chews men up and spits them out. She's so fake, and he's so naive. He's being taken in by her games, and she's going to break his heart. I just know it.*

"I've got an idea," Chad said, rubbing his hands together. "There's a vintage diner that serves old-fashioned malted milks and cheeseburgers. My treat."

"Sounds good. Let's do it." Isabella clapped her hands.

Ashley bit her lower lip. *I was going to tell him I had to go home and study if he asked to do something after the meeting. Now I hate to leave him alone with that man-eater. Isabella's not his type. She's ruthless. She'll use him and hurt him and then dump him. I can't let that happen.*

"I'm in," Ashley said. "I love malts and cheeseburgers."

The burger joint smelled like fried onions and was decorated like a fifties diner. The waitresses looked like they had been working since 1955 and had names like Faye and Bernice, and their breath smelled like stale coffee and cigarettes. They called men 'hon' and women 'darling.' The greasy spoon's specialty was cheeseburgers, served hot and tasty with a plateful of french fries and a large bottle of Heinz ketchup. The waitresses served old-fashioned malts that they delivered to the tables along with the excess in the aluminum containers used to mix them. The malts chilled the throat and caused instant brain freeze.

Chad sat on one side of the booth, Ashley and Isabella on the other. Each booth had a mini jukebox directory so patrons could select three songs from the jukebox by inserting a quarter.

"This place is old-school, isn't it? Let's play some music. What do you girls want to hear?"

Isabella spoke up first. "Anything by Taylor Swift or Katy Perry? 'Dark Horse,' 'Roar,' or 'I Kissed a Girl?'"

Chad sat up straight. "'I Kissed a Girl?' Is that a song?"

"That's one of Katy's good tunes."

"That's strange. I'll check." He started flipping the menu pages. He shook his head. "No. Sorry. They only have oldies in their jukebox. Something else?"

"Elvis Presley?" Ashley asked.

"They've got Elvis. How about 'Love Me Tender,' 'Hound Dog,' and 'Peace in the Valley?' What do you think?"

"It works for me," Isabella said.

They listened to the crooning of Elvis while scoping out the food menus. They all decided on cheeseburgers, fries, and malts. Their food came out quickly, and they polished off their burgers and slurped down their malts like they hadn't eaten in days.

"Isabella, did you know that Elvis had eighteen number one hits, but the only Grammys he got were for gospel songs?"

"No, Chad, very interesting," she chirped. "You're really knowledgeable about music, aren't you?"

"Oh no. I just know a few things about Elvis."

"Chad, I'm interested in learning from you. Please share more."

Ashley rolled her eyes.

"He was nominated for many Grammys, and he won a Lifetime Achievement Grammy, but his only three Grammy wins were for his gospel albums *How Great Thou Art, He Touched Me,* and the live recording of *How Great Thou Art.*"

"Oh, Chad, those are amazing facts. Thanks so much for sharing. You're so smart."

Ashley glanced away and muttered under her breath, "Dear God."

Chad noticed. "Did you say something, Ashley?"

"Oh, nothing, Chad. I'm just singing along with the music."

Isabella put her hand on Chad's arm. "Go on, Chad. This is fascinating."

"I guess I'm an old throwback when it comes to music. To me, Elvis is still the king of rock and roll."

"No. You're not a throwback. I'm loving this. I've learned so many things from you tonight. You're such an inspiration. Go on. More, please."

"That's about all I can tell you about Elvis. I like a lot of gospel music too."

"I love gospel too," Isabella said. "I listen to it all the time."

Ashley couldn't keep quiet any longer. "Since when?"

"Since always, Ashley. I thought you knew." She pouted.

Chad stared at her. "Who's your favorite gospel performer?"

"Oh, I like so many. It's hard to pick just one. I'd say Amy Grant, but I'm also into all the new secular music. I could give you a real music education on the new artists, Chad." Her eyes suggested she'd like to do a lot more for him than that.

Chad recognized the look—it was one he'd seen many times before—and responded with a warm smile. "I'm sure you could, Isabella. I'm sure you could."

Ashley frowned. *This isn't going well. The dude is clueless, and she's playing him like a fiddle.* "Hey, you two, let's talk about the cancer walk. Isn't it exciting to do something for the community? I can't wait to start getting donations."

"I've already raised five hundred dollars from my friends who are sponsoring me," Isabella said as she flicked her hair back. "My aunt is a cancer survivor, and I'm walking in her honor. My whole family is behind me."

"That's amazing," Chad said. He caught the eye of his cochair. "You should know that Ashley and I are in it to win it. The Ax Handle crew is planning to raise the most donations of anyone. Right, Ashley?"

"Right." She managed to force a slight smile.

The server brought the check, and Isabella grabbed it before Chad could. "My treat. I'm making big bucks these days."

Ashley straightened up in her seat. "Doing what?"

"I'm repping for a pharmaceutical company. There's a lot of money in opioids."

"Isn't the government beginning to crack down on opioid abuse and doctors who overprescribe?"

"There are some bad actors in every profession, Ashley. The medications I represent are lifesavers for people in chronic pain."

"That's great that you're helping people who need it," Chad said.

Ashley started drumming the table with her fingers, and her jaw visibly tightened. Neither Isabella nor Chad noticed. They were too busy making eye contact. When her friend began telling a long story about their escapades in high school, Ashley could take it no more.

"This has been enjoyable, but it's getting kind of late. I better be heading home."

Isabella put her hand on Chad's arm. "I'm not tired at all. If you want to stay out longer, I could bring you home."

When Chad glanced at Ashley, she glared at him.

"No. Thanks anyway, Isabella. I'll go back with Ashley."

Her delight at his response morphed into exasperation when she spied them exchanging phone numbers. They drove to Chad's place in silence until they got near his apartment, when Ashley opened up the conversation. "What did you think of tonight?"

"The walk is really organized, and I think it will be fun."

"I think we'll have a great time and raise a lot of money in the process."

"Isabella is really something, isn't she?"

"What do you mean?"

"You know. She's really psyched about the walk and everything."

"Chad, I'd be careful with Isabella if I were you."

"What do you mean?"

"I've known her for a long time, and there's stuff about her that... well, she's not what she seems."

"Like what stuff?"

"Oh, just stuff. I don't want to bad-mouth her. We're friends. Not so much now, but in high school we hung out. I know she makes a good first impression, but just be careful with her."

"Thanks. Not sure what you mean, but I appreciate your concern."

"You're a good guy, and I don't want to see you hurt. That's all I'm saying."

"Ashley, I'm a big boy. I can take care of myself."

"Good. You do that."

"While we're on the subject of relationships, I've been meaning to ask you how serious you are with the ex-bouncer. I've heard conflicting stories. Some say you're hot and heavy. Others say not so much. Are you open to getting into a relationship with someone else?"

"I think you're a good guy and a gentleman. Can we just be friends and leave it at that?"

"Sure. Whatever. It's just that I'd like to get to know you better outside of work."

"Chad, we're doing that right now."

"I mean, what if I want to ask you out sometime?"

"What if you do?"

"Will you say yes?"

"It depends."

Ashley turned into Chad's apartment complex. When she stopped the car and put it in park, she noticed her hands were shaking. Taking a deep breath, she leaned over and hugged him. "See you tomorrow, cochair."

"Thanks for the ride, friend." He got out, and when he closed the door, it sounded like a sigh.

After returning to her apartment, Ashley went to the fridge for a beer and settled on her couch with her phone to check her messages, hoping to hear from Caleb. There was only one message: *I had a gr8 time wit u 2 nite. Thx 4 looking out 4 me wit Isabella. I'll be careful with her but she seems really sweet. Not as sweet as u. Chad*

She took a deep breath and closed her eyes.

49

The morning sun shined on the Upper West Side of Manhattan as the city's dwellers pursued their passions on an exceptionally gorgeous spring day. Caleb slept in late, finally stumbling into the kitchen midmorning to make himself a cup of coffee. After he swallowed the last of the brew, he glanced at Flash, who sat at his feet. "Hey, boy. Happy Saturday. Wanna go for a walk?"

Flash barked excitedly.

"I thought so. Let's go."

Caleb led Flash to an isolated area of the park so he could let him off the leash. They walked along a stream until it came to a tunnel under a bridge. As they entered the tunnel, Caleb spied three guys holding down a young girl whose legs kicked wildly as she screamed.

"Hey!" he shouted. "Get your hands off her."

They stopped and stared.

"Now!"

They let go of the young girl, who scrambled to her feet, straightened her torn blouse, and pulled up her shorts.

The three stepped menacingly in his direction while Flash retreated from under the tunnel to the grassy area above.

"Who the hell do you think you are?" the leader asked.

"None of your business. Leave her alone and get the hell out of here before I hurt you."

"You're going to hurt us?"

"If I have to."

"Bring it on."

The three guys spread out and slowly circled him, then they lunged at Caleb at the same time. The leader grabbed him from behind. Caleb spun around, delivering a spinning backfist that made a cracking sound when it broke his jaw. Ducking a roundhouse right from the second punk, Caleb drove his fist into the guy's gut, causing the thug to double over and fall to the ground, moaning. The third teen, the biggest one, lowered his head and charged Caleb, dragging him to the ground, then felt both eyes getting poked by Caleb's strong fingers.

They both jumped to their feet, but the young ruffian staggered, rubbing his eyes, unable to see anything clearly. Caleb grabbed him and choked him out. He fell to the ground, unconscious. Caleb noticed that the other two had fled.

Shaking his fist, still numb from the gut punch, he turned to the girl. "Are you okay, ma'am?"

"I'm fine. Thanks to you. In another minute or so—I hate to think. You got here just in time. I went for a walk in the park, and they grabbed me and dragged me here. They asked for money, and when I said I didn't have any, they started trying to take my clothes off."

"You should only go to the park with someone else."

"I know. Did you kill that man?"

"No. I just choked him out. He'll be fine. He'll have a couple of black eyes, and his vision will be blurry for a couple of days, but I didn't do anything permanent to him."

She managed a smile. "Your dog took off right away. He was no help at all, was he?"

"No. He's a golden retriever. They're lovers, not fighters. Come on, let's get you out of here. I'll walk you back to the street."

As they emerged from under the tunnel, they saw Flash lying on the ground chewing on a dandelion. He got up smiling, tail wagging, happy to see them.

The teenage girl, who had been composed up to this point, suddenly broke down, trembling and crying.

Caleb put his arm around her. "I know. What happened just hit you. You're safe with me. Come on. Let's get you home."

He leashed Flash, and they walked her to her apartment building. Before she went in, she stopped. "I don't even know your name."

"I'm Caleb. This is Flash."

"I'm Mindy."

"Hi, Mindy."

"Hi, Caleb. Hi, Flash. Thank you."

"No problem. Bye now."

50

Caleb and Flash trekked across the park to their bench next to the tennis courts. They could watch the matches and had a spectacular view of the hill and the pool, two famous landmarks of Central Park.

"It's fun to watch tennis, isn't it?"

Caleb swiveled around to see a man standing behind him who appeared to be fortysomething. He wore a two-button suit on his medium five-foot, ten-inch frame with a tieless dress shirt buttoned to the top. His black slicked-back and neatly combed hair framed the serious expression on his face, which featured a well-trimmed mustache and goatee.

"Yes."

"Pleased to meet you. I'm Eli Burns."

"I'm Caleb Sinclair."

"I saw you rescue that poor young girl under the bridge. Thank you for doing that. She was terrified."

"Thanks for saying that. My friend told me Central Park is a lot more dangerous than it used to be, but that's the first time I had a problem."

"The park is going through some dark times. I'm seeing more attacks all the time. I like the name Caleb. Do you know what it means in Hebrew?"

"No."

"Dog."

"Dog?"

"Yes."

"That's kind of insulting to be named dog."

"It doesn't mean you're a dog, Caleb. Think about the characteristics and traits of dogs."

"Let's see. They chew things up. They make messes. They spend a lot of time sleeping and licking themselves."

"They're good companions. They're faithful protectors. They're trusted friends."

"I see what you mean." Caleb scratched his neck, then reached down to stroke Flash's back. "You're all those things, buddy."

"Caleb can also mean 'like his heart,' from the Hebrew word *leb*, for heart, indicating that Caleb was a man who acted like his heart or followed his heart. It's a good thing to follow your heart—if your heart is in the right place, that is. Caleb was one of Moses's spies who checked out the promised land and agreed with Joshua that the children of Israel could conquer it."

Caleb leaned back on the bench and folded his arms. "Are you a Hebrew scholar or historian? You seem to know a lot about ancient history."

"No. I'm in the communications field. I'm a messenger. What about you?"

"I guess you could say I'm a messenger too. I work for an old guy who is dying and wants to make amends before he croaks."

Burns folded his arms and turned his gaze to the pool. "Did you know that the pool is man-made?"

"No. Really?"

"It was created by enlarging Montayne's Rivulet, one of New York's original streams. Most of the rest of the water you see in the park is actually fed from the city water lines."

"It's all city water? No kidding. I didn't know that. You know a lot of stuff, Mr. Eli Burns."

"What brings you to New York, Caleb?"

"I'm dog sitting for my friend Anthony while he's on a business trip. I'm actually from Briggs Lake, Arizona. Are you from New York, Eli?"

"Yes and no. I'm from a lot of different places. It depends on the job. I do a lot of traveling in my line of work."

"I do a lot of traveling in my work too, except my job is temporary. I don't know what I want to do when it's over. How did you choose your career?"

"Everyone's path in life is different. Embrace the path you find yourself on. Do your best in your current job, then when doors open, walk through them. When they close, look for another open door. There will always be an open door somewhere else—keep doing that in your life, and you will end up where you need to be."

"It sounds too simple. Is that all there is to success?"

"It depends on your definition of success."

"Work that I enjoy. An income that allows me to do the things I like to do. A loving family life, a wife and kids—you know, that kind of stuff."

"Those are good goals, Caleb. However, you're missing something very important."

"What's that?"

"Keep on seeking, and you'll receive the answer when you're ready."

Caleb took a deep breath. "Truth is, I am missing a lot of things. I would like to have a wife, but I'm afraid of choosing the wrong person and being miserable. So I've always been afraid to commit myself in relationships, trying to keep my options open in case a better person comes along. How will I know when I've found my soul mate?"

"You'll know. And when you do find your soul mate, don't waste a minute. Time is a precious commodity that can't be bought, sold, or stored. It must be used now because it's in a constant state of expiring. Time waits for no man or woman. It marches relentlessly forward. If there's something on your heart, do it without delay."

"Marriages are made in heaven."

"So are thunderstorms and tornados. Nature hates a void. Empty spaces will be filled. If you leave empty spaces in your relationships, others will fill those spaces."

"I see what you mean. You have a lot of wisdom for a young guy."

"I'm not that young."

"Whatever. I'll remember what you said."

"Later." Putting his hands in his pockets, Eli marched toward the pool.

After walking a few steps with the dog, Caleb turned to take a final look at Eli Burns. He had disappeared.

51

Caleb and Flash joined the busy sidewalk packed with people in a hurry to go to various destinations nearby.

"How old's your dog?" the chain-smoking man in the lawn chair asked.

"Ten."

"My dog's ten too."

"Cool."

Back at the apartment, Caleb checked his phone, which he had left on the charger by mistake. There was a voice mail.

After getting the pooch some water, Caleb sat in the chair by the front door and listened to the message asking him to call his buddy Anthony.

Punching Anthony's number, Caleb took a deep breath, waiting for his friend to answer.

"Hi, Caleb. How's it going there in New York?"

"We had an interesting morning. I saved a young girl from getting raped in the park by three punks."

"I hope you didn't kill them, bro."

"No. Just broke a jaw, gave a stomachache, and temporarily blinded a guy. Nothing serious."

"Good."

"And for the record, Flash was no help at all."

"Not surprised. Were you?"

"Nope."

"I'm calling to confirm that I'll be coming back on Thursday."

"Good. I'll give my boss a call and let him know I'll be available for another assignment. I've enjoyed it in New York. It gave me a lot of time to think."

"For you, that could be a dangerous thing."

"I know, bro."

"I'll text you my flight information so you can get the apartment cleaned up and all the women out of there before I get back. If you can stay through the weekend, I'll take you to Times Square to see the sights and take your picture with the Naked Cowboy."

"No thanks. If you had a naked cowgirl, that might work for me."

"Sorry. You're the flirt king, not me. You don't need my help finding women. They find you. Talk to you later."

Placing the phone on the end table, he watched Flash drinking water. The food bowl already empty, Flash busied himself with emptying the water bowl.

"Well, buddy. I'm going to have to say goodbye soon."

The dog trotted back to his sitter and licked his hand.

"You're welcome, Flash."

52

That night, Caleb decided to give Ashley a call to try to talk to her. After speaking to Eli, he realized he could lose her forever if he didn't make a decision soon. If she didn't hang up on him, he would insist that they have a conversation. He knew for sure he wanted to get back together with her and hoped it wasn't too late. Taking his shoes off, he put his feet on a stool and reached for his phone to call Ashley. Before he could hit number one on his speed dial, the phone rang.

"Hi, Caleb. How are you?"

"Lily? I'm fine. How about you?"

"Not so good. I'm sorry to bother you, but I can't get ahold of my friends, and I need help."

"What's going on?"

"I took a cab to Manhattan to scout a location where I'll be auditioning. A random woman walked up and punched me. I fell down and hit my head, and she grabbed my purse, which has all my credit cards, driver's license, cash, and the key to the apartment where I'm staying."

"That's terrible. I'm so sorry."

"Luckily, I had my phone in my jeans, so I called the police. But none of the people I know are picking up, and my battery is getting low."

"Where are you?"

"I'm in a Duane Reade, a twenty-four-hour drugstore." She gave him the address.

"I'll text an Uber and be there as soon as I can. Don't worry. I'll take care of you."

"Thanks. You're so sweet."

When he put his phone down and grabbed his jacket, Flash ran up to him with eyes full of expectation.

"Sorry, buddy. You can't come along on this mission. I need you to guard the apartment. I'll be back soon."

When the car arrived at the drugstore, Caleb told the driver to wait until he returned. Near the front door by the cash register stood the shaken victim of the purse snatching. Lily ran up to Caleb, threw her arms around him, and started crying.

"It's okay." He held her for a few minutes until she could compose herself.

"I can't tell you how glad I am to see you. Thank you so much for coming, Caleb. I'm so scared."

"No problem. Why don't we come back to my apartment? It's not far. You can wait there until you can get ahold of your friends. Without the key to your apartment, you'll be locked out anyway."

She hesitated for a second. The more she thought about it, the more it sounded like a good idea. "Okay. You're probably right."

Once inside the Uber, her strawberry perfume filled the car with its sweet fragrance. Caleb patted her on the knee. "Everything will be fine, Lily. How's your head?"

She lifted up her blond locks to reveal a bump on her forehead.

"That's not so bad. We'll put some ice on it at the apartment. You're still gorgeous. No worries." He held her hand.

She smiled and rested her head on his shoulder.

"What did the cops say?"

"A female cop came and filled out an incident report, but she didn't sound very positive about recovering the purse or finding the woman who robbed me. She offered to call an ambulance, but I declined."

"I'm really sorry. That's an awful thing to happen. When we get back to my apartment, I'll fix you something to eat and you can rest up. The golden retriever will be glad to have someone there besides me."

Flash greeted them with an excited bark and wagged his tail, licking Caleb's hand before scurrying to Lily and nudging her leg with his snout.

"He wants you to pet him."

"Oh. Of course." She reached down and patted him on the back. "Good boy, Flash." He turned and started licking her hand.

Caleb sauntered to the kitchen to heat up chicken soup and make sandwiches. "Just relax, Lily. I'll get you some ice for your forehead."

She called her friend Jenny and left an updated message that she was having dinner with a friend and that she was unhurt.

He returned to the living room with a plastic bag filled with ice. "Soup's on. We've got some red wine. Would you care for a glass?"

"I'd love that. Thanks, Caleb."

She called her credit card companies and reported the theft. She got a new Visa account number that she could use until her new cards came in the mail.

With some difficulty, he popped the cork off the bottle and poured them both some wine. He raised his glass. "Here's to the future Broadway actress, Lily Lofton. Now you'll have a story to tell when you're famous."

"Right."

They touched glasses.

"I better check the soup."

He dashed into the kitchen, poured the soup into a couple of bowls, brought them out, and placed them on the coffee table. Returning to the kitchen to retrieve grilled cheese sandwiches, he also set that tray on the coffee table. She stayed on the couch, sitting next to the pooch, and he pulled up a chair.

Taking a big bite of the sandwich, she said, "What great service. This is delicious. I feel so much better already, Caleb. I haven't eaten all day since a yogurt for breakfast. Thank you sooooo much."

"Glad you like it. You know, it's getting late. If you'd like to spend the night, I can set you up in the bedroom with some clean sheets. I can sleep on the couch with Flash. It's not a big deal."

"Thanks for the offer. I don't want to impose."

"It wouldn't be an imposition. This couch is comfortable if I can just keep Flash from hogging it." He saw Flash sitting on the sofa with his new best friend.

The wine warmed her on the inside, and she studied this man—clean-cut, strong, and so protective. His blue eyes pierced right through her.

"More wine?"

"Sure." She held up her glass while he filled it.

"I had an incident myself today. Flash and I were walking in Central Park and came upon three jerks assaulting a young girl."

"What happened?"

"What do you think happened?" he said, chuckling. "I kicked their asses and gave them a few souvenirs to remember me by."

Lily burst out laughing. "You are such a cool guy. I absolutely can see you doing that. You are such a badass."

"Aside from this adventure, how's everything else going with you?"

Before she could answer, her phone started playing music. She jumped up and answered it before returning to the couch. "Jenny. Good to hear from you. Something terrible has happened. As I said in the last message, I was robbed and my purse was stolen…yes. Just a bump on the head…but the key to your apartment and all my credit cards were in the purse…I'm with a friend who lives on the Upper West Side. He's invited me for dinner…no, that's all right."

Caleb studied this woman on the couch and envied Flash sitting next to her. Despite all she had been through, she still had that spark that had attracted him when they first met on the plane. Their eyes met while she was listening to Jenny, and they smiled at each other.

"He's invited me to spend the night, so I think I'll just stay here, and we can reconnect in the morning."

Caleb's smile widened.

"Thanks, Jenny. I'll call you in the morning."

Caleb set his wineglass on the coffee table. "I guess I better get to changing those sheets on the bed."

"Thanks so much for the offer, Caleb. Jenny spent the day with her boyfriend and left her phone at the apartment. She felt terrible."

"I'll get the bedroom fixed up for you and set out a bathrobe, toiletries, and some clean towels. You can take a shower if you want. There's good water pressure. My buddy's got soaps, shampoos, and creams from every hotel from Los Angeles to Istanbul. He travels a lot."

"What does he do?"

"He visits businesses his company wants to buy and kicks the tires, drills down, does due diligence, and recommends whether to buy them or not."

"Your friend must be intelligent."

"He's very smart, but his heart is even bigger than his brain. You ought to meet him sometime. He's good-looking, in an Italian sort of way. You'd love him."

"You have a big heart yourself, Caleb."

"Not really. Just trying to treat people the way I would like to be treated."

"It's not always easy."

"Tell me about it." They smiled at each other, still making eye contact.

53

By the time Lily stepped out of the shower, Caleb had changed the sheets and organized the bedroom, setting out a couple of small bottles of body lotion. She found the oversize white cotton bathrobe in the bathroom, slipped into it, and joined him in the bedroom.

"Thanks for everything, Caleb. That shower was just what I needed."

"Good. I've laid out one of my T-shirts and a pair of sweatpants on the bed. They'll be a bit big, but they're clean."

"Thanks a lot."

"Can I get you anything else?"

"No. I'm good. I think what I need now is a good night's sleep."

"Sounds good to me too."

She waved and smiled. "Thanks again for everything. Good night."

"See you tomorrow. C'mon, Flash, let's hit the rack." They returned to the living room and settled down on the couch. He listened for the bedroom door to close but didn't hear anything but the ceiling fan.

She must have left the bedroom door open. Why? Does she want me to come back? Is that an invitation?

He waited longer and heard her walking around in the room. Then he heard her slowly close the door. He listened carefully to hear if she locked it. She didn't. She left the door unlocked. He would have heard that sound. Did she forget? Was it an invitation, or did she simply trust him?

She said what she needed was a good night's sleep. Did she mean that, or did she mean something else?

He got up and slowly tiptoed to her room. The door was closed, yes, but it was unlocked. He was sure of that. He stood by the door trying to decide what to do next. *Should I knock, or should I just walk in and make love to her?*

Lying on her back with her hands behind her head, Lily heard purposeful footsteps coming toward her. She listened as he stopped outside the bedroom door. Her breasts heaved with each deep inhale, yet she felt out of breath, like she wasn't getting enough oxygen. Unhooking the diamond necklace around her neck, she set it on the nightstand. Untying the drawstrings on the sweatpants, she pulled the bed covers back, let her arms fall to her sides, and waited.

On the other side of the door, Caleb stood like a statue for a full minute, then shook his head. *I can't do this.*

He quietly stepped back to the living room and slid under the covers. Flash was gently snoring. Caleb soon fell into a deep sleep.

Caleb's buddy Nick is shot and crumples to the ground a few feet away. Ducking under a blizzard of steel projectiles, Caleb presses a bandage against Nick's stomach to staunch the blood. When the UH-60 Black Hawk finally lands, the helicopter is greeted by a hail of bullets. Caleb cradles Nick like a baby in his arms and charges through the gunfire toward the chopper. Crew Chief Big Jim Robinson hoists Nick inside at the door, and Caleb jumps in behind, nearly falling out as the chopper lifts upward with a roar. Rocket-propelled grenades detonate around the rising copter, engulfing it with smoke and the smell of sulfur and ammonia. The explosions launch shrapnel into Caleb's right leg. He's so focused on encouraging Nick that he doesn't feel the steel shards lodged in his calf. When they land at the field hospital, Nick is dead.

Caleb screamed. Lily and Flash came running out of the bedroom. "What's wrong, Caleb?" She shook him awake. "Are you okay?"

"I'm fine. I just had that nightmare I had on the plane. Did Flash sneak into the bedroom with you?"

"He scratched on the door, so I let him in with me. He was whimpering."

Caleb patted the pooch on the head. "You big baby. What a whiner you are. He'll do anything for attention, especially from a beautiful woman." He turned back to Lily. "Since we're all up, can I make you some hot chocolate?"

"Sure."

They sat on the couch, Flash at their feet, sipping their drinks. Gifted at impersonations, Lily imitated directors and other actors during the auditions to share stories about the humorous things she'd seen. Caleb laughed until his sides hurt.

After two hours, things got serious, and he finally felt comfortable enough to talk about the dream. Opening up about Nick, he explained how much their friendship meant to him and how much he missed him. He started weeping. She grabbed him in a big hug and held him.

"You did all you could do to save him. Stop blaming yourself."

He didn't say anything. She held him until his breathing got steady, and then he fell asleep. She pulled the covers over the young war veteran before sneaking back into the bedroom with the dog. In the morning she got up early and, using her newly minted credit card account number, called an Uber. By the time Caleb woke, she was in the apartment with Jenny.

54

After sleeping in, Caleb showered and got ready to take Flash for his morning walk in Central Park when Stockbridge called.

"How's everything in New York, Caleb?"

"Can't complain. I was going to call you today. My friend is coming home for the weekend, so I'll be ready for another assignment."

"Good. That's why I'm calling. Since you're already on the east coast, you can pick this one up before you come back to Arizona. When are you free to leave?"

"Anthony comes back Thursday night, so Friday morning, I suppose."

"Good. I want you to fly to Richmond, Virginia. Rent a car and get a hotel in Chesterfield County. There's a professor at John Tyler Community College named Dr. Hua-Chang Huang, who is one of the world's foremost Aramaic scholars."

"How do I get ahold of her?"

"I'll send you a text with her office contact information. I don't have her personal phone number. The best place to find her might be to just go to the school. She's leaving for the Middle East on Monday or Tuesday, so it's very important that you meet with her this weekend."

"Roger that."

"I may have another one for you in that part of the country, but let's get this one done first. Any questions?"

"No, sir."

"Keep me posted."

As planned, Anthony returned on Thursday night. They ordered pizza and hung out at the apartment. Caleb explained that he had to leave Friday morning for Virginia, so they decided to make an early night of it.

"How was the trip, bro?"

"Good. The business I checked out was a rural cable company. Their spreadsheets can get complicated to sort out between monthly revenues and expenses. You have to examine free cash flow per subscriber and not just the overall debt. Cable is a capital-intensive business, but once the lines are in, the recurring cash flow is amazing—it continues coming in month after month like a goose that keeps laying golden eggs. It was a good business, and I'm going to recommend it." He lifted his bottle of Stella Artois toward Caleb. "What about you? How'd things go with Flash?"

"We had a good time. He's a constant companion and seems to understand everything I say. I wish I could take him home with me. I have a better relationship with him than I do with my girlfriend—excuse me, I keep forgetting, my ex-girlfriend."

"I appreciate you coming out here to give me a hand. I hope you can patch things up with Ashley. She sounds cool."

"Probably not. It's pretty much over. Nothing's changed. She still won't even talk to me. Traveling for this job doesn't help either."

"Welcome to my world. Now you know why I'm still single. With an unpredictable schedule and extensive traveling, I don't have much time for relationships."

"That, and women find you repulsive."

Anthony threw a pillow at Caleb. "Watch it, man. I'm a trained killer."

"So am I."

"Oh. That's right. I forgot." Anthony took a swig of beer. "Remember the old saying that absence makes the heart grow fonder. Being separated may cause her to appreciate you more."

"Absence makes the heart grow fonder, all right…for somebody else."

"You're a pessimist."

"Nature hates a void. Empty spaces will be filled by something."

"Speaking of voids, my bottle's empty. I hate it when that happens. Want another?"

"Sure."

Anthony walked into the kitchen to get a couple more beers while Caleb petted Flash on the couch. "You're a good boy. I'm going to miss you."

Flash slobbered over Caleb's hand as if he understood every word.

Anthony handed Caleb another beer.

"Thanks, man. Say, I dated one woman while I was here. I met her on the flight to New York, and she's an aspiring actor. I took her to dinner at Al's Place, that restaurant you suggested. You were right—Ivory Williams put on a spellbinding show."

"I told you. Almost a hundred and she's still got it."

"Lily is the name of the woman I took out. She got mugged, and her apartment keys and credit cards were stolen, so she called me. I picked her up, made her dinner, and let her sleep in your bed."

"Did anything happen?"

"What do you mean?"

"Did you sleep with her?"

"No. I thought about it, but it didn't feel right."

"You're slipping."

"Either that or maybe I'm just growing up. Lily was vulnerable after the mugging, and I didn't want to take advantage of the situation."

"Do you think Lily wanted something to happen that night with you two?"

"I do. Maybe I'm reading too much into it, but I showed her how to lock the door from the inside, and she didn't lock it. I took that as an invitation that she wouldn't mind if I tucked her in."

"Someday you may regret that you didn't make a move."

"I already do!"

They laughed.

The friends turned in for the night, Anthony to his bedroom and Caleb to the couch he shared with Flash.

55

Caleb flew to Richmond Friday morning and contacted John Tyler Community College for Professor Huang. He was told she was out of the office until Saturday, so he left a voice mail on her business line. After checking into his hotel, he took a shower until he heard his phone. Jumping out dripping wet, he saw that Lily was calling.

"Hi, Lily. How are you?"

"I'm well. Sorry I didn't answer your message earlier. I wanted to thank you again for putting me up that night. I really needed a friend, and you were there for me. I'll never forget that."

"No problem. I was kind of shocked that you left so early before I woke up. But I did see your note with the explanation."

"I felt it was better to let you sleep in. You had a hard night and needed to rest."

"You could have woken me up, though. Then I could have said goodbye. Being with you that night was one of my best nights in New York. The only night better was when we went to Al's Place and listened to Ivory Williams."

"I feel the same way. Except for the mugging part."

"Yes, of course, except for the mugging part."

"The other reason I called is that I think I left a diamond necklace in the apartment. It's the most expensive piece of jewelry I own, and it was given to me by my grandmother, so it has sentimental value. Have you seen it?"

"No. I would have called you. When I made the bed and cleaned up the apartment, there was nothing there like a diamond necklace.

I'll give you my buddy's phone number so you can call him and ask if he's seen it. His name is Anthony."

"Where are you? I thought you were still in New York at the apartment."

"I'm in Chesterfield County, Virginia, just south of the James River near Richmond."

"Back to work already?"

"Yeah."

"If I had known you would be leaving New York, I definitely would have woken you."

"I didn't know it myself at the time." He gave her Anthony's phone number and asked her to repeat it to make sure she got it right.

"Thanks. I'll give Anthony a call."

"If it's in there, he'll find it. You'll like him. He's a good man."

"If he's anything like you, I'm sure he is. Will you be coming back to New York?"

"I'm not sure, Lily. It depends on my work, I guess."

"Call me if you do, please. I've got a small part in a Broadway show with only a couple of lines, but it's a start."

"Congratulations. Now you're a working actor."

"Yes. At least for six weeks. How's the bad dream?"

"Haven't had it since that night."

"Good. I hope we see each other again someday, Caleb. Remember, you promised me a tour of Briggs Lake."

"I remember, and I will. I'm a man of my word."

"I know you are. I wish I could give you a hug."

"I could use one."

"Then I'll give you a virtual hug and a kiss on the check. How's that?"

"Oh, that felt wonderful. Thank you, Lily. Good luck with the career."

"Take care."

"You too."

"Bye."

"Bye. Will you please hang up first?"

"Sure. Talk soon, Caleb."

He placed his phone down and stared out the window at the parking lot, remembering Lily's eyes and the smell of her strawberry perfume.

56

On Saturday morning, he called the office phone number for Dr. Hua-Chang Huang and got voice mail again. After leaving a message, he decided to go to her office at John Tyler Community College. A security guard stopped Caleb at the front door.

"May I help you?"

"Yes. I'm here to see Professor Huang."

"Do you have an appointment?"

"No, I don't, but it's important. I understand she's leaving for the Middle East on Monday or Tuesday."

"Let me call her and see if she's available." He picked up the phone. "There's a man here to see you." He put his hand over the receiver. "What's your name?"

"Caleb Sinclair."

The guard relayed his identity to the professor, then hung up the phone. "Come on. Follow me. I'll take you to her office."

The newly waxed floors reflected the heavyset shape of the guard like a mirror. His image, interrupted by flashes of light when they passed windows, stopped at an open door. The guard pointed at the doorway. "Right in there, sir."

"Thank you."

Caleb walked in and saw the professor hunched over her computer. Her coal-black hair was pulled back by a red ribbon and extended midway down her back. When she saw him, her thin red lips parted into a wide smile, showing perfect teeth. Taking off her glasses, she stood and extended her hand. "I've been expecting you. Nice to meet you, Caleb."

"Pleased to meet you, Dr. Huang."

"Please call me Chewy. My husband gave me that nickname, and it stuck. It's much easier to say than the name my Chinese parents gave me."

"I've left a couple of messages on your work phone because you never picked up."

"Sorry about that. I turn my work phone off when I'm busy so I don't get interrupted. I'm leaving in a couple of days, and I have a lot to do. But I've been expecting you ever since I received a call from a man who said he'd send a representative named Caleb Sinclair who would help me with anything I needed. At first I thought it was a prank call."

"Oh. That would be my boss who you spoke with."

"Just who is your boss, and why didn't he identify himself?"

"He prefers to remain anonymous, but he's rich, and he likes to help other people out with things. He has his reasons for keeping his identity private."

"Why does he want to help me?"

"I don't know. He didn't say."

"What I need you can't help me with, Mr. Sinclair."

"Try me."

"I need a security detail of about a dozen contractors with combat experience in the Middle East. They must meet me in Iraq and travel with our archeological team to Syria for a week or possibly more."

"We might be able to make that happen."

"I'm an Aramaic scholar and have discovered a series of ancient monasteries in those countries that have stored and hidden some of the oldest Aramaic and Hebrew scrolls in existence. I'm scanning them—digitizing them as fast as I can to preserve them for other scholars and for posterity. Warring tribes of Islamic fundamentalists are destroying ancient biblical manuscripts whenever they come across them. It's a race against time."

"I never thought about that. By scanning them to a computer and digitizing them, they will be preserved even if the originals are destroyed."

"Exactly. I translate ancient Hebrew, Syriac, and Aramaic languages and am creating an online library so other scholars can research these ancient texts and compare them with newer manuscripts to create more accurate translations of the Bible. Generally speaking, though not always, the older scrolls tend to be more accurate because they are closer to the time period in which they were written."

"With all the fighting going on with various Muslim groups, I can see why it would be risky for you and your staff."

"For sure. That's why I need a security team. They think they're doing their God a favor by killing people like me."

"When are you leaving?"

"Tuesday morning. Flying to Baghdad first."

"I'll talk to my boss. I'm sure he'll try to help you if he can. I'll give you my number. Since you don't always pick up your business line, would you mind giving me your phone number?"

"Sure. Give me your private number, and I'll call you and leave a message. Then you'll have mine."

When he handed her the slip of paper with his phone number, hotel, and room number, she grinned. "That's a good hotel."

57

Back in his room, Caleb called Stockbridge. "This request is probably the toughest one yet. The professor needs a security team for a week or longer to protect her and her staff. They would meet in Iraq and travel to Syria."

"What are they doing there?"

"They're scanning ancient biblical scrolls before they get lost or destroyed by Muslim extremists. Scholars study them and compare them with other manuscripts to get a more accurate translation of the Bible."

"I'll see what I can do. What is the time frame we're dealing with?"

"She flies to Baghdad from Richmond on Tuesday morning, so I imagine that she would want to know as soon as possible but no later than Monday night."

"Sit tight for a day or two. I'll call you when I get a security team together."

"Sounds good. I'll find something to keep me busy."

"Good. Bye now."

"Later."

Caleb laid his head on the pillow and drifted off to sleep. His phone rang. "Hello, this is Caleb."

"Caleb, this is Chewy. I've just finished my work, and since you're stuck in a hotel, I thought you might like to join me for dinner and a taste of Southern hospitality."

"That sounds good. I haven't eaten anything all day. Where do I meet you?"

"There's a cute restaurant in the Shockoe Slip, the old tobacco warehouse section of Richmond. It's called the Tobacco Pub. Meet me there at six."

"I'll be there. Thanks. You've saved me from a long night of watching bad television."

This comment inspired a laugh from the professor. "Is there any other kind of television?"

"It depends if you're a sports fan. I'll see you at six."

While Caleb spent Saturday in Virginia, Ashley's cancer walk got underway in Arizona.

The walk started on time early in the morning, and the teams enjoyed the fresh desert air and cool breeze as they trudged along in groups with their teams, children, and dogs. Each team wore colorful T-shirts, some featuring pictures of loved ones who had lost their battle with cancer.

Ashley and Chad led the Ax Handle team in the middle of the pack, carrying on an animated conversation, occasionally separating to encourage other walkers. She couldn't help but notice his muscular frame and his upper-body strength. *This dude must spend a lot of time in the gym.*

"Did you ever lose anyone to cancer, Chad?"

"My mother got breast cancer, but she beat it and is still kicking. Did chemo and radiation, the whole nine yards. Prayed a lot too, and God healed her with all of the above."

"That's a success story that should be shared to encourage others."

"Yes, and I tell it every chance I get. A cancer diagnosis used to be a death sentence, but not anymore. Every day there are more successful therapeutics that are less invasive."

The Ax Handle cancer walk team didn't win any awards for shirt design or total donations, but that didn't matter to Joyce Benson. Pleased with the effort put forth by her crew, she wanted to reward them. She invited all the employees to the bar for a couple of free drinks and a catered chicken dinner. The boss even hired a cover band to play dance music and allowed employees to bring a guest.

Before the dinner started, Joyce grabbed the band's mic to thank everyone for their involvement. "We're a community-based business, and I believe it's important to support local nonprofit organizations. I'm so proud of you all. Thanks."

Everyone clapped.

As an afterthought she returned to the mic and said, "Let's have a toast to our cochairs, Chad and Ashley!"

All raised their glasses to Chad and Ashley, who eyed each other with embarrassed looks at the special attention.

"Now let's eat," Joyce said.

Chad sat at a table with his buddy Artie while Ashley, who didn't have anyone special to be with, volunteered to be the bartender for the night. She wanted to make sure everyone had a good time, so she really turned on the charm. Chad's eyes followed Ashley everywhere she went. She couldn't help but notice his interest, and she had to admit that it made her feel good on the inside.

Artie noticed his friend's fixation on the auburn-haired bartender. "You've got feelings for her, don't you?"

"What do you mean by that? We're just coworkers."

"You can't take your eyes off her. That's what I mean. I feel like your body is sitting with me, but your mind is following that girl around the place."

"I'm sorry, Artie. I didn't mean to check out on you. I believe she's got a boyfriend—the guy who had my job before I did. Ashley doesn't like to talk about him. I'm just trying to be a good friend to her with no ulterior motives. I will confess, though, that I'm attracted to her. How could I not be? She's friendly, compassionate, and as cute as can be."

"I'm friendly and compassionate, but I'm not so sure about the cute part. Since I became a Christian, my love life kind of dried up, so show some sympathy."

"Are you blaming God because you can't get a date?"

"No. Just saying my love life dried up."

"You mean your lust life dried up," Chad said as the corners of his mouth turned up.

"Whatever you want to call it. You're not being very helpful, you know, smart guy."

"Did you ever think that the love of your life may be sitting in this bar tonight?"

"No. That hadn't occurred to me, Chad. This doesn't seem like a good place to pick up the mother of your children, if you know what I mean."

"Keep the faith and stop whining. This could be your day."

"Either that or my day could end by you driving me to my parents' house for the night so you can be alone with Ashley."

Chad laughed. "I wish. I'm not making much headway with Ashley. I'll introduce you around to some of my coworkers and will do my best to help you get connected, but keep in mind, I'm not a miracle worker."

"It shouldn't take a miracle if it's the right one, don't you think?"

"Yep."

58

The Tobacco Pub had been an old tobacco warehouse, and the walls were made of bricks from the 1800s and smelled like tobacco. The cozy booths were lit by a single candle, and the glossy finish on the wooden tables accentuated the wood grain and the reflection of the dim ceiling lights. The waitresses wore ankle-length dresses from the Civil War era and had Southern accents to match.

Caleb arrived fifteen minutes early and waited near the front door. Chewy walked in and, after checking the place out, greeted him with a big smile. "There you are."

"Here I am." He smiled back.

Turning to the hostess, she said, "We have a reservation for two under Chewy."

As they followed the hostess to their booth, Caleb noticed her long, shiny black hair on the back of her red blouse. After ordering, she gave the young man a history lesson on the restaurant and pointed out some of the antiques that added to the atmosphere.

"I really appreciate the way you've been open to meeting me and letting me see if I can help you with your project...you know, being a stranger and all."

"Normally I would have been suspicious of an anonymous caller announcing the visit of a stranger to 'help me' with anything I need," she said. "But I had just been praying for an answer to the security problem with my work in Syria when your boss called me. I think it was an answer to my prayer."

"I'm glad we can be of assistance. If there's a way to pull it off, my boss will find it. He's on the level too."

"I do have to ask: why is your boss helping me? What's in it for him?"

"Good question. He wants to remain anonymous, but I can tell you that there is no selfishness in his motives. I've been working with him for a while now, and this is just something he wants to do. He wants to help people. He wants to make a difference. He asks for nothing in return."

"How does he know about me?"

"I don't know. He seems to have a history of some kind with everyone we've helped."

"What about you? What's in it for you?"

"It's a job, and I need one. I spent years fighting in those Middle East wars, and I needed to find a way to support myself. This job is temporary, but I hope it lasts until I find something permanent."

She stared at him.

"What?"

"Sorry. You remind me of my husband—a younger version of my husband, but you look like him."

"Thank you. I'm sure that's a compliment. Does he teach too?"

Her eyes teared up, and she gazed at the table. "He passed away a couple of years ago. We were working in Syria, actually, searching for ancient scrolls in separate locations. His was more dangerous than the place I worked. He was kidnapped, tortured, and then killed when they couldn't get a ransom."

"I'm sorry. Why would you ever want to go back there?"

"To finish the work we started together. We shared a love for the Aramaic language and similar dialects, which is how we met. Then we felt called to preserve the manuscripts. We believe Jesus spoke Hebrew but also Aramaic."

"I didn't know that. Very cool. So you and your husband learned Jesus's language?"

"Yes. I guess you could say that. When scholars compare the oldest texts with each other, they can interpret the original meaning more accurately. Ever heard of the expression 'lost in translation?'"

"Yes."

"If something is translated improperly, even one wrong word can change the whole meaning of a text."

"I see what you mean."

"Getting the security force lined up was the last piece of the puzzle. Syria is still a dangerous place."

"Wouldn't it be better to wait until the fighting dies down? It would be safer then."

"Time is of the essence. These irreplaceable ancient manuscripts are being destroyed whenever they're discovered by the Islamic extremists. Biblical and archeological history have been major casualties of these endless, senseless Middle East wars. Some have estimated that over fifty percent of the ancient manuscripts and scrolls have already been destroyed."

"That's tragic."

"These scrolls are priceless and unique. That's why we want to digitize them so they can be preserved."

Their waitress arrived with their meals. They both had ordered steak and had wine served with dinner. The wine was selected by Chewy, who had taken charge of the ordering and suggested the steak.

"Caleb, you seem like an enterprising young man. Have you considered attending college?"

"Not really. It's too expensive, and I don't have any money. Anyway, I'm not sure what I want to study. I really admire people like you who know what they want to do in life, who find their passion."

"It is fulfilling to work at something you love doing. Our work was even more than a passion. We considered it a calling from God."

"You have conviction about your work. I don't have that about anything."

"You will, Caleb. Keep searching your heart and explore the opportunities that present themselves. May I ask you a personal question?"

"Sure."

"Do you have a girlfriend?"

"Good question. I thought I did. She cut me loose before I came here on this trip to the east coast."

"Why?"

"She wanted to take our relationship to the next level, get more serious and plan for the future. I just wanted to continue dating and have fun together for a while. I haven't been out of the service that long and don't have a career yet or anything permanent."

"What's she like?"

"She's a knockout——"

"I'm sure she is to attract a man like you."

"I'm the lucky one. Her heart is as beautiful as her body, and that's saying a lot. I actually took a bottle over the head for her, but that's a long story. She's five feet, eight inches tall and weighs about one hundred thirty-five pounds. She's very strong, athletic, and articulate."

"She told you her weight? That gal's got confidence."

"She's studying to be a nurse. Right now she's a bartender, and she's the best."

"She must be a remarkable young lady."

"She's got brownish hair, and it's thick. I guess the color is more like auburn than brown. In the morning sun, her hair looks like it's glowing, since it's filled with red highlights. Sometimes it looks brown, sometimes red, depending on the way the light hits it."

"Auburn hair. Got it."

"She's tough but sweet, mentally sharp, and a hard worker. She's a good judge of character and not afraid of many things. That's a quality I admire in her. I guess you could say she's fearless."

"She sounds like an amazing young lady."

"She wanted us to go on life's journey together and help each other. I wasn't ready for that, so she dumped me."

"She's a smart young lady."

"For dumping me?"

"Relationships have to be developed together. It doesn't work to develop yourselves separately. She's right about that."

"I can see that now. Being separated on these assignments was tough on our relationship, more for her than for me."

"She sounds like a catch. Do you love her?"

"Good question. I think I do. Ashley, that's her name—"

"Lovely name."

"Yes. Ashley told me she has feelings for me and loves me, but I couldn't say it back to her."

"Now you have lost her?"

"Probably."

"Go home and tell Ashley you love her. Life's too short to spend even one day without telling the ones we care about that we love them. Then tell her you love her every day for the rest of your life."

She took a bite of food and chewed silently, then continued asking probing questions regarding the young man's childhood, military service, and last gig as a bouncer. With each answer she listened carefully before asking another question.

When the server brought the check, Chewy snapped it up.

"Professor, you don't—"

"Chewy, please. Call me Chewy."

"Chewy. I can pick up the tab."

"I'm sure you can, Caleb, but I got this."

"If you insist."

"I have some work to do in the morning, but if you have nothing planned, I could give you a tour of Richmond's historical sites in the afternoon. Interested?"

"Sure. I'm just waiting around until I hear from my boss about your security detail."

"Good. Then I'll call you tomorrow afternoon when I finish."

"Thanks, Chewy. And thanks for dinner too."

She held out her hand, and he shook it, surprised by the softness of her fingers. He felt warm on the inside and wasn't sure if it was the filet mignon or the good company. Maybe it was both.

"See you tomorrow, Chewy."

"See you, Caleb."

59

The employee party wound down, and only a few stragglers remained, Chad and Artie among them. Rosie chipped in to help Ashley clean up the bar area.

Chad approached them. "Thank you both for the prompt and friendly service."

"You're quite welcome," Rosie replied. "You were both very good boys tonight."

Ashley, who was wiping down the bar, smiled without looking up.

"Say, Artie and I were wondering if you two would like to go out and do something with us."

"We sure would, Chad," Rosie said. "My kids are with their father this weekend."

Ashley stopped wiping the bar.

"Cool. We'll be right back. We need some fresh air." They walked outside.

"Rosie, why did you accept? I need to get some sleep."

"Oh, Ashley, you may not be interested in Chad, but I am. This could be my only chance to be out with him away from this place."

"It's not a double date. It's just friends—"

"I know. But it will give me some extra face time with the stud muffin. Maybe I can win him over with my seductive charm. Come on. Be a friend. Support me."

"Oh, all right. You'll owe me big-time."

"Fine. I'll owe you one."

When the guys returned, the group decided to go to Chad and Artie's place to hang out. Artie brought home a new recording from his band, Armor of God, that had two new songs he wanted everyone to hear.

"We'll follow you guys to Chad's place," Ashley said as she removed her apron. "I can't stay late, but I would like to hear the band's latest tunes."

Once in the car, Artie checked behind to make sure the girls were following them. "Which one do I get?"

"You don't get either one. We're not shopping. You asked them to listen to your band's latest music. That's all this is about."

"You say that now, but I know you have feelings for Ashley."

"Did it ever occur to you that I might just be trying to win her for the Lord?"

"Sure. But can't both things be true?"

"Not in this case," Chad replied.

Artie stared at his friend and thought he saw a slight smile.

In Ashley's car, Rosie asked if she could turn up the radio.

"Sure."

Ashley's phone buzzed. She saw Caleb's picture.

"Do you need to get that, Ash? I can turn the radio off."

"No. I don't need to answer it."

60

Chad and Artie's apartment was small, organized, and clean. A sofa, two easy chairs, and a couple of wooden chairs formed a circle in the living room. Instead of framed sayings on the walls from Eastern gurus, as the faint smell of wisteria suggested, the living room was adorned with posters of athletes in action. Two large speakers on either side of the flat-screen TV had a cradle for an iPhone to enhance the sound quality of the device.

Ashley and Rosie asked for water instead of the soft drinks and coffee offered, which Chad cheerfully served up while Artie grabbed the CD from the kitchen counter.

"We think these may be the best songs we've ever recorded. The first one is called 'Cast Your Care,' and the second one is 'My Cup Runs Over.'"

Chad held up his hand. "My friend here forgot to mention that he wrote both of them."

"I had help. To God be the glory."

The four listened intently until both songs were played.

Artie looked around. "What do you think?"

Rosie spoke first. "I loved them, Artie. The melodies are catchy, and the words are deep and heavy."

"Thanks." Artie smiled. "We have a good feeling about them. What do you think, Ashley?"

"I liked them, Chad. Very good. I liked the first one best."

"'Cast Your Care?'"

"The message that we can take our worries and give them to God is uplifting."

"I think so too, Ashley," Chad said. "I like that one best as well."

Chad popped some corn and served everyone while Artie engaged Rosie in a conversation about their favorite music groups. Ashley walked around the apartment, studying the posters and asking Chad about some of the items on display in the apartment.

She pointed toward a large trophy on top of a bookshelf. "What's this for?"

"I was a state cross country champion in high school."

"Very nice."

"When I got to college, I played football and was a pretty good wide receiver until a knee injury changed the course of my life. During the many hours I spent in the gym rehabbing the knee, I developed a passion for fitness and weight training, which has led me to being a personal trainer. I guess you could say it all worked out. Or as I like to say, God had other plans."

Ashley shook her head. "You're saying God had your knee broken so you would become a personal trainer?"

"Not at all. God didn't hurt my knee; I did. But he turned the negative into a positive. I discovered I enjoyed working in the gym helping other people more than my own athletic accomplishments."

Ashley had never shown that much interest in Chad. He felt good about the attention she was giving him now. His heart beat faster, and he broke out into a sweat.

"What I hear you saying is that God turned lemons into lemonade because he had other plans for your life."

"Yes."

Ashley took a long swig from her water bottle. "I wish I could be that sure about God's will for my life. How do you know if you're really doing God's will?"

"You'll know. Everything fits together."

Silence.

"Hey, ladies, would you like to see my gym?" Chad asked.

"Sure," the girls responded almost simultaneously.

Chad led them to the spare room that he had converted into a home gym. An orange-colored mat was rolled against the wall. He had a weight bench with a bar over it resting on side supports with a selection of weights nearby. One wall had five-, ten-, and fifteen-pound dumbbells lined up along the floor.

Ashley stopped at an Exercycle and pictured Chad on the seat, peddling furiously. "I'll bet you spend a lot of time on this bad boy."

He stepped next to her. "Yes, as a matter of fact, almost every day as part of my cardio workout. My offer stands—if you ever want to work out with me, just let me know."

"You never know. I just might—"

"Hey, you two. Am I missing the next part of the tour?" Rosie jumped in front of Chad. "Amazing room. So this is your secret for how you got to be so strong."

"This and other things. I run a lot, every morning, and use the machines at the gym where I work. Diet is important. It takes a commitment to keep on a training schedule, but the benefits make it worth doing."

Rosie lifted the five-pound dumbbells. "These are perfect for me. Should I lift them over my head?"

"If you want to," Chad said.

She did.

"Good. Now don't lock your arms, Rosie."

"How's this, Chad?"

"Perfect."

"Someone take my picture."

Rosie posed with the weights over her head, proudly displaying her ample bosom and muscular build. Her long black hair framed her bright blue eyes. At five feet, eleven inches, she was the tallest woman at the Ax Handle and probably the strongest.

Artie moved directly in front of Rosie, holding his phone. "I'll get your picture. Say cancer walk!"

He took several pictures and showed them to Rosie. "You look athletic."

She lowered the weights to the floor and stood up. "I played field hockey in high school, and I was pretty good, but life got in the way of my sporting career. Two kids and a divorce later, my main goal now is raising Seth and Sarah."

"There's nothing more noble than that," Chad said as he moved the weights back to their correct spot on the floor.

"I agree, Rosie. I don't know how you do it," Ashley said.

"I don't know either. Maybe I don't."

Artie moved closer. "Do you have any pictures of your kids on your phone?"

"You'll regret asking me that, Artie. We may be here all night." She whipped out her phone and began sliding her finger across its surface to find her favorites. "As luck would have it, I do have a few— thousand. Here's my son, Seth. He's ten, and Sarah's eight."

Everyone surrounded her and passed the phone around in a circle.

"They're blessed to have such a beautiful mom," Chad said.

Ashley smiled but felt a knot in her stomach. *He's sure giving her a lot of attention for some reason. What am I? Chopped liver?* "It's late. Rosie and I need to get going."

Rosie shook her head. "The night is young."

"It may be for you, but I feel old right now. I've got to spend the day studying tomorrow. I have tests on Monday."

The group started migrating toward the front door, and the girls slung their purses over their shoulders. Chad followed behind with his hands in his pockets. When they got to the front door, Ashley turned around and said, "Thanks for inviting us over, Chad. I like your place, and the music was stimulating."

***

Once in the car, Rosie leaned back in her seat and took a deep breath. "That was fun. They're both super guys. I wish we could have stayed longer. Chad and I were just getting started."

"I know you don't get to go out that often with Seth and Sarah at home, but as I said, I have to study. Tonight wasn't planned, and I'm not prepared to make a late night of it."

"It's fine. I think I detected some chemistry between Chad and me. You know, when I lifted up those dumbbells. The way he was staring at me. I think he was impressed. What do you think?"

"Artie seemed interested in you."

"Yes. He was quite attentive, especially when he took pictures of me. They're both great guys. I'll have a tough time choosing between them."

"You sure will, Rosie."

61

Caleb slept until the call from Chewy woke him up.

"I'm all done with my work. You ready to see some of the sights of Richmond?"

"Sure."

"I'll pick you up at your hotel at one p.m."

"I'll be waiting out front."

As promised, Chewy arrived just before one o'clock, driving a red Corvette with the top down. She wore oversize sunglasses, her glistening black hair pulled back in a ponytail. Her simple sky-blue blouse with fringes on the short sleeves and form-fitting jeans revealed an athletic body twenty years younger than her biological age of forty-six.

Caleb, outfitted in a Diamondbacks cap, polo shirt, jeans, and cross-trainers, smelled eucalyptus when he climbed into the passenger seat. "College professors must make pretty good money to drive a car like this. What a sweet ride."

"It gets me around. No complaints. This is my husband's dream car. He saved for a lot of years to buy it. I only wish he was here to enjoy it."

"I'm sorry. I was only trying to give you a compliment on the car."

"I know. Don't worry about it. I miss my husband every day, but I know he died doing what he loved—preserving ancient texts. I feel close to him, knowing that I'm completing some projects he wasn't able to finish. I know that would please him."

They started with a tour at Maymont, a one-hundred-acre American estate formerly owned by James and Sallie Dooley, who lived there from 1893 to 1925. They toured the manicured gardens, colored with blooms, and tramped through the mansion before sitting outside on a bench to watch the otters.

Caleb folded his fingers together and stretched his arms over his head. "This place is really something. I've never seen a park like this with such beautiful gardens—it's all free."

"The mansion is spectacular, and I love the museum. It gives you a taste of how the wealthy landowners lived. Bless their hearts. Unfortunately the rest of the people didn't live so well. Glad things have changed."

The next stop was the Virginia Capitol building, which was designed by Thomas Jefferson and modeled after a Roman temple in France.

"See that sculpture of George Washington?" Chewy pointed in its direction.

"Very cool."

"It's the only statue of Washington produced during his lifetime."

"That's an amazing fact."

They saw the White House of the Confederacy, the mansion where Jefferson Davis lived, and went to the Historic Saint John's Episcopal Church, where Patrick Henry gave his "give me liberty or give me death" speech. They arrived just in time to see a reenactment. Finishing the tour at Carytown, they got out of the Vette and browsed through all the shops and small museums.

Holding up a handmade bracelet, Chewy called to Caleb, "Isn't this a beauty? Ashley would like this."

"Probably. I'm never sure what women like."

"Women like a man who is authentic. Someone who is caring and kind and has a good sense of humor."

"That's good, because I have all those things." He laughed.

"I guess I should have added humility to the list. You do have the sense of humor part anyway." Her eyes smiled as she said it. "Say, do you have time for dinner before I take you back to your hotel?"

"Sure. I'd like that. I'm kind of hungry now, come to think of it. But only if you let me buy."

"Deal. I just want to pick up a souvenir first. I'll be right back."

"Sounds good. I'll wait by the front door."

A short while later, she returned and led him to a small eatery that featured antique furniture from the 1800s and an aroma to match. After ordering, she folded her hands in front of her. "My husband was working in an old monastery when Islamic militants surrounded it for two days, not letting anyone in or out.

"Rafael discovered a scroll that may be the oldest version of Zechariah in existence. This manuscript translated *echad* in Zechariah chapter fourteen, verse nine as 'alone.' *Echad* is normally translated as 'one.' For example, *echad* in Deuteronomy chapter four, verse nine is 'Listen, O Israel! The Lord our God is one Lord.'

"Many theologians argue that *echad* in this verse should be translated as 'one' because then it implies a 'compound unity.' This find was a big deal to Rafael because he always felt that translating *echad* as 'one' opened the door to polytheism, the worship of multiple gods, or pantheism, the worship of nature.

"If *echad* is more accurately translated as 'alone' instead of as 'one,' the verse would correctly read, 'Hear, O Israel! Yahweh is our God. Yahweh alone.' This nuance changes the meaning to close the door on worshipping multiple gods, which is important because Orthodox Jews recite this sacred verse every day as part of the Shema."

"I see why it was a big deal to Rafael. You're saying that the older scrolls are more accurate, right?"

"In most cases. The older manuscripts are closer to the original meanings. Rafael was afraid the militants would destroy the manuscripts if they took over the monastery, so during those two days when it was surrounded, he and a monk hid the manuscripts in one of the concrete walls and covered the opening with cement. At the time, I was working in another location. He texted me where they hid the scrolls in case something happened to him."

"He cared more about those scrolls than his own life."

"Ancient scrolls were his life. Unfortunately, after two days, his security guards abandoned them, and the monastery was taken over. Rafael was captured, tortured, and murdered."

"Did you get his remains?"

"No. His body was burned, according to the locals. They poured gasoline on him and set him on fire. That monastery is no longer held by the terrorists. If I can find those scrolls, I'm going to retrieve the manuscripts from the walls and scan them. Discovering a more accurate translation of Deuteronomy chapter six, verse four would excite scholars around the world and prove that the 'compound unity' argument was false. It would be Rafael's crowning achievement."

"It sure would."

Neither had ordered alcoholic beverages. Instead, they had a pitcher of sweet tea. The server brought Chewy a chef's salad and a cup of clam chowder while Caleb got shrimp scampi and a dinner salad.

After a spoonful of chowder, Chewy paused and looked him in the eye. "I'll bet you have a few stories to tell."

"From the war?"

"Yes."

"I do. But I'd hate to spoil this beautiful day and dinner with talk of war."

"I understand. Do you think your boss is going to come up with a security detachment for my team?"

"As a matter of fact, I do. He's been able to fulfill every request I've given him so far, although yours is the most difficult one we've had."

"We'll need to know by tomorrow because the next day, Tuesday, we're scheduled to go."

"I told him that."

"Caleb, how do you like this job of yours?"

"It's fine. It's a job, and I didn't have any other people knocking my door down."

"I have a proposition for you. I'd like to hire you to be my personal bodyguard. Your knowledge of the Middle East and your ability to use weapons, if necessary, would really enhance my safety."

He hesitated before speaking, taking a deep breath. "I appreciate you thinking of me, but—"

"Let me finish. You'd be in charge of security on this trip, and afterward, you could stay on as my research assistant and help me with special projects. I have the position in my approved budget. It's open and needs to be filled. I could pay you a good salary, and it's not a temporary position. It's permanent."

Caleb glanced across the dining room as images rolled through his head of life in Briggs Lake and auburn-haired Ashley smiling at him. "I'd have to give that some thought."

"I understand. I think you would be fabulous on our team, and I think you and I would work well together. You don't have to give me a final answer now. Promise me you'll think about my offer. If you have any questions, let me know."

"Will do."

"Thanks for the lovely dinner."

"Thank you for the wonderful tour of Richmond."

After she dropped Caleb off, he watched the Corvette dart off into the dark. *She's a brilliant researcher and dedicated teacher, but there is such sadness in her eyes. I know she misses her husband terribly. He must have been a great guy. He had good taste in cars and women. Do I see myself as her partner and bodyguard?*

62

The next morning, as Caleb was doing push-ups, Stockbridge called. "You sound out of breath."

"You caught me in the middle of my morning push-ups."

"How many do you do each morning?"

"A hundred if I have time. I was at fifty when you called."

"No wonder you're so strong. I didn't know that about you. Do you do other things in the morning?"

"I do a hundred sit-ups and a lot of stretching. They keep me in fairly good shape, especially when I'm traveling."

"I'm calling to say everything is set up. I have a security team on the way to Baghdad right now. They're contractors, all ex-military with combat experience. They'll be able to protect Dr. Huang and her group. They'll have all the necessary clearances from our embassy too. The diplomatic bases are covered. After we terminate this call, I'll text you the name and number of the team leader. Pass the information to Dr. Huang so they can coordinate their schedules. She's only got them for two weeks, so she better make good use of the time. Tell her to ask him for the password, which is strawberries."

"Wow. How'd you pull that off?"

"I still have some pretty good contacts from another life, but it wasn't easy. I had to call in all my chits with some old colleagues. These security guys I've sent are the best, but they're pricey."

"I can imagine. Can I leave today after giving her the information?"

"Not yet. I want you to see her off at the airport tomorrow. Then you can head for home any time after that."

"Roger that. She offered me a job working with her."

"She did? Doing what?"

"I think she had in mind for me to be her personal bodyguard on this trip and then to become her assistant after that—a permanent job."

"What did you tell her?"

"I told her I'd have to give it some thought."

"It's your decision, Caleb. I'll leave it up to you. That said, I have a couple more people for you to follow up on for me. We're almost done."

"I understand. I'm not too sure that's the right thing for me right now anyway. But she asked me to think about it, and I said I would."

"I appreciate your help with these projects. I know it's not easy, but you've met these strangers, and by gaining their trust, you've gotten them to reveal to you what they needed the most. It's fun helping people, isn't it?"

"It sure is."

"When you get home, mail me a summary of your activities with your expenses for reimbursement to date."

"Copy that."

"We'll talk soon."

As soon as he hung up, he called Chewy.

"Hello. This is Dr. Huang."

"Chewy, it's Caleb. I just got confirmation that your security team is in place. They're already on the way to Baghdad. All of them are experienced military and combat veterans. I'll give you their commander's number, and when you call him, before you tell him anything, ask him for the password. He should say strawberries. They will meet you at the airport so you can coordinate your schedule with them in person. It's safer to do that face-to-face than trusting the phone lines or the internet."

"I can't thank you enough. You've made this trip possible, Caleb. I didn't think we were going to be able to pull it off, but I didn't want to cancel until the last possible minute."

"I knew my boss would come through if he could. He always does."

"Now, what about my offer to hire you for my personal security and to be my assistant?"

"I've thought about it, and it doesn't seem right to quit my current job until we're finished with all our projects."

"Fair enough. How can I ever thank him and you for all you've done?"

"I guess the best thank-you is to finish the work you and your husband started."

"We'll do just that. I guess this is goodbye, huh, Caleb?"

"Not exactly. My boss wants me to see you off at the airport, so I'll go with you to the security checkpoint."

"Marvelous. Then let's have breakfast before we go."

"Let me take you to the airport in my rental. Then you won't have to leave that beautiful Corvette in long-term parking."

Chewy's smile came through over the telephone. "That sounds good. I'm meeting my team at the gate, so I was taking myself to the airport. I'll text you my address, and you can pick me up at home. I'll show you a good place where we can have breakfast."

"Perfect."

63

Tuesday morning Caleb picked Chewy up and they went to Mama Flo's Diner, which was filled with everyday working people from professionals, tradesmen, and blue-collar workers to laborers and students. The eclectic gathering had two things in common—the need for a good breakfast before going to their jobs and the need to be around other people. They enjoyed their fellow diners as much as Mama Flo's pancakes and grits.

Chewy led Caleb to a booth in the back. "This is my spot. You can see everything going on, but it's quiet enough to have a conversation. Sometimes I come here with my iPad and work. Being around all these busy people helps take the edge off loneliness."

"I met a woman in New York who told me being alone and being lonely are two different things. She said she had been alone but never lonely until her husband died."

Chewy teared up.

"I'm sorry, Chewy. I didn't mean to make you cry."

"I'm not crying, Caleb. The accuracy of that statement just kind of hit me. What the lady said is true, and I can relate to that."

An awkward silence followed. Chewy was relieved when the waitress came to take their orders. It changed the subject and gave her a chance to compose herself. "You should order the pancakes. They're Mama Flo's signature dish. Grits come with every order."

"I love pancakes, even the bad kind the army makes." He laughed. "Which, by the way, is the way I prepare them—not good. Cooking isn't exactly my forte."

"You are so funny. What's next for you? Do you have another errand of mercy coming up?"

"I'm sure there will be something. He wants me to see you off first."

"I've never been to Arizona. I hear it's beautiful, with warm winters and dry heat in the summers."

"I love it. Where I live in Briggs Lake there is a lot of desert, which I like, but we have all the watersports you could want. Why don't you come and visit sometime, and I'll show you around there like you did for me in Richmond?"

Chewy paused. "Better be careful, young man. I just may take you up on that."

"I'm serious, Chewy."

"Thanks for the invitation. For now, I'm pretty busy, but when I get back—"

"You've got my number, Chewy. The offer stands."

"And you have mine. Let's keep in touch, Caleb."

"That would be great."

"Is something wrong, Chewy?"

"No. I guess I'm just emotional. If we pull this off, it will be my last trip to the Middle East and the conclusion of Rafael's work."

"Then what?"

"I'll keep teaching. I'm thinking about writing a book about my research experiences."

"Let me know if you do. I'll read it. I've thought of writing a book about people who have served in the military. We've made so many sacrifices for America's freedom. I want people to know."

"That's an admirable idea. I'll read your book too."

She held up her hand, and he slapped it. "Agreed!"

Flo's mouthwatering pancakes were delivered at that moment, golden brown, smelling sweet, and tasting even better than they looked. They ate in silence, each alone with their thoughts about their respective futures. Chewy contemplated the long flight to Baghdad while Caleb wondered when he'd be able to sleep in his own bed.

Caleb broke the silence. "How about you? Anyone special in your life now?"

"No. You don't replace the kind of love Rafael and I had. I don't know if I'll ever find love again, and I don't care if I don't. We experienced a love that people dream of. We were connected on so many levels—academically, personality-wise, sports, we even both loved to play chess."

"That's awesome. Who won?"

"He did most of the time, but not without me giving him a hard fight." At the thought, Chewy grinned and, after studying her plate, rescued a lonely strip of bacon, making short work of it.

"Are you scared to go over there again knowing that it's so dangerous?"

"To be honest, I'm scared to death. I have a bad feeling about this trip."

"Then cancel."

"It's too late for that. My husband would want me to finish the work."

Chewy picked up the check, and they were off to the airport. When they arrived at the outside baggage check-in, they got out of the car.

"You can only come as far as the security checkpoint anyway, so we might as well say goodbye here."

Caleb wasn't prepared to say goodbye so quickly. Should he give her a handshake or a hug? Chewy took over and grabbed him in a tight embrace, followed by a kiss on the cheek, then she whispered in his ear, "Thank you for everything, Caleb. You're a good man. If you get another chance with Ashley, don't let her go."

"I won't."

Still holding him tight, she patted him on the back, not wanting to let him go. Then she turned abruptly and marched through the front door of the departing flights entrance, pulling her carry-on. Turning around, she came back to Caleb.

"I almost forgot. Give this to your Ashley as a gift from me." She handed him a gift-wrapped box.

"What's this?"

"It's the handmade bracelet I saw at Carytown. I bought it for Ashley."

"Oh, thank you so much, Chewy." He took her in his arms and hugged her. They locked eyes and smiled until the tears started.

"I better go now."

She grabbed the handle of her carry-on and walked away. He watched her until she disappeared from sight.

64

Returning to his hotel room, he called Stockbridge to inform him that Chewy was on the flight to Baghdad and that he would check out and book a flight to Las Vegas.

"Not so fast. While you're on the east coast, I have another one for you in Nashville, Tennessee. Ever been there?"

"No. Can't say that I have."

"You'll love it. When you get settled in your hotel, I want you to call a man named Frank Marchese. His number is unlisted, but I'll give it to you now. Got something to write with?"

"Yes. Go ahead."

After getting the number, Caleb booked a flight to Nashville that afternoon. When the aircraft landed, it was raining. Unprepared, with no coat or umbrella, Caleb made the walk from the parking lot to the hotel lobby drenched from head to toe, and he looked like he had emerged from a swimming pool instead of a rented car.

It's been a long time since I've been caught in the rain.

The hotel room was comfortable and clean, which was all that mattered to him. He took his wet clothes off, showered, then made the call. "May I speak with Frank Marchese?"

"Speaking."

"I wonder if I might meet with you briefly."

"Regarding what?"

"You have an anonymous benefactor who wants to help you. There are no strings attached. He just wants to help you. He wants nothing in return."

"Don't tell me. He's a Nigerian prince who has a million dollars burning a hole in his pocket. This is a scam. Nobody does that kind of stuff. Who are you anyway?"

"My name is Caleb Sinclair, and I work for the man. He wishes to remain anonymous and asked me to contact you to see how we may be of assistance."

"That's nice, but I don't believe in Santa Claus or the tooth fairy. Tell him thanks but no thanks."

He hung up.

Caleb flopped down on the bed, exhausted. He wanted to set up an appointment for tomorrow before taking a nap and going to dinner. He grabbed his remote and started surfing through the channels. It was four o'clock in the afternoon, and there wasn't anything worth watching. He was too tired to sleep and too tired to enjoy TV, so he decided to call Stockbridge. Getting off the bed, he sat in the desk chair and made the call.

"Caleb. What's up?"

"Gas prices, but that's another story. I'm in Nashville and checked into my hotel. When I called Mr. Marchese to set up a meeting, he turned me down. Doesn't want to meet, says it sounds like a scam. He even hung up on me, thinking I was a whack job. I haven't run into this before, and I'm not sure how to handle it."

"I don't blame him. No one does what I'm doing, so naturally he's skeptical."

"Exactly. I introduced myself, and that didn't matter either."

"I've got it. Tell him I was a friend of his mother's when she gave birth to him. I know something about him that very few people do. He lost a couple of toes on his left foot when he was mowing the lawn as a kid."

"I'll give that a try. I assume you still want your identity kept from him?"

"Of course."

"All right. I'll call you tomorrow."

Caleb hung up the phone and dialed Marchese again. "This is Caleb Sinclair. I spoke with you earlier. I've got proof that my boss sincerely wants to help you without expecting anything in return."

"What?"

"When you were a boy, you lost a couple of toes on your left foot trying to mow the lawn."

"How does he know that?"

"He was friends with your mom."

"Who is he?"

"He wants to remain anonymous. I think he doesn't want you to feel like you'll owe him anything. He just wants to help you with whatever you need. Can I meet with you somewhere tomorrow?"

"All right. I'll meet you at the West Long Branch Café. It's on Wall Street."

"In New York?"

"No. Here in Nashville. Are you out of your mind?"

"No. I'm sorry."

"Nine o'clock sound good?"

"Yes. Perfect. See you then."

Caleb grabbed the remote and started surfing the channels again, searching for something good to watch, hoping the rest of this job would go more easily than setting up the appointment. Checking his watch, he saw that Ashley would be starting her shift now. He wondered if he should call her and say hello, finally deciding on sending a text instead.

Hope u r good. I'm in Nashville. Will be home sometime this week. Want to get together? C

He mindlessly watched an old movie and munched on pork rinds until he fell asleep waiting for her response. It never came.

65

The West Long Branch Café was a trendy, local hot spot in more ways than one. It catered to those addicted to their phones who could plug in, recharge, and use free Wi-Fi to search the web. A bank of outlets on a countertop was filled with coffee drinkers on stools immersed in their smartphones and iPads.

Sitting near the door, Caleb's eye was caught by a man with materials spread out in a booth using a laptop to write. He was so intent on his work that his latte sat unattended, like a lonely survivor on a battlefield. *He's probably working on the next* New York Times *best seller. I wonder if I could ever muster the self-discipline to write like that?*

His reverie was interrupted by the entrance of a tall man with prominent brown eyes that scanned the coffee shop. *That must be him.* Making eye contact, Caleb asked, "Mr. Marchese?"

"Yes." The man came to the booth, extending his hand.

"I'm Caleb Sinclair. Pleased to meet you, sir. Have a seat."

"Thank you. How do you like this place?"

"Very interesting people in here. I've been watching them and trying to determine what they're all doing on their devices."

"Solving the problems of the world…or at least reading about them. Excuse me. I'm going to go to the counter and get a cup of coffee. Can I get you anything?"

"No thanks. I've had some coffee already."

When Marchese returned, they got to know each other. "Here's my story, Caleb. I'm a computer expert, in charge of IT for an international corporation. Fortunately, I can work from home and live anywhere I choose."

"Sounds like a sweet gig."

"It wasn't always sweet, and I worked my tail off to get to this place in my life."

"I understand."

"My partner, John Emanuel, and I have this idea to start a business selling homemade doughnuts, cookies, and cupcakes with a personal touch. John is retired and an excellent baker. I'm planning to retire myself in the next few years, and our goal is to run the business out of our home, like an old neighborhood grocery. We want to run a bakery shop where neighbors can just walk to the house, have a friendly conversation, and purchase homemade pastries."

"That's unique in this age of online ordering and brick-and-mortar chain stores."

"We think so. Of course, our model won't ever produce the same kind of revenue as online marketers or the chains, but we're not doing it for the money. We want to restore the personal touch in a business, which originally was about establishing relationships through providing good products or services."

"That's an incredible idea."

"Thanks."

"Do you need a small business loan to get started—is that how we can help?"

"We've got plenty of money for the start-up. We've been saving for years."

"What then?"

"I don't think you can help with this, but I'll tell you anyway. Our request for the certificate of occupancy was declined. Remember, we want to bake and sell the cookies from our home. That's an important part of the concept."

"Right. I get that."

"But here's the obstacle, and it's one we never dreamed would be a problem. Our home is in a residential zone, not a commercial one, so the city won't grant us a certificate of occupancy to run the business out of our home."

Caleb laughed. "We could have used a zoning commission where I'm from. We have warehouses and storage units on prime shoreline of the Colorado River. It was like first come, first served in Briggs Lake, Arizona. Hell, we even have trailer courts adjacent to mansions. We must have the most dysfunctional zoning laws in America."

Nodding, Marchese smiled. "Yes, of course. We understand why there are zoning laws; however, our business will not pollute the air, nor will it create excessive neighborhood noise or traffic. The city fathers don't see it that way. They're afraid if they give us a variance, it will open the door to other businesses to ask for the same kind of exception."

"Maybe that's where we can help you out. My boss has a lot of contacts everywhere. He may be able to grease the skids for you."

"That would be wonderful. Would you like to stop by the house and see our operation?"

"Sure."

The next day Caleb visited Frank and John's house, which was located near the West Long Branch Café in an upscale neighborhood. From the outside their home looked like the others in the neighborhood. On the inside it was filled with personal touches that made the house seem much larger than it appeared from the street. The finished basement had commercial exhaust fans and a built-in fire suppression system protecting a gourmet kitchen that would be the envy of any chef in a five-star hotel.

"You seem to have spared no expense."

"We wanted our kitchen to be top-shelf, like our baker."

"Are you talking about me?" A man with light blue eyes came down the steps with a newspaper in hand and a big smile on his face. "Hi, I'm John Emanuel."

"Hi, John, quite a place you have here. Frank's giving me the cook's tour—pun intended."

"What do you think of our gourmet kitchen?"

"It's world-class, John. You guys seem to have thought of everything."

Frank folded his arms. "Everything except the zoning."

"So I hear. We'll see what we can do about that. I'll be in touch. Thanks for the tour. You've got a beautiful home and a novel business model."

"One more thing, Caleb. I have a gift for you."

"What?"

Handing him a brightly covered bag labeled 'Frank and John's,' he said, "Here are a dozen of our assorted doughnuts."

"Oh my gosh, I love doughnuts. You'd think I was a cop. Thank you so much, Frank."

"And another thing. They're fat-free and sugar-free, so you won't gain weight eating them."

Caleb grinned. "If you say so. Good to know."

66

Back at the hotel, Caleb called Stockbridge and explained the situation. "They'd already built the kitchen in their basement, thinking it would be no problem with the city. Selling their baked goods in a neighborhood setting is what the business model is about, so going downtown or to a commercial strip mall doesn't work for them."

"I see. I do have a contact in Nashville, a lawyer friend of mine. He won't take the case unless he's sure he can win it. He doesn't come cheap, but neither does anyone who's worth it. Sit tight for a day or two while I work things out."

Caleb stretched out in his bed, remote in hand, and ordered room service. While he waited for his grilled cheese sandwich, he channel surfed for a good movie.

Since he had a couple of free days in Nashville while he waited for Stockbridge to make an arrangement with a local lawyer, this would be the perfect time to take the backstage tour of the Grand Ole Opry. He stood in the circle and saw the green room and the stars' dressing rooms. He heard stories about what happens backstage and saw a video. He wished he was in town on a performance day to actually see a show, but this was pretty good. He vowed one day to return and sit in the audience.

He stopped at a honky-tonk for a late-afternoon lunch and sat at the bar. Behind the bartenders were guitars of all kinds hanging from the ceiling, autographed by the musicians who'd played them. Instead of barstools, each seat was a saddle, and the patrons straddled them while drinking beer.

Stockbridge called and said arrangements had been made for a special meeting at city hall to request the zoning variance for Frank

Marchese at ten a.m. the next day. The lawyer representing them would be there. His name was Scooter Evans, and he was considered one of the top lawyers in Nashville, known by judges as a courtroom maestro who guided witnesses and trial juries the way a conductor directs an orchestra, always one step ahead and firmly in control.

"I'll be there, boss. Wish us luck."

"With Scooter Evans there, you won't need much luck. Just get out of his way and do what he says."

"Yes, sir."

"How do you like Nashville?"

"I haven't seen too much of it. It's rained since I got here, but everyone is friendly. I took a backstage tour of the Grand Ole Opry this morning, and I loved it."

"Good. I'm glad to hear it. After your meeting, if all goes well, you can head for home."

"Sounds good. I can't wait to sleep in my own bed again."

When he got back to the hotel, he put on his workout clothes and went to the gym for some cardio on the StairMaster as well as upper-body weight work. After he got back to his room and took a shower, he ordered room service. While he was waiting for his food, he called Chewy; it went straight to voice mail, so he left a message.

67

The meeting room was small but had large picture windows with views of the busy streets below. On one side of the table were two staff members wearing white cotton shirts with ties but no jackets. The older man, whose sleeves were rolled up, took charge.

Scooter Evans sat directly opposite the senior staffer. His large black cowboy hat sat to the left side of the table in front of him, his legal pad with a folder on the right side. He wore a bolo tie with a multicolored Western shirt with a lot of fringe on the front pockets. Caleb thought his flamboyant attire was more suited for the stage of the Opry than for a business meeting. However, the government officials knew of Scooter's reputation for winning tough court cases and showed him sincere respect.

Frank sat to Scooter's left and Caleb to his right. The older staffer read the appropriate portions of the zoning laws pertaining to businesses such as the one planned by Frank and John.

When Scooter spoke, it was his custom to begin with a sincere compliment and a courteous tone of voice. He knew that you make more progress quickly by being congenial at first and saving the tough talk for later in case the meeting went south.

The older man started the proceedings. "Mr. Evans, as you can see, the language in the ordinances is clear." He passed out copies of the relevant documents.

"Thank you for bringing copies of the statutes to this meeting," Scooter replied. "You're saving us time. I'm most appreciative of your preparation today."

The older man glowed after the compliment and continued. "We would need a compelling reason to give you a variance."

"Our reason goes to the heart of our argument for an exception to your laws. Those concerns don't apply in this situation. You see, this business is personal, friendly, and neighborly. The city's code was written so the neighborhoods don't have the noise, traffic, and parking problems that businesses generate. See where I'm going with this?"

"Go ahead," the older man said, his arms folded in front of him.

"What we have here is a couple of guys who want to make doughnuts for their immediate neighbors. They are going to both be retired and will not need a large volume to generate an income. Their goal is simply to be of benefit to their neighbors, like the corner grocery stores used to be in American neighborhoods not that long ago."

"If we make an exception, we'll have to do it for every small business."

"No, you won't. Frank and John's setup is small, and their idea is that people can walk to their home. Their business isn't going to generate traffic jams, make loud noises, or pollute the air."

"Is that right, Mr. Marchese?"

"Yes, sir. We might even deliver for shut-ins and others who can't drive or walk to our home. We only want to share our love of bakery goods with our neighbors and make enough money to cover our costs."

Scooter added, "Give them a year, sort of like probation—an experiment. We'll all meet in twelve months to assess the impact this business has had on the neighborhood. We can also meet any time before that if an issue arises. When the year is up, if there have been problems—the kind the zoning law was meant to avoid—you can close us down."

"In that case, with those assurances, we'll make that recommendation to the zoning commission along with our approval of a zoning variance for Frank and John's doughnut shop. They meet tomorrow night in open session. Be there in case they have any questions."

Scooter glanced at Frank, who nodded. "Frank and I will both be there. If you want John to come, he can be there too."

"He can come if he wants to. It's an open session, but we only need Frank to speak on behalf of the business, or you, Mr. Evans. See you tomorrow."

When the older staff member stood, everyone else followed suit. The younger man said, "I'll show you the way out. Please follow me."

In the parking lot, Caleb, Scooter, and Frank huddled by Scooter's Mercedes. Frank shook Scooter's hand. "I can't thank you enough, sir."

"We're not done yet. We have to go through the formal review process in the public hearing tomorrow night. We'll celebrate after that, but I think we've convinced them to give you a variance. You'll be asked some softball questions. Some of the zoning commissioners feel like they have to ask questions to show they're on top of things, even though the staff recommendation will be sitting in front of them. It's a bit of theater, but go along with it. Be polite—yes, sir, no, sir—and whatever you do, tell the truth. But just answer their questions and then stop. Don't elaborate or expound on anything more than you have to. And finally, don't bring up anything that you don't want to explain in detail. Got it?"

"Yes, sir."

"Tomorrow I'll announce that we're posting a voluntary bond with the city to cover any unexpected expenses they might incur to regulate your business. We know there won't be any costs. I'll say that the tough negotiators on the staff got us to put up the bond and that there is also a one-year probation before final approval. These facts will be in the papers for public consumption and will make the city government staff look good, like they squeezed us. We have to give them a win in this too."

"Sounds like a good idea," Frank said.

Scooter shook Caleb's hand. "I'll take it from here, Mr. Sinclair. Thanks for joining us. We won't need you tomorrow. I got this."

"Good. Thank you so much, Mr. Evans."

68

Tired of room service, Caleb decided he'd celebrate by having dinner at a restaurant. Randomly selecting the first one he saw on the way to the hotel, it turned out to be the perfect place to have a quiet meal alone. It was a cross between a coffee shop and a fine dining room with a menu as diverse as a New Jersey diner. He believed one should order Southern fried chicken while staying in Nashville. His phone rang.

"Chewy! How are you?"

"Pretty good. I'm calling from Mosul in northern Iraq. I'm fine, but we've had several clashes with jihadist fighters in Syria and Iraq. Thanks to our security force, we've stayed safe and escaped their clutches. That said, we've had to move quicker than planned and need to get out of here as soon as possible."

"Did you complete the mission?"

"Yes. That's what I wanted to tell you. The monastery where my husband hid the ancient scrolls of Zechariah was burned down by ISIL, but the scrolls were in a steel box encased in concrete right where my husband told me they would be. It survived the fires. It took us the better part of a day to dig them out, but when we opened the steel box, the manuscripts were unharmed."

"That's a miracle."

"I don't want to mention any more details on the phone, but we scanned the scrolls, and they have been exported not only to my website but also to several universities and museums for further study. The original manuscripts are now hidden in a safe place under the care of a monk. We're on our way home."

"That's epic news. Congratulations."

"We're experiencing some bad dust storms right now, so we're going to stay in Mosul until the weather breaks before returning to Baghdad and flying home."

"Get out of there as soon as you can. The longer you stay, the more danger you're in."

"That's true. Things here are unstable, and we don't know who we can trust. There are bounties on Westerners so that they can be used for ransom. There is a strong incentive to betray us and collect the bounty. I'm not going to allow myself to be tortured and killed like my husband."

"What will you do?"

"Kill myself."

"Don't talk like that."

"I don't mean to alarm you. Share our joy. We found the scrolls and scanned them so that they will be saved from destruction by ISIL, Daesh, or whatever they're calling themselves these days."

"That's great news. I'm so glad you called."

"How are you?"

"Fine. I'm in Nashville."

"How is it?"

"It's been raining since I got here, but the people are friendly. I've spent most of my time in the hotel, but I did take the backstage tour of the famous Grand Ole Opry."

"Don't forget. You promised me a tour of the famous Briggs Lake, Arizona."

"Your ticket is punched."

"Someone's at my door. I'll be in touch."

"Thanks for calling. Take care."

"You too."

When he got back to his room, he gave a full report to Stockbridge and concluded with a comment about the attorney. "You picked the right guy. Scooter is a powerhouse. He bowled those city staffers over. It's a done deal. They just have to give a public presentation at the zoning board meeting."

"I knew Scooter would come through for us."

69

The featured comic that night, Sweaty Palms, shared humorous observations about relationships that got the crowd going.

"You probably met our bouncer, Chad, when you came in. Let's hear it for Chad."

Everyone clapped. Chad raised his arm from the bouncer's station and made the peace sign with two fingers.

"What you may not know about Chad is that he's a chess player. That's right, a chess player. The last time I played chess with a friend I said, 'Let's make it interesting,' so we quit playing."

The audience giggled in waves as they caught the joke.

"Just think…down for it and up for it mean the same thing." He walked back and forth across the stage. "Doing the same thing over and over again has been called the definition of insanity, but if you get paid for it, we call it a job. How many of you live in Briggs Lake?"

The majority of the audience raised their hands.

"I have a theory that the greatest salesman who ever lived was the realtor who sold all those empty lots in Briggs Lake. This was probably his sales pitch to prospective buyers: 'I'll sell you a lot in the desert sixty miles away from the nearest utilities. You'll live among snakes, lizards, coyotes, and scorpions. It will be one hundred twenty degrees in the shade. There will be wind storms that blow away everything not tied down. Someday there will be signs all around this town that say 'Welcome to Paradise.' And you know what? He was right."

Everyone in the audience laughed. Joyce Benson beamed as she worked the room, talking to customers and making sure they were getting good service.

Artie stopped by. "Hey, man. Do you want to do anything when you get off work?"

"Stick around and have a beer, and we'll see how the night winds down. Maybe you can get Rosie to talk to you while you're waiting."

"Why? Am I so hideous that Rosie would avoid me?"

"I didn't say that." Chad grinned. "Lighten up. I'm just joking."

"Where can I sit so that Rosie will be my server? Are there assigned stations tonight?"

"Yeah." Chad gestured to a table of two next to a wall. "Sit there. Then she'll *have* to talk to you."

"Boy, are you hilarious. You should be doing stand-up instead of Sweaty Palms."

"His job is secure."

Artie took a seat, and Rosie came right over to get his drink order. When she left, Artie smiled at Chad, who flashed a knowing grin. Nothing else needed to be said.

Rosie returned with a beer and a chilled glass. "Here you go, Artie."

"Chad and I are going to do something tonight after work. Would you like to join us?"

"Can't, Artie. I've got a babysitter who has to go to school tomorrow—unless you and Chad want to come over to my house after work, but we can't wake my kids. They have school tomorrow too."

"We just might do that."

"My house is probably a mess right now."

"I don't care. I'm sure it's fine."

Rosie smiled and went back to work. A half hour later, she got Ashley's attention. "Could I see you for a few minutes in the restroom?"

"Give me a minute." She passed out a drink order, then met Rosie in the bathroom.

"Artie said he and Chad were going to get together after work and wanted to know if I wanted to go with them. I told them that I can't because I have to relieve the babysitter, and I threw out that they could come to my house. To my surprise, Artie thought that was a good idea."

"So they're going to your house?"

"You want to come along?"

"It might be fun. I could sure use a break from studying. I wouldn't be getting in the way of you and Artie, or is it you and Chad?"

"I'm attracted to Chad, always have been, though he seems more interested in you."

"If I'm not mistaken, Artie has his eye on you. Why else would he be sitting in your station tonight?"

"Maybe Chad asked him to sit there so he could invite me out on Chad's behalf. Ashley, please come with us. If both guys come to my house, I'll never get a chance to be alone with Chad."

"I don't want to give either of them the idea I'm interested in dating them. And I'm not thrilled with how religious they are—bringing up God all the time. It makes me uncomfortable. I want to be able to say 'shit' without feeling like someone's judging me."

"We'll steer the conversation away from religion."

"I'll come for a while, but then I'm going home. I'll give you an hour to get Chad's interest, then I'm leaving. I don't want a relationship right now. You can have both of them as far as I'm concerned."

70

Artie scanned Rosie's living room as he sipped a Michelob while she went upstairs to check on her kids. She had described her home to Artie and Chad as "decorated in early ten-year-old." He thought "kid-friendly" would be a better description, since anything that could hurt a child had been relocated to the garage or safely put out of sight.

Rosie emerged from the stairway and sat in her big, comfortable chair, eyeing Ashley, Artie, and Chad. "What do you think of my messy home?"

Artie's answer began with a smile. "I think it's a place for kids who feel loved, which is more important than an organized house."

"That's what I say to people. I'd rather have my home be a happy place for my kids than an uncluttered and organized one."

Chad got Ashley's attention and whispered, "Could we go for a walk? I need to talk to you."

"Not far. I need to go home. I'm tired."

"Thanks."

Raising his voice, Chad said, "Excuse me, Rosie. Would you mind if Ashley and I took a short walk? There's something we need to discuss."

"Sure."

———

Once outside, they walked in silence for a few minutes. "What did you want to talk about, Chad?"

"I think we could really enjoy each other's company if we spent time together, and I would like to do that. You never say anything about your ex-boyfriend. I know it's none of my business, but are you still together?"

"Caleb is doing a lot of traveling."

"That's not what I asked you. Are you still a couple?"

"Why are you asking?"

"If I have to spell it out for you, I will. I want to date you, hang out with you. Do things with you besides work. We worked well together on the cancer walk, and clearly we have chemistry. You must have noticed that too."

"We do have a connection, for sure. I really respect your faith and your manners. But—"

"But what? Do you still have feelings for the other guy?"

"To be honest, I do. He's been through some horrible war experiences, and I'm giving him time to sort his life out. I really care for him, and I'm hoping we can get back together someday."

Chad took a deep breath and then sighed. "At least I know where I stand. Thanks for being honest with me. I don't want to waste your time or mine. It takes two to have a relationship, and I won't force myself on you."

"I know you won't because you're a gentleman. I don't want to hurt your feelings, yet I have to tell you the truth."

"I know."

"You're a good man. You deserve a woman who can give you her whole heart. I'm not that woman. I'm sorry."

"I understand. Can I just say one more thing?"

"Go ahead."

"If things don't work out with Caleb, I'll be here for you in case you change your mind. Remember that."

She patted him on the back. "I'll keep that in mind. You'd be a prize for any woman."

"Except you."

She punched him. "Stop it. Let's leave it like this and be friends."

"If that's what you want."

"I'm going home. When you go back in the house, would you please tell them I had to leave?"

"Sure."

"Thanks."

71

When Chad popped back in the house to relay Ashley's message to Rosie and Artie, he added his own. "I need to go home too. You kids have fun and don't stay up too late. See you back at the apartment, Artie."

"Thanks for coming over, Chad. Sorry you have to leave early. Artie, if you can stay, I'd love to keep talking."

"So would I. See you back at the apartment, Chad."

Chad smiled and waved. Rosie escorted him to the door and gave him a hug. He grinned as he walked to his car.

"Artie, I wish you could have met my kids. It was too late to get them up, and they have school tomorrow."

"I love kids. My degree is in music education, and I'll probably end up being a music teacher if Armor of God doesn't make it, but I try not to think of that possibility."

"Since your gigs are only on the weekends, how are you able to support yourself?"

"I'm a substitute teacher for the school district, and I get a small salary from our church to be the music director."

"It sounds like you've got it together, Artie. You know what you want, and you're working toward it."

"Like anyone else, I have my doubts at times. Do your kids have any interest in music?"

"Seth, my ten-year-old, has a beautiful singing voice and loves to serenade us in the car when we go on trips."

"I hope it's not 'Ninety-Nine Bottles of Beer on the Wall.' I used to torment my parents with that when we went on car trips."

"No. It's songs he's picked up on his iPod."

"He sounds like a music lover."

"He is. So is Sarah. She's a Swifty—a fan of Taylor Swift. She also likes Carrie Underwood and Martina McBride. Sarah wants to take piano lessons next fall. Her fingers are small right now—she's only eight—but in another year or so, she should be able to start lessons."

"That's wonderful to hear. I think introducing children to music at an early age is very important. My parents started me on the piano when I was about Sarah's age, and I've been hooked on music ever since."

"You're really a good bass player, and I sincerely enjoyed listening to your band. I love the name Armor of God. How did you come up with that?"

"It's from a verse of scripture from the Bible, Ephesians chapter six, verse eleven, which says to put on the whole armor of God."

"Do you have any brothers or sisters?"

"No. I'm an only child. After my parents had me, they said, 'No more children for us. We don't want to take the chance of getting another Artie.'"

"I have two sisters, both older than me. A lot of women in our family too. Poor Seth is surrounded by girls." She got up from her comfortable chair. "I'm going to get another Michelob. Want one?"

"Sure."

Rosie returned from the refrigerator with two bottles. After handing Artie his, she sat down next to him on the couch. "I hope you don't mind me asking you this, but if you're a religious guy, how can you drink?"

"I read the fine print."

She laughed. "Oh, there's fine print? What does it say?"

"The Bible never says drinking is bad; it only says getting drunk is bad. Do you know what Jesus's first miracle was?"

"Healing a blind man?"

"He turned water into wine when he was at a wedding reception. His mom told him they ran out of wine and wanted him to do something about it. He turned water into wine. Not just any wine either. The best-tasting wine."

"I never heard that in Sunday school."

"If drinking was wrong, Jesus never would have done that."

"I wish Jesus worked at the Ax. We run out of stuff all the time 'cause Joyce tries to save money by ordering the bare minimum of what we need."

Rosie felt relaxed and comfortable with this man. She rested her hand on his arm and leaned toward him. After a few minutes of contented silence, he pulled her close to him and lost himself in her eyes before giving her a long, wet kiss.

When they came up for air, she snuggled against his chest and sighed. "I needed that. Thank you. It's been a long time."

"For me too. You're a good kisser."

"So are you, my friend. More, please."

He kissed her again and again and again.

72

When she got home, Ashley threw herself on the bed and cried herself to sleep. A few hours later, she heard a noise that woke her up. She held her breath and listened carefully. *I don't remember what woke me up, but the sound was different from a car going down the street or a barking dog. I think someone's outside my door. I may need to call the police. Where's my phone? It's not on the nightstand.*

She slipped out of bed and searched for her phone, then pulled on her shorts and a sweatshirt and crept toward the bathroom. Hearing footsteps, she stopped. Her front door slowly opened, and she heard two people entering her living room. She barged into the bathroom and locked the door. Seconds later someone banged on it.

She sat in silence, her heart pounding like the hooves of a thoroughbred. The knocking continued—getting louder and louder. The door shook with each blow.

"Come out, come out, wherever you are," a voice growled.

More knocking. A higher-pitched voice said, "We know you're in there, little girl. Come on out and play. You don't want to get us mad at you, do you? Lenny gets real mean when he's mad. You don't want to see Lenny mad."

"What do you want?"

"We won't hurt you. Just open the door. You don't have a thing to worry about. Just come on out."

"Get out of here, or I'll call the cops."

"Why don't you call your boyfriend? His name's Caleb Sinclair, right? We'd love to meet him."

"I don't know who you are, but I don't want any part of this. Get out of my apartment."

More banging erupted on the door.

If he breaks the door down, that might wake the neighbors, and they'll call the cops. That's my only chance. Dear God, if you're there, save me.

Ashley's phone rang underneath the bed.

The man with the high-pitched voice answered. "Hello. She can't talk now. Can I give her a message? Sure will. Bye now."

The pounding on the door started again.

Ashley gripped her hair dryer, planning to use it as a club if they got in the bathroom.

"Hey, little girl. The manager just called to bitch about the noise in here. She's getting complaints from the neighbors. Will you keep it down in there?"

They banged on the door again, more loudly this time.

"You said you had a phone in there, but I'm holding it. You lied, didn't you? I don't like it when people lie to me. It gets me really mad, and then I do terrible things. I got an idea. Let's call your boyfriend. Maybe he'll come and join us."

Caleb's phone rang. Ashley's face appeared on the display. "Ashley! It's so good to hear from you, honey. How are you doing?"

"Ashley's busy right now in her bedroom. She can't come to the phone. She's got company, and it sounds like she's having a lot of fun in there. We had no idea how flexible her body is. You probably know, don't you? Why don't you come over and join us?"

"Who are you? What are you doing with Ashley?"

"We've come over to play. Ashley's very fun to play with—as you know."

"Listen. I don't know who you are or what you're doing there, but get the hell out of there, you son of a bitch. I swear I will track you down and hurt you so badly, even your mother won't recognize you."

"When you leave her alone all the time, do you think she just waits for you to come home, Caleb? You don't mind if I call you Caleb, do you, Caleb?"

"Put Ashley on the phone. Now!"

"She can't come to the phone right now. It's playtime, and she's having way too much fun to talk to you. Why don't you come on over and see for yourself? We'll wait."

"Whatever you're doing there, stop it now and get out, asshole."

"Come over here and make us, big man."

Click.

Caleb called Ashley's number back. It went straight to voice mail. *What am I going to do? I'm in Nashville, Tennessee.*

73

Caleb called 911. That led to local law enforcement in Nashville. He asked them how to reach Briggs Lake's emergency number.

"Sir, I'll have to search the internet to find the number. Please give me the state, city, and county if you know it."

"Briggs Lake, Arizona, in Mohave County."

"This may take a few minutes. Please stand by."

"Please hurry. This is an emergency. Someone's life is in danger."

After what seemed like forever to Caleb, the call was patched through to the Briggs Lake Police Department. "911, may I help you?"

"Yes. There's a hostage situation in the city. The person is Ashley Bivens. At least two men are holding her hostage and may be hurting her. They sound like really bad dudes. She's in apartment 212 at Lakeview Terrace Apartments."

"What's your name and number, sir?"

Caleb gave her the information. "Will you call me back when someone has been there so I know she's okay?"

"Yes, sir."

The dispatcher's protocol for hostage situations required her to call the home of Chief of Police Louis Strollo if it occurred after hours. He picked up on the third ring.

"Chief Strollo."

"Chief, I received a call from a man named Caleb Sinclair in Nashville. He said a female is being held hostage at the Lakeview Terrace Apartments by at least two guys, maybe more."

"We'll send SWAT right away. What's her name?"

"Ashley Bivens."

"Ashley Bivens! I know her. She was a team leader on our cancer walk. Thanks."

The SWAT team woke the tenants on either side of Ashley's apartment and evacuated them.

After securing the adjacent streets, they waited for Strollo. He came in his Explorer a few minutes later and approached the SWAT commander, Jack McColaugh.

"We're probably going to wake up all the residents in the middle of the night, but we can't wait much longer. There's no telling what they're doing to the hostage."

"Yes, sir," McColaugh said.

"Lead your four SWAT members up there and use a battering ram to smash open the door if you have to, but follow our required legal protocol."

McColaugh led his team to the second-story apartment. Dressed in black uniforms with matching helmets, they carried automatic rifles and pistols. One of the team members brought the battering ram. The commander slammed his fist on the door.

"Police department, search warrant, demand entry."

No answer. They tried again.

"Police department, search warrant, demand entry. Open the door, or we'll break it down."

Still no answer.

McColaugh turned the door handle. It was unlocked. He motioned for the team to follow him. He raised his rifle to his shoulder and moved into the room. His team followed in single file. Once inside, they saw no one.

While the officers pointed their rifles at the closed bedroom door, McColaugh yelled, "This is the police. Come out."

"Help! I'm in the bathroom!"

After entering the bedroom, McColaugh knocked on the bathroom door. "Ms. Bivens, this is the police. You can unlock your door. It's safe to come out."

"How do I know you're really the police?"

"We were sent by Chief Strollo. I understand you know him."

The door swung open, and a shaking Ashley Bivens stumbled into the arms of McColaugh and started sobbing. "I thought I was going to die. I've never been so scared in my life."

"Ma'am, nobody's going to harm you. Do you know who those men were?"

"There were two of them. I dived into the bathroom and locked the door. The first one who talked at me through the door had a deep voice, and I think his name was Lenny. The other guy had a high-pitched voice. I've heard that voice somewhere before, but I can't recall where. There might have been more guys, but those are the only two who talked to me. They kept pounding on the door and woke up the neighbors."

"Do you have any idea why they came to your apartment?"

"They found my phone and threatened to call my ex-boyfriend to ask him to come here. I think he's traveling somewhere. We're not together anymore anyway. I think he was the one they were after and they were trying to take me hostage so he would come to the apartment."

"Did they call him?"

"I couldn't tell. One of the guys left for a while and probably went to my living room. I couldn't hear anything when he left the bedroom."

"Why would anyone be after your ex-boyfriend?" McColaugh asked.

"I have no clue. He's the kind of guy who'd give you the shirt off his back."

Strollo bounded into the apartment, followed by two officers. "Is everything all right?"

"I'm fine, sir. I thought I was going to die, though. I've never been so scared in my life. I was afraid they'd knock the door down and kill me."

"Did they steal anything from you?"

She surveyed the bedroom. "Everything seems to be in order. Let me see if my purse is still here. It was sitting on my vanity." She hurried to the vanity. "No. They didn't steal my purse." She took out her wallet. "My money is still there. They must have taken my phone. I don't see it anywhere."

Strollo glanced around. "We'll run a tracer on your number. The phone may help us find them. You're a lucky lady. We'll get these guys."

"I'm afraid to stay here. I'm going to call a friend and spend the night with her."

"That's probably a good idea for the time being," Strollo said. "Sergeant McColaugh is going to ask you some questions for his report. After that, you're free to go. We'll leave a couple of officers here for the rest of the night in case the perps return."

"Chief Strollo, how did you know to send people to my apartment? I wasn't able to call 911; the bad guys had my phone."

"The 911 dispatcher got a call from a man in Nashville."

"Who?"

Strollo pulled a note out of his pocket. "The man's name was Caleb Sinclair."

"Caleb! Oh, Caleb!" She broke down, crying and shaking. "That's my ex-boyfriend."

"He left his number with the dispatcher and asked for a callback when this was resolved. Would you like to call him yourself? You can use my phone."

"Yes, please."

74

Caleb had been pacing the floor since he got off the phone with the 911 operator. He imagined the brutality that could be inflicted on Ashley, and he felt powerless to protect her. His worry turned to anger and then rage. He envisioned the beating he would inflict on anyone who harmed Ashley. *If only I had been there with her. This would never have happened.*

His phone went off.

"This is Caleb."

"Hey, dude. Remember me?"

"Ash! Are you okay?"

She started crying. After a few seconds, she composed herself. "Yes. I'm fine. Thanks to you. You saved my life by calling 911 when you did."

"Please don't cry, honey. Before I say anything else, I want to tell you something."

"What?"

"I love you."

"I love you too, dear boy. I always have, and I always will."

"I want to be with you forever."

"Then come home to Briggs Lake, mister. I'm here waiting for you. I've been waiting all along, and I knew you'd come back to me someday."

"I'm coming home today…this afternoon, and I have a gift for you—all my love."

"I've got something for you too."

"What the heck happened?"

"At least two guys broke into my apartment, maybe more. I woke up and dashed into the bathroom, and they tried to break the door down a couple of times. They found my phone and must have called you from the living room. I didn't hear the call. I was in the bathroom the whole time."

"Did you know the guys?"

"No. I don't think so, but then I didn't see them. One of them had a high-pitched voice, almost sounded like a woman. Creeped me out. I've heard the voice before, but I couldn't place him. Their names were Geno and Lenny."

"What did they want?"

"They wanted you for some reason."

"Me?"

"They were trying to hold me hostage so you would come here to rescue me. It was a trap. They probably had a plan to ambush you."

"Why do they have it in for me? I don't even know them."

"Beats me."

"Are you sure you're all right?"

"I'm fine. I'm a bit shaken up, but overall I'm fine. Let me put it that way. I don't want to stay here tonight, though. I'm going to call Rosie and see if I can spend the rest of the night with her. I'm going to hang up now, dude. Get yourself back in my arms as soon as you can. That's an order."

"Yes, ma'am. Copy that."

"Chief Strollo wants to talk to you. Call Rosie when you get to Briggs Lake. She'll know where I am."

She gave him the number before handing the phone back to the chief.

"Caleb, this is Chief Strollo of the Briggs Lake Police Department. Don't worry about a thing. We're going to leave a pair of officers here to watch the apartment complex and another car that will follow Ashley to her girlfriend's place. They'll be watching her for the time being until we're sure we've eliminated the threat."

"Good. Please keep Ashley safe until I get home."

"I will. Listen, I overheard her say the guys were after you. Why would these thugs be out to get you?"

"I have no idea. I've been working out of town for most of the last two months."

"Do you have any enemies, someone holding a grudge against you or Ashley?"

"No."

"Have you been in any fights? Is there someone out there who might be seeking revenge?"

"No fights either, unless you count kicking someone out of the Ax when I was a bouncer."

"Tell me about that."

"Not much to tell. This guy had too much to drink, and the bartender, who was Ashley, cut him off. He broke a bottle over my head, and I removed him from the bar and punched him a few times. I guess I knocked him out."

"How long ago?"

"About six months. It was a couple of days before Christmas, on December 23."

"Do you remember the guy's name?"

"Derek Snerd."

"Derek Snerd! Are you sure about that?"

"Absolutely. Why?"

"When you get to Briggs Lake, I want to meet with you and Ashley right away to discuss this case in more detail. We have an ongoing investigation and surveillance activity regarding this individual. Please don't say anything to anyone about this."

"I won't."

"I'll make sure you and Ashley are safe. Your lives are in danger, so be careful and let us know if you see anything or anyone unusual."

"Thanks for everything." Caleb hung up and sat down, shaking his head. "Wow. This is unbelievable."

75

Rosie and Artie had fallen asleep in each other's arms on her couch. Her phone chimed, and it woke up Artie.

"Rosie. Rosie, wake up. Your phone."

She rolled over and reached for it on the coffee table. The name Private Caller made her suspicious. "Artie, I don't usually answer phones with no caller ID."

"Answer it."

She picked up the phone. "Hello."

"Rosie, it's Ashley."

"Hey, girl."

"I lost my phone and am using someone else's. Listen. Some guys broke into my apartment tonight."

"Oh my gosh, that's terrible."

"They didn't lay a hand on me, but they escaped before the police got here, and I don't feel safe staying in my apartment. Can I spend the rest of the night with you?"

"Sure, sweetie. Come on over."

"I'll pack some things and will be over in about a half hour."

"See you then." Rosie set the phone down.

"From what I heard, it doesn't sound good," Artie said with a grim expression.

"Someone broke into Ashley's apartment tonight. They got away before the police came, so she's afraid to be alone and wants to spend the rest of the night here."

"I don't blame her. I'll get out of here. We must have fallen asleep. I didn't realize how late it was. I'm sorry."

"Nothing to be sorry about. We had a blast, didn't we?" She smiled and hugged him.

"We sure did. Thank you for the hospitality and everything. I'll get going now so you can get ready for Ashley."

"How about a kiss goodbye, Artie?"

"Are you sure? I may have morning breath."

"Who cares?" She threw her arms around him and gave him a long kiss.

After waking up, Chad stumbled into the kitchen to make coffee. Seeing Artie's door ajar, he poked his head in. "Are you up in there?"

"I haven't been to bed yet. I just got back."

"Things must be going well with you and Rosie."

"We had a good time, but we fell asleep. Otherwise, I would have been home earlier."

"Your prayers must have been answered, buddy."

"Let me tell you something. Robbers broke into Ashley's apartment last night, but she must have called 911 because the police chased them off."

"Whoa. Really?"

"Truth. Ashley called Rosie to see if she could spend the night with her. She was afraid to be alone."

"I'll wait awhile, then give her a call to see if she needs anything."

"She's fine now. She probably could use a bodyguard, though."

"Artie, I'm a professional bouncer."

"If these guys have guns, you're going to need more than your muscles, champ."

"I already have the armor of God and the power of prayer."

"Whatever. I'm burned out. Good night."

"See you later, buddy."

76

Derek Snerd sat at a ceramic picnic table at Lakeside Park opposite Geno Schlubb.

"So what happened this time, Geno?" His cigarette dangled out of his mouth and jumped up and down as he spoke.

"We had some extensionating circumstances, boss."

"What? That's not even a word." Snerd wasn't pleased, and his tone of voice and body language made that quite clear. Geno had failed again, and Snerd's patience had run out.

"She heard us coming and got in the bathroom. We couldn't break the door down without waking up the whole apartment complex. The manager called while we were there saying they were getting complaints and threatened to call the cops. You said to keep a low profile."

"In other words, you failed."

"She left her phone under the bed, so I called her boyfriend in the living room where she couldn't hear me and tried to talk him into coming over so we could get him. While we waited for him to come over, someone must have called the cops."

"Go on."

"I posted a lookout near the entrance of the complex, and he buzzed us when the cop cars rolled into the parking lot. We ran down the back stairs and into the woods before they got in the building. Our car was parked about a mile away in a secluded spot. No one saw us."

"Don't you know the cops can trace us using her cell phone?"

"We thought of that and threw the phone into the lake. They'll never find it."

"You didn't lay a hand on the guy. Is that what you're telling me?"

"No. But I'm sure we scared the life out of his woman. They're going to be worrying about when we're coming for them again."

"Let's take a walk down memory lane, Geno. I told you guys that I thought the bouncer was feeding the cops information about our drug deals. Somebody was, and it was probably him."

"I remember, boss."

"The bouncer knocked me out in front of the other patrons that night he punched me. If I let him get away with that disrespect, the word goes out that I'm soft. How long before someone comes along and takes over my crew?"

"You said we had to get revenge. I remember."

"Right. I send you and Lenny to get him at the burger joint, and he beats you both up. Then I told you to bring more muscle, so you get three guys on him and he still gets away. By the way, your idea of more muscle is just one more guy?"

"The bouncer was bleeding out the nose. We roughed him up good."

"You guys got the worst of it. I didn't ask you to give him a bloody nose. I asked you to take him out."

"I see what you mean, boss." Geno wished he could crawl in a hole.

"Then this time, I got the girl's home address from my spy at the Ax. You were supposed to take her hostage and then call the boyfriend for help, and when he comes, you nab him."

"We did call her boyfriend."

"But someone called the cops before he came over, and you two ran for your lives."

"Okay. I get that."

"I even promised you a twenty-five-thousand-dollar bonus, and you still couldn't get it done."

"Right."

"That's the third time you failed. Three strikes and you're out."

"Give me one more chance. No foul-ups next time. Promise."

"You're a moron. Get out of my sight. You make me sick."

"Yes, Mr. Snerd." He turned and left for his car.

Snerd lit another cigarette and watched Geno drive away. He inhaled and blew a long cloud of smoke toward the sky. Picking up his phone, he punched a speed dial number.

"Yes, Mr. Snerd. What can I do for you?"

"Hey, Lenny. Geno just left and told me what happened last night. I'm not happy."

"Sorry, boss. I've been meaning to talk to you about Geno."

"What?"

"Remember when you said you thought there was a rat? Things were leaking out and cops were showing up during transactions?"

"Yeah."

"Geno just might be the rat."

"You got any proof?"

"He went into the living room of the girl's apartment. He said he was going to call her boyfriend while I stayed in the bedroom outside the bathroom door."

"Go on."

"The next thing I know, cop cars are pouring into the parking lot and the lookout calls us and says to get the hell out of there."

"What are you saying, Lenny?"

"Geno may have called the cops. Then they'd have an excuse to arrest us and interrogate us about our operation at the Ax. Just sayin'. Can't prove it, but that's what I think."

"I'll give you a chance to redeem yourself, Lenny."

"Sure, boss. Whatever you want."

"I want you to do a hit for me—a loyalty test."

"Sure. Who do you want me to knock off?"

"Geno."

"Like I said. I have my suspicions about him but nothing I can prove, or I would have come to you before now."

"We have a rat who's leaking things to the cops. If Geno's the rat, we eliminate him. If he isn't, it sends a signal to the rat that we're coming for him."

"What if I'm wrong and Geno's not the stoolie?"

"He's no good to us anyway. He's lost his edge. He'll get someone killed."

"If that's what you want."

"That's what I want. Do the job clean. I don't want cops looking up my ass, got it?"

"Got it, sir. I'll take care of everything."

"We're done here, Lenny."

Snerd hung up on Lenny, crushed his cig out on top of the table, then called his girlfriend. "Hey, Ginger."

"Hello, Derek. How's my man? It's good to hear your voice. You've been working too hard. Mama needs some sugar from her big stud."

"That's why I called. We're going out tonight. Put on that dress I like with the sparkly things on it."

"The red one you bought me? Sure. I'll put on the matching shoes too."

"You do that, sugar buns. I'll pick you up in about two hours. You be ready. You know I don't like to wait for anything."

"I know. You hate to wait for anyone."

"That's my good girl. See you soon."

77

Chad called Ashley a number of times, only to get her voice mail. He texted her. No answer. As the day progressed, he got more worried. He went into work early to see Joyce and was told she was behind closed doors ordering supplies.

Crystal Glade worked the bar and offered him a soda, which he gladly accepted.

"A little early for your shift, aren't you, Chad?"

"Some guys broke into Ashley's apartment last night, and I want to tell Joyce about it."

"That's awful."

"The cops came and chased them away."

Joyce came out of her office.

"Joyce, may I talk to you for a few minutes?"

"Sure, Chad. Come on in."

He followed her into the office.

"Have a seat."

"No thanks. I'll stand. Something happened to Ashley last night. Some guys broke into her apartment."

"Was she hurt?"

"No. The cops came and chased them away before they did anything to her. She was scared, so she spent the rest of the night with Rosie."

"How do you know all this?"

"My roommate was with Rosie when Ashley called to ask if she could spend the night. I've tried to call Ashley since I woke up, and she's not picking up. I'm getting worried."

"Thank you, Chad. I'll get in touch with Ashley and make sure she's all right. Don't speak about this to anyone."

"I did mention it to Crystal. I'm sure she'll keep it to herself."

—※—

When Crystal got off work, she drove straight to Snerd's house and knocked on the door. He peered through the peephole and swung the door open.

"Hey, Crystal. Come on in. I thought I told you to call first before dropping in on me?"

"Sorry. This was a spur-of-the-moment decision, Derek. Are you going out?"

"I'm wearing dress pants. How'd you know, Captain Obvious?"

"What happened last night with Ashley?"

"What do you mean?"

"There was a home invasion at her apartment. Everyone at the Ax is talking about it. Chad said something to Joyce, and it spread like wildfire. Were they your boys?"

"I don't know what you're talking about. What makes you think it had anything to do with me?"

"I'm asking you a straight-up question, Derek. Did you order your boys to do this?"

"I'm not interested in Ashley or her boyfriend, for that matter. But, sweet cheeks, my business is none of your business. I've told you that before."

"I know. I just don't want any of my coworkers hurt."

"Nobody's going to get hurt."

"I'm not comfortable with all this, Derek. I don't mind giving you intel on the Ax, but I don't want it used to hurt anyone. I don't want any part of that."

"It's too late for that now, Crystal. You and I are in this together— up to our necks."

"No one gets hurt, right?"

"Come here."

"No."

"Come here, now."

She inched closer. He grabbed her and held her tight.

"Derek, you're hurting me."

He let up on his embrace, pushed her against a wall, and pressed his lips against hers until she opened her mouth and gave him her tongue as she relaxed into his arms.

"Is that better, Crystal?"

"Yes. Much better. I'm sorry, Derek. I guess I just overreacted."

She rested her head on his shoulder while he stroked her hair and then flicked it playfully.

"I love how compassionate you are and the way you care for other people. Don't worry about a thing, Crystal. I got this under control." He rubbed her bottom with his other hand. "You know I love women with big butts, and yours is a beauty."

"Thanks, Derek."

78

A layover at the DFW airport gave Caleb the chance to call Mr. Stockbridge.

"Hello, Caleb. How are you doing? I appreciate your quick work on the Nashville job. Everything is on track for the variance."

"Thanks. There was a home invasion at Ashley's last night. A couple of guys broke into her apartment. She heard them come in and locked herself in the bathroom until the cops came. She's terrified to be alone. This wouldn't have happened if I had been in town. I love her and don't want to leave her alone anymore. I'm ready to make a commitment to her, and…well, I think I need to quit working for you."

Silence.

"Did you hear me? I need to resign."

"I heard you. I'm thinking. The home invasion doesn't have anything to do with your work with me. You two had broken up. You wouldn't have been at her apartment anyway."

"I'm not saying that, Mr. Stockbridge. I need to stop traveling so I can start over with Ashley—begin building a life with her. I know now that's what I want to do. And she'll know I really mean it if I quit working for you. Hopefully it's not too late, and she'll take me back."

"We're almost done, only one or two more jobs at the most. Take some time off to focus on your relationship with Ashley. I'll give you three weeks of paid vacation to get squared away with her. How does that sound?"

"That will work. We'll have time to find a place and move in together, but I only want to do one more project."

"You're serious about her, aren't you?"

"I am."

"Give me a call in three weeks. If you need anything else, call me before that. Any questions?"

"Mr. Stockbridge, if you don't mind my saying so, you sound down. You've paved the way for Frank and John's doughnut shop. You should be happy. I know I am."

"Caleb, I've got some bad news. Dr. Huang's team and the security detail are missing. I haven't been able to contact them."

The concourse seemed to move. His mind flooded with images of Chewy, so alive and vibrant and brainy. He remembered her loyalty to her husband and their mission, eating breakfast with her at Mama Flo's, riding in her red Corvette, her long black hair, soft hands, and perfect white teeth.

She had a premonition that something bad was going to happen. She was scared to death, but she went anyway. So faithful to her husband and his mission, even at the risk of her own life. She knew it was dangerous. That's why she wanted me to be her bodyguard. If I would have taken the job offer, would I have been able to save her? I'll never know.

"Caleb, are you all right?"

"I'm fine…um…do you know anything else?"

"I don't know any details."

"If she was captured, she would have killed herself rather than be tortured to death like her husband."

"If she was captured, she may not have had an opportunity to do that. Try not to worry. I'll let you know if I hear from them or from anyone else who has information about them. Thanks for taking care of Frank."

"Whatever."

"Caleb, what's the matter?"

"Nothing."

"You helped Professor Huang fulfill her deepest need, to scan the scrolls her husband wasn't able to get to. Remember that. If she died, she was doing what she loved and felt called to do in life."

"Was scanning old scrolls worth risking her life?"

"She thought it was, and so did her husband. Call me when you get to Briggs Lake."

Stockbridge didn't tell his young protégé that he thought Chewy was probably already dead and that his health was failing fast. He needed to spend more time in bed. As he stared out the window at the lake, he wondered if he would be able to survive the three weeks until Caleb could work again.

He pulled the covers off, swung his legs over the side of the bed, and sat until the room stopped rocking back and forth. He set one foot on the floor, then slowly eased the other one down. He rose to his feet, quivering, his eyes searching for his cane, which had fallen on the floor. Turning around to the bed, placing both hands on it, he lowered his knees to the floor. The joints made cracking sounds. Head throbbing, hands shaking, he leaned to the right to grab his cane, then used it to prop himself back up to a standing position. To Stockbridge, the bathroom seemed like a mile away, but he had to go. He felt like he was walking through three feet of snow.

Finally arriving in the bathroom, he set his cane against the wall and caught his breath. *Time's running out on me. It's time to tell Caleb the truth—the whole truth. If I don't tell the boy soon, he may never know what this has all been about.*

79

When Caleb's plane touched down in Las Vegas, he called Rosie, who gave him Ashley's new number.

"Hi, babe. I called Joyce and got the next couple of weeks off the schedule, so I can spend time with you."

"That's good news, Ash. You know what? I have three weeks paid vacation from Stockbridge, and I've only worked for him for about six months."

"Awesome. We need the time, Caleb. Chief Strollo feels our lives are at risk and wants us in a safe place for a couple of days, and he wants to meet with us about the threat."

"Who would want to hurt us? We're adorable."

"I know. I am, at least." She giggled. "These guys must be out of their minds. Strollo said he would explain when he meets with us."

"This is getting weirder all the time."

"Exactly. Anyway, you're supposed to go to your apartment and get some things together so you can stay with me at an undisclosed location."

"Where are you?"

"I can't say on the phone. There will be two cops in an unmarked car at your apartment, and they'll lead you to where I am. One of the officers will say to you, 'Ashley sent me.' Got it?"

"Affirmative."

"When I called Joyce to let her know what happened and asked for the time off, she was casual about it and didn't seem too concerned about what I had been through. Another thing that's strange is that she already knew what happened to me and said all the employees at the Ax were talking about it."

"How would they know?"

"Exactly."

"What if Derek Snerd is the one behind my home invasion and he has an accomplice working at the Ax—giving him information about me and you?"

"Who would do that? I can't imagine who would give Snerd information about us."

"It could be Joyce. Remember, she backed Snerd up when you removed him from the bar that night. When he threatened to sue the Ax, she fired you for doing your job. Besides, he hit you first. You were only defending yourself."

"And protecting the staff and customers from his physical violence." Caleb scratched his head. "That doesn't make sense to me. Joyce is a better person than that. She's a business owner at heart and has never been malicious to me or anyone."

"Maybe Snerd and Joyce are in a secret relationship."

"That's a stretch. How could she be with that sleazeball with the greasy ponytail and soul patch? That area under his lower lip is probably the only place the dude can grow facial hair."

"Then who?"

"Rosie?"

"No way. I asked her if she told Joyce about what happened to me, and she said she didn't tell anyone."

"Chad?"

"No way. Too religious for that."

"Those are the kind you have to worry about," he said with a laugh.

"Who's the jealous one now? By the way, I want you to get to know Chad. He's a good guy."

"So he can push his religion down my throat?"

"He doesn't do that. He's not pushy. Besides, Chad wasn't there. It was just Rosie and her kids. They were sleeping in their bedroom."

"Whatever. It will all come out. I better hit the road, honey. Can't wait to hold you in my arms. See you soon."

Ashley texted Strollo to let him know Caleb was on the way from Vegas so he could send the unmarked car to Caleb's apartment to wait for him.

I wish I could have told Caleb that we'll be staying in a five-star hotel on the Parker Strip, but he'll have a fantastic surprise when he sees it for himself. I wonder if Rosie did spread it around after all? I better call her to make sure she didn't.

Ashley grabbed her phone and called her friend. "Rosie, I have to ask you a serious question one more time to confirm what I thought you said. Did you tell anyone at the Ax what happened to me last night?"

"Nope. I didn't, and I wouldn't do that."

"That's good to hear. Has anyone been asking questions about Caleb or me?"

"You mean besides the legions of heartsick twentysomethings out there who still miss seeing 'that stud who used to check our IDs?'"

"Right. I guess that's what I'm saying."

"Snerd. He's asked me a lot of questions about you both."

"You don't tell him anything, do you?"

"No way. He's a low-life scum."

"That's what I thought. Thanks. I just wanted to make sure."

"Why? What's going on?"

"Oh, nothing. Just wondering."

80

The main thing on Ashley's mind now was getting herself ready to see her man. She ran a warm bath, lit scented candles, and played soft music. After easing herself into the tub, she closed her eyes and pictured them together. She visualized them in cars, in restaurants, on walks in forests, and getting their kids ready for school.

Ashley dressed like she had the first time she'd visited his apartment, wearing the tight-fitting orange crop top, a faded pair of cutoffs, and her Boston Red Sox cap.

When she answered the knock on the door, there he was—tall, dark, and handsome, grinning from ear to ear, wearing cargo shorts, flip-flops, and a T-shirt—the Briggs Lake uniform. She jumped up, threw her arms around his neck, and wrapped her legs around his waist. "I missed you so much, babe. Welcome home."

"I missed you too, Ash. I had forgotten how beautiful you are in person. And you have charisma, intelligence, and class to go along with your killer body."

"I'll bet you say that to all your girlfriends. Flattery will get you everywhere. Is that your Glock I feel, or are you just happy to see me?"

"Can't it be both?"

With that, she gave him a big kiss that took their breath away. All Caleb could say was, "It's good to be home."

"Bring your suitcases in so we can close the door. Would you like something to drink?"

He set his bags down. After closing the door behind him, he dropped to one knee.

"First things first. Ashley Rebekah Bivens, I love you with all my heart, and I want to be with you the rest of my life. I want you to have my children. I want to grow old with you. I want to share my life with you, the good, the bad, and the ugly. I want to go on life's journey with you. Whatever happens doesn't matter as long as I'm with you." He held an engagement ring up to her. "Will you marry me?"

She put her hands on her cheeks and then on his shoulders. "Yes."

"Then please put the ring on." He handed it to her, she slide it over her finger, and it fit perfectly.

"How did you know my ring size?"

Still kneeling, he looked up at her with a toothy grin and watery eyes. "I have my ways."

"Would you please stand up, dear boy, so I can kiss you?"

He rose and held her in his arms for a few seconds, looking into her bright green eyes, before bending down to land his lips softly on hers. After the kiss he whispered, "I love you forever."

"Me too. I mean, I love you forever, not me forever. You're my man, and you'll always be my man, and I'll always be your woman, no matter what life throws at us. That's what I meant to say."

Except for the words "I love you," which were spoken over and over, there wasn't a lot of conversation for the next several hours, only a lot of hugs and kisses.

The next day, Joyce Benson and her lawyer, Steven William White, were at the police station being interviewed by Captain Emily Alvarez, who had recently been assigned to the case. Alvarez's close-cropped, pitch-black hair accentuated her muscular frame. Working her way up from the ranks, the officer appeared to be much younger than her actual age of forty-five.

Strollo made it a point to sit in on the interview, which surprised Alvarez, since the chief didn't usually participate in interrogations. It had been a grueling couple of hours filled with surprises for Benson. Someone had fed the cops inside information about the drug ring headquartered in her bar. Alvarez's questions, aimed at discovering Benson's role, if any, in the criminal activity, probed every aspect of the owner's workday.

Attorney Steven White, a lean, energetic man in his seventies, projected a quiet confidence that came with decades of experience defending clients. "Mr. Strollo, can my client and I take a break?"

"Sure. Mr. White, Ms. Alvarez and I will leave the room for fifteen minutes, and then we'll resume. Do you need coffee or water or anything like that?"

White checked with his client, who shook her head. "No, we're good. And if I have another cup of coffee, I'll be up all night."

"Good. See you in fifteen." Strollo and Alvarez exited and went to an adjoining room that had one-way glass and a speaker so they could see and hear everything said between Benson and her attorney.

"Mr. White, I'm really getting stressed. They keep asking the same questions over and over again."

"That's right. I told you they would do that. They'll ask the same questions in different ways to catch you lying."

"What unnerves me is how specific and detailed the questions are. A drug operation has been happening under my nose all this time, and someone knew more about it than I did. I honestly didn't know anything about it, but they don't believe me. Someone's setting me up."

"Maybe there isn't a mole and they're bluffing, just trying to get you to talk. Remember, I told you before it's not against the law for a cop to lie to you. They do it sometimes to get you to spill your guts. If they can get you to think Snerd is setting you up, they can get you to drop the dime on Snerd—give them the information they need to prosecute him. He's the one they're after, I think. Not you. If you've done nothing wrong, you have nothing to fear."

She took in a deep breath. "I hope you're right. I'm scared, though."

He patted her on the shoulder. "Trust me. It will be all right."

Strollo and Alvarez reentered the room. Alvarez addressed Benson. "Shall we begin?"

"Sure. Go ahead."

"Good. Let's go back to the beginning. What is your relationship with Derek Snerd?"

"He's a good customer and a big tipper."

"Did you know anything about his drug business?"

"No."

"How did you think he made his money?"

"He's a realtor."

"How would you describe your relationship?"

"He's one of my customers."

"Do you have a personal relationship with Derek Snerd?"

"What do you mean?"

"Is any aspect of your relationship with him personal?"

"No."

"So are you stating that the only relationship you have with him is business-related?"

She hesitated. "Yes."

"Why did you hesitate?"

"We're friends, I guess I could say. Friends, nothing more."

Alvarez folded her arms. "How would you define friends?"

"We're friendly in our communications, Captain Alvarez; that's all. He's kept his business to himself, and I run the Ax Handle as I decide, with no interference from him or anyone."

Strollo's eyebrows raised. "So when you fired Caleb Sinclair, that was on your own? You didn't have any consultation with him about the punishment for your bouncer?"

White put his hand down on the desk. "Wait a second, Mr. Strollo. I advised Ms. Benson in that matter. Mr. Sinclair beat up Derek Snerd outside the bar, leaving him unconscious. Snerd was ready to file a civil lawsuit against the Ax Handle. We negotiated with Snerd's lawyer that the lawsuit would be dropped if we terminated Mr. Sinclair."

"I see." Strollo nodded. "We're done for now. As we develop more information on this case, we may bring you in again for questioning."

"That's fine," White said.

"I want to remind you that everything you said has been recorded and may be used in court," Strollo added.

"Understood," White replied.

Benson and White rose, shook hands with the two cops, and left.

Alvarez rested her chin on the palm of her hand. "I think she's holding information back. I don't think she's telling us everything she knows, Chief."

"You're probably right, Emily. That said, I don't think she was helping Snerd in any way."

"Why do you say that, Louis?"

"I have an informant on the inside of the gang."

81

A couple of days after Caleb joined Ashley at the hotel, he got a call from Police Chief Strollo inviting them to his home for dinner so they could meet and discuss the threat to their lives. The chief's home stood alone on a cliff overlooking Briggs Lake. The large house with the landscaped yard, composed of decorative stones and blooming cacti, was the focal point of the surrounding desert scene. Caleb and Ashley slowly motored up the driveway so they could take in the view of the house and the stone wall encircling it.

"Like a fortress on the top of a mountain, don't you think, Ash?"

"I'd love to have a view like that." Wearing her hair down, she smoothed the sides.

"So would I." He put the Frontier in park and walked around to get her door.

Wearing a cream-colored crop top and white cotton pants held up with a drawstring, she slid out of the front seat, sparkling sandals first, and placed a small white purse with a skinny strap over her shoulder. "Thank you, Mr. Sinclair."

"You're welcome, Miss Bivens—or should I say the future Mrs. Sinclair?"

Strollo opened the door to welcome them before they got near his home. His driveway alarm and one of his thirty-six television monitors had alerted him as soon as the truck approached. His German shepherd stood at his side, swinging his tail back and forth like a hairy windshield wiper. "Come right in. Glad you could join us. This is Duke. He's friendly but annoying."

The couple entered through a large wooden door that resembled a medieval castle gate. "Thanks for inviting us," Ashley said as she shook his hand. "It's good to see you again."

Then, smiling broadly, the chief gripped Caleb's hand. "You must be Caleb. My wife, Samantha, will be right out. Please have a seat anywhere." He gestured toward a love seat and several chairs placed in a semicircle facing a huge window with a panoramic view of the lake below.

Ashley and Caleb sat on the love seat.

Strollo's arms rested at his sides. He wore baggy dad jeans and a Hawaiian shirt. "Care for something to drink? We have water, coffee, tea, beer, wine, and Diet Coke."

"What are you drinking?" Caleb asked.

"Diet Coke."

"I'll have that."

"Me too," Ashley said with a big nod of her head. "You have a lovely home, and the view is awesome."

"Thanks."

Samantha glided into the room in a brightly colored silk pantsuit. She brought a fragrance of spring into the living room, and the world seemed to pause for a moment to acknowledge her presence. Her slender shape and graceful movements reminded Ashley of her ballet teacher, Julz Bayless. When Samantha extended her arm to shake Ashley's hand, her shapely fingers crowned with colorfully polished nails momentarily took the young bartender's attention away from her mahogany eyes.

Caleb stood up and felt her warm, soft skin when she squeezed his hand. No one had mentioned Samantha's exquisite beauty, so his face reflected surprise. "Nice to meet you" seemed to him an inadequate response to the stunning woman in front of him, although it was all he could think of at the time.

"I see that Louis gave you Diet Cokes. That's all he drinks. Just because he does, that doesn't mean you have to. I'm having wine myself. Anyone care to join me?"

Ashley raised her hand.

"I'll be right back with some wine and snacks. The lamb will be ready in about an hour. Louis told me you have some business to take care of before we eat. Excuse me for a minute."

When she left for the kitchen, it felt like someone had turned off a light in the living room.

Caleb's first impression of Louis Strollo was a positive one. He appeared to be a good guy, and his name sounded familiar. The fiftysomething cop sported a mustache that punctuated his sentences when he talked. When compared to his wife's bedazzling appearance, Strollo appeared plain and average.

This guy is the chief of police of Briggs Lake. He must have something going for him to snag a hot woman like that.

82

Samantha returned with a tray of shrimp, crackers, and cheeses, and she handed Ashley a glass of wine. Checking to see if anyone needed anything else, she settled into a chair near her husband.

"Ashley, you did a marvelous job preparing your team for the cancer walk. The Ax Handle walkers were enthusiastic and inspired the rest of us."

"Thank you, sir, but I had a partner, Chad, who shared the responsibilities. Our team was filled with good people too. I didn't have that much to do with our team spirit."

"You're too modest, young lady. Your team stood out for its enthusiasm, and when a team excels, I think it's a reflection of its leaders."

"Thanks." She shifted uncomfortably on the love seat.

"Now there is another matter I need to discuss with you both that is more serious."

Caleb leaned forward. "What's that?"

"Caleb, you and Ashley are being followed by a Mafia gang led by Derek Snerd."

"Derek Snerd's a mob boss? Why would he be interested in us?"

"He's based in Las Vegas, but he's the biggest drug dealer in western Arizona and has ties to the Sinaloa drug cartel in Mexico. We've been busting their street dealers and gathering information on the gang for eighteen months. All roads lead to Snerd, the one we're really after. When you told me you kicked him out of the Ax and got into a fight, I put the pieces together, and it started to make sense."

Caleb straightened up. "I still don't understand why he would have it in for me. It wasn't that big of a deal. I got fired and needed staples to put my scalp together."

Ashley touched his arm. "You did knock him out, dude."

Strollo continued. "His crew hangs out at the Ax and does deals there."

Ashley studied his face as he spoke.

"They're good. Real pros." Strollo took a deep breath. "His soldiers weren't there that night, or they would have murdered Caleb. They heard about it, though. Snerd's lost face and has to show his outfit he's still a tough guy by taking you down. If he doesn't, his wise guys will think he's getting soft, and someone will challenge him for the leadership. In a way, he has no choice but to put a hit out on you, or even better, to knock you off himself."

"Shut the front door!"

Ashley's jaw dropped. "Where did you get that one, dude?"

"From the Mormons. They've got a lot of good ones like that they say instead of swearing."

Strollo continued. "It's a good thing you've been out of town recently. We knew they were following you two, but we didn't know why."

Caleb folded his arms. "Let me get this straight. You've been following the guys who are following us?"

"As much as we could. Obviously, we don't have enough manpower to give you twenty-four-seven protection. That's why they could get to Ashley's apartment that night."

Ashley gripped Caleb's thigh until her knuckles turned white. "Babe, I'm scared."

"I can handle myself." Turning to Strollo, he made eye contact. "What do you want us to do?"

Strollo took a sip of his Diet Coke. "Keep us informed of your schedule. Let us know when something or someone seems suspicious—if something doesn't seem right or is out of place. Even if it's a little thing. Let us know."

"Will do."

"Can you remember any other unusual run-ins with Snerd or with people who might be working with him?"

"Wait." Ashley hit her forehead with the heel of her hand. "Caleb, what about that night we went out for burgers and those two guys attacked us?"

"They could have been Snerd's men. They asked us for money and tried to rob us."

Strollo set down his Diet Coke. "They asked for money to distract you. If you would have pulled out your billfold, they would have pounced on you."

"They jumped us anyway, and I can tell you they regretted messing with me."

"You may not be so lucky next time. They don't play fair."

"I carry a Glock everywhere I go. They better not come after me."

"Let the police do their job, son. We've almost got what we need to start making arrests. When the prosecutor feels we have enough evidence, we'll stop the surveillance and take him down. It could even be just a matter of a couple of days. We'll move as soon as we can. Until then, don't go it alone. Stay in the hotel where we have you. We're closing in and will get them soon. Just be patient."

Ashley turned to Caleb. "I just remembered another thing. As I've thought about those two guys who came to my apartment that night, they were really trying to lure you to my place. I think I was only the bait to get you there so they could do bad things to you."

"Definitely what they were up to," Strollo said.

"When I was locked in the bathroom, I recognized one of the men's voices, but I didn't know from where. The high-pitched voice was the same one I heard from one of those guys that night at the burger joint."

"Yeah, Ash," Caleb said. "Probably the same guy."

"Their names were Geno and Lenny," she added.

"Yes, and that's in the police report from the interview you gave to Sergeant McColaugh."

"Lenny and Geno, and Geno had the high-pitched, creepy voice. I'll never forget that voice."

Caleb hit his forehead. "What a dummy. I almost forgot. Three guys jumped me one time after I had a meal with my boss. At the time, I thought it was because of his past involvement with the CIA, but there was no connection. The same hoodlums were trying to get me."

83

Over the lamb dinner, the conversation shifted to more pleasant topics like love and marriage—Ashley and Caleb's newest favorite topic. They caught each other's eyes. "Do you want to tell them, Ashley, or should I?"

"Go ahead, Caleb."

"Ashley and I are getting married. When I got back home, I proposed, and she accepted. We can't wait to tie the knot. You're the first people we've told. It's a secret until we make a public announcement."

"Congratulations. This calls for a toast." Samantha raised her glass. "To Ashley and Caleb: may your marriage bring you happiness, health, and prosperity."

Strollo raised his Diet Coke can. "Here. Here. Whatever that means."

After dinner, Strollo asked Caleb if he'd like to see his gun collection, and the two went off to check out Strollo's man cave while Samantha and Ashley cleaned the kitchen and put everything away.

"I heard you were a news anchor early in your career. I can believe it. You're as attractive as a movie star."

"Thank you, Ashley. So are you. Although I'm proud that I was Miss Arizona in my youth, beauty can be a drawback in the news business. Some think you're a mini-mind who only got the job for your looks. Women assume you're some kind of bimbo who slept her way to the anchor chair."

"I never thought of that."

"Good thing I'm not blond. It would have been way worse."

"Indeed."

"An attractive woman has pressure on her to demonstrate her knowledge and ability. We almost have to be twice as good at everything as men. In news, credibility is everything, and I had to establish that."

"I'm sure you did."

Samantha grinned. "Oh yeah."

"Now you're in human resources, right?"

"Yes, with the local television station."

"Samantha, I noticed at the cancer walk that you and Chief Strollo are a good team."

"Thank you. We are a good team. We have our problems like everyone else. I'm a neat freak, and he's a slob. My husband can manage to make even his Hawaiian shirt look disheveled. I eat healthy, loading up on vegetables and avoiding food that has been genetically modified. By contrast, Louis is hooked on Cheetos, potato chips, and Diet Coke. He could eat hot dogs and pizza every day if I'd let him. But I love that man dearly. He's got a heart as big as Briggs Lake and would do anything for anybody."

"Do you have kids?"

"No. Not together anyway. From our previous marriages, he has a rebellious daughter, and I have a clinging son. It's a good thing we have each other to commiserate with. They're not exactly model children."

Ashley's green eyes seemed to light up when she asked, "What makes a good marriage, Samantha?"

"Communication is a big key. We make time to be together. We're best friends. If something takes us away from each other for too long, we avoid it. That's why I joined him at the cancer walk. I'm glad to honor his deceased wife because she's a big part of the man I love. And that dog of his, Duke, gets hair all over my clothes, but Louis loves the pooch, so I love him too. In marriage you have to compromise. Another thing is that we don't try to change each other. We accept each other as we are."

"Thank you for sharing all this with me, Samantha. I'll take it all to heart."

⁂

Meanwhile, Strollo showed off the weapons, stored in three separate gun safes, that he had collected throughout his law enforcement career.

"Caleb, tell me about this job of yours. I hear you're working for a philanthropist."

"He's an old rich guy who wants to use his money to help people before he dies. It's been quite a learning experience for me."

"I can imagine. What are you going to do when this job ends?"

"I have no idea. I've thought about it a lot, Louis."

"Have you ever considered law enforcement?"

"Being a cop? No. Not really. My run-ins with MPs didn't inspire me to take up that line of work. Maybe that's because I was on the wrong side at the time." He laughed.

"There are bad cops, but they're in the minority. No one hates a dirty cop more than a good cop. There is a bond we share, probably similar to the one you had with your fellow soldiers. It's something special. I've done some research on you, and I think you have the qualities I look for in a police officer."

"I don't know about that, sir."

"You're a protector of other people. You served in the military protecting our country and your fellow soldiers. You're honest. You're physically fit and strong and have proven yourself in life-threatening situations by keeping a cool head. You've been trained to properly handle firearms. You seem to have a heart for service, which is required. Our motto is 'To Serve and Protect.'"

"Surviving war doesn't make me anything special. A lot of better men and women weren't so lucky."

"My research shows you were awarded the Distinguished Service Cross, the second highest military decoration. You only get that for extraordinary heroism in combat, risking your life."

"I was part of team, and I share it with my guys. Some of them made the ultimate sacrifice. They're the heroes, not me."

"I know what you mean, but I don't believe in coincidences or luck. You stood up to the biggest drug dealer in this part of Arizona. You've been entrusted with the wealth of a man you don't even know."

"Thank you for your confidence in me, but I'm not sure I could do that job."

"Caleb, law enforcement isn't just a job. It's a calling. I have two slots available for the next class at the police academy in January. I'd like to give one of them to you. I'll have my assistant drop off an application at your hotel tomorrow. You can call him with any questions. You've got until the end of August to make a decision. What do you think?"

"It's an open door. I'll think about it and talk to Ashley. She may not like the idea of me risking my life every day at work."

"All I ask is that you consider it."

"I will. Thank you for believing in me, Louis."

84

As they headed down the hill from the Strollo house, Ashley and Caleb were still trying to process that people were following them in hopes of killing Caleb. The magnitude of the threat shook them both.

Ashley took a deep breath. "Caleb, I'm worried about how this is going to end."

"Don't worry, honey. I can take care of myself, and I can take care of you too."

"I know you will, Caleb. Just be careful, mister."

"Yes, ma'am."

"What did you think of the Strollos?"

"I think the chief is a good man, no frills, the real deal. He's probably forgotten more about law enforcement than most people know. At heart, he's a good cop. He wants to serve and protect. And..."

"And what?"

"He wants me to apply for the police academy. He thinks I have what it takes to be a cop."

"A cop?"

"What do you think about your future husband being in law enforcement?"

"You mean when I send you off to work each day, I'll never know for sure if you're going to come home?"

"I can handle myself."

"You keep saying that. But what about me? What about my stress in worrying about you all the time?"

"He just asked me to think about it. I haven't made a decision yet."

"If you decide it's what you really want to do, I'll support you. In marriages couples have to compromise, and I'm willing to compromise. I learned that from Samantha."

"I'm willing to compromise too."

"Good. What did you think of Samantha?"

"I didn't know she was African American. They're like the odd couple. She's smoking hot, and he's an average Joe. He must have something going for him to snag a woman like that."

"Did you know she was Miss Arizona?"

"I believe it. What does she do for a living? Is she a fashion model?"

"She works at the local television station, Briggs News 20. She runs the human resources department, although she used to be a news anchor. A strong, powerful woman married to a strong, powerful man. They're a power couple."

"When those two fight, it must be like Armageddon."

"What makes you think they fight?"

"Every couple fights."

"We don't fight."

They both started laughing. When Caleb caught his breath, he turned to her and said, "Whatever you say, honey."

"Good. Now I'm getting somewhere, dear boy."

85

Johnny Jerman's monologue had just gotten underway, and the crowd showed their appreciation with unbridled laughter.

Johnny took a deep breath. "Before we go any further with this show, I have a sad announcement to make."

The crowd hushed, waiting for the news.

"Someone broke into the Ax Handle last night and stole our limbo stick." Shaking his head, he said, "Man, how low can you go?"

The audience cracked up, their laughter interrupted by the noisy entrance of Geno and Lenny as they stumbled toward a vacant table. Johnny stopped speaking and stared at them. "How did you guys get here? Did someone leave your cage open?"

The audience chuckled and stared at the two thugs who looked like their pictures should have been in the post office along with the FBI's most wanted.

"Oh, by the way, quick question—do you still love Mother Nature after what she did to you?"

Lenny's faced turned red. "Who the hell do you think you are, baldy?"

"My friends call me Johnny. You can call me Mr. Jerman."

"You think you're smart, don't you?"

"If you were twice as smart, you'd still be stupid."

Geno pointed at the comedian. "Oh, shut your face."

"If your brains were dynamite, there wouldn't be enough to blow your hat off."

The audience laughed.

Lenny threw his arm like he was air slapping the comedian. "That ain't even funny, chrome dome."

"What are you going to do for a face when the baboon wants its butt back?"

The audience chuckled again, glancing from the comedian to Lenny.

"Hey, funny boy, you're talking yourself into an early grave. Keep going."

The comedian folded his hands to his chest. "Oooooh. I'm scared. You're like Moby Dick…only without the Moby."

Lenny stood up. "You want to take this outside?"

Chad came out of nowhere. "That's enough. I'm sorry, gentlemen, but I'm going to have to ask you to leave."

Lenny shook his head. "We just got here. Mind your own business."

"I'm the bouncer. This is my business." Chad held his arms out. "Sorry, fellas, but people paid good money to see the comic, and you disrupted his set. We can't have that."

"We paid the cover, so we don't need to evaporate," Geno said and folded his arms.

"I'll refund your cover, but you can't stay here. Let's go, or I'll call the cops."

Lenny raised his arms. "What's wrong with you people?"

Chad stood his ground. "Let's go, guys. Now!"

The mobsters reluctantly followed the bouncer out to the applause of the audience. Geno turned around at the doorway and gave the crowd the middle finger salute with both hands.

Chad refunded their money and led them outside to the parking lot.

Lenny pulled a 9mm Smith & Wesson. "You disrespected us in front of a lot of people tonight, and we're not happy about it."

"I don't want any trouble here. I didn't mean to embarrass you. You were disrupting the show that people paid good money to watch. I'm just doing my job. It's nothing personal."

The hoods looked like they were trying to decide if they should answer or shoot him.

Chad remained calm and stared at them while saying a silent prayer.

Geno put his hand on Lenny's arm. "Let's get out of here, Lenny. It ain't worth it."

The two walked to Lenny's car and drove off. After traveling in silence for a few blocks, Lenny turned to Geno. "Why did you back down? We should have wasted that guy."

Geno shrugged. "I couldn't care less about the guy."

"I wasn't going to shoot him—just hold the gun on him while you beat him up, but I guess you're getting soft, Geno."

"The guy we're supposed to illiterate is the old bouncer, not the new one."

"If you say so. Whatever. I got an idea. Let's go to the Parker Dam. I've got some coke. Let's do some blow and watch the waterfall."

"That's a good idea, Lenny. Now you're thinking."

86

Water rumbled over the Parker Dam, and the area was dark and deserted. After snorting some coke in the car, they got out to watch the water go over the dam. Geno walked to the edge and observed the running water below. "What a beautiful sight, Lenny. This beats listening to some no-name comic." He turned around and saw Lenny pointing his pistol at him.

"What's this about?"

"You're a rat, Geno. Snerd put a contract out on you, and I'm doing the job."

"I didn't give up nothin' to nobody. I'm not the stoolie." He started walking toward Lenny. "We're pals. We came up together, Lenny. Remember all we been through."

Lenny fired. The bullet went through Geno's chest and ripped a gaping hole in his back, throwing him to the ground faceup. Lenny dragged the bloody corpse to the edge of the walkway and kicked it over the dam. *Sorry, Geno. Nothing personal. This is business. I was just doing my job. The funny thing is, you were killed for being a rat—by the rat.*

87

"Mr. Stockbridge, this is Caleb. How are you feeling?"

"I've been better, and I've been worse."

"We need to talk. Feel like going for a boat ride?"

"I can't go anywhere right now. Not up to it. Let's talk now."

"Remember when I was jumped by those three goons after we met for lunch?"

"They beat you up so badly you thought they broke your nose."

"Right, but I put a hurt on them too. And there was the time I told you when Ashley and I went out for burgers and we were jumped in the parking lot by two guys."

"You thought they were trying to rob you."

"Yeah. You told me you did some work for the CIA. You were going to check to see if you had an old enemy out to get you. Were you able to learn anything?"

"Nothing. I couldn't find any evidence of someone coming after me for my past undercover work. That's why I never brought it up again."

"That's what I thought, Mr. Stockbridge. Those incidents don't have anything to do with you. They're coming after me. Derek Snerd, the guy you saw me throw out of the bar that night, is a Mafia don, and he put a contract out on me."

"Mafia? In Briggs Lake?"

"Turns out Snerd's based in Las Vegas, but his territory includes western Arizona, and he's connected to a Mexican drug cartel. The police are investigating his operation and closing in. His boys have been tailing me and Ashley, and the cops have been tailing them, if you can believe that."

"You're being followed?"

"They're watching me for opportunities to kill me. Ashley and I are in a secret place for a couple of days. The cops will be springing the trap soon. Until then, we have to lay low."

"Please keep me posted."

"Heard anything about Chewy? She's not answering my calls or texts. I'm afraid something's happened to her."

"I haven't heard anything from Chewy or Sean, her head of security. It was a dangerous mission; everyone knew that. Maybe they're not near a cell tower, or it could mean—"

"That they're dead. One more thing—I asked Ashley to marry me."

"Congratulations, Caleb. That's great news. I'm happy for you both."

Stockbridge's young employee couldn't see his face, but he felt the smile and the happiness that emanated from the other end of the phone.

88

"Are you about done on the phone?" Ashley yelled from the kitchen. The mouthwatering smell of fresh popcorn permeated the air and made its way to the bedroom, where Caleb sat on the bed. When he joined her in the kitchen, he took a deep breath and inhaled the aroma. "Popcorn. I hope you're slathering all sorts of butter on it."

"I am. Who were you talking to?"

"Mr. Stockbridge. I wanted to fill him in on what we learned from Chief Strollo and share the good news of our engagement."

"What did he say?"

"Congratulations and that he's happy for both of us."

"What's wrong? You don't look good."

"One of the people I helped for Stockbridge was a college professor who's gone missing in Iraq. I'm afraid she might have been killed."

"I'm so sorry. Maybe she's just lost. At any rate, there's nothing you can do about it. Let's watch some old movies and try to take our minds off all the drama."

They stayed up late watching flicks on the hotel couch, munching popcorn, and taking breaks to make out until finally falling asleep, leaving the television blaring infomercials in the darkened room.

89

Chief Strollo worked late that night. He sat at his desk sipping a Diet Coke and munching on Cheetos as he went over in his mind all the details of the next day's operation. He called Samantha, informing her that he would fix himself something when he came home, so she should eat dinner by herself, go to bed, and not try to wait up for him.

With the danger to Caleb and Ashley more acute, he made the decision to spring the trap on Snerd the next morning. A late-afternoon call to the district attorney confirmed there was enough probable cause to get the warrant for Snerd's arrest. At the same time, Strollo planned to arrest Lenny Colleti and Geno Schlubb. The plan was to arrest the three at their homes at four o'clock a.m. Each would be squeezed to be informants on the other two in exchange for lighter sentences.

This would be the culmination of a nearly two-year operation to trace the drug cartel's street revenue to the man at the top, Derek Snerd. Caleb and Ashley would be safe tonight, and by tomorrow the threats to their lives would be removed. Strollo wanted to make sure he hadn't missed any evidence or detail in planning the takedown that would hinder the prosecution of the case. There would be no chances for do-overs, so this had to be done by the book. If defense attorneys found one technical illegality, no matter how minor, or one procedure not consistent with the department's protocol, they could get these criminals off, and they'd walk.

Across town, Artie and Chad followed Rosie home after work. After paying the babysitter and checking on Seth and Sarah, she offered drinks to the men, which they gladly accepted.

"Is there anything you can tell me about her? I've been trying to call her, but she doesn't pick up."

"Chad, that's because the guys who broke into her apartment stole her phone. She had to use my phone at first, and then she got another number, but she asked me not to give it out."

"Artie told me what happened when he got back to our apartment, so I let Joyce know when I went into work."

"Why did you do that?"

"I thought she should know."

"That's why everyone knew all about it. You should have let Ashley call Joyce. Please don't say anything else. Ashley will share what's going on at the appropriate time."

"I won't. Sorry. Just trying to be helpful. I'm worried about her."

"We all are. Ashley will be in a secret place for a few days. That's all she told me, so please don't spread that around."

"If you talk to her, tell her if she needs anything to let me know."

"Sure."

"I'll be going back to our apartment so you and Artie can have some time alone."

The roommates touched knuckles, and Chad left.

90

With the precision of a military operation, the SWAT members divided into three groups to simultaneously arrest Lenny Colleti, Geno Schlubb, and Derek Snerd. Captain Emily Alvarez led the ten-man Alpha team to Derek Snerd's house and circled it. They knew their target was armed and dangerous, so they took their time getting into place.

She pounded on the door. "This is the police."

Wrapped in his girlfriend Ginger's arms and more than half-drunk, Snerd wasn't sure if he was dreaming.

"This is the police. Open the door, please."

That left no doubt this was real. Snerd scrambled out of bed and glanced at his Smith & Wesson .38 Special. It was loaded and ready on his nightstand.

"Give me a minute. I'm coming. Calm down." He slipped on a bathrobe and stuffed the handgun in the right pocket. He noticed that Ginger was sitting up in bed, horrified. "No worries, sugar buns. There must be some mistake."

I shouldn't have given my bodyguards the night off so that I could have privacy with Ginger. Big mistake. Now what do I do? I'll either have to escape if I can or shoot my way out.

"Hey, Ginger. Put on your robe, sweet cheeks. Let's answer the door together."

"Derek, it's late. I'm tired." She slipped on a beige silk robe that Derek had given her from one of his trips to Mexico. "The things I do for you."

When she got close to him, he held her hand, and they walked down the hallway to the front door. He unlocked it and then backpedaled, grabbing Ginger and putting the .38 to her temple. "Do what I say, Ginger." Then to the police: "Come in. The door's unlocked."

The door slowly pushed open, and the cops saw Snerd standing about twenty feet away with his left arm around Ginger and his right arm holding the .38 Special to her temple. Four SWAT members entered and took positions, two on each side of the door. Alvarez stood in the open doorway.

"If you step any closer, I'll blow her brains out."

"I'm Captain Emily Alvarez. You're under arrest. Cooperate and no one will get hurt. You can call your lawyer. If you've done nothing wrong, you'll be set free."

"It's not that simple. I want a safe escape out of here, or I'll kill her. Understand?"

Ginger started shaking and crying. "Please don't kill me, Derek. I love you."

"I want to talk to the head guy."

"Who are you talking about?"

"The police chief. What's his name—Stiletto or something like that?"

Alvarez took a deep breath. "You mean Chief Strollo. I'll give him a call." She backed out of the house, went to her cruiser, and called Strollo on the radio. In fifteen tense minutes, Strollo was on the scene. After being briefed outside by Alvarez, he entered the house.

"I'm Louis Strollo. You asked to talk to me?"

"I want to negotiate a safe passage out of here. Let me go, and I won't hurt her."

"How do you expect to escape? Even if we were to let you get in the car and go somewhere, law enforcement in other jurisdictions will pick you up. Your best option is to surrender. You can call your lawyer and start a legal defense."

Snerd's head cleared, realizing the futility of his situation. He was outnumbered and outgunned. He figured he had only two options—surrender or kill as many cops as he could.

Ginger broke free from his grasp and ran for the door. Snerd shot her in the back, then turned the gun on Strollo and hit him twice in the chest. The top cop dropped to the floor, pulled his Beretta 92 out of its shoulder holster, and fired one shot into the center of Snerd's chest, blasting his body back twelve feet and killing him instantly.

Alvarez ran up to Strollo. "Are you okay, Chief?"

He got up and holstered his pistol. "I'm fine. His bullets hit my Kevlar vest. It was like getting punched in the chest twice, but I'm all right."

A siren announced the arrival of an ambulance. Snerd was pronounced dead at the scene. First responders worked on Ginger for a half hour to stabilize her heart and staunch the blood before carrying her to the ambulance. She died on the way to the hospital.

The Bravo team, led by Sergeant McColaugh, arrested Lenny without incident in the home he shared with a woman and her young son. He proclaimed his innocence all the way to the police department.

When no one answered the door, Juan Romero's Delta team broke into Geno's home. The putrid smell of spoiled leftovers in the sink indicated he hadn't been there in quite a while. The San Bernardino Sheriff's Department recovered his body the next day when it floated to the surface of the Colorado River.

91

With the threat to their lives removed, Caleb and Ashley used their time off to get settled and develop their relationship. They bought a house on the south side with a view of the lake. When the bank turned down their mortgage for lack of income, Richard Stockbridge pulled some strings and provided enough financial guarantees to get the loan approved. It would be several months before the couple realized he had paid off the mortgage so that they would own it free and clear.

Crystal Glade quit the Ax without notice, so Joyce asked Ashley to return earlier than expected. Ashley and Caleb decided to announce their upcoming wedding and celebrate their new home before Ashley had to go back to work. The couple invited Artie, Rosie, Chad, and the Strollos over for a barbecue. The house had a shaded swimming pool and a sound system that could entertain the entire neighborhood. Caleb cooked the steaks while chatting with Louis Strollo at the grill.

"Those steaks smell delicious, Caleb. You might even get Samantha to eat one."

"She should. It's not every day Chef Caleb works his magic."

Chad and Artie played catch with the Frisbee in the pool while Ashley, Rosie, and Samantha sat in lounge chairs wearing big hats, chatting and drinking white wine. They could have been in the front row at the Kentucky Derby. Rosie thought Artie looked pretty good in a swimsuit and watched him closely while talking with the other women.

Samantha noticed Rosie eyeing Artie. "Are you and Artie dating?"

"We're seeing each other a lot, but we haven't defined it. I like him, and he likes me. He's good to my kids. We're taking it one day at a time and enjoying each other's company."

"I can tell you think a lot of him by the way you're watching him. I'm in HR. People and their motivations are my business."

Ashley smiled. "I thought HR departments were designed by management to keep the unions out and the company from getting sued."

"What a cynic you are, Ashley," she said with a smile. "To me, I'm helping to foster and maintain a fair and safe workplace that provides all employees an equal opportunity for training and advancement."

"Steaks are done! Everyone out of the pool. I don't want them to get cold." Caleb wielded his barbecue fork like it was a sword.

Ashley sprang into action, pulling her salad out of the refrigerator while Caleb put the steaks and baked potatoes on several platters and brought them to the table. Their guests waited for Ashley to direct the seating.

She placed Artie, Rosie, and Chad on one side, Samantha and Louis on the other side, and herself and Caleb on each end. "Before we get started, Caleb and I have an announcement to make. Caleb?"

"Yes. One of the reasons we invited you all over, besides the housewarming, was to announce that Ashley and I are getting married. I proposed, and she said yes."

Everyone clapped and congratulated the young couple. "Now let's eat," Ashley said. "Who would like to say grace?"

Chad raised his hand. "I will. Heavenly Father, thank you for your blessing on this food, on the people who prepared it, and on everyone in the food chain, from the growers to the supermarket. May we receive good nourishment and strength while we enjoy the fellowship of our friends. Amen."

Ashley lifted her fork. "Thank you, Chad. Bon appétit."

Samantha took a big bite. "Delicious, Caleb. You're a man of many talents."

"Thank you, Samantha. Glad you're not a total vegetarian."

"It's hard to be a vegan when smelling steaks grilled to perfection." She turned to face Chad. "Nice prayer. I understand you and Artie are religious and go to the same church."

"Yes, ma'am. Though we don't consider ourselves religious. We believe true Christianity is not a religion but a relationship between a

Heavenly Father and his children. In our view denominations spend too much time finding fault with each other over their different interpretations of the Bible and not enough time on the common mission—to spread the good news about Jesus."

"What church do you go to?"

"New Life Christian Fellowship. It's an ecumenical ministry based on Jesus's teachings. The Bible says the church is the Christian believers—not the building where they worship. While it's good for Christians to hang out together, going to church doesn't make you a Christian."

"What does?"

"The Bible says in Romans ten that when you make Jesus your Lord and say it out loud, and when you believe God raised him from the dead, you're saved—you're a Christian, and you'll have everlasting life."

"Interesting."

Ashley set her fork down. "Samantha, Chad gave us the name of the person who had this house for sale."

Caleb pointed at Chad. "We needed to find something fast before we went back to work, and you came through. Thanks again, buddy."

"Glad I could help. The previous owner of this house, Lonnie Elswick, goes to our fellowship."

Samantha's mouth widened, and her eyes got brighter. "I know Lonnie. He's the chief engineer at our TV station, Briggs News 20. Good man. He knows his stuff. We nicknamed him Eastwick because most people mispronounce his name that way—and it stuck."

"He told us that," Chad said.

"One of our Briggs News 20 viewers called one time for help getting a cat out of a tree, so Lonnie went over there to do the job, and a camera crew followed him."

Chad smiled. "Did he get the cat down?"

"Yeah, and the story made the eleven o'clock news. It was a slow news day. Artie, I understand you're a musician. Rosie and I were talking about that earlier."

"Yes. I play bass in a band called Armor of God, but I'm a substitute teacher in my day job. Our band taped a music video and recorded a studio album, but they flopped. We're trying to become a money band so we can play music full-time."

After putting down her fork, Samantha pointed her finger at Artie. "Never judge something by its immediate response. The movie *It's a Wonderful Life* was released on Christmas Day in 1946 and lost five hundred twenty-five thousand dollars, which was a lot of money in those days. No one went to see it. Hardly anyone. There was no buzz about it. Critics tore it apart, and it didn't win any big awards. But now it's considered one of the best Christmas movies ever made."

"Thanks, Samantha. I'll keep that in mind."

"Save room for dessert, everybody," Ashley interrupted.

Louis folded his napkin and placed it on the table in front of him. "That was a tasty steak dinner. You're a master chef, Caleb. Thank you so much. I'm going to go outside before dessert and smoke a cigar. Anyone care to join me?"

"You men go out with Louis. We'll clean up the dinner so we can engage in some girl talk," Samantha said.

"That way we can gossip about you guys," Rosie said.

The men followed Louis over to the pool area, and he passed out cigars to Caleb, Chad, and Artie. Caleb enjoyed a good cigar occasionally and had just quit cigarettes. Chad and Artie were nonsmokers but didn't want to turn down Strollo.

"Chad, you and Ashley did an exemplary job at the cancer walk with your team. We saw so much enthusiasm and excitement. Your leadership stood out."

"Thanks, Louis, but it was mostly Ashley. She has a way with people, and everyone at the Ax loves her." Chad turned his gaze to Caleb. "You're a blessed guy to have a woman like that. When I first started working at the Ax, I had a crush on her, but she only had eyes for you."

"Chad, Ashley has always spoken highly of you. She said you were always a gentleman. That actually made me jealous. I kept wishing you weren't such a good guy."

Chad laughed. "Lot of good it did me. You won her heart, not me."

"I had a head start, and I'm grateful I did," Caleb said with a smile. "Louis, how did you and Samantha meet?"

92

"I was doing a murder investigation at Briggs News 20, and she helped me set up interviews with some of the staff. We were both doing our jobs in a professional manner, yet I must admit, we were definitely attracted to each other."

"Was it love at first sight?" Artie asked.

"No. I thought she had a boyfriend. It turned out to be her son. Couldn't imagine she would be single. I liked her a lot, but I was a widower and had my hands full with a teenage daughter. We weren't looking for love, but it found us."

"Right after Ashley and I connected, I was fired for protecting her from Derek Snerd," Caleb noted.

"Are you seeing anyone, Chad?"

"Not right now, Chief Strollo. I'm focusing on putting God first in my life."

Artie held his hand up. "I'll translate. What he's saying is that he prays night and day for God to get him a girlfriend."

Chad puffed his cigar and blew smoke in Artie's direction. "Very funny, wise guy."

Artie wasn't finished. "He prays a lot because he knows it will take a miracle from God for any girl to be attracted to him."

Everyone laughed.

"Forget the music career," Chad said. "You should be doing stand-up at the Ax Handle."

"No. It's more entertaining just making fun of you."

Ashley poked her head out of the sliding patio door. "Come on inside, guys. Dessert's ready—chocolate cake and ice cream."

"My favorite," Strollo said as he put out his cigar in an ashtray. Caleb set his cigar aside so he could finish it later. Chad and Artie followed suit, thankful for an excuse to ditch the stogies.

Caleb hustled to the sliding door. "Honey, why don't we have the dessert out here and watch the sunset? I'll help you bring everything out."

"No. Stay there. We'll bring it all out."

Turning to the guys standing near the pool, Caleb motioned for them to stay where they were. "Dessert is coming to us. It would be a shame to waste a beautiful Briggs Lake sunset."

"Go ahead and start without me." Artie ran into the house.

"What's with him?" Strollo asked.

"He doesn't normally smoke," Chad explained. "I think he went to toss his cookies."

The ladies brought out the dessert plates. Everyone settled back and enjoyed their cake and ice cream while watching the Arizona sunset, marveling at the reds, oranges, purples, and yellows as the sun said goodbye for the day.

93

The next night after an early dinner, Caleb and Ashley sat by their pool sipping a couple of beers, reminiscing over their first dinner party.

"It turned out even better than I thought," Ashley said. She tilted her can to Caleb. "We're pretty good at this hosting thing, aren't we, babe?"

He lifted his Coors Light toward her. "Yes, we are, honey."

"I think the Strollos are a phenomenal couple. I asked her what the key to a good relationship was, and she mentioned two things that stuck with me—communication and compromise. Even though they are two different people, they make the time to communicate, and when they have conflicts, they compromise."

"Speaking of communication, remember when I explained that I had to keep my work for Stockbridge on the down low, you assumed I was hiding things from you—not being honest? After you broke up with me, he told me I could share things with you if that would help our relationship. Stockbridge made a point that he didn't want his assignments to hurt us."

"I wish you would have told me that then, dude."

"I did tell you, remember? But you said we were through. If I would have pursued you any more after that, you would have had me arrested for stalking you."

"I don't think I was that bad."

"Oh, you were. You had already made up your mind."

"I may have said that, but only because you weren't as serious as I was about taking our relationship to the next level. You had my heart all along, but I knew you had decisions to make about your future before we could go on."

"You had my heart too, although I didn't realize it. Anyway, I want to share about my work now, especially about three of the women I spent time with. Are you okay with that?"

She smiled. "Three women, huh? I see you kept yourself busy, dude."

"It's not like that. Can I tell you about them?"

"You don't have to share anything. I'm over all that jealousy. I trust you."

"I want you to know you can trust me in the future because even when you dumped me, I still was faithful to you."

She set her can down, jumped up, and hugged him. "You sweet man. I love you so much."

"And I love you. Now sit down, and I'll give you the short versions, and you can ask any questions you want."

"All right. Let's go for it." She sat back down in her patio chair. "I'm listening."

"Danielle Stevens had a dream of owning her own coffee shop. I had to get to know her to find that out. Once I knew that was her dream, Stockbridge came up with the seed money to get her started. On the side, she's a children's author, and I found out later she has a daughter."

"And no boyfriend?"

"Not that I know of. She said if I sent her my address, she'd send me a signed copy of her book. That's all there was to that. Any questions?"

"No. Go on."

"There's another woman I was with three times, and it had nothing to do with my work for Stockbridge. I met her on the plane to New York; we sat in the same row. Lily's from Parker and went to the big city to audition for acting roles."

"I imagine since she's an actress, Lily is gorgeous."

"She's okay."

"Just okay?"

"She's good-looking in an actress sort of way—photogenic with engaging eyes, and she enunciates her words. Not as attractive as you, though."

"Good answer, dude. It's kind of shocking that you had this little relationship in New York when you were supposed to be dog sitting."

"It wasn't a relationship. I had a conversation on the plane. Then we talked about going to dinner while we were there."

"Go on."

"Remember, you had broken up with me. I was single and unattached."

"Aren't they the same thing?"

"Don't nitpick me. Talking about this stuff is hard enough."

"Go on."

"So we went to dinner one night to a dive bar and listened to a blues piano player, Ivory Williams, who was quite the entertainer. We had a pleasant evening together."

"And?"

"And nothing happened except a hug at the end of the night. Then a while later she got mugged and couldn't get in her apartment, so I picked her up and brought her to Anthony's, gave her dinner, and she spent the night."

"And?"

"And nothing happened. I slept on the couch with the dog, until the dog abandoned me to go in the bedroom so he could sleep with her."

"That's pretty funny. The dog got more action that night than you did."

He chuckled. "Honestly, I had the same thought myself. Anyway, I had my dream in the middle of the night—you know, about Nick. If there was any thought in her mind about us getting together, that was kind of a buzzkill. No woman wants to be with a man who has those kinds of psycho dreams."

"I do."

"I know. You're special."

"You may not realize this, dear boy, but she was hitting on you and wanted you to sleep with her—dreams and all."

"I doubt it."

"One hundred percent. Now I'm starting to get jealous—for real."

"Nothing happened, honey. She did call me after that and said she left her diamond necklace in the room and asked if I could I find it for her."

"That's an old trick women use. They leave something at a guy's house that will require him to see her again. It also marks the territory in case another woman comes over."

"Do you really think women are that devious?"

"You don't? Go on."

"When she called, I was already out of town and on my way to another job, so I gave her Anthony's phone number. He found her heirloom necklace, and they arranged a dinner date for him to return it. The rest is history. He'll be my best man at the wedding, so you'll get a chance to meet her."

"I can hardly wait."

"Ashley!"

"Go on."

"The third woman I spent time with was a Virginia professor of ancient languages, named Dr. Huang—her nickname was Chewy. You remember me mentioning a professor I helped who was missing?"

"Did they ever find out where she is?"

"No. I'm afraid she probably killed herself when she was captured. We went out to eat a couple of times, and she gave me a tour of Richmond."

"I imagine she was a beauty too. You never seem to be around ugly women."

"She's a nice-looking woman but much older, I'd say midforties. Her husband was recently tortured and killed by Islamic militants. They were in the Middle East to scan ancient scrolls, and she still grieves for him."

"I'm sorry to hear that."

"We retained a security detail to protect her in Iraq and Syria. Her goal was to finish the project she and her husband were on when he was killed." He shook his head. "Now she and her security team are missing."

"I'm so sorry. Sounds like you two had a connection."

"We did. Considering the fact we were only together a handful of times, I feel like we really developed a friendship. Chewy asked all about you. I told her about your beauty, brains, and heart and that you had kicked me to the curb. I told her I thought I loved you but had never said it to you."

"What did she say to that?"

"She said to go home and tell you I love you and then tell you I love you every day for the rest of my life."

"It's hard to be jealous of a woman like that."

"And another thing. When she gave me the tour of Richmond, she bought a handmade bracelet that she really loved. When I said goodbye to her at the airport, she gave the bracelet to me and said she had bought it for you."

He reached under his chair to fetch a small gift-wrapped box and handed it to Ashley.

When she opened it, her eyes lit up, and her mouth broadened into a big smile. "Thank you so much. I love it."

"Chewy said you would." He looked at the ceiling. "Thank you, Chewy."

Ashley smiled as she admired the bracelet.

"Any more questions?"

"No."

"That's it—all my contact with other women while we were broken up."

She reached over and hugged him. "You didn't have to tell me all that, but I'm glad you did."

94

At the housewarming party, Chad had invited Caleb to a free personal training lesson at Sampson's Gym, where he worked part-time. Taking his new student on a circuit of the weight machines, he gave precise instructions, concise corrections, and constant encouragement.

"I've done a lot of PT in the military, Chad, but you've shown me a lot today about getting stronger without injuring myself by over-doing it. You know your stuff, and your passion for physical training is contagious."

"Thanks, Caleb. I love doing it. It's fun helping others get stronger, and it keeps me fit and flourishing. If you like people as I do, it's the perfect job."

"After doing a few of the machines, I got exhausted. Now I'm feeling stronger and seem to have more stamina than when we started out."

"That's the phenomenon we call a second wind or a runner's high. When you push yourself until you're out of breath and exhausted, suddenly you can find renewed strength and can perform better with less effort."

"Yeah. It's weird. I'm not tired at all now."

"I've experienced a second wind running marathons. They kick your butt—you run more than twenty-six miles. Any marathoner will tell you that something kicks in about the twentieth or the twenty-first mile—runners bottom out. Then the second wind hits, and they can run those last six miles at a faster pace and with less effort than the first twenty."

"That's amazing."

"Research indicates that during rigorous exercise, the body's release of endorphins and the dynamics of aerobic metabolism are two of the drivers that trigger the second wind. Whatever the cause, when athletes push themselves to exhaustion, the second wind kicks in, giving them renewed strength and energy."

"Army training taught me that our minds underestimate what our bodies are capable of doing. In combat, when the adrenaline jacked me up, I did things physically I never thought I'd be able to do."

"Adrenaline also gives us a physical boost when we're under stress—it's called the fight-or-flight reaction. Consistent physical training, aiming for optimal fitness, is important because the more strength and stamina a person has to begin with, the more they will benefit from the second wind and an adrenaline rush in emergencies."

"That makes sense. I've been meaning to ask you about something. You and Samantha Strollo were talking about your church at the barbecue. Are you studying to be a minister?"

"If you mean going to a seminary and getting a degree to preach from a pulpit—no. To minister means to serve. Any believer can minister without going to a seminary and getting a degree. My church is the gym, and I work best with people one-on-one, not in groups. Not everyone is called to run a church or to preach. That's not my calling. Jesus didn't always preach to thousands either. A lot of times, he ministered to one person at a time."

"You're good at working with people individually in a gym setting. I can see that."

"Thanks. I'm licensed to officiate at weddings, but otherwise I'm not a paid clergyman. There are people whose occupation is to run religious organizations who work full-time building churches and equipping the believers. Pastoring wasn't always a profession or an occupation.

"Jesus started out in life as tradesman—a carpenter and builder. Paul, the apostle who wrote most of the letters of the New Testament, supported himself in a secular job as a tentmaker and leather craftsman during the week. On the Sabbath he preached in the synagogues and sometimes in marketplaces."

"That's amazing. I never heard that before."

"Paul didn't want to be a financial burden to anyone or to be accused of doing it for the money, so he offered his ministry free of charge."

"You're planning to go full-time as a trainer?"

"That's the goal. What about you? What do you do, if you don't mind me asking?"

"I represent a wealthy guy and run errands for him. I like it, but it's temporary. Chief Strollo invited me to apply for the police academy."

"I think you would be good at that. It's easy to see you as a policeman."

"Why do you say that? Is it the short hair?"

"Maybe." He smiled. "No. Not that. You're a warrior with training in self-defense and weapons. You like to help people. You have experience thinking on your feet in life-or-death situations. What does Ashley think?"

"She's not thrilled about the idea. She'll support me if that's what I decide."

Chad spotted Caleb while he did more reps on the bench press. Another trainer approached. Blond streaks cascaded throughout her brown hair, which she'd pulled back in a ponytail. "Prayer Power" was scripted in white letters across her forest green tank top. A pair of black yoga pants and Asics trainers completed her outfit.

"Chad, I see you've got another victim in your clutches."

"Hi, Carol. I'd like to introduce you to Caleb. He's trying to do bench presses and would say hello if he could, but he has an oxygen deprivation problem right now and can't speak for himself."

"Nice to meet you, Carol. I've got plenty of oxygen, no thanks to this sadistic monster, who is doing his best to give me a heart attack."

"Don't worry. If you have a heart attack, I'm trained in CPR."

"Good to know. Thanks."

She swaggered toward the front desk.

"Carol's husband's a police sergeant. You should ask her what it's like being the wife of a cop. Let's get to work on those abs. You're too young to get a potbelly."

"I don't have a potbelly. I do a hundred sit-ups every morning, my man."

"Consider this preventive maintenance."

95

The next day Caleb got a call from Stockbridge. "How did the housewarming party go?"

"Perfectly, Mr. Stockbridge. I wish you could have been there. How are you feeling these days?"

"I've been better, and I've been worse. I appreciated the invitation, but I'm limited by my health. Are you ready to get back to work?"

"Yes, sir."

"Good. I had hoped to do three more, but your next assignment will be your last. It's in Puyallup, Washington. It's the location of Washington's state fair, which happens to be in the top ten of all state fairs in America. Over a million people attend. The whole city is built around the fairgrounds."

"I'm going to the fair?"

Stockbridge laughed. "No. Just telling you what the city is famous for. There's a man there named Ari Hassan who gave me a break when I needed one. I was so distraught at the time, I even had thoughts of suicide."

"I can't imagine you ever being in that place."

"Oh yes, I was. Hassan not only gave me a job but also gave me hope that things would get better—and they did. One of the greatest things we can give someone else is hope."

"Right."

"He and I reconnected while you were on break, and I tried to give something back to Hassan in return for how he helped me when I needed it. He refused anything personally, but he asked me to pay it forward with his son, Ali."

"What's going on with his son?"

"He wants to kill himself."

"Why?"

"He's lost hope. Ali has recently been fired after a long and prosperous career, and he can't accept it. He's at the point of ending his life over it."

"Excuse me, sir, but I can't wrap my head around a guy killing himself over a damned job. That makes no sense."

"Suicide never makes sense. You would be surprised by how many people take their own lives each year after losing a job. For those people, their job was their purpose in life, their only reason for living."

"I'd never do it."

"Imagine putting your job ahead of your health, your family, your friends, your hobbies—making it your God—and sacrificing everything else in pursuit of your career. Then one day, the career is taken away from you, and you have nothing."

"That's sad."

"Yes. Your final project is Ali Hassan, my friend's son. Ali was laid off after serving his Fortune 500 company for twenty-five years. He's devastated and suicidal."

"How can I help?"

"I want you to set up a counseling session with one of Washington's top psychiatric counselors, Holly Starr. She's got the professional training and experience to help Mr. Hassan."

"When do I go?"

"Tomorrow. One more thing. I've told my friend that I want you to sit in on the counseling session, and he and his son have agreed to that."

"Why do I have to sit in on it?"

"I want you to listen and learn from the discussion. There will be things said that will help you for the rest of your life."

96

When Caleb broke the news to Ashley that he would be going to Washington, she wasn't happy.

"Why do you always have to do jobs out of town? Can't Stockbridge send you on assignments closer to home?" Ashley's veins were bulging on her temples, and her face was crimson.

"This is the final job for Stockbridge."

"Where the hell is Pollywog, Washington, anyway?"

"It's not Pollywog. It's pronounced pew-AL-up, and it's about twenty miles from Seattle."

"Where's Seattle?"

"Oh, stop it, honey. You're messing with me now."

"And I've said over and over that I need you here with me. That's how we drifted apart the last time. What about that police academy application?"

"I filled out the application, and I'll mail it before I go. We need this income to pay for our house, remember? Are we going through this every time I go to work for the rest of our lives?"

"The very last job. Are you sure?"

"Yes. He's never lied to me."

Ashley started crying. He walked over and hugged her.

97

When Caleb landed at Sea-Tac International Airport, he contacted Holly Starr and Ali Hassan and arranged a meeting at her office. Caleb arrived ahead of time and briefed Starr on the client from information he received from Stockbridge. They retreated to her conference room, and she left instructions with her assistant to call her when Hassan arrived.

"I'll get Mr. Hassan pointed in the right direction and away from thoughts of suicide. It may take several meetings, but if he'll embrace my process, I'll get him out of this funk."

"I think he will. From what I can gather, he really wants the help."

"People need to admit they have a problem and be willing to ask for help. Then they must cooperate and follow the suggestions offered to overcome the crisis."

"Makes sense."

"If you don't mind my asking, how does your boss know this guy?"

"He's the son of my boss's friend. His father helped my boss when he was down and out. Unfortunately, the man isn't able to do the same thing for his own son that he could do for his friend."

"That happens. Why does he want you to sit in on the session?"

"He thinks by listening I will learn things that will help me the rest of my life."

She frowned. "Unless it's a family member, third parties are rarely allowed to attend counseling sessions."

"My understanding is that the client has agreed in advance to this arrangement."

"All right. You'll have to sign a nondisclosure agreement promising to keep the session confidential. You'll also need to indemnify me if your involvement causes any legal problems for either Mr. Hassan or myself by signing a hold harmless agreement. Understood?"

"Yes."

She slid the documents across the table to him. "Sign where the arrows are pointing."

Starr's phone rang, indicating Hassan's arrival. She hustled to the lobby and escorted him back to the conference room.

Ali Hassan's silver-colored hair and well-trimmed beard made him appear more like a distinguished university president than a top-level executive for an international corporation. His gray, 100 percent worsted wool suit revealed an elegant taste and a shirt that did not need a tie to dress it up.

"Mr. Hassan, this is Mr. Caleb Sinclair, who will be sitting in on our meeting. He signed a confidentiality agreement and a hold harmless document that will indemnify both of us for any legal matters that arise from his involvement in the counseling session. I understand you have agreed to this in advance. Is that correct?"

"Yes."

"Then please sign this." She handed him a document, and he signed it.

Ali Hassan extended his hand to Caleb. "I have no problem with you sitting in on this session, sir. I've got nothing to hide, and I know you are part of a team that wants to help me. Please call me Ali."

Caleb smiled, then stared at Ali's watch.

"I see you like my watch."

"Yes, sir. It's a beauty."

"It's called a Ulysse Nardin Diver Deep Dive. It's a special edition Navy SEAL watch. It's worth about twelve thousand dollars."

"Awesome."

"I collect expensive watches. It's my guilty pleasure."

"I wouldn't feel guilty about owning that," the young veteran said with a smile. He held up his wrist. "I'm a Timex man myself."

"The dirty little secret is that cheap watches keep better time than expensive ones—in most cases."

"Who knew?"

Eager to get on with the counseling session, Starr held out both arms. "Gentlemen, please be seated." They sat around her solid oak table with the shiny finish in comfortable leather chairs—bottled water, yellow notepads, and pens in front of them.

Ali Hassan sat quickly and folded his hands on the table. Caleb settled into his chair and rocked it back and forth as though taking it for a test ride.

"Ali, why don't you start by telling us what the situation is and what emotions you are feeling? We'll come up with a game plan to help you adjust to the situation."

"After getting a degree in computer programming, I got my dream job in a Fortune 500 company. For the next twenty-five years, I worked tirelessly, sacrificing time with my family and my wife, working long hours, and neglecting my health. I've served as the vice president of our most profitable regional operation."

Holly tilted her bottle and took a sip of water, then wiped her mouth with a napkin and set the bottle down. "Congratulations. It sounds like you've been quite successful, Ali."

"I've been rewarded richly in dollars, honors, and perks. There's been chatter that I could become the next CEO."

"So what is the problem with all that? It sounds like you knew what you wanted in life and you got it."

"True. I made choices that cost me in other ways. If you want something as bad as I wanted my career, it becomes the priority. I've sacrificed everything for it."

"It's a balancing act. We want to be successful in our jobs, and at the same time we want to have good health, friends, family relationships, and fun."

Ali began rubbing his fingertips on the table in circles, trying to find the words to start relating his problems, finally deciding just to say it. "I gave up all those things. Then I got fired. Now I have nothing to live for."

"People get fired every day, and most people have been fired at least once."

"My termination was part of a reorganization. They played musical chairs with the company's management team, took my chair away, then stopped the music."

"That happens every day, Ali."

"Yes. But to a man who served with distinction and gave his all?"

"As a matter of fact, it does. Your employment is at the will of the company."

"I know that, but I was a top producer. I got results."

"Unless a person owns their own business or has a professional position, like a lawyer or a doctor, they eventually will be forced out whether they get results or not."

"Why is that true?"

"A lot of reasons. Salaries get too high, and their work can be done by less expensive workers. The company's strategic goals may be changing, which will require employees with different skill sets. In some cases, companies may want to make room for younger talent who can be developed and who can give more years to the business."

"I just wish they would have told me why they let me go."

"Companies aren't obligated to tell an executive those reasons. When they feel they no longer need your services, they have every right to let you go—with or without an explanation."

"I know that. Employment is at the will of the company, but in my case, I didn't do anything wrong."

"How old are you?"

"Fifty-five."

"Wasn't your compensation among the highest in your firm?"

"Of course, Holly, and I was worth it. There were only five of us at that level. After the reorganization there are four, now that I'm gone."

"Ali, it really wasn't about you; it was about them and about who they wanted to anoint to be the next big star of the company. If bosses pick the winners and losers by restructuring, they can take the credit for the accomplishments going forward."

"But I was a producer."

"A highly paid producer. Think of the money they saved by terminating you." Holly started writing on her tablet. "Ali, are you set up financially? Have you saved your money, invested it?"

"I have all the money I would ever need for the rest of my life. It's not about the money; it's about the job and my reputation. My job was my life."

"There are other things in life besides jobs."

"Other things don't interest me. My job is what I loved, and they've taken that from me. I feel like I have no reason to live. I've got nothing else."

At this point, Caleb wanted to crawl under the table. He felt like a voyeur seeing this man, so rich and powerful, brought to his knees by this life change beyond his control.

This guy's rich. He's got all the money in the world. He never has to work another day in his life. And yet he has nothing to live for and wants to kill himself. I'd trade places with him in a heartbeat.

Holly Starr saw Caleb's awkward body language and noticed that Ali was on the verge of an emotional breakdown, having just bared his soul to two strangers. "Why don't we take a break and reset. I'll have my assistant, Joe, bring in some menus. We'll order lunch and then resume."

98

While Joe passed out the menus, Starr addressed Caleb. "Have you ever been to Puyallup?"

"No, ma'am."

"You'll have to visit the Meeker Mansion while you're here and at least drive by our famous fairgrounds. We're in the top ten of the largest fairs in America."

"That's huge."

"I suppose you've already noticed our city has a fabulous view of Mount Rainier."

"Yes. I got a great look at it on the plane coming in."

When the food arrived, they made small talk until they finished. Then Holly pushed her plate to the side and called her assistant. "We're finished, Joe. Would you please remove our trays and hold my calls?"

"My sandwich was delicious. Thanks," Caleb said.

"Gentlemen, let's get back to work. Where were we?"

"I was telling you that I have no reason to live and want to kill myself."

Caleb burst out laughing.

Holly and Ali glared at him.

"I didn't mean to laugh. So sorry. It was just the timing—"

Holly took over. "We understand, Caleb, but please refrain from interrupting the session. Again, I appreciate your candor, Ali. When people are as open and honest as you are, healing comes a lot faster."

"It's helping me just to talk to someone about it."

"I speak to many people who go through what you're experiencing. It's a common occurrence, and there are two basic reasons for it, although companies never will admit that. In a nutshell, you're getting older, and your salary is high. It comes down to a coldhearted business decision. Your company would rather invest in a younger person who can give them another twenty to thirty years and who is willing to get paid less now."

"Yes, but I was willing to put in all those hours."

"So will the people who take your place. Let me rephrase that: no one can replace any of us because we're all unique. However, a football team, a company, an army, a country—they go on after their best and brightest leave. It's next man up. Or to be politically correct, the next person up. That's the way it is in all organizations."

Ali rubbed his temples, took some deep breaths, and spent a few seconds studying the wood grain on the table as he tried to process this. "After all I've done for them. And they always talk about the company being a family. That's a bunch of bull crap."

"You can't fire your family, although sometimes you wish you could."

"That job was my life."

"You'll have to create another one. Develop your hobbies."

"But I don't have any hobbies."

"Then develop some interests, go on a long vacation, take a cruise, volunteer at a local soup kitchen, start your own business or nonprofit. There's a big wide world out there that you haven't even seen or experienced. This is your opportunity to try out all sorts of things. Be thankful you're healthy and that you have the money to do whatever you want. Most of the world would like to trade places with you."

"I know I would," Caleb said.

Ali and Holly stared at him, surprised that he'd interjected his comment at this point in the discussion.

"I'm sorry. I guess I got carried away." His face turned red, and he looked at the tabletop, wishing he could crawl under it.

"Holly, I understand your answers, although they aren't satisfying. You may be right. I'll need some time to think about everything you said. I know this—I really don't want to kill myself. I want to live."

"I know you do, Ali, or you wouldn't be here. You've come for help, and I'm going to work with you to lift this cloud. You've let your job define who you are. Your identity is wrapped up in your employment, which is not uncommon for high achievers like you."

"That's probably true."

"You're much more than your job. Let me put it another way. You didn't achieve your goals because of the position you held. Your position was a by-product of your accomplishments—your track record. It was you, not the job. You're leaving your company and position behind, yes, but you're taking 'you' with you, which is where the success came from in the first place. Do you see what I'm saying?"

"Yes. I guess so."

"There's one final idea I'd like to leave you with. In rising to the top of your company and earning one of the highest salaries paid, you must have influenced, motivated, trained, groomed, and inspired hundreds or even thousands of people." She paused and continued to stare at her client. "Let that sink in."

"Not to boast, but I did help mentor many people along the way."

"I'm sure you did. Life is a marathon. You've exhausted that career—there's nothing left to do, you're tired, you're done. Then what happens? You get your second wind, and you feel fresh and strong again. Ali, your life is about to embark on its second wind. You're getting a fresh start. Isn't that exciting?"

Hassan rested his hands on the table, talked out and resigned to the fact that the answers to his questions wouldn't change.

Caleb tried to process this new information. *Sounds like Holly is right. How would this apply to me? Stockbridge is terminating my job. Maybe I'm due for a second wind too.*

Holly checked her watch. "I think we're done for now. Ali, I want you to go home and think about all we've talked about. Make a list of activities you believe would interest you. Think about your childhood, the things you did then, before you started working. Take the time to revisit those childhood dreams and passions. Come up with some new goals and a plan, then call me in a couple of days, and we'll set up another appointment. I'll help you fine-tune your plan, and we'll put specific targets and objectives to it that we'll review periodically. I'll get you out of this. You simply need to replace the void left by that job with something new. The key to retirement is understanding that you're not retiring *from*; you're retiring *to*."

"I'm willing to give it a try, Holly. Thank you."

"That's all I want from you: to try. And that means taking action. Talk is cheap, as the old saying goes."

"Yes, of course. I'll apply the principles I used in my career to my retirement."

"Exactly, Ali."

The three stood.

"Thank you, Holly, and you too, Caleb, for setting this meeting up. I do feel better."

Caleb extended his hand. "Ali, I wish you good luck in your new endeavors. I just left the military and am sort of starting over too, so I know the feeling of not being sure what to do next. By the way, I really do love your watch."

"Thanks. Here, you take it." He removed his beloved Ulysse Nardin Diver Deep Dive and handed it to Caleb, who immediately put it on his wrist and held it up in awe.

"Are you sure?"

"I want you to have it."

99

Holly came between them. "Joe will show you out, Ali. Caleb, will you please stick around?"

"Sure."

After the door to the conference room closed, Holly and Caleb sat back down.

"What did you think of that?"

"It sort of blew my mind, Holly. I really didn't know what to think. I thought you made a lot of good points."

"Thanks. A lot of men and women who are high achievers have trouble accepting their terminations. In most cases, their work is exemplary. There's a lot of politics in companies because managers are competing for the top jobs, the high-paying jobs, so blame gets shifted around, and credit is taken by people who don't deserve it. In the competitive environment in which Ali worked, it's like a stable of racehorses—the adrenaline rush is addictive. No one likes to walk away from that kind of money and influence. It's hard to accept that one is of no further use to the company because of age, a high salary, or skills that are no longer in demand."

"Copy that."

"Ali really wanted help, and he was open and honest. If I can get him to focus on his new goals the way he focused on his company, he'll be fine."

"I'll be sure to relay all this to my boss. I know he'll appreciate all you did here today."

"It's what I do."

"If you don't mind, I have a personal question. I don't know if I have PTSD or not, but I do have a recurring dream that comes randomly in my sleep or when I'm awake and feeling stressed. I'm saving my buddy, and I put him in a helicopter, but when we land, he's dead. I have it over and over."

"It's natural to have moral injuries after war experiences. Survivor's guilt is one of those moral injuries. You feel guilty because you didn't do enough to save your friend, and you probably feel guilty that you survived while he didn't. You never addressed these reactions at the time, so they will keep coming back to haunt you until you do."

"So, how do I address them?"

"You need to change the conversation in your mind. Your self-talk. You're telling yourself over and over that you didn't do enough to save your buddy, which makes you feel guilty. Start telling yourself over and over that you did your best to save him and that he knew that."

"Thanks. I'll try that. If there isn't any more need for me to be here in Puyallup, I'll schedule my flight out tomorrow morning. I'd like to do some sightseeing, but I have a fiancée at home waiting for me. Someday I'll return here with her."

"Enjoy your trip home."

He handed her a check and a card. "Here's the retainer you requested. If future counseling exhausts this, just invoice the address on the card."

"Perfect. Thank you, Caleb. It's been nice meeting you."

"You too."

When he got back to his hotel room, his phone rang.

"Caleb?"

"Yes."

"It's Chewy."

"Chewy! Where are you? I thought you were lost. I've been so worried about you."

"It's a long story that I can't get into now. I just wanted to let you know that I didn't return your calls because my phone was destroyed. This is a special, secured phone line. We were detained, security team and all. I'm safe and will return to the United States soon. I'll call you again when I have more time and can speak freely."

"This is huge news. I'm so relieved."

"Before I go, how are you? Is everything good?"

"Ashley and I are getting married. We just bought a home together, and I've applied to the police academy. I gave her the bracelet you bought, and she loved it."

"Congratulations on all that, and I'm glad Ashley loved the bracelet. I knew she would. I'm delighted you worked things out. She's a very lucky woman to have a man like you."

"I'm the lucky one."

"It's so wonderful to hear your voice, Caleb. Best wishes on everything. Talk soon."

"Take care, Chewy. Thanks for calling. I'm so relieved that you're alive."

She handed the phone back to the commander of the security detail. "Thanks, Sean. I think I'm going to take a walk."

100

Sea-Tac smelled of freshly brewed coffee and mouthwatering pastries. Everyone hurried to get something to eat while waiting for their flights. Caleb bought a cup of coffee and a chocolate chip muffin. Finding a quiet corner next to the window, he speed-dialed Stockbridge after taking a big bite out of his breakfast.

"Morning, boss. How are you feeling today?"

"I've been better, and I've been worse. How about you?"

"I'm good. Glad to be going home."

"Sean called to tell me the good news about Chewy and her team. I understand she called you last night."

"I've been worried sick about her, and it was hard not to think the worst."

"Two of the security team were injured, but they'll live."

"That's good to hear."

"You've taken care of some unfinished business for me, and you did a good job. Thanks for everything."

"No. Thank you. I appreciate you giving me a chance when I was down and out. I learned so much from the people you helped and the ones I met along the way."

Stockbridge laughed. "I knew you would. I'd like to meet with you when you get squared away and conclude the final piece of our business together."

"Sounds good. I'll give you a call when things quiet down."

Caleb finished the muffin and washed it down with cold coffee. He knew Ashley would be ecstatic that this job with its out-of-town assignments was over. He decided to surprise her when he saw her in person, so he texted her instead.

Honey, Coming home 2–4 pm. Love, Caleb

———

As the road wound through a rock-edged area of rolling desert hills, it curved around a bend to a majestic view of Briggs Lake down below. Caleb had seen the sight many times upon return trips, and the scenic view, always inspiring, meant even more this time. He was going home to the woman he loved, who was now his fiancée. She was waiting in their house, and he had a promising future in law enforcement.

Around the next corner, an oncoming pickup truck driven by a distracted driver barreled at him in his lane. On each side of the highway, deep crevasses in the rock formation would swallow up his vehicle out of sight and send him to instant death. He chose to jump on the brakes and hope for the best. He saw the vehicles collide, heard the sounds of metal crashing and glass smashing, smelled burning rubber and leaking gas, and then everything went dark.

101

Ashley touched up their home in preparation for Caleb's arrival. She vacuumed the carpet for the second time and even washed the windows. She was so proud of their new house that cleaning it wasn't work. It was a time to enjoy the things in her home.

Someone knocked. When Ashley opened the door, Chief Strollo stood in his uniform, a grim expression on his face. "Hello, Ashley."

"Good to see you, Chief Strollo. I'm afraid Caleb isn't here right now, but I do expect him anytime if you'd like to wait."

"Ashley, Caleb has been in a serious accident on the highway coming into the city. He collided head-on with a pickup truck. The other driver wasn't wearing a seat belt, and she is deceased. Fortunately, he had his seat belt on, but he's been hurt pretty badly."

"Where is he?"

"He's in the hospital, in surgery. If you want to go, I'll escort you."

"Yes. Give me a minute." She gathered her purse and phone and turned to Strollo. "Let's go."

At the hospital, she paced in the waiting room. Subjects of her nursing coursework paraded through her brain—broken bones, casts, medications, treatment options. These sterile classroom topics suddenly became real matters of life and death.

She called Rosie, who asked Artie to watch her kids so she could join Ashley at the hospital. The two waited in silence, occasionally hugging one another, hoping for the best yet fearing the worst.

After a couple of hours, a man in green scrubs with a mustache and short brown hair parted on the side came out with a nurse, who directed him to Ashley. He paused in front of her chair. She stood up. "My name is Dr. Randy Miller. I understand you're Mr. Sinclair's fiancée. He's had multiple fractures in his arms and a broken bone in his lower leg that needed surgical repair. We inserted a titanium rod to support the bone."

Ashley had held her breath when Dr. Miller gave his report. Now she exhaled with a deep sigh. "Thank you, Dr. Miller. Is he going to be all right?"

"We think the prognosis is good. We won't know for sure until he wakes up. He's heavily sedated right now. His vitals and brain activity appear normal, but we won't be able to fully evaluate any brain damage or cognitive problems until he's conscious."

"Can I see him?"

"He's in recovery now. When we put him in a room, you can see him there. He'll be in an induced coma for a day or two. You won't be able to talk to him. The next twenty-four hours are critical. We'll do everything we can for him."

"Thanks, Dr. Miller."

He walked back through the double doors. The nurse stayed.

"Ma'am, I'll come get you when he's put in a room."

"Thank you very much."

"He'll be sleeping through the night, though. I suggest you go home, get some rest, and come back in the morning."

"No. I'm staying here with Caleb." Ashley turned to Rosie. "You don't need to stay. Your children need you. I'll give Joyce a call later and tell her I won't be able to take my shift for the next couple of days."

"I'll go home now, but I'll be back in the morning. Call me if you want me to bring you anything from home. After I get the kids off to school, I'll be back."

"Thanks. I really appreciate your support."

102

Rosie stopped for pizza on the way home. When she walked into the house, her kids were watching a movie with Artie and Chad. "Anyone want pizza?"

"We do," Seth said.

Sarah yelled, "Yay! Can we eat in the living room? We're watching a good movie."

"Sure. You can eat in the living room." She gave them their food. While the kids ate, they were glued to the animated movie about Willie, the lonely burro. The adults took the opportunity to slip into the kitchen so they could talk.

"There's a large pizza for you guys too. I ate something at the hospital, so I'm not really hungry."

Chad's forehead wrinkled. "How's Caleb?"

"The doctor said he's got multiple fractures, one of which needed surgery to repair. Other than that, his vital signs are good, and his brain activity seems normal. That's all we know for now. We won't know more about any brain damage until he wakes up, which hopefully will be soon."

"Things could be worse, considering how bad it was," Artie said. "The accident has been all over the news, especially that one of the drivers was killed. We've been praying for all the families involved and hoping the deceased person wasn't Caleb."

"Good. Keep praying, and pray for Ashley too. Poor thing. She's a wreck."

Ashley kept a vigil for the next three days, leaving the hospital only to shower and change clothes. Caleb still hadn't regained consciousness, even after Dr. Miller discontinued the medically induced coma.

On the fourth day, Dr. Miller examined Caleb while Ashley was there. He studied the green screen that monitored Caleb's vitals, then used a small flashlight to stimulate eye movement, looking for any sign of consciousness.

"Dr. Miller, thanks for coming. It's been more than three days, and Caleb is still asleep. I'm worried that something's wrong."

"I know you're concerned that he's still asleep. This happens sometimes with brain traumas. The body needs to rest itself. Overall, he seems to be recovering. Let's give it some time. This is not unusual in cases like this."

Those words were comforting at the time. Then two more weeks passed, and Caleb was still unconscious. Returning to work, she resumed her vigil at his bedside when she wasn't at the Ax. She stopped going to her nursing classes and withdrew from school.

Ashley read the faces of the nurses and the doctors who attended Caleb, and they looked worried. Everyone avoided eye contact and seemed to go out of their way to avoid talking to her. When she did get someone to speak to her, she had more questions than they had answers.

103

Caleb's buddy Nick is shot and crumples to the ground a few feet away. Ducking under a blizzard of steel projectiles, Caleb presses a bandage against Nick's stomach to staunch the blood. When the UH-60 Black Hawk finally lands, the helicopter is greeted by a hail of bullets. Caleb cradles Nick like a baby in his arms and charges through the gunfire toward the chopper. Crew Chief Big Jim Robinson hoists Nick inside at the door, and Caleb jumps in behind, nearly falling out as the chopper lifts upward with a roar. Rocket-propelled grenades detonate around the rising copter, engulfing it with smoke and the smell of sulfur and ammonia. The explosions launch shrapnel into Caleb's right leg. He's so focused on encouraging Nick that he doesn't feel the steel shards lodged in his calf. When they land at the field hospital, Nick is dead.

 A man dressed in white glowed as he approached Caleb and placed his hand on his shoulder. He said, "Nick's death is not your fault. If you will stop blaming yourself, you will stop having this dream. You did your best."

 Caleb took a closer look at the man. "Where have I seen you before?"

 "In Central Park. I'm Eli Burns."

 "The last thing I remember was heading home to Briggs Lake and getting in a head-on collision, then things went black. Am I dead now? Is this heaven?"

 "No, Caleb. You're alive. Do you want to stop this dream?"

 "In the worst way."

 "Then stop blaming yourself. Whenever you think of the day Nick died, remind yourself that you did all you could do."

 "I will. I want this dream to stop."

 "Remember in Central Park when I asked what your definition of success was?"

 "I told you it was having a good job, a wife and children, and enough money to do the things I want to do."

"Then I said you were missing something that is important to any definition of success. Now, do you know what was missing from your definition?"

"God. None of those things, a job, a family, or money, means anything if God isn't a part of my life."

"That's right."

104

One afternoon, Chad, Artie, and Rosie arrived at the hospital while Ashley dozed in a chair by Caleb's bed. The noise startled her, and she woke up. "Hi, guys. Thanks for coming. Nothing new here, but seeing you sure makes me feel better."

Rosie sat in the other chair while the guys remained standing. "We were thinking about you and decided it was time to form a prayer circle around Caleb and lay hands on him."

"What's that?"

"It just means we'll all stand around him, touch him, and take turns praying for him," Chad said. "Would that be okay?"

"Of course. I've never prayed so much in my life. It doesn't seem to be doing much good, though."

"Prayer always does good," Artie said. "Even if we don't see the results right away. Healing isn't always instantaneous. Sometimes it's a process and takes time."

Ashley stood up and put her hand on Caleb's shoulder. "Let's all pray for Caleb together."

Chad put his hand on Caleb's other shoulder, and Artie stood next to him and placed his hand on the leg that had the titanium rod. Rosie stood and put her hand on the opposite leg, completing the circle.

Chad looked around. "Who wants to go first?"

"I will," said Artie. "Father, thank you for saving our buddy's life and for starting the healing process in his body. Now we ask you to wake him up, if it's your will. If he needs more rest, let him sleep. Amen."

"God, this is Rosie. I love you. I don't know what to say, but you know what's in my heart. Do what's best to get this wonderful man back to living his life. Amen."

"Hi, God. It's me again, Ashley. Sorry to keep bugging you, but I need you to heal my man. Heal him completely. Let me bring him home so I can love him for the rest of my life. I want to be with him when his hair turns gray and his face is filled with wrinkles. Thank you."

Chad closed the circle of prayer. "Heavenly Father, we give our thanks and praise to you for all you have created, including this brave man. Thank you for saving his life in war and in this truck accident. We pray for the woman who died, that she is in your bosom in eternal glory, and for her family, that they can find comfort and strength. May your will be done. Amen."

They opened their eyes and remained in their positions, watching Caleb, looking for signs that he was waking up. Suddenly he took a deep breath and exhaled in a sigh. Then his eyes blinked and opened. He turned to his left and focused his gaze on Ashley.

Everyone in the circle gave a collective gasp.

"Ashley. Where am I?"

"You're in a hospital, babe. You've been in an accident. You broke some bones, but you're going to fully recover." She rested her head on his chest and sobbed. "I love you so much, Caleb. Thanks for bringing him back to me, God."

Caleb looked around and saw Ashley's three prayer partners, who were grinning and tearing up. "Hi, Caleb!" they all said simultaneously.

He smiled. "Hi, everyone. I suppose you're wondering why I called this meeting."

"To sell us Amway?" Artie asked.

They all laughed.

"Group hug," Ashley said.

The circle closed around Caleb, and they all cried tears of joy.

105

Sent home from the hospital to heal, Caleb spent his days with Ashley talking about their past and their future. His bones recovered, and in six weeks, the casts came off. Then came the process of rebuilding his strength. The young veteran committed himself to daily rehab at Sampson's Gym with Sam, his physical therapist.

Sore and hurting everywhere, he decided to pay a visit to Chad at his apartment.

"Why am I hurting more since I started therapy, Chad?"

"That's normal, so don't worry about it. You're using muscles you haven't used for a while, and they need to be torn down again so they can be built up."

"It seems counterintuitive to hurt myself to make the pain and stiffness go away."

"I know. But that's the way rehabilitating your muscles goes, my friend. Be patient. Who's your therapist?"

"Sam."

"Sam's good. Just follow the plan—stay faithful to it—and you'll see results soon. I'm glad you stopped over. How are the wedding plans coming?"

"The accident has kind of slowed everything down, but we're back at it."

"Yes. I can imagine. Glad to hear things are coming together with the wedding. If you're serious about Ashley, and I know you are, make it official as soon as you can."

"We sort of feel like we're married in the eyes of the Lord."

"Marriage is a public declaration to your family and friends that you're making a commitment to forsake all others till death do you part. Living together without marriage may seem to work for some, but it gives you an out when things get rocky. In marriage, you vow to stay together no matter what."

"I see what you mean. I don't want an out. I want Ashley as my wife."

"Great."

"Would you be available to officiate?"

"It depends on the date. If I have no conflicts, I would be honored."

"We'd like to get married on December 23 because that's the first night we were together—almost a year ago now. I start at the police academy the first week of January, so that seems to make the most sense."

Chad found his calendar. "I'm clear on that day. It might be tough to find a church that time of the year because it's so close to Christmas services. Any thoughts on where you'd like to have it?"

"We'd just like to do it at a local hotel. They're all decorated for the holidays, and the guests can stay there. No one will have to drive after drinking. We'll just rent a room."

"That's a good idea. Would your parents approve of a nonchurch wedding?"

"My foster parents are in a nursing home in Iowa. They're in frail health and both have dementia. They really shouldn't travel."

"What about Ashley's folks?"

"They could pay for a big wedding, but Ashley and I want to pay for it ourselves and make it small, simple, and personal. I've never met her mom, but Ashley says she would take over the whole thing and push her preferences. Ashley says her mom's heart is in the right place, but it's just that we want to do the wedding our way."

"I understand. We should have a counseling session before the wedding. I'd like to share some thoughts on marriage from a biblical point of view and have a discussion about topics and issues you'll deal with as a married couple."

"That's fine. Whatever you think would help us prepare would be okay with us."

"Good. How about tomorrow, here at my place? Artie will be at a rehearsal."

"Sounds good."

When Caleb shared the conversation with Ashley, she hugged Caleb. "Babe, things are coming together."

———

The next day at the start of their counseling session, Chad instructed them to take notes, so he gave Ashley and Caleb a notepad and a pen. He used a big study Bible containing commentaries, research, notes, and passages underlined in ink.

Caleb raised his eyebrows. "You actually write notes in your Bible itself?"

"Sure, Caleb. Why not? That way, when I come to a passage, the note is right there."

"I don't know. It just seems kind of sacrilegious."

"Good. I'm sacrilegious. I'm a follower of Jesus, and that's what counts."

Ashley shot Caleb a look.

Chad continued. "First, marriage is honorable in the sight of God, and it is a commitment to forsake all others till death do you part. You are declaring publicly to love each other, honor each other, protect each other, and sustain each other."

"And doesn't it say she's supposed to obey me?"

"No, Caleb. She should respect you, and you should respect her too."

He held up a finger. "Wait. I thought wives were supposed to obey. I want to see the fine print."

"Caleb, stop it." Ashley raised her pen to a throwing position. "This is serious."

"I am serious."

"No, you're not."

Chad smiled. "All right, you two. Let's get back to work. Marriage is a fifty-fifty proposition. You are equals in the marriage. And marriage isn't always fifty-fifty. Some days it's thirty-seventy and others seventy-thirty. Unconditional love means never keeping score. It means always having each other's backs no matter what."

"Absolutely," Caleb said and caught Ashley's eye. "I know we'll each give our all to make it work."

She smiled.

"Good. We'll be having a salt covenant ceremony. The salt covenant dates back to ancient times and has its roots in the Bible. When two people make a salt covenant together, they commit to an alliance that lasts until death. The pledge of unity to each other is unchanging no matter what circumstances or situations arise. We'll combine two vials of salt into one container, symbolizing the unity pledge you are making to be one flesh for the rest of your lives."

"That sounds great," Ashley said.

"Marriage is a commitment to forsake all others. You don't keep old relationships going on the side as a backup plan. There is no plan B, only plan A."

"That sounds good," Caleb said.

"Marriage lasts until one of you dies. Divorce isn't part of the deal. There is biblical justification for divorce in only three instances, which I call the three As—adultery, abuse, and abandonment. Understand?"

The couple nodded.

"Adultery doesn't have to end a marriage if the behavior stops and the partner can forgive. When it comes to abuse and abandonment, there's no going back."

Chad then read to them all the verses in the Bible regarding marriage before giving them a checklist of issues they needed to discuss before the wedding ceremony in order to resolve any conflicts ahead of time. Then he explained the meaning of each aspect of the wedding ceremony, from the vows to the exchange of rings.

"Now that we're finished, do you have any questions?"

The couple shook their heads.

"Caleb?"

"No."

"Ashley?"

"I can't think of any."

"Good. If questions come up, give me a call. One final suggestion. I always recommend Charles Buck and his assistant, Stephanie Angel, as wedding photographers. They take good pictures, and they work cheap."

Ashley hugged Chad. "Thanks."

Caleb gave him a fist bump. "Thanks, man."

106

It was December 23, and there was no snow on the ground. There wouldn't be any snow on Christmas day either. It rarely snowed in this part of the Arizona desert, and this year would be no different. Caleb Sinclair stood to the left of Chad Blake, who wore a powder blue suit, and on Caleb's left stood Anthony Victorino, his best man.

Caleb and Anthony wore their army dress blues—dark blue, single-breasted, four-button jackets over lighter blue trousers with yellow stripes on the outside of each pant leg. Both staff sergeants wore their medals received for valor and courage under fire.

Armor of God played a bridal processional on acoustic guitars. In the next instant, Rosie appeared at the doorway in the back of the room, carrying flowers and wearing an ivory-colored, floor-length chiffon dress with ruffles. Her black hair was curled and waved, which highlighted her bright blue eyes that were outshined only by her smile.

When Rosie reached the front of the room to Chad's right, she left a space for the bride, then turned to the right until she also faced the open doorway at the back of the room. The music stopped, and a hush came over the guests.

The three men kept their eyes on the back of the room, waiting for the bride's entrance.

In that eternal moment, Caleb took a deep breath. Time stood still. He felt his buddy lightly touch his left hand as if to say, "You got this, bro." Caleb smiled. *What's taking her so long? Come on, honey. Get a move on.*

The band started playing "Here Comes the Bride." There was Ashley, beaming and glowing, holding her father's arm. A rustling sound reverberated throughout the room as everyone stood up and turned to get a good view of the bride. She paused; at that moment she looked like a goddess.

Photographer Charles Buck began snapping pictures like he was firing an automatic pistol. Careful not to distract from the service, he considered himself a master at photographing scenes and not making a scene himself. He liked to say discretion was his middle name—although it was Gregory.

Caleb had never seen Ashley so stunningly beautiful, and his eyes filled with tears. She locked her eyes on his, and she teared up too as she came down the aisle with her dad. She was as graceful as a doe walking through a meadow on a spring morning. The bride wore a white, A-line, floor-length wedding dress with three-quarter sleeves made of chiffon lace. The bracelet from Chewy was on her wrist.

Her dad, wearing a classic black tux, extended his daughter's hand toward Caleb, who gently took it in his and turned his bride toward Chad, who told everyone they could be seated. The bride's half of the room filled every chair on the left side.

Chief Strollo sat in the aisle seat in the front row on the groom's side of the room. His wife, Samantha, sat to his right, and on her right was Joyce Benson. Next to Joyce sat Lily Lofton. She wore a yellow chiffon dress and the diamond necklace she'd lost in Anthony's apartment. On Christmas break from show rehearsals, Lily had flown in from New York with Anthony, whom she was dating. On Lily's right sat Clinton Devers in his wheelchair; he was also wearing his army dress blues.

Behind them in the second row sat Danielle Stevens and Sam, Caleb's physical therapist. Next to Sam sat Alvin Larsen in his Marine Corps dress blues. To his right sat Ali Hassan, John Emanuel, and Frank Marchese. Chewy, wearing an A-line, scoop-neck, floor-length red silk dress, her long black hair in braids, sat at the end of the second row.

Since Caleb had no family in attendance, employees of the Ax Handle occupied most of the remaining chairs on his side of the theater-style setup, although the last two rows were vacant.

It was time for the couple to say their vows. They faced each other, holding both hands.

"Caleb Sinclair, you're the man I've always dreamed of since I was a little girl, and I promise to be worthy of your love. I will dedicate myself to be your loving wife, partner, best friend, confidant, and anything else I need to be to support you. I want to go on life's journey with you, always at your side, whatever comes our way.

"I'll train you to eat better and to lay off the Slim Jims and pork rinds—how can anyone eat that stuff?—will enlarge your vocabulary beyond saying 'very cool' or 'wow,' and will teach you that there are other responses besides 'affirmative' and 'copy that.'

"I'll be with you in good times and in bad, when you're healthy and when you're not. I will never quit on us, and I will give you all I have. I want to be the mother of your children, and I want to grow old with you."

When it was Caleb's turn, he drew a blank. The words weren't there. He had written them down for an emergency, but he thought it would be too weird to drop her hands and dig into his pocket for his cheat sheet. He waited, hoping the words would come to him. They didn't. He decided to wing it and hope for the best.

"Ashley Bivens, I promise to give you my unconditional love for the rest of my life, even on the days when you're bitchy. Everything about you turns me on—your ponytail coming out the back of your Boston Red Sox cap, the way you smile with your green eyes, which look blue to me. I love to see your facial expression when you call me 'dear boy.' And when you call me 'dude,' your tone of voice is affectionate...and at the same time, kind of like you're kicking my butt. You're the most beautiful woman in the world, and your auburn hair has fire streaks in it when the morning sun hits your red highlights. I love that. As gorgeous as you are physically, you're even more stunning on the inside—if that's possible. You're quick-witted and wise and a hard worker. You make me laugh when I'm not expecting it. That in itself is a gift. You have compassion for other people and are a giver. You know me better than I know myself. As I protected you in the Ax a year ago tonight, I promise to protect you like that every day for the rest of my life. I dedicate myself to you, and only you, forever."

Chad asked them to kneel in front of him. He placed his right hand on Ashley's head and his left hand on Caleb's.

"Father, thank you for blessing the marriage of Ashley and Caleb, that it will be pleasing in your sight and pleasing to them. May they always help each other to live their best lives. May they be companions throughout life's journey in the good times and the bad times. May they share with each other an intimacy deeper and more special than with anyone else as they strive to become one flesh in body and soul. May they love each other, honor each other, cherish each other, and sustain each other for the rest of their lives. Amen."

He motioned for them to stand up. "I now pronounce you husband and wife. You may kiss the bride."

With tears running down both of their cheeks, Caleb gently pressed his lips against Ashley's and held them there, holding her tight, wishing this moment would last forever. As he pulled away, Chad turned them around to face the audience.

"Ladies and gentlemen, I present to you Mr. and Mrs. Caleb Sinclair."

Armor of God began playing Mendelssohn's "Wedding March." Caleb held out his arm, Ashley took it, and they walked out of the room. Cell phone cameras went off, and everyone clapped and cheered. Once outside the room, the newly married couple turned around and waited to greet everyone as they left before getting their group photographs.

107

By Christmas Day, all their wedding guests had checked out of the hotel. Caleb and Ashley set up a late checkout with the intention of attending the hotel's holiday brunch first and then going home. While they were eating, Ashley asked Caleb if he still had the bad dream about the day Nick died.

"No, I don't, Ash."

"That's what I thought. You've slept peacefully through the night, and I don't remember you having any bad dreams at all lately."

"The last time I had the dream was when I was in the hospital in a coma. It started like it usually did, with the helicopter ride and Nick dying by the time we got to the field hospital. Then this guy appeared, Eli Burns, who I had met in Central Park. Only in my dream, he was dressed all in white. I asked him if I had died in the crash, but he said I was still alive."

"That's amazing."

"Eli told me if I would stop blaming myself, I would stop having the dream. I decided to follow his advice, and the bad dream stopped."

"Wow."

"He asked me what I learned about success. I told Eli that I learned that any definition of success had to include God, and he said, 'That's right.'"

"Do you think Eli is an angel?"

"Could be."

As they finished their meal, Caleb's phone rang.

"Mr. Sinclair?"

"Yes."

"This is Sheliah, Mr. Stockbridge's personal assistant. He's asked me to call you. He wants you to come to the hospital as soon as you can."

"I just got married a couple of days ago, and we're still celebrating our honeymoon."

"He understands that and said you could bring your new wife."

"It's really not convenient right now, Sheliah. Can I reschedule for another time?"

"Mr. Stockbridge is dying."

"We'll be right there."

108

Caleb ran a red light in his haste to get to the hospital. He got the room number from the receptionist. Unwilling to wait for the elevator, he and Ashley bounded up the stairs. Doctors had treated his war wounds in field hospitals that had the same smell, which made him nauseous.

Stockbridge had oxygen tubes in both nostrils and an IV in his arm. A green video screen next to his bed displayed all the numbers his heart was generating and whether those numbers were within healthy metrics. A nurse sat in a nearby chair and smiled when they entered.

"He's not asleep. He's awake and wants to talk to you." She got up and whispered in his ear. "Mr. Stockbridge, Caleb is here."

Stockbridge's eyes opened, and he managed a weak smile. "Hello, Caleb. I see you brought Ashley. Congratulations on your wedding. I'm sorry I couldn't attend."

"We understand," Caleb said. "No problem."

"Marcy, would you please raise my bed up and give us some time alone?"

"Of course, Mr. Stockbridge." She used the button by his bed to raise his head and set the call button near his hands. "Remember, just push this red button here if you need anything."

Stockbridge raised his arm. "This is Marcy, the best nurse in the world. I'd like you to meet these newlyweds, Caleb and Ashley. They just got married two days ago."

Caleb rested his hand on the bed. "Is this guy giving you any trouble?"

"Oh no. He's a model patient."

"Marcy, you can leave us now. I'll call you if I need anything."

"Very good, sir."

"Ashley, it's good to see you. I'll bet you were a beautiful bride." Caleb beamed. "She was, sir."

Ashley moved to his bedside. "How are you feeling?"

"I've been better, and I've been worse. The doctors say there isn't much more they can do for me except keep me comfortable. That sucks."

"I've been rehabbing from the car accident, and we've been planning our wedding. I should have been checking up on you."

"You've had a lot going on. I did want to see you today, even though it's Christmas. I have a few things to tell you before I check out."

"Of course."

"First of all, take good care of Ashley. She's a good woman."

"I plan on it."

"The next thing you need to know is that I'm your grandfather."

"What? That can't be."

"Oh yes, it can. Your father was my son. He was a wild child, and I was an absent dad—bad combination."

"I tried to find Dad before I went in the service and took a DNA test and everything. No luck. By the way, you weren't in my list of DNA matches either, so how can you be my grandfather?"

"My name didn't show up in your DNA matches because I made my account private. If you choose to have a private account, your name isn't disclosed to others. I took the DNA test too, searching for my son, and that's how I found out about you. It took me over a year to track you down. My permanent home is Fort Myers, Florida, but I moved to Briggs Lake temporarily to be near you."

"Did you ever find Dad?"

"No. He disappeared off the face of the earth, and he had not taken a DNA test, so I couldn't connect with him the way I was able to with you."

"This is unbelievable."

"I sat in the bar that night you got in the fight because I had been watching you work. I must say, I was impressed and proud of you."

"All this time—"

"All this time you were working for gramps." He chuckled. "Now, let's go over all your assignments, starting with Danielle. She's your second cousin."

"How can that be?"

"You share the same great-grandparents, John and Emma Stockbridge. They were my parents."

"That blows my mind."

109

Ashley put her hand on Stockbridge's arm. "I was so jealous of Danielle and thought they had something going on. I even broke up with Caleb over her—and here she's his second cousin."

"You see, Ashley, Danielle's grandfather is my younger brother, Henry. He gave me a job with his car detailing business. I repaid him by quitting without notice when I had the chance to go with his competitor, who offered me twice the salary. I revealed company secrets, rates, and client information to my new company. My information was used to steal Henry's customers, which drove him out of business."

"Why didn't you give Henry money to start a new business?"

"Too late for that, Caleb. After his business failed, he filed bankruptcy and killed himself. He was a broken man. He left behind a wife named Barbara and a son named Bobby. Henry never blamed me, although Barbara and Bobby did. They never spoke to me again."

"That's awful."

"I'll say. It's one of my biggest regrets. From what I've been able to learn, Barbara and Bobby had rough lives. Barbara is now deceased. Bobby became a hopeless drunk and met a woman named Nancy Stevens. They lived together for a few years, and then Nancy gave birth to Danielle. A short time later, Bobby abandoned them. Nancy never married and raised Danielle by herself, supporting them as a waitress until she was killed in a car accident a few years ago."

"Thanks to the seed money you gave her, Danielle was able to buy a coffee franchise, and it's quickly becoming the hottest place to get coffee in Briggs Lake."

"I know. I used to go there and watch her before I got too sick to leave the house." Stockbridge smiled. "Now, tell me, Caleb, what did you learn from her?"

"Not to judge people by their outward appearance. As you know, Danielle wears all black and has tattoos and piercings. She looks like the poster girl for Marilyn Manson. In reality, she's a kind person who writes children's books and serves coffee with a heart full of love."

"That's a good lesson to learn. When we judge someone's appearance in a negative way, we can cut ourselves off from developing a relationship with them that would enrich us and them."

"True."

"Your next assignment was Alvin Larsen, the Vietnam veteran. Tell me about him."

"Alvin is an interesting guy. He's an old leatherneck who shared a lot of his experiences in Vietnam as well as his thoughts on war. He's a crack shot too. He came to our wedding, and he can still fit in his dress blues."

"I asked you about any war correspondents he remembered."

"Yes, there was a reporter with his unit. Alvin saved his life, and he wrote a hit piece on the marines. They felt betrayed after sharing the battlefield with him."

"That journalist was me, and what Alvin told you was true from the marines' point of view. It's another one of my regrets. I was young and naive. I thought the war was wrong, but it wasn't those marines' fault. I should have made that clearer in my article. I misled them on how I was going to frame the story."

"It really hurt him at the time as well as the guys in his unit."

"I know. Caleb, the lesson there is to always be honest with people. The truth always comes out anyway. And I should have honored their service instead of jumping on the bandwagon of blaming them for the war. Never turn your back on people who helped you in the past, especially if those people saved your life."

"I should also add that Alvin holds no resentment about the past. He's moved on. He knows who he is and what he did and why he did it. It doesn't matter anymore to him what others say or write about him."

"That's a good place to be, isn't it, Caleb? We need to remember the mistakes of the past so that we don't repeat them, but we shouldn't live in the past and let it define us. We can't change the past anyway. Now he has his own home in which to live securely for the rest of his life. Your next assignment was Clinton Devers. Tell me about that."

110

"Clint has no bitterness about his war injuries, which cost him the use of his legs. Apparently, he's a fantastic pool player and uses a customized cue stick. He also plays wheelchair basketball. He has a passion for life. I learned from Clint that a person should focus on what they can do, not on what they can't. If people adapt and adjust when life throws them a curveball, they can do almost anything they make up their minds to do."

"Profound advice."

"He doesn't dwell on the past either. He started a nonprofit and works with the federal government to catch online pedophiles as a way to honor his grandfather, who did the same thing."

"Yes, I know all about his grandfather. Clint was named after my older brother, Clinton. My brother's daughter is Clint's mom. That makes Clint your second cousin, same as Danielle."

"Oh man. This is unreal. I would have never guessed that one. Clinton's African American."

"You noticed?" He smiled. "My niece married a black man named William Devers, who was a Vietnam War hero. He joined Lockheed after his military service. He's a brilliant engineer. They've not let racism stop them, nor have they ever used it as an excuse either. She just retired from a thirty-year teaching career."

"That's awesome."

"Getting back to my older brother, he was a brilliant writer and mentored me growing up. I wanted to be like him and investigate corruption, expose it, and write about it. He taught me the ropes and helped me get my first writing job at a small newspaper in Cody, Wyoming."

"Clint impersonates children to catch online predators."

"Right. He's following in the footsteps of his grandfather, who cracked a child trafficking and porn ring in the San Francisco area. His series of articles exposed the gang behind it and the support it got from some top politicians. Over seven hundred were arrested, and Clinton was up for a Pulitzer Prize in journalism."

"That's really cool."

"He was gunned down in broad daylight. A mob hit. A guy with a silencer came up behind him and fired a .22 hollow point round into the back of my brother's head."

"I'm so sorry."

Stockbridge gripped his covers to compose himself. "It was a terrible blow to our family, especially me. I've kept in touch with the younger Clinton over the years; however, I wanted to give him help without him feeling indebted to me. Doing it through you seemed like the best way to facilitate that. I'm pleased Clint is continuing his grandfather's work. I've set aside an endowment to keep the foundation going."

"Clint doesn't see himself as disabled. He says he just does things differently. He was awarded the Silver Star, which is the third highest decoration a military man can receive. It's for gallantry in action against an enemy. He showed conspicuous bravery in holding off a dozen enemy fighters, killing five of them while being wounded himself. He's credited with saving the lives of three guys in his squad."

"Yes, I know. I'm very proud of him. My brother would be proud of him too. Your next assignment was Karmen Klosser. What did you think of her?"

111

"As I told you, she's a knockout. I couldn't believe she didn't win the pageant. Karmen's mother, Haley, and grandmother are attractive too."

"You should have seen her grandmother when she was young. Helen was a beauty."

"They're good people. I do have one question on that assignment."

"What?"

"In every other job, you had me find out what they needed. In this case, you knew beforehand that Helen Moberg needed money. How did you know?"

"I've been following Helen Moberg for years, and I know from public records that she recently filed bankruptcy."

"Karmen shared about her grandmother during the onstage question part of the competition when asked who her hero was."

"Really?"

"Apparently, Helen got pregnant at seventeen. The man she was supposed to marry split, leaving her to raise the child by herself. She never got married and raised Karmen's mom as a single parent."

"Pregnant? I never knew that. Oh my goodness. That man who walked out on her was me."

Caleb and Ashley glanced at each other in disbelief, not knowing what to say.

"We were engaged, yes, but I got cold feet. I just wasn't ready for a relationship. I didn't know how to tell her, so I just left one night and never came back."

"Wow," Caleb said.

"But honestly, I didn't know she was pregnant."

"Would that have made a difference?"

"I don't know, Caleb. I don't know."

"Since she never married, I wonder if she was waiting for you to come back all her life?"

"I'll never know."

"Maybe you should try to visit them and tell them you're sorry."

"It's too late for that now. It would only stir her up. She'll ask why I left, and the answer I would give sounds so weak and selfish."

"It's never too late to say you're sorry, and it's never too late to act in love."

Stockbridge stared at his young grandson. "I didn't want to hurt Helen then, and I don't want to hurt her now by stirring up the past."

"You could at least tell her you were the one who gave her the check, so she doesn't spend any more of her life thinking you're a donkey's rear end and hating your guts."

"Why? So she could return it and tell me I couldn't buy off my guilty conscience that cheaply? The damage was done years ago, and it's too late to fix it now."

"Maybe the thing Helen Moberg needed the most wasn't your money but for you to man up and tell her you were the world's biggest jerk and ask her to forgive you."

"I know what you're saying. I've thought about Helen all my life and wondered what if. I got married once. The union produced your father and lasted fifteen years. I gave her half my money and paid the legal bills but chose not to spend years fighting for custody."

"Maybe you should have married Helen Moberg and lived happily ever after in Utah."

"Hindsight's twenty-twenty."

As Stockbridge began to process this new information about his past love, he clammed up. A lonely tear trickled down his cheek. "Would you help me sip some water, please?"

"Sure." Caleb got up and held the water glass up to Stockbridge's mouth so he could reach the straw.

"Thank you. And thank you for the information and suggestions. I'll give some thought to contacting Helen and apologizing for being a lowlife. She deserved much better, to say the least. I guess you and Karmen are half-first cousins. Let's go on to Dr. Hua-Chang Huang."

112

"I really liked meeting Chewy. She's a cool lady. She grieved for her husband and viewed the trip to the Middle East as something she had to do to finish his dream—their dream. She was scared to go. I think she had a premonition that something bad was going to happen. She took the risk and fulfilled the dream she and her husband had."

"Yes."

"How did you know Chewy? She didn't seem to know who you were, and she pressed me, but I told her you preferred to stay anonymous."

"Remember when we had lunch in the cove at Briggs Lake and I told you I worked undercover for the federal government collecting intelligence?"

"Yes. After those three guys jumped me. You said you spied for the government."

"Right. Chewy's husband, Dr. Rafael Hernandez, was a noted expert on the ancient Hebrew and Aramaic languages, and he was also an intelligence agent. We were partners on a few jobs."

"Her husband was a spy?"

"Yes."

"Did Chewy know that?"

"No, she didn't. I don't think his death was just a random attack from an Islamic extremist group either. You see, when I got the security team together, I found out that Rafael not only went over there to scan ancient scrolls but also to gather intel on the location and the number of Islamic militants in the area. He knew it was dangerous, but he thought it important enough to risk his life."

"Are you sure she didn't know?"

"Yes. He wouldn't have told her. That way she would have what the CIA calls plausible deniability. The spooks withhold information from higher-ups and special people so they can say they had no knowledge of an operation in case the shit hits the fan."

"She taught me that when a couple shares a dream, it unites them in a powerful way. Even after her husband died, she stayed committed to the dream, risking her life to complete it."

"That's a valuable lesson. Her husband was a good man, and we were close. I'm grateful we could help her finish their mission and that she came home safely. Your next job was Frank Marchese in Nashville. How did that go?"

"That one was smooth. That lawyer you hired, Scooter Evans, was worth every penny. He had those government employees from the get-go. It wasn't even a fair fight. He's not just a flimflam guy either. He's a gentleman who showed respect for everyone and tried to see it from all points of view."

"There's your lesson, Caleb. See things from the other person's perspective by stepping in their shoes for a while. There's nothing like empathy to find a starting place for negotiations or for making a sale. You have to be sincere and respectful in the process, though, because people can smell a phony a mile away."

"Scooter was all those things and so persuasive. He thought of the objections and arguments ahead of time."

"Frank's a good guy too. His mom and I have been friends for years. We met in a local business group. She's a fabulous realtor, and I helped her out when Frank cut off his toes in the lawn mower accident."

"That must have been terrible."

"As you can imagine, she was a hot mess about it, feeling guilty. Things happen, and they can't all be explained by your religion or your philosophy. You have to adapt and adjust and play the hand you're dealt."

"That's for sure."

"Frank and John share a vision for a down-to-earth neighborhood bakery, and when I heard about it, I just loved the idea. They're going to be such a blessing to their neighborhood."

"And the doughnuts are out of this world."

113

"What did you think of Ali Hassan, your seventh assignment?"

"A sharp dresser and a nice man who is brokenhearted that his company has no use for his services."

"That happens to people every day, Caleb. In fact, it happens to us all several times in our working career. We get crushed because we can't imagine that a company we work for can get along without us. The truth is, they can." He laughed. "Boy, can they."

"Holly Starr explained that companies have many reasons— older age, higher salary, shift in emphasis, new leaders with a new direction. It could be a lot of things. What I got out of it was that we can all be replaced, even if we do a competent job."

"If you and I were doing the same job, we would be expected to get similar results, but we would each go about it in different ways depending on our talents and personalities."

"Something else about Mr. Hassan. He gave me the most expensive watch I've ever seen in my life. It costs around twelve grand. It's a Ulysse Nardin Diver Deep Dive watch. Check this baby out." He held out his wrist.

"Impressive. Did you learn something besides the fact that it's common—even for top producers—to be laid off by their companies?"

"Yes. Mr. Hassan was rich, but it wasn't the money he loved. It was the job. I guess that means jobs make you happy but money doesn't?"

Stockbridge laughed until it hurt him, and he abruptly stopped. "Money has made more people happy than poverty has, to be sure, my boy. Money isn't bad. It helps you do things and gives you freedom in some ways. The love of money as an end in itself, however, becomes problematic. What motivated Hassan was his love of his work and to excel; the money was a by-product."

"I see. Earning a lot of money shouldn't be the goal; instead, if you work hard at something you love, the money will be a by-product of your good work."

"Exactly. I'm sure he appreciated every penny he made and enjoyed it with things like his watch collection. Money is one of the report cards we get in life for our accomplishments—not the only one, necessarily—but one of the ways that our culture measures success. Now, what is the common thread in all these stories?"

"They all had problems."

"It's more than that. Everyone has problems."

"I don't know where you're going with this."

"I'll explain what I mean. Every person you helped was at a turning point in their lives. They were at the end of something, which also signals the beginning of something else. The things we did for them laid a foundation for the start of something new."

"I see what you mean."

"In each case, they had lost something. For Danielle, she lost her business. Alvin lost his house, Clint lost his military career, Helen lost the dream of Karmen being Miss Utah, Professor Huang lost her husband, Frank lost his business permit, and Ali lost his career. Our gifts helped give them a new season in their lives, a fresh start—a second wind, if you will."

"That's right. They all had those things in common. There's also something else they had in common, Mr. Stockbridge."

"What's that?"

"Each one of them gave me something. I wasn't expecting anything from them. I was there to do my job, which was to find out what they needed and try to give it to them. Yet they all gave me things too."

"Like what?"

"Danielle gave me an autographed children's book. Alvin gave me one of his most prized possessions: a bank note he got from his Vietnamese girlfriend on their last night together worth one thousand dong. Today it's worth only four cents in American currency, but when she gave it to Alvin, she said, 'Now you'll never be without money.' He passed that promise on to me with the bank note. Clint gave me a piece of shrapnel to remind me that war couldn't kill me and that it's not going to stop me from living the life I want to live. Helen gave me a headshot of Karmen that Karmen also signed. Frank gave me a dozen of the best doughnuts I ever ate. Chewy gave me a handmade bracelet for Ashley, and Ali gave me the twelve-thousand-dollar watch."

"That's interesting. There's an ancient saying that applies here: give, and it shall be given to you. In addition, you got a fresh start. You've got a house, a wife, and a career in law enforcement ahead of you. You've also changed a lot in the last year. You've become very wise about life. I'd say you got a second wind too."

"Roger that. I had no idea what was in store for me this year."

"There's something else you should know. I've put all my assets in a trust fund and made you the executor. You will be allowed to withdraw a designated amount each year as a salary; however, you will be required to give away that same amount to others, either individuals or nonprofits. If you do that, you'll never be able to spend it all before you die."

"I don't know what to say."

"You've proven to me you can do it. This was a test, and you passed it."

Caleb approached his grandfather and held him tight. "Thank you for all you taught me. It was fun working with you, and I can honestly say that my life will never be the same after the time I've spent with you."

"I know I wasn't there for you growing up, but we did change seven people's lives...together. We will always have these memories of working as a team."

"Yes, we will."

"I'm so glad we took this journey together. My race is almost run, and I'll cross the finish line a satisfied man. Someone who made mistakes, tried to learn from them, and made amends wherever he could. I'll leave this life with some regrets but also with a peaceful heart."

"Thanks for coming into my life when you did. I really needed it."

Pulling himself away so he could look into his grandson's eyes, Stockbridge took a deep breath. "I needed it too, Caleb. Working with you gave me a second wind."

EPILOGUE:
A YEAR LATER...

It was December 25, and there was no snow on the ground. There wouldn't be any snow on the ground tomorrow either, or the next day or even on New Year's Eve. It has never snowed on Christmas day in this part of the Arizona desert, and this year would be no different. Caleb Sinclair stood at the table, raised his glass, and cleared his throat.

"Before we begin our dinner, I'd like to propose a toast to Richard Stockbridge. He taught me a lifetime's worth of lessons in one year and gave me a second wind. In the last year I graduated from the police academy—"

"With honors!" Ashley shouted from his side.

Ashley, Artie, Rosie, Chad, Anthony, and Lily clapped.

"Thank you all. Ashley returned to her nursing classes, got her license, and was offered a job in the pediatric ward. She's going to work for a few years, and then we're going to start a family."

Everyone clapped.

"Artie popped the question, and Rosie said yes. Maybe she loves him, or maybe she just wants to keep getting those free piano lessons for Seth and Sarah. Artie's band, Armor of God, has a number one hit on Christian radio stations around the country, and the band is going on tour next summer."

Artie acknowledged their applause with a nod before raising his glass in a salute to the toastmaster.

"The man who believed in us, prayed for us, counseled us, and married us has had a good year also. Chad received his certification as a fitness instructor and has been hired by our local gym to start a youth fitness program. As you know, Chad and Isabella Rodriguez dated for a long time after this year's cancer walk. I think their relationship fell apart because he was trying to lead her to Christ, and she was trying to lead him to the alter.

"Last but not least, I'd like to include my army buddy, Anthony Victorino, and Lily Lofton in this toast. He's been promoted to vice president in his firm, and I'm pleased to report that Lily has moved in with him. He thinks it's love, and I think she loves his dog, Flash. You may think she loves you, but remember, buddy, she is an actress after all—a Broadway actress.

"To our second winds! Thanks, Mr. Stockbridge! Merry Christmas, everyone."

None of them, except Ashley, knew that Caleb had another job, a secret job that he never disclosed. He was paying it forward, giving anonymously without any need for recognition or return. This life principle continued to open doors and allowed him to reap the rewards in his and Ashley's lives.

He became a shooting partner with Alvin Larsen, and they racked up a series of wins at the gun club. Caleb stayed in touch with Chewy, and, as promised, he and Ashley gave her the tour of Briggs Lake.

He never saw Eli Burns again and came to believe he was an angel.

Caleb finished writing his book about war, and he profiled a veteran in each chapter. He dedicated the book to his best friend, Nick, and the closing chapter was Nick's life story.

Continuing to enjoy pork rinds and Slim Jims, Caleb never again dreamed about the day Nick died and their last ride in a helicopter; however, he had many dreams about their happy times together.

Acknowledgments

Stephanie E. Dopp

My wife of forty-eight years, first reader of *Second Wind*, editor, and muse. I'm incapable of doing almost anything without her help and support. She has brown hair with red highlights.

Second Readers

Their feedback made *Second Wind* more readable and realistic. They caught and corrected many mistakes in the kindest manner possible.

> David Bellomy
> Stephen Dopp
> Bonny Meyers
> Sally McClure
> Susan and Jack McColaugh

Consultants

Major James L. Keyes (ret.): My mentor in the Army ROTC, who generously shared his knowledge and experience as a Ranger.

Sergeant James J. Robinson (ret.): He was the inspiration for the helicopter crew chief, Big Jim. He fought in the largest helicopter assault in the Vietnam War at Lam Son 719.